Fill The Chalice

Sean Mott

PROLOGUE

I am a corpse floating through space, lost with the other
dead debris. I'm withered, my body curling in on itself.
My limbs are limp, drooping down like a misplaced
jacket on a chair. I can see only half-images and blurry
impressions. I am lost. I could stay here forever, slowly
rotting away. I would never be found. My body would
decay. I would be nothing.

I am close.

I open my mouth, letting the liquid rush into my
mouth. It flows past my teeth, pooling around my gums
and tongue. It's a miniature pond. My personal world. I
destroy it as I blow the liquid out.

I am cold. My body hair sways back and forth,
brushing against my skin. I blink, giving my chilled eyes
a respite. My teeth chatter, nipping my tongue. I curl
into a ball, clutching my knees into my chest. This is
torture.

I am very close now.

I flare my nostrils. Bulbous globs rise above me,
bursting as they reach the surface. I sink to the floor,
toes pushing into the ground. Weeds wraps around my
legs. I am seated.

It is quiet. I am alone.

I stare at the watery ceiling. I see vague outlines
of shadows. Jagged rocks point down like daggers.
Flames burn in tiny cages. People are gathered in a

circle, looking down. Or are they looking up? I can't tell. Do they even know I'm here? If I stay here, will they ever know?

I put my hand in front of my face, blocking them out of my eyes. I need to focus.

I stare at the darkness. It sits there, waiting to envelop me. In a few seconds it will have me. My whole body is screaming.

I'm almost there.

I look deeper into the darkness. It hates me. No, worse than that; it doesn't care about me. I'm a speck. I'm nothing. Everything I've ever accomplished means nothing here. I'm just a body submerged with the muck.

I could stay here, resting with the decay. The world wouldn't notice. People could build statues of me, pray to me, die for me, but the world wouldn't notice. It would just keep turning, waiting for people to die, waiting for more soil.

I'm finished.

I swim upwards, puncturing the ceiling. I swallow a gulp of air, savouring it. The water washes over my eyes. Everything is still blurry. I float on my back, staring at the jagged rocks.

I am reborn.

CHAPTER ONE

I am standing backstage.

I can hear the murmur, the constant hum that echoes in my bones. I bounce my knee in time with it. I brush my fingers on the curtain, feeling its faded velvet, worn-out after decades of use. It's perfect.

We found the curtain in a tool shed by the river. It was bundled under rakes and shovels. Spiders had made a web labyrinth in it. Its faint red colour peaked through the layers of white silk. Dust enveloped it like a second skin. We wiped the webs away, sending the spiders scattering through the floorboards, and we unrolled the curtain on the grass. It reeked of mildew and urine. We threw the curtain into the river, letting the dust wash downstream. It sat on the bank, half submerged. I held onto the edges of the curtain with my fingertips. Joseph just watched.

I felt the curtain sag and dip below the surface. The water weighed it down. I yanked on it and hauled it to the bank. I dug my feet into the mud, slipping and sinking. The current tugged on the curtain, but I held fast. I crawled, inch by inch, back onto the grass. I flopped the curtain on the ground. Joseph never helped.

I rolled up the curtain and we walked back to the buildings. I hanged it in the auditorium. It's stayed here since.

I push my face against the curtain, closing my eyes. It's rough, coarse and itchy. I can still smell the mud and grime clinging to the fabric. We've hosed it down and scrubbed it with soap. We've dried it in the sun and hanged it back up. But the smell returns. We've stopped cleaning it. It refuses to change.

It keeps me focused. The crowd is far away. They sound muffled. I'm back under water. I'm surrounded by weeds, mud, and fish. I'm sealed in a jar of water. This is my sanctuary.

I feel a tap on my shoulder. Time to come up for air.

"Ready, sir?" It's Greg, clutching his clipboard. Black bags cling to his eyes.

"Of course. Always." I touch his shoulder.

"Whenever you're ready." Greg flips through crumpled pages on his clipboard.

"Will you be watching?" I bounce on my toes and crack my neck.

"I need to get back to-" Greg looks at me. He's dead on his feet. He needs a nap. He's seen hundreds of my sermons. He doesn't need to be here. But that's the point. I look into Greg's eyes. They're a steely blue. But they're weak. I stare at Greg. No judgment, no pressure; I'm just peering into him. He looks away, noticing something on his clipboard. I've won.

"It's up to you." I wink at Greg. That's all it takes.

"I'll see you in the audience, sir." Greg rubs his eyes and smiles.

"Wonderful." I massaged my jaw as Greg slinks back into the shadows.

My robe is draped over a chair. I slide into it, letting it envelop me. I fasten the front belt, leaving the top collar open. The robe flows with me, breathes with me. It's my second skin.

I catch myself in a mirror. The edges are grimy, but I stand in the clean middle, surrounded by filth. I look good. Sharp, cutting, powerful. I'm almost ready.

I roll my sleeves up to my elbow. I raise my hand next to my head. I look myself in the eyes and nod. I strike my hand across my face, hitting my cheek and nose. First slap. I haul my hand back. I never stop looking at myself. I recite the words. My hand careens past my face, bumping into my eye. Second slap. My hand goes back to its place. Strands of my hair have been knocked loose. My palm reaches the other side of my face, clipping my ear and making it ring. Third slap. I look at myself

again. My cheek is red. I push the loose hair back in place. I tug
my sleeves down to my wrists, straightening out the creases on
the arm. The man in the mirror nods. I'm ready.

I place my fingers through the small opening in the
curtains. I twirl them. The noise grows. They see me. It's time to
meet my audience. I pull the curtains aside and run to the stage.
The crowd is loud. Not as loud as they should be, but it's been a
busy week, so I let it slide. I stand at center stage with my hands
on my hips. I tilt my head. The applause builds. That's better.

Hundreds of faces stare up at me. Familiar, loyal faces.
Ready and willing. Faces lined with hope. Faces that want
something different. Young enough to believe, but not old
enough to question. The perfect age.

Sweat pools on their faces and clothes. A stale stench
accompanies them. It's barely midday and people are marinating
in sweat. I just came from the river. My body is cool, but I can
feel the heat surrounding me, ready to pounce. It must be torture
outside. Everyone should be irritable. Good. I can use that.

An aisle runs through the middle of the audience from
the stage to the door. The builders sit on the left side of the aisle.
They breathe life into our buildings. They chop the lumber,
hammer the nails, hoist up the frames, and suffer the injuries.
They're the lackeys, the tools, the sweatiest people in the room.
The planters sit on the right side of the aisle. They harvest the
crops, tend the gardens, prick their fingers on flowers. They keep
us alive. Anywhere else, they'd be hippies, free spirits,
dependents. They reek of manure and corn.

I don't play favourites. I deny myself that pleasure. I
must be impartial. So I created another division. The first few
front rows are for the best members. The hardest workers, the
most devoted, the faithful. I give them the best seats in the
house. The back rows are reserved for the sloths, the
lackadaisical, the doubtful. I let them know their place. They're
put on notice.

But it's more than that. After months of front row
seating, even the most passionate follower may find themselves

in the back row. They don't know how they got there. No explanation is given. They are asked to sit in the back and they must earn their way back up. There's no reason for the switch. I keep everyone on their toes. They can't afford to be lazy or complacent. Nothing is ever handed to them. Everything is always on the line.

Sometimes I'll elevate a back bencher to the stage-side seating. They'll see what it's like to be close to the spotlight, to be important. They'll sit with the others, thinking they're one of the elite. They've finally arrived…until they're shunted back to the end chairs. Their rise is over as quickly as it began. Why? How? They don't know. But they've had a taste. Now they want more. So they'll scratch and claw their way back to the front. They'll do whatever it takes to get that close to the spotlight again.

I soak in the cheers, nodding at select members. I'm standing next to a microphone stand, towering over everyone. I squint my eyes to get a good look at the faces, but the spotlight is too bright. The audience looks like jittering silhouettes. I won't find anyone from here.

I leap off the stage into the darkness. I stroll down the aisle, shaking hands and smiling. I reach the end and peer over the crowd. I see one man at the edge of his seat near the door in the builder section. His head is bent over, his elbows leaning into his bouncing knee. He's rubbing his hands together. He's chewing on his lower lip and cracking his neck. I nod. I've found my target. I run back to the stage and yank the microphone from the stand.

"Whoo, I don't think Hell could get hotter than today." I smile, flashing my teeth.

Respectful laughter. I untangle the microphone cord from the stand and drag it like the leash of a limp dog as I walk across the stage.

"No, I can't recall a hotter day here than today. Can you?" I hold the microphone to the audience. I hear some smatterings of "no" and "not around here."

"Exactly, exactly. I thought so. Day like today could melt your eyes out of your sockets." I hold a hand up to my eyes and make a popping motion. More respectful laughter.

I walk to the edge of the stage, dangling my toes over the empty space. I spot a builder near the front row covered head to toe in sawdust and perspiration. Something to work with.

"Of course, some of us are hotter than others." I point at the man. He smiles and raises a dust powdered hand.

"We applaud your hard work, sir." Polite clapping.

"But don't sweat too much. It'd be hard to scoop you off the ground if you slipped off a roof." Chuckles and snickers.

I sway on the edge of the stage, tossing the mic between my hands. I drop it, jump down to the floor and start pacing.

"But I'm sure you've all seen some hot spots. What's the warmest place you've been to?" I point at a planter. She reeks of soil, naturally. Her eyes light up as she stammers into the mic.

"Me? Uh, um, well, I lived up north for a long time. Most of my life. But we went to Cuba once. My family, I mean. We went for a vacation. That was the hottest spot. Until I came here…"

"Cuba? Don't supposed you brought cigars for any of us?" I wink at the planter, ruffling her hair. I walk over to the left section, spotting a brick house in the front row. His arms are crossed and flexed, his whole body nearly bursting out of his uniform.

"Now I know you've been somewhere warm." I rest my elbow on his shoulder. His eyes widen for a second. He could turn my insides out and fashion my rib cage into a xylophone. But he won't. He knows his place. He grins.

"Texas. Absolutely. Hotter than hell." He looks to his friends for approval.

"Sounds like we've got a steer in the audience." I pat the builder on the cheek and walk to the centre aisle. I lick my lips; I'm starting to feel the heat. I widen my stance so my thighs don't rub against each other; they're already a little tender.

"We've all felt the heat. We've endured." I wander deeper into the crowd. People lean out of their chairs. They look at me, breathless and smiling. I brush my hand on a man's forehead, dragging three fingers through his layer of sweat. He shudders. I hold up the fingers, nodding. Everyone nods with me as if they're aware of some shared experience.

The crowd is comfortable. They're relaxed, at ease. Playtime's over. It's time for something that will stick in their minds. It's time for an investment.

"We've worked." I wipe my sweaty hand on my sleeve, forming a light stain. People stick their heads out expectantly. I look at the door. I walk towards it, holding out my hands with outstretched fingers. I bump into heads, arms, shoulders, necks. All drenched. All quivering. I tap my fingers against my robe. My chest, my sleeves, my back, my face.

Sweat drops splash on my clothes, drying and leaving small wet circles. Some stains streak across my chest and arms, like brush strokes dragged over a long canvas. The circles widen and deepen, connecting to one another. The streaks overlap and crisscross. I'm soaked in everyone's sweat.

It's absolutely disgusting. I'm covered in bodily fluids, coated in layers of germs. I want to hurl. I want to leap into a pool of soap and never emerge. I want to tear my skin off and toss it into an incinerator.

But I won't. This is important. This is a test, like any other. I have to overcome my revulsion, my disdain. I have to overcome myself. I stare at the door. It's the only thing that exists. Everything else is superfluous. I'm wading through a parade of perspiration to get to the door. It's all that matters.

Some hands grab my fingers. I squeeze them and pull away. I can't be delayed. I have to get to the door. I've reduced my life to this narrow corridor. I need to make it another ten paces and I'm free.

The sweat makes my body itch. My flesh is roasting. I can feel everyone's heat radiating on me. Their breath is heavy and thick. I'm in an oven. Eight more steps.

The smell. Good Lord, the smell. It's like plunging into reheated soup. It wraps around my nostrils, forcing its way inside. I breathe through my mouth, gulping like a fish. But this is the easy way. I inhale deeply through my nose, inviting the stench in. It's sheer agony. Five more steps.

I've worn these robes for years. Every sermon, every speech, every rally. A follower weaved them for me. They spent months on them, perfecting the design and the fabric. Their hands trembled when they gave the robes to me. I smiled and squeezed his shoulder. He died two weeks later. Slipped off a roof and split his skull open. Co-workers said he was exhausted. Never slept. Stepped on a ladder that wasn't there. He sacrificed. He suffered. So I wore the robes.

They're a reminder. They've been a constant. They're more than clothes. And now these robes that a man died to make are coated in sweat. They're sagging me down. They've been tainted. I will burn these robes tonight. I will douse them in kerosene and watch the flames devour the fabric. I will throw a man's life work away. Two more steps.

I blink. My own sweat is rushing into my eyes. They sting. I blink again but the sweat keeps coming. I want to wipe my face, but my hands are preoccupied. And I probably don't want to rub my lips and eyes with germ-coated fingers. But it won't stop burning. I need to clean my face. I need to—

A hand squeezes me. It's full of bumps and ridges. I look down and see a builder staring at me. His face is devastated. His lower teeth are missing, and a yellow layer covers his upper teeth. There is a pink tattoo on his cheek. It's a poorly-done star. One point barely reaches his jaw while another grazes across his hairline. The centre looks deeper than the points, as if it's coated with ink. It's like something exploded next to—It isn't a tattoo. His neck and arms are the same. Scarred-over gashes and faded cuts. Other wounds are fresher, red and deep. His skin is jagged terrain.

Sweat covers his body, seeping into his cuts. His body must be on fire. He should be scratching every inch of his skin.

He should run out of here and jump into the river. No one would blame him. I sure wouldn't. But he just stands there. He smiles at me. His eyes are dancing. He's grateful. He wants to be in this oven. He shames me. I stop blinking. I nod at him and look forward. One more step.

I reach the door. Hands brush my back. I close my eyes. I raise my arms to my sides. The hands fall away. I hear the chairs squeak. People scuffle their feet to get a better view. They stare at me. I make them wait.

A breeze worms its way through a crack in a window. It's heaven. The door is right there. I could push it open, run into the woods, throw my clothes in a bush, and leap into the river. I would sink to the bottom. The cold would wrap around me. There's nothing I want more.

But I can't. Not now, not when I've got them in my palm. I sigh, shake my hands, and turn around.

"We've all sacrificed." I hold my arms above my head, showing off the drenched sleeves.

Applause. Laughter. Relief.

I smile and wipe my forehead, flicking beads of sweat into the crowd. I fan myself, rolling my eyes. More laughter.

Everybody's chuckling, except for one. I see him in the corner of my eye. It's the man from before. Still stooped over, still bouncing his knee, still chewing his lip. He stares at the floor, hands gripping his elbows. I'll get to him.

I wade through the crowd. I squeeze shoulders and pat cheeks. Keep things light. I run down the aisle, jump onstage, grab the microphone, and rub my brow.

"Now, that's how you work up a sweat." I hold up my soaked fingers.

Nods and smiles. They watched me soak myself with their sweat. I look like a moist, deflated balloon. And they're smiling at me. Incredible.

"That's what I wanted to talk about today: Hard work. Denial. Sacrifice." I hold the microphone in both hands, drumming my fingers on it. There is a constant thumping echo in the room. A pulse.

"But isn't that what I always talk about? Isn't that what I preach, day after day after day, right on this stage? Isn't that why we're here?" I look over the crowd, raising my eyebrows. I keep drumming my fingers. People nod in unison with the thumping. Synchronized agreement.

"Of course it is. Without a shadow of a doubt. You all know what it means to sacrifice. You all left everything behind and you came here." I clap softly.

"But I'm talking about a certain kind of sacrifice. Something special, something important. The next step." I quicken my drumming.

"It's easy to sacrifice. Well, no, that's not right. Sacrifice is painful. But when you're sacrificing something evil, spiritually evil, it comes pretty easy. How hard was it to give up your jobs? Your condos? Your morning commutes? Incredibly hard. To let go of your shackles is no simple feat. But it was the natural choice, the right choice." I pace across the stage. "And how did that sacrifice feel? When the pain faded, when you realized your choice, how good did it feel? It was a relief. For the first time in your life, you felt at peace. It was a just sacrifice." Faster drumming.

"But what about the other kind of sacrifice? The one that doesn't relieve, doesn't soothe, doesn't have a clear answer. What then?" I stop drumming.

"When it hasn't rained for three weeks and your crops are dying, what then? When you break your arm and you have to finishing roofing, what then? When you can't stand up, when you're barely clinging to life, what then? All your sacrifice has led to this: Suffering. There is no relief, there is no point. What do you do?" I clutch the microphone stand, leaning into the audience, teetering on the stage's edge.

"I know what most people would do: They'd pack it in. Throw in the towel. Crawl back to their apartments, their jobs, their massage chairs. They'd slide back into the life they'd sacrificed. They'd return to their old, dead selves. They'd rather be docile than defiant. They'd rather be asleep than awake. They'd rather be dead than alive." My knuckles are white. "But you're not like them. You don't turn away from the struggle. You know what true sacrifice is, don't you?" Silence. They crowd is confused. They need encouragement.

"Don't you?" I slam the microphone stand on the stage. I storm across the stage, wrapping the microphone cord around my fist.

"Don't you? Don't you? Don't you? Don't you? Don't you?" I stomp my foot with each question. I bore my eyes into every person I see. They're quiet, unsure. I keep pushing. I keep asking. They nod. First to their neighbours, then to me. The clap along with my stomps. All those hands, all at once. The clapping overtakes me. It's a sea of noise. They're standing, their bodies shaking. Their eyes are on fire.

"Of course you do, of course you do." I yell to rise above the din. It's deafening.

"You know what sacrifice is. It's more than giving up your possessions, your job, your family. It's about sacrificing yourself, denying yourself. It's about holding yourself to an impossible standard." An ocean of heads nod in agreement.

"It's about going to sleep with an empty stomach. It's about working in the field with no shade. It's about hammering wood on a roof as your arms scream. It's about living in pain, living with nothing, and giving more. Sacrifice is your life." I'm spitting into the microphone. I pause and watch the crowd clap and cheer.

I part my hair to the side. My heart bangs on my chest. I'm high on my own brand. I lick my lips. Life is simple here. No complications, no bullshit, just raw power. I pick up the stand and put the microphone back in its slot. I release my grip on it, letting my knuckles darken.

"You understand sacrifice. You know it's about more than what's out there. It's about what's in here." I jab my thumb into my ribs. I nod, letting people calm down and return to their seats.

"You sacrifice yourselves every day. You find the strength to give up what you want. You turn away from distractions, from easy answers. You have the power to let it all go. But sometimes, it's not enough." The crowd murmurs; they know what's coming.

"Sometimes, there are insurmountable temptations. Sometimes, our strength falters. Sometimes, we lose sight of the path. But there is always a way back." I hop off the stage, holding my arms out wide.

"Who wants the Honour?"

I walk through the crowd with my hands above my head, fingers twitching. People surge towards me. I pause in front of a few members, miming consideration. I shake my head and move on. I can hear them deflate as I leave. They might need it, they might even deserve it, but I have a goal. This ceremony is just extra flair.

I reach the end of the audience and turn left. The builders grin as the planters sigh, shuffling back to their seats. I walk through a back row, tapping my fingers on twitching heads. I close my eyes, feeling for the "right" person. I bump into a bouncing knee. I look down and point.

"You deserve the Honour." It's the anxious man. He's still stooped over his folded arms. Surprise washes over his face.

The crowd stares at the man. He blinks and unfolds his arms.

"Are you ready? I hold my palm out. He stares at me, lost. Panic fills his eyes. I squeeze his shoulder and smile at him. I lean into his ear.

"It's just the two of us. No need to be afraid." I pull back and nod.

"Are you ready?" I widen my palm. He looks at it, panting, and clasps it. The crowd applauds as I lift him up.

I lead him through the audience as they pat his back. He smiles and gives a quick thumbs-up. I bring him to the center stage and push him down to his knees. He waves at the crowd as I crouch beside him.

"Name?"

"Josh Pinter, sir." His voice is squeaky, stuck in a permanent puberty.

"Good to meet you, Josh. Just follow my lead and you'll be fine." I pat his chest. I place my hand on his head. His hair is coarse and knotted. His skin is bumpy and rough. He's quaking. He's almost too perfect.

"I think he's ready, friends. Josh, what're your sins?" I look straight ahead at the crowd. I feel Josh tense up.

"I, uh, well, I'm not sure, really. I suppose I-"

My hand lashes out at Josh's face.

The crowd gasps, not in surprise. Josh reels back, stopping himself by planting his hand on the floor. I'm standing in front of him in a wide stance with both hands flexing at my sides. Josh touches his face and looks at me. He knew this was coming. He must have. He's been here long enough. But he's afraid.

"What are your sins?" I gesture to my hand. Josh flinches and I can see the gears turning in his mind.

"I-I um, I... Fuck, I... Oh, I left the roof unfinished. I was working on a roof. We all were. And I had one section left. But I was tired. And I knew the man next to me would do it. He always helps. So, I went to bed. And when I woke up, it was done. He had finished it. I, I avoided my responsibility." Josh shifts his eyes to the ground, ashamed. He shirks away from me, trembling. He's almost convincing.

My knuckles graze Josh's nose this time.

Blood streaks down his lips. He wipes his face and blinks, breathing fast. I can hear his heartbeat from here. His head tilts forward as he speaks. He's looking at my hands.

"I-I slept in. It was a big project. We were setting up the barn. I was tired, so tired. I'd been working for four weeks straight. I pretended to be sick. Said I'd help later. I just wanted a

break. I slept in. I didn't work that day. I just slept." Josh
swallows and nods.

"How did it feel?" I raise my eyebrows.

"Awful. It was terrible. I never should—"

The red mark on Josh's cheek grows.

"Honestly." I wipe my hand clean.

"It was wonderful." Josh is surprised with himself.

"Good, good, now we're getting somewhere." I pat
Josh's cheek. Carrots and sticks.

"Josh, these are minor sins. They are shameful, no
doubt, but they are symptoms. We're looking for the root." I
gesture to the crowd. They nod and grunt.

"We want to know your secret, Josh. The one you won't
even admit to yourself. Can you do that, Josh? Can you be
honest?" I crouch in front of him. He shuffles his knees away
from me. I lean forward.

"Can you, Josh? Can you?" I brush a stray hair out of his
eyes.

"I don't know what—" My fingers flick the bridge of his
nose.

Josh grimaces as I tower above him. I shake my head,
trying to look disappointed. It's hard though; I'm having a blast.

Josh grabs my robe. He bunches them up in his hands,
tugging on them.

"I skip sermons." Josh lets the words hang in the air. He
thinks he's dropped a bomb.

"When?" I ease his fingers off my robe. His blood's
going to stain the fabric.

"All the time. I skip it all the time. I, I want to g-get to
meal hall early. After sermons, I get stuck behind the crowd. I'm
always late and the best food's gone. No meat, no bread, j-j-just
corn and soup. Corn and soup every day. So I skip sermons."
Josh eyes pool with tears. His voice cracks and squeaks. Not bad.

"I wait outside the hall. When the sermon's done, I just
join the crowd. Right at the front. And the food's mine. It-it's

easy. I'm sorry." Josh whispers this last part. The crowd is quiet. I flex my hand.

"Is that everything?" I step an inch closer.

"Yes, yes, that's it. I'm sor—" My next slap sends Josh falling to his side. He lands on his elbow and grunts. I kick him over onto his back and plant my feet near his shoulders. Neither of us say anything. The entire room is silent, except for one sound.

There is no pause between the slaps. I strike his left cheek and catch his right one as it jerks away. My arms pump back and forth. It's poetry. Josh's face gets redder with each turn. My palms are numb and sore. I pull Josh up by the collar.

"Why am I doing this, Josh?" I wipe blood off his lips.

"B-because, because I skipped a sermon. Because I was se-selfish. I took the easy way out." He's close.

Josh's head flops. I crank my hand up and send his head hurtling down onto the floor. I wait as Josh wipes the tears and snot from his face. I send another hand down. And another. And another. Josh is on the edge. He's going to crack or throttle me. I speak between the slaps.

"Josh, I'm not doing this because you slept in."

Slap.

"I'm not doing this because you skipped a sermon."

Slap.

"I'm doing this because you're lying. You know the sin. Confess."

Slap.

"What."

Slap.

"Is."

Slap.

"Your."

Slap.

"Sin?"

I step back. I fold my hands behind my back, massaging the knuckles. Josh crawls away from me, inching towards the edge of the stage. He's babbling.

"I don't, I d-don't know. I don't know what I diiiiiiiid. God, please, I don't know. What did I do? What did I do?" Josh leaks saliva and blood.

I prop my hand on the microphone stand, drumming my fingers. Josh is propped up on his elbows, lost. All I can hear is his breathing. I flip the stand and hold it like a club. I stalk towards Josh and loom above him.

"You know your sin." My voice fills the room. The voice of God.

"I don't, I don't, I don't." Josh is seeping fluids.

"You do. Confess." I bare my teeth as I hold the stand. I will smite him.

"Please." Josh locks eyes with me. He doesn't want to admit the truth. Not to me, not to himself. He's afraid. I understand. Who wouldn't be? But he has no choice.

"Confess." I hold up the stand for the final blow.

"I doubt." Josh flinches, horrified.

Josh spits a glob of bloody mucus on the floor and rubs his eyes. He grabs his leg to stop its shaking. The crowd lean and whisper to themselves, licking their lips. A gang of dogs cornering a fox.

I tilt my head up and close my eyes. I collapse my hand over my face and hold my breath. I hear Josh's weeping, the crowd's panting, the rats scurrying under the floorboards. I can hear the river. Gurgling and chugging along, beckoning me. I ignore it. I wait. My chest tightens but I wait. Josh fidgets and squirms, but I wait.

And I feel it. The Surge. The righteous blast in my soul. The signal that what I'm doing is just. That I have chosen the right man. I am vindicated. Just as always.

I exhale and open my eyes. I place the stand against Josh's leg. I kneel in front of him and nod.

"Explain." I lift his chin up.

"I-I can't. I don't—" He's falling back on bad habits.

I clasp the stand and flex my arm. Josh follows my veins and meets my eyes. Pure steel. He swallows and jerks his head. A nod, I'm sure.

"I doubt. I-I'm not sure I should be here. I come to sermons and I don't...feel anything. It doesn't seem real. I don't believe."

Gasps from the crowd. You'd think Josh had just shot a puppy.

"I'm living a lie. I-I can't do...I don't believe. I'm a liar."

"So, you're a nonbeliever surrounded by fanatics. Why have you stayed?" Everything hinges on his answer.

"I tried to leave. I mean, I thought about it. I packed my bags, I waited until everyone was asleep, and I snuck out to the entrance. I was going to leave—"

"And what happened?"

"I just stood there. I was right on the edge. I could lift my foot and cross the line. I could leave. But-but, I wouldn't. I just stood there all night. I stood there until the sun came up. Then I went back to my cot."

"Why didn't you cross that line?"

"I don't know. Something was keeping me here..."

"What was it, Josh? Think."

"I felt this...pull. This force. It kept nagging on me. It wouldn't leave. It just hammered on me. This feeling, it wouldn't let me go."

"So you stayed. You couldn't defeat this...force. It imprisoned you, left you powerless."

"...Yes."

"Then there's still hope for you."

I jump to my feet and grab Josh's shoulders, hauling him up. His eyes have dried and there's a small blood stain under his nose. I clasp his cheeks with both hands.

"Are you willing to try? Do you want to unleash this feeling? Do you want my help?" I squeeze Josh's head and purse my lips. He stares at me, his knees buckling.

"Are you ready to overcome yourself, Josh? Are you ready to be more?"

Josh's mouth moves, emitting a sharp squeak. I shake him and lean in close. He's blubbering, gasping for air. I hear one word.

"Say it to them." I push Josh to the edge of the stage.

Josh stands there, dumbstruck. His lips move, but he can only squeak. His whole body shakes, his hands flapping at his side. He might have a stroke. Did I push him too far? Did I—?

"Yes." Josh collapses to the floor, hugging himself.

"Yes, yes, yes, yes. Please, I want it. Please. Yes, yes, yes, I do, I do. Please. Yes, yes..."

The crowd explodes, stamping their feet and applauding. Josh rocks back and forth, smiling and trembling. I stand over him and place my hand on his head.

"This man was lost. A dead soul. He was filled with doubt and misery. He was ready to commit the ultimate betrayal: the betrayal of his beliefs. He thought himself beyond redemption. And he's come back to us. There is always hope. There is always a way back into the fold. We welcome you with open arms."

I stride into the crowd, leaving Josh to his delirium. Some followers comfort him. Most of them cheer for me, watch me, touch me. They swarm around me. I clench my fists and shove my arms above my head.

"You can all be saved. You are all welcome."

They bow their heads as they part before me. They would march into the pits of Hell for me. No drug is better than this. I'm ecstatic.

CHAPTER TWO

I'm miserable.

My body reclines in a stiff wooden chair. I wriggle my toes and stretch my legs, crossing them. One hand droops like putty over the armrest. My fingers idly pick at the grooves in the wood. My other hand props up my head, pushing against my cheek. My eyes are watery; it's like looking through smeared glass. I blink. My eyes are shut for five, ten, twenty seconds. A power nap. I heard that phrase once. I blink again. I can see. I couldn't look calmer.

My head is screaming. My brain is pounding on my skull, smashing the walls, begging for a pardon. It wants to run, fuck, kill, eat, destroy. In that order. It snarls at me. It chafes against this silence. I gave it a taste of adrenaline; now it wants the full course.

My heart beats in rhythm with my brain. It shoots fiery blood through my body. It wants to send me into overdrive. It wants my brain to devour itself. It threatens to explode if I stay in this chair. I uncross my legs.

"...which brings us slightly below par, but I think we can manage fine if we..."

Every goddamn day. After every sermon, I'm filled with righteous energy. I'm feeding off the crowd. We're a surging mass of fervor. I have a massive erection. I could storm the Vatican, throw the Pope off his throne, lead a march into

Jerusalem, and climb Vesuvius. I want to spread the gospel across the world. I'm alive.

I can barely control myself. My mind is barely functional. Something else takes the steering wheel, something primal. It doesn't want to think, or wait, or reflect. It just wants to go forward. It'd be so easy to give in... I have to wrestle control from the beast every day. I force it down the pit. I lead my followers outside as I smother it. It shakes my body, screaming for freedom. It wants to run, to swim, to fuck... But I suppress it. I deny myself. I have to.

I directed my people to the dining hall. They passed me and shook my hand. I squeezed tight, hoping they don't notice my trembling arm. They smiled at me and I smiled back. Perfectly normal. Perfectly restrained. They left me there. I exhaled, and I walked to my office. I wanted to run. No, it wanted to run. But I'm in command. I sat down at my desk and breathed. Slowly, I extinguished it. For today.

"...noticed a pack of wolves on the border but they didn't seem too..."

I flick off a wood chip from the chair. It lodges in my fingernail. I pull it out with my teeth tasting its musky flavour. I launch it through my lips, watching it land on a stack of papers. My robe hangs above the bookshelf across the room. It's still damp with sweat. I'll have to dunk it in the river. I'm wearing a black turtleneck with grey pants. Professionalism is key.

"...progressing along nicely, although we had a slight hiccup when Gerald forgot to..."

I scratch my arm, massaging my bug bites. I trace my finger around the rim of a glass of water. I numb myself with tedium. Boredom builds up a wall. Boredom keeps the beast in the pit. Boredom keeps me sane.

I plunge my finger into the water. A halo of ripples form around it. I stare at my warped and enlarged fingernail.

"...but I told him that would cost us a significant yield and he said..."

I outdid myself today. I was incredible. It was a stroke of genius. But where can I go from here? I twirl my finger, creating bigger ripples.

I always do this to myself. I find some new way to preach the truth. I'm struck with this bolt, this surge of creativity. I raise the bar. I make a perfect moment. And then I torture myself trying to surpass myself. What if they get bored? What if that was the best I'll do? What if that's my peak? What if they all leave before...before I can save them? What if I'm a...?

"...that about covers the preliminaries. Questions, sir?"

I hold my thumb on glass rim and dip all four fingers in the water. I scoop upwards, splashing my palm. What can I do next? What can I do...?

"Questions, sir?"

I run my fingers down my face, letting the water roll to my shirt. A mask of water, a mask of...

I could cut my palm. Long and deep. Let it open and turn red. I would hold it up onstage. I would ask for a volunteer. They'd approach, afraid, naturally, and kneel before me. I'd pat their cheek with my clean hand, talking about strength, about passion, about fury. I'd raise my crimson hand and bring it down...

"Sir?"

They'd lie on the stage, stained, weeping. The room would reek of iron. I'd wrap my hand in the robe and walk through the crowd. I'd hold my bandaged hand out, parting the sea. Red drops would paint the floor. I'd leave everyone in silence. Marvelous, just marvelous...

"Sir."

I reach for the water and my finger bump into the desk. The glass is gone. I look up. Greg is holding it, smiling.

"Good trip, sir?" He drinks the water.

I'm back in the office. My hand is sealed. Greg is standing here, drinking my water with a smug—No, don't think that. That isn't me. I shake my head and grin.

"Just thinking up new sermons."

"Anything good?" Greg sits down across from me.

"You'll have to wait and see." I wipe my face and adjust my posture.

"What is it? Test of endurance? Ritual chants? A chain of trust falls?" Greg licks his lips.

"Well, you're giving me plenty of ideas." I inspect the glass. Empty.

"Oh, please, sir, just a hint." Greg leans forward.

I chuckle and meet him at the middle of the desk. The wood creaks beneath our weight. I crook my finger and he strains his ear towards my mouth. I rest my chin on my hand, listening to his heavy breathing. I open my mouth. His smile gets wider. I flick his ear.

"No spoilers." I fall back into my chair.

"But, sir-"

"No, no, that would be cheating. No special treatment." I stand up with the glass.

Greg massages his ear as I walk to the sink. I crank the handle and the faucet shudders, releasing a slow stream of water. I rub my eyes. The high is gone. Time to get back to work.

"What did I miss while I was brainstorming?" I sit on the edge of my chair.

"Well, there's not too much happening. Construction's on pace, water supply's fine, some wolves were spotted in the woods."

"Standard stuff."

"There's one major item: Our crops are underperforming." Greg hands me a folder.

It's full of numbers, charts, descriptions, day-to-day performances. I nod and stroke my chin and mumble as I read through it. I pause on certain pages and flip back to others, comparing sections. I stop at one point to look at Greg and raise my eyebrows. I close the folder and drum my fingers on it, staring off thoughtfully. I can't understand any it.

"What happened?" I slide the folder back to Greg.

"Bad soil, mainly. The planters said the land just wouldn't cooperate. Everything grew...wrong. Then we had that accident with the fireworks, which cut into our total yield. Add that to a late season and we're looking at a reduced crop selection." Greg blinks as he talks, adding and subtracting every factor. A human calculator.

"How reduced?"

"It's going to be a lean winter." Greg shifts in his chair and looks at the ground.

I sigh. We both know what this means. "Lean" only has one definition here. Last year we had a surplus. Barely, but we had it. And still there were...

"Well, we're not here for the easy life." I walk to Greg and raise his chin.

"No, sir." Greg's eyes tremble.

"Everyone here knows the risk. That's why they come. They throw it all away for the risk, for the sacrifice. They're ready for anything. And if the time arrives, they'll know what to do." I look at my robe as I speak.

"Of course, sir. Just thought you should know." Greg gathers his notes and stands up.

"Besides, winter might not matter. The time is getting near." I smile and clasp Greg's shoulder.

"Ah, yes, sir, that's actually the last thing I wanted to talk with you about. See, we—"

I raise my hand and Greg falls silent. I gesture to the door behind my desk. A strand of light beams through its plaid curtains. I pick up my glass and turn the door handle. We step into my paradise.

The sun lands on my face, peeking out past the tree branches that droop over from the forest. Even at midday, shadows stretch far here. Wooden fences surround us, sealing us in a square. They're planted deep into the ground and still they tower over us. They're separated by half-inches, allowing for faint gusts of air. It's sealed off from the world. My private garden.

I empty my glass on a pot of dirt and rest it on a bench. I push past the sunflowers, holding them open so Greg can walk through. We step into a circle of stalks. Three rows of soil lay in front of us. I bend down and prod a flower, the tallest of the bunch. It bounces as I poke a thorn at its base. Most of the flowers are starting to rise from the ground. They were a good batch of seeds. They're almost ready.

"Is it ready?" I tug at a petal. Quite firm.

"Yes, I've made the order. It's on its way." Greg shields his eyes from the sun with his clipboard.

"Good, good."

Greg taps his fingers and drags his feet, covering his legs with a dust cloud. He scratches his arm, digging for an itch that's gone. He sniffs, scrunching his face, trying to pin down some imaginary odour.

"Say what you have to say." I stare at the flower.

"Sir, is this necessary?" Greg starts pacing.

"It's absolutely necessary." I trace my finger down the stem.

"But we've made so much progress. Look at how many people are here." Greg flips through his clipboard.

"I know the stats. It's wonderful, it really is. But there's more to do." I pinch the flower at its base, bunching up dirt in my fingernails.

"I know, I know. I'm just not sure if we should throw it all away." Greg's voice cracks.

Throw it all away? Does he think I'm collecting trash for curbside pickup? Who's he to—? Let it go, let it go.

"Greg, do you believe in this?" I look up at him.

"Of course I do." Greg stops fidgeting.

"Do you trust me?"

"Yes, yes, absolutely." Greg doesn't hesitate. Good.

"Then keep doing that. You know we're doing the right thing. It seems scary, and it is, but it's right. It's vital. We're doing something meaningful. You can feel that, can't you?" I gesture around the circle.

"I can." Greg is completely still now.

I bend my fingers and he kneels beside me. He stares at me. I guide his eyes to the soil.

"What do you think of this flower?" I give the stem a jerk back and forth.

"Um, quite nice, sir. Looks a little lopsided on the right. Those petals are frayed just at the edges. Not sure why, could be-"

"Just say it looks nice." He could have gone on for another ten minutes.

"It looks nice, sir." Greg bows his head.

"Yes, it does. It took months of work to get here. It was planted, watered, and nurtured to get to this point. It clawed its way out of the dirt and grew its limbs. Piece by piece, hour by hour, it fought to get to this point. At any moment, it could have withered, or snapped, or been chewed to bits by insects. Every day was a struggle. And now it's here." No flower's had its own epic before.

"So, what do we do now? Do we leave it here, comfortable in the dirt? Do we leave it in its rut? Do we let it stay?" I tighten my grip at the base.

Greg shrugs. I rip out the flower. It lets out a groan as it's torn from its hole. Tangled roots and globs of dirt dangle at its bottom. Beauty at the top, filth at the end.

"No, we don't leave it. We pluck it out and stuff it in a bouquet. We rest it in a jar of water. We lean it on a windowsill. We take it beyond its trappings, beyond its rut. It's not meant to stay in the dirt, reaching its peak before wasting away in the muck. We don't allow it to do so. It's meant for something more. It has a purpose. Do you understand?" I dangle the flower in front of Greg's face.

"We're meant for more." Greg nods and smiles.

"Exactly, Greg, exactly, you've got it. We've reached our peak. We're at the top. It's time for the next level." I feel a shiver down my back.

Greg's eyes are dancing. His knee is bouncing. I place the flower in his hand, folding his fingers around it.

"A reminder. Now, is there anything else?" I stand up, patting the dust off my pants.

Greg squeezes the flower and jumps to his feet. He glances over his clipboard and shakes his head. I clap his shoulder.

"Wonderful. Now, could you give me a moment alone?" I walk him through the sunflowers.

"Of course, sir, of course." Greg opens the door to the office.

I grab the watering can by the bench. I feel its contents slosh around. Plenty for one trip.

"Sir, there is one more thing." Greg stands in the doorway, peering over his clipboard.

Just one moment of peace, please. I nod.

"I've noticed a compound across town. It's fairly new, just bought a few extra acres, called Zaan, run by a guy named Smit." Greg flips a page.

"Can we get to the point?" I drum my fingers on the can.

"Sorry, sir. It looks like they've poached a few members"

"Poached?" I grip the can tighter. We've lost members? To a new compound? How? Why? What do they have? How have I not heard of them?

"Yes, it seems three members have gone there in the last six months. At least, that's where they said they were going." Greg tucks the clipboard under his arm.

I loosen my grip. Only three. In six months, they've only gotten three. Three misled, easily-suggestible people, I'm sure. They'll be back here before long, begging for forgiveness. Now that'll be a show…

"Not a priority." I wave to Greg as he disappears into the office.

After all these years, there's another compound. How did it take this long? I thought we'd be swamped with pretenders. Everybody wants to get in on the act. I'm not complaining. One compound is more than enough.

Three members… What were they offered? How'd they even hear about this compound? Doesn't matter. They can tell me when they come back. And they will come back.

Every few months, we wake up to a couple of empty cots. Runaways. The first time it happened, I wanted to track them down, buy some bloodhounds, find them in their two-bit motel, ask them why. But Joseph let them go. Told me to forget about it. Said they'd figure it out. Joseph…

He was right. The next week, they slunk back into the compound. Tried to blend back into the crowd and go about their work. But I spotted them in a sermon and gave them the Honour. They couldn't handle it out there, that world out there. Its pain, its greed, everything. It was too much. As hard as this place can be, it means something. And that's what brought them back. That's what always brings them back. Sure, there are permanent runaways, cots that are reoccupied. They force themselves back out there, trying to fit in, trying to hold it together. Maybe it works for them. But most return. These three will be the same. I'm sure…

Where did this compound come from? I haven't heard anything for months. The whole town's been quiet. A construction company tried to build a strip mall down the road, but they packed up weeks ago. Couldn't raise the money. Where did Zaan come from? Did Greg just find out about it? He should have known when they laid the first brick. Is he slipping? He looks focused, but… I heard those doubts. Maybe he's split, can't think straight. No, no, Greg's a professional. He doesn't make mistakes.

So he decided to keep me out of the loop? He thought it wasn't worth my attention? He tells me everything. All the ins and outs of this place. Something happens in this compound, in this town, he'll have a full report on my desk in the morning. I'll pretend to read it as he gives me the gist. It's a beautiful system.

Why did he wait until now to tell me about Zaan? What did he gain by holding out on me? Did he think he could handle this on his own? He tried something and when it failed, told me about it? Did he want some glory of his own? Steal my thunder? Steal my—

I unfurl my fingers from the can handle again. I'm living in possibilities. I need to stay here. Greg's just doing his job. No need to panic. Let him do his job and keep an eye on him. He knows what he's doing. Zaan shouldn't be a problem. Still, I didn't get here by being reckless. I'll get Greg to double his intel on them. We need to be prepared for anything. Besides, they might be the dose of antagonism we need. A little friction would keep things interesting.

I tilt the can and walk around the edges of the garden. Water splashes the flowers. Everything here runs like clockwork. They sprout, they flourish, they die. Endless rebirth. It's beautiful. This place is my cocoon. I give to my people every day. I give my time, my energy, my attention, my wisdom, I give it all. I'm more public than private. But I need time to reflect, to rest. I deserve this place. This garden is my sanctuary.

This garden is hypocrisy. I preach sacrifice, denial, self-control; then I retreat to a personal paradise. I tend to flowers, I bask in the sun, I sleep. Everyone's out there chopping wood and gathering crops while I'm snipping petals in here. This is a gift from me to me. I'm sick every time I slink back here, but it's vital. I force myself to come here, force myself to indulge. I have to remind myself what it feels like to submit. I have to confront temptation. I need to enjoy this place, because one day, I'll burn it all to cinders and stand in the ash. And it will feel wonderful.

I've finished my circuit. I drop the can on the ground. I crack my neck as I look at the sun. I could lose myself in this place. The quiet and the seclusion are intoxicating. It'd be easy to just lie down…

I feel a sting on my neck. I catch a mosquito between my fingers as it tries to escape with its loot. I hear more buzzing around my ears. I'm back in reality. Back to work. I open the door to the office.

Ken is sitting on Greg's desk. What a specimen. His muscles look chiseled out of stone. I've seen him crush apples with one hand. Messy but impressive. The desk groans under his weight. He's a behemoth.

He came here years ago, some hayseed hick from the Bible Belt. He was wearing overalls and a straw hat. I'm not joking. This Mark Twain character showed up at my compound and asked to join us. Looking at him, I bit my lip to keep from laughing. The hat, the denim, the gap tooth; it was all too much. I thought he was lost and told him to move on.

He followed me around the compound. He kept asking questions, kept staring at every building like they were monoliths. He spoke with monosyllabic words. I told him to leave.

But he stayed. Day after day he followed me, asking an endless barrage of questions. On the fifth day, I considered his request. He wasn't leaving and I had to do something. I asked him why he was here. He said he had gotten tired of the farm, wanted something more. He'd heard about us at a gas station. He'd thought it sounded too good to be true. As he talked, I watched his eyes. They didn't waver. He just stared at me. He didn't hide anything. He was dull and malleable. He was the perfect bodyguard.

Ken leans in close to Greg, who's sorting through papers on his desk. I lean against the door frame.

"What's that?" Ken traces his finger over a sheet.

"Nothing, just technical stuff." Greg pulls the papers closer. His cheeks are red.

"Like what?" Ken crooks his head to read the papers.

"Making sure we have enough supplies for the month." Greg's clears his throat.

"Oh. Can I help?" Ken flicks at Greg's hair.

"Probably not." Greg's chair scratches on the floor as he fidgets.

I clap my hands together. Ken jumps to his feet, looking at me. Always good to see.

"How are you, Ken?" I peel off the door frame.

"Good, sir. Can't complain." He flashes that gap-tooth smile.

"Excellent, excellent. Well, if you're done bothering Greg, I'd like to see my people. Would you join me?" I glance at Greg's files. Walls of nonsense words.

"Of course, sir." Ken's eyes sharpen.

"Would you mind waking me up?" I present my cheek.

I brought Ken onboard for many reasons. His commitment, his passion, his...suggestible nature. He's the most loyal man here. He's a man of action, not questions. He's always ready to do what has to be done. But above all—

Ken's hand streaks across my face like a mallet, destroying my garden stupor.

Above all, he's strong as an ox. And that has endless benefits.

"Shall we?" I fling open the door and dash outside. Time to see the people.

CHAPTER THREE

I nearly decapitate myself.

The plank is a foot away from my head. I'm about to jam my neck into it. It'll crush my windpipe. I can't stop moving. I duck under it, clipping my forehead. The plank wobbles but stays afloat. I hunch away from the board, nursing my hairline. No blood, no splinters. It stings. I shake my head.

Two builders are holding the plank. I could fit my fists in their mouths at this moment. The one on the right looks like his soul was just consumed in front of him. The one on the left is shaking, bouncing the board up and down. They're ready to collapse.

Ken is beside me. His eyes are racing. He grabs my chin and tilts my head up. He runs his fingers across my hairline. His grip hurts more than the plank. I pull his hand off my jaw.

"Are you alright, sir?" Ken keeps leaning into my hairline.

"I'm fine, give me some space." I walk to the other side of the porch.

"Are you sure?" Ken takes a step to me and I raise my hand.

"I'm sure. It's just a bump. If I can't take a few of those, we've got bigger problems." I touch my forehead; it's definitely going to bruise.

Ken nods and his eyes slow down. He faces the builders. He flexes his fingers and lowers his head. Those boys would run if their legs weren't noodles.

"You dumb fucks. You could've... You stupid fucks." Ken stalks towards the builders, whose eyes resemble dinner plates.

Ken stands over the builder in the right, breathing down on him. The builder fumbles over his flailing lips. His friend isn't much help; he keeps clearing his throat and coughing. Ken's hands curl into fists.

"Oh, Ken, lay off them. It was just a mistake." I pat Ken's shoulder, pushing him to the side. The builders are still terrified.

"We're, we're so, so, so, sorry, s-sir." The right builder shoves the words out. His colleague nods.

"I know you are. Look, no harm done." I pull up my hair. They squint their eyes and nod.

"Why were you here in the first place?" I rest my elbows on the plank.

"We had an extra piece, sir." The right one looks at his friend for support.

"I heard Greg say that you needed some wood for, for, for..." The left one can't look me in the eyes.

"For a sermon." I touch the left one's arm.

"Yes, yes, just that, exactly that." The board dips and I jerk towards the left one. He smiles as he lifts it back up.

"So, we thought we'd bring this board to you. Since it was just lying around" The right one drums his fingers.

"Not that it's scrap." The left one tightens his grip.

"No, no, no, of course not. It's excellent wood, perfect, really. Not a single knot." The right one raps his knuckles on the plank.

"Yes, we just didn't need it. It'd be a shame if it went to waste-"

"A terrible shame."

"Yes, exactly. We finished our section-"

"With a week to spare."

"We finished and we had some spare parts so naturally we thought..."

I slap my hand down, feeling the vibrations. They stop talking.

"That was quite considerate. Wouldn't you agree?" I glance at Ken. His arms are folded as he leans against a porch beam. He bobs his head; close enough to a nod.

"Yes, this was very considerate. I appreciate it, honestly. Thank you, boys." I pat their hands.

"You're welcome, sir." The right one flashes his pearly whites.

"Sir, I want to apologize again for—" The left reaches out to me. I move off the board.

"No, I won't hear it. The whole thing was an accident. My fault, really. How could you have known I'd run out the door at the exact moment you'd walk up here? You're not clairvoyant, are you?" I raise my eyebrows. They shake their heads and chuckle.

"No, I didn't think so. There's no reason to apologize. I should thank you. That hit woke me up." I clap the left one's shoulder.

"Now, put that board in the back. Greg will show you where to go. Then get back to work. We're wasting light." I wave them away.

"Yes, sir, thank you, sir." They disappear into the office. I hear Greg grumble.

"You don't waste time, do you?" I smile at Ken as I walk to the edge of the porch.

"No." Ken joins my side.

"One of your better qualities. Now, let's get going…" I step off the porch.

It's a beautiful beehive. Everyone streams in and out of buildings, carrying supplies and gear. People stop to talk, to trade, to listen, then return to their post. There are no wasted moments. Everybody has a purpose, a goal. This is a good day.

I'll be honest: Most days are crap. Usually, someone lags behind. They're tired, or incompetent, or lazy. It's common with the new recruits. They don't understand the routine and the structure. They start strong, to be sure. They'll go weeks, even months, without failing. But when they mess up, and they always do, it throws everyone off. The machine stutters. There are days where one errant buffoon destroys the whole schedule.

But today, the machine purrs. Everybody is where they should be. We haven't had that many new recruits to slow us down. Not many recruits in a while…

The planters are beyond the buildings armed with scythes and bags as they walk through fields armed. They're almost silhouettes strolling across the horizon. Builders fluttering around the main compound. Some carry boxes overflowing with tools. They pop in and out of buildings, pointing at the ground and each other, yelling. They're the handymen. They make sure a roof doesn't cave in on us during a sermon. That happened once, so I keep an eye out. It was one of my best sermons, but still…

Most of the builders are working on our new living quarters. It's right across from the sermon hall. Prime real estate for the best members. That's what I call motivation.

This is the biggest project we've ever done. We decimated part of the forest to make it happen. We've never had this many builders working together on one structure. But it's worth it.

Joseph was exact when he designed this place. He poured over the maps, laying out every building. It all had to be perfect. And we followed his instructions to a "T." It's taken years, but we've built the compound from his mind. No, from my mind. I helped with the planning, I edited, I led, I saw it through, I stayed. This is my vision. These living quarters are the last pieces. It's a complete thought, not a half dream.

I take a deep breath. This energy is intoxicating. I wander to the side of the path as Ken steps on my shadow. I walk along the edge of the ditch, passing by workers carrying lumber, saws, and shears. A woman lugging a bag of mulch over her shoulder walks towards me. Behind me, a man holding a bucket of water approaches. They lock eyes and nod. The woman drops the bag and extends her hand. The man passes the bucket and picks up the bag. They continue walking. Perfection.

I see a faint stream. Runoff from the river. Grass and rocks cover most of it, but I can hear a light gurgle. Four people are hunched over, kneeling into the water. Baskets of clothes lay next to them.

"Good work?" I squat down.

The workers squint their eyes. They smile and hold up their wrinkled hands. I chuckle and salute them.

I return to the path. I sidestep hurried planters running to the fields with water jugs. I nod at slower members, who smile and quicken their pace. Two people run past me, making a beeline for the living quarters. They're the boys who nearly chopped my head off. Ken grunts as they disappear.

I'm at the compound square. Our focal point. I can see every building from here. You step forward here and you're going somewhere. We built a small box filled with flowers here. I sit on it and watch.

Workers zip by, engrossed in their work. They don't see me. I notice one man leave a woodshed with a paper slip. I rotate in my seat as I watch him circle the center. He ducks under a moving plank and nearly bumps into a woman holding an axe. He reaches the living quarters and hands the paper to the foreman. He nods, spits, and rips half the slip. The man glances at the paper and runs back to the shed, dodging incoming wheelbarrows. I could sit here all day.

A woman is hauling two water buckets across the square. She stops near my box and stretches her back, groaning. She's got large biceps and a better-than-average face. She winces as she carries the buckets behind a building. Let's follow this vein.

I pop out of my seat. I reach the side of the building and hold my hand in front of Ken. He starts to speak and I wag my finger. He sighs, nods, and leans against a fence. I wipe the sweat layer from my face and round the corner.

The woman is pouring the bucket of water into a sprinkling can. She hunches over a patch of dirt and tilts the can. Dozens of wooden stakes dot the patch. She rocks the can back and forth over the soil as she walks. Sloppy form. She shuffles through rows of small orange specks. She inspects the garden, holding the sprinkling can at her waist, smiling.

"Now that's a nice patch." I step out from the building's shadow.

The woman looks up and blinks. The sun is in her eyes. I inch to the right, tilting my chin up. She smiles and nods. I walk to the garden's edge.

"How's your day going?" I tap a pile of dirt, spraying flecks over my shoe.

"Can't complain." She shrugs.

"So, what do we have here?" I brush the soil off an orange speck with my foot.

"Carrots, mostly. Tried growing cucumbers, but it didn't work out. They look warped." She contorts her hand, pointing her fingers in random directions.

"Shame." I grab a carrot and tug on it, revealing a web of dirty roots.

"Guess there was only room for one phallic vegetable." She chuckles.

I don't know what she means, but I smile. I wrap my fingers around the carrot and press my foot against the root. I tear the carrot away from the ground, dusting the dirt off.

"Sorry, I wanted a better look." I wipe my hands on my pants.

"No problem. They're about ready, anyway." She bites her lower lip and holds her arm.

"This looks good, quite good. You've been doing this long?" I step closer.

"As long as I've been here. I mean, I started in the field, but they moved me here after a week." She clears her throat.

"Why did they do that?"

"I accidently hit a worker with a shovel."

"I don't see why—"

"Well, it wasn't an accident, really. I swung it and her face happened to be there."

"Happened?"

"She kept getting in my way. She was so damn slow, every day, holding up the line. I was stuck behind her and I told to pick up the pace and she told me to calm down."

"Did you?"

"I hate it when people say that. 'Calm down.' Like it's any of their business. They don't know where I'm at. Don't you hate that?"

"Completely."

"Well, I kept telling her to hurry up and she kept telling me to relax. 'Calm down, what's your rush? We'll get there soon enough.' So I picked up the shovel."

"I think I remember this. That woman needed ten stitches."

"Nine. She was back in the field the next day."

"Commendable. I think she's a coordinator now.

"Assistant coordinator."

"And they sent you here."

"For the best. I like it back here."

"And all that happened in a week."

"Six days, yeah."

"I see."

The woman flexes her fingers on the watering can handle. I take a step out of swing range.

"Sorry for all that. What a terrible introduction. I can't shut up sometimes." She walks towards me, brushing hair from her face.

"Clearly." I raise my eyebrows.

"Someone asks me a question and I go on and on and on…" She makes circles with her hands.

What am I doing? Backing away from my own follower? Stop it.

"And I appreciate it. That was...informative. Thank you." I squeeze her shoulder.

"So, what brings you here?" She steps out of the garden.

"Curiosity. I like to check in on everyone and you caught my eye. Besides, I haven't been back here in awhile and I wanted to see what you've done with the place." I shake dirt loose from my shoe.

"And what's the verdict?" She fills up her watering can.

"Only one way to find out. Would you mind?" I hold up the carrot.

She takes it from my hand and points the tip at the ground. She tilts the can and soaks the vegetable. She rubs her thumb against it, pushing away the dirt. She grips the larger top and flicks off every speck. She drops the can and brings the carrot to eye level, rotating it. She gives it to me and I bite off a chunk. It makes a beautiful crunch as I chew. I push it around with my tongue, savouring the flavour. The woman stares at me as I finish off the piece. I swallow. She leans forward.

"Damn good." I take another bite.

"I thought so." She folds her arms.

We stand there in silence, aside from my chewing. I'm trying to think of what to say next when I hear shouting. A mob of yelling. I round the building corner and see Ken craning his head past the building. He turns around and I raise my hands.

"They're lifting a support beam for the living quarters." Ken peaks around the building again.

"Pretty big?" I take another chunk out of the carrot.

"Yeah, it's a shaved trunk. Looks like about twenty people are around it." Ken ticks off his fingers, counting.

"Sounds like a show. Let's give it a look." I salute Ken as he disappears past the building.

The woman is sprinkling water on the patch. She wanders into the field, wiping her forehead. She bends down, examining a dirt hole. She's lost in her work, like I was never here.

"What's your name?" I cup my hand around my mouth.

"Sandra." She doesn't look up. She stays crouched, holding her can for balance.

"Keep up the good work." I snap the carrot in half, biting into one piece and throwing the other into a bush. I round the corner.

They're ants swarming a carcass. A mass is huddled in front of the living quarters worksite. They jostle and surge. People dash to new spots, squeezing between fellow members. They're yelling "lift," "hold," "stay," "pull," in a messy swirl. Voices overlap each other, drowning out everyone.

I jog to catch up with Ken. I manoeuvre past onlookers and reach the fringe of the mob. The tallest members are back here, a human wall. I stand on my toes, straining my neck to see into the centre, but it's just a collection of flesh. I try to push past two hulking brutes but they're too focused to see me. I fall back, panting. Ken is beside me, smirking. I smile back and roll my eyes.

I circle the edge of the group, looking for an opening. It's a tuna can of tightly-packed people, all turned toward the focal point. I see an empty space. I bolt forward, worming to the middle. I see it.

It's a trunk thicker than my torso and longer than the office. It could batter the gates of Heaven. It's been sanded and shaped into a rough rectangle beam. Its edges are jagged and gnarled, but it'll keep the roof up.

People meet at this opening and grab the beam. They push it, gritting their teeth and snorting. Their feet tear into the ground...

One member spots me and stands up, smacking his friends' shoulders. The lifters release the beam, looking up at me. They breathe through their mouths. I shake my head.

"No, no, I'm not here to sermonize. I'm just a spectator. Now, get back to work. I want to see that beam held high." I slap a builder's chest.

"Yes, sir." He arms bulge, nearly ripping his shirt. God, where did we find this one? He could pulverize Ken. Maybe.

"Get to it." I raise my hands.

The men fall back on the wood, tightening their grips. They dig under it, inching it above the ground. It starts to rise.

"That's it, that's it."

Other builders stand above these groups on an elevated platform. Their feet are eye-level with the lifters. The gaping hole of an entrance looms behind them. They're reaching for the beam. They'll drag it inside and haul it into the rafters. It'll be the spine of the building. These men just need to raise it above their heads.

"Keep at it, you're halfway there."

The men gasp as they bring the beam to their waists. They pop out their thighs for support. They're still for a moment, repositioning their hands. They nod and begin again.

"Wonderful, you're supermen. Yes, just like that…"

They bring the wood to their chins. Several people duck under the beam and push it up. They grind the grass to mush. They're shiny with sweat. Gorgeous…

"Yes, yes, yes, yes, yes, yes…"

It wobbles over their heads. The platforms builders grasp for the beam. The men below extend their arms, making the final shove. They look up, straining. The trade-off is almost done.

"You've got it. You've done it. You're unstoppable, you're-"

The beam tilts away from the platform. Workers shuffle and scramble, trying to stabilize it. The men on the platform jump down for support. It dips to the ground and slides down, slipping from their hands. The beam crashes on the ground. Right on a man's leg.

My hands are frozen above my head. The man's eyes are glued to his leg. His lips let out a sharp whistle. The workers are lying on the ground, panting. Some hold the beam for support; others are collapsed on their knees. Builders jump from the platform. We're statues. The screaming starts. The man's voice splits my ears. It's a guttural screech. He rocks back and forth, banging his head on the ground, writhing in agony. He grinds his teeth together. He tears out clumps of grass, trying to escape.

The beam has consumed his left leg. It starts just below his waist and stretches past his feet. Red seeps out beneath it, pooling around the man. I step away from the liquid.

The man's voice cracks. He slams the beam, slobbering over his chin as he tries to move it. The wood doesn't budge. He rams his knuckles into it. It doesn't budge. He tears at the sides, ripping off splinters. It doesn't budge.

He falls to his back. His eyes are full of tear as he looks at me. He gasps, jerking his head at the beam. The workers are still frozen in time. They stare at me, waiting for...something.

Okay, okay, I can do this. I need to comfort this man...no, no, not comfort, guide, yes, that's it. I have to guide him, show the, the point of it. Just until they get the beam off. No problem. I wipe my face and point at the wood, nodding at the builders. I kneel beside the man, inching away from the blood. I grip his hand and he nearly crushes my fingers.

"I know this is scary. But you're...you're strong. You can make it through this. And after, you'll be, you'll be...better for it. You'll be on the other side."

Workers crowd around the beam, trying to get an angle. The man bangs his head on the ground. He looks at his leg and gags, howling. I focus on his finger wrapped around mine. I don't look away. He squeezes tighter, slamming the earth with his free hand. He's not listening; how can he? I can't hear myself.

"You're a soldier. This is a test, yes, a test you're going to pass. Pass with flying colours. You'll be a... beacon to others. 'There's someone who's been through it.' That's what they'll say. They'll know you're real. You'll be an example, something to follow. You'll show us..."

My lips move, but only air comes out. I barely notice as Ken shoves me out of the way. My fingers slide out of the man's grip. I land on my ass as he stands over the man and seizes the beam. He shouts at workers to get ready. Ken exhales and bends his knees. His legs straighten, inch by inch, and the beam rises with them. The man's leg is attached to the beam for a moment before falling down. Ken brings the wood to his thigh level. The builders drag the man away and Ken drops the beam. He bends over, panting and moaning.

They lay the man next to me. His eyes flutter; he's not here. I pat his chest, muttering an apology. Everyone's moving around me, shouting for help, trying to be useful. They sound submerged. My gaze traces the man's body, reaching his left leg. It's ruined, beyond mangled. He'll be lucky to keep it. It's coated in gore. His pants are shredded, revealing cuts, bruises, and gashes. Wood chips are everywhere. His leg looks like it's been drained. It's been reduced to a noodle.

My stomach contracts. My throat burns. I press my chest, regaining my center. I'm fine. I'm here.

The workers lay a stretcher beside the man and drag him onto it. He whimpers as they bring him up. I stand with them, clutching the man's shoulder. His eyes are half-closed but I see a glimpse of his pupils. His head rolls away.

I tell the carriers to get going. They haul the man through the compound, flanked by onlookers. They enter the infirmary. Silence hangs over everyone. They slowly turn to me. I blink.

"That was horrible. But it's the risk we all run. And we can overcome it. We're strong. Strong enough." I have no idea what I'm saying. My brain is grabbing words and shoving them in my mouth.

"Now, let's get back to work. He'll be fine, he'll be fine. Back to work everyone." I pass through the crowd, squeezing arms and smiling. Pure autopilot.

They all look down at the ground. They're appalled. They don't know what's happened, and I'm making it worse. They saw their friend get brutalized and I'm telling them to work. I should be comforting them, giving them something, anything, to help. But I keep walking and smiling. This is the best I can do.

The crowd fades away, muttering. Their disgusted eyes disappear. It all melts away. Now I'm standing in the forest. I shake my head and clench my eyes shut. My throat tingles.

"Are you alright, sir?" Ken is beside me.

"Yes, yes, of course I'm fine." My stomach growls.

"Are you sure? Do you need to-?"

"I'm fine, really. Just give me a moment, will you? I have to...process everything." I smile at him and I duck behind a tree.

My throat is on fire. Something's rising. Oh, God, that was so much blood. His leg, his leg, it's gone. My stomach is churning. I hunch over, resting my hands on my knees. His eyes, he was begging me for help. I just stared at him. I held his hand and let him suffer. I didn't do anything. I was worth—

No. Stop this. I did what I could; it simply wasn't enough. But I tried. I'll learn from this. I'll be better for it.

The burning subsides. My stomach settles. I stand up and exhale. I'm fine. I'm here.

Vomit erupts out my mouth.

CHAPTER FOUR

I'm standing at the edge of the river.

The sun is dipping below the trees. A cool breeze rustles the leaves and bushes. Faint voices weave through the forest. Everyone's going to dinner. I'm alone. I sent Ken away. I needed my space. He walked to the compound, protesting the whole time. I watched him disappear. I stood still, listening for footsteps or snapped twigs. I was met with silence.

I wandered along the river. I followed its flow, stopping at a small clearing. I planted my feet and stared at the water, watching the gentle currents. I've been here for hours.

It was a single burst of vomit. No repeated blasts, no dry heaving. I didn't drool and lean on a tree for support. I wiped my mouth and moved on. Nothing major. But why did I do it? I saw the beam fall, heard the crunch, smelled the blood. I listened to every scream. I held his hand and watched them carry away his limp body. I even managed to talk. It was rambling nonsense, but I talked. I went through all that and I was fine. I came to the woods and emptied my guts.

It was a delayed reaction, I guess. I could hold it all together when I really needed to. I spaced out, but I was basically there. The main functions worked. I walked to the forest and I didn't have to hang on. So everything went loose.

But why did I throw up? It's not like I haven't seen blood before. I've cut myself open, I've fractured my arm, I've been hurt. I saw a man fall off a roof once. He landed right on his shoulder, popped it out. He couldn't work for a month. I don't have a weak stomach. We live in the woods with no toilets; I've seen and smelled, some questionable things. I covered myself in sweat this morning, for fuck's sake.

But that was different somehow. The adrenaline, the crowd, the performance, they all added distance. I wasn't really there. I was protected. Today there was no distance. The blood, the screaming, the pain; they all got shoved in my face. I was in it. I panicked.

I'm a two-bit liar. I stand on that podium, I talk about sacrifice and penance and suffering, I tell everyone to try harder; then this happens. I'm faced with an actual moment of agony and I turn away. I retreat. I have a chance to feel something real, and I puke.

What did that man feel? When that beam fell on his leg, he became pain. All his life, his troubles, worries, loves, regrets, they all melted away. His focus narrowed down to one thought: Suffering. What a pure experience. Nothing clouded his mind, nothing distracted him; he was totally in the moment. And where was I? Holding his hand and mumbling to myself.

What did I miss back there? I could have learned so much. I had an opportunity to see the agony up close. It could have been revelatory; or, at least, sermon material. It was a perfect chance; now it's lost.

I failed today. I let this moment slip away. I'm still weak. All these years and I have so far to go. I'm crawling when I should be running. Why do these people follow me? I'm no better than them, no different than them. I'm just as lost, just as confused. I shouldn't be a leader. I should—

No. That's not true. I'm here for a reason. I'm in charge for a reason. I'm feeble, weak, afraid, same as everyone. But I can see my flaws. I can see everyone's flaws. I know what's killing us, what's driving us insane. I'm ruled by the same diseases, but I'm working on a cure. I'm digging out of the muck. I deserve this position. I built this place from nothing. I'm surrounded by followers, by believers. They trust me. I'm showing them the way.

I failed today. I fail every day. But tomorrow is another chance. I'll find a new way to fail. I'll dig to the bottom and build our future on monument of failures.

I remove my shoes and socks, tossing them behind a bush. I shake my feet, letting go of the tension. I lean forward and dip my big toe into the water. I shiver. I strip naked, stretching my arms. I close my eyes, holding one foot above the river. I penetrate the water. I exhale, releasing a flurry of bubbles as I sink to the bottom. I float down in a spiral, pushing my hands away from the surface. My feet squish against the soft floor as I sink into the mud. Dirt pushes between my toes. I open my eyes. I see a distorted outline of my body and dim fragments that surround me. I look up at the water shimmering against the distant light. Faint ripples, remnants from my splash, are the only evidence I'm here. Shadows creep at the edge of my vision. It's a black tomb. I'm home.

I half-curl into a ball. I jerk my hands out, carving a path. I kick my legs and stroke, slowly turning upside down. I wrap my fingers around a collection of weeds for stability. I let my legs float down to me so I'm parallel with the floor. My stomach brushes the mud. I swim forward.

My lungs are burning. I wasted a lot of air in the descent. I part the water with my hands, pushing the ground with my legs for momentum. My shoulder bumps against something sharp. It scrapes my skin, but doesn't break it. I reach out for the object and I break a piece off. It's a wood chip. I grab onto a branch and pull myself along the log. It's rotted and decayed. I rip off another chunks of wood as I travel down it. The log's been down here for years. How have I missed it? I run out of branches and grip the log's sides, pushing further into the dark. My lungs are screaming.

The log ends. I'm floating alone. I peer into the dark. I'm enveloped by the blackness. It gazes into me. It's everything I'm afraid of. It could swallow me whole. I'm in a pit. I want to scream, shut my eyes, and scramble to the surface. I never want to be here. But I stay, suspended in space. The darkness stares at me, and I stare back.

God, my lungs are dying.

This is why I'm a leader. Who else could do this? Who else could gaze into this hole and not blink? Who could see their insignificance laid bare and soldier on? Me. I have the strength. That's why I come here. It humbles me, it silences me, it terrifies me. It reminds me why I'm in charge.

My lungs are slamming on my chest in protest, so I swim to the top. I break the surface, gulping back air. I stroke to the bank and haul myself up, collapsing on the ground. My stomach rises and plummet. I keep my feet in the water. I want to hold on to that feeling.

I'm not the first one to use this river. Villagers, hunters, and passersby have all been to this place. To them, it was a rest stop, a watering hole, a food source. They didn't understand it, didn't really use it. But Zeke did.

Hundreds of years ago, this place was about the same. A town was nearby. Nothing special, a few dozen people, mostly farmers. You'd have to go out of your way to find it. Not that it'd be worth the trip. It was just another village in a country teaming with them.

Zeke lived in these woods with his twin daughters. His wife died during childbirth. Zeke built a cabin on the other side of the river, right across from me. They grew crops, hunted game, and netted fish, all near the river. They went into town from time to time for supplies. People steered clear of Zeke. He didn't talk to anyone, he didn't know anyone. That worked for everybody. He'd arrive, get what he needed, and leave. Zeke's world revolved around this river.

One day, Zeke went into town with his daughters. They were in their earlier twenties at this point. Zeke kept to himself as usual, but the girls were curious. They'd never seen this place before. Zeke had to drag them away from store fronts and stalls. They came at morning and were still there at dusk. They didn't want to go home.

They met a butcher boy who was about their age. He took a shine to them. He showed them how his shop worked, how he skinned the animals, how he prepared the meat. He even taught them how to swing a cleaver. They hung onto every word.

Zeke was getting angry. He'd been standing in the town square for hours. He told the girls it was time to go, but they waved him off. He screamed at them, but they ignored him. He glared at the butcher boy and said the girls were on their own. He stormed into the woods.

The daughters and the butcher boy talked as their shadows grew. The girls were very curious about one thing. It was something they'd never done before, something Zeke could never do with them. They wanted the boy to show them how it was done and asked him to follow them into the forest. How could he resist?

They walked ahead of him, weaving between trees. He clutched his lantern tight. They looked back at him and giggled. They quickened their pace, vanishing into the woods. The boy called to them and they answered. He followed their voices and arrived at the river's edge. He could hear the girls giggling. He saw them on the other side of the water. They waved at him and disappeared. Then Zeke spilt his guts with a knife.

The boy fell into the river. Water rushed inside the wound. The boy tried to swim away, but Zeke pounced on him. He held the boy's head underwater and opened his throat. Zeke and his daughters ate well that night.

They did the same thing a few more times. Always men, always at night, always by the river. The deputy, the preacher, the shepherd, they all made it to the dinner table. Of course, it didn't take long for the villagers to suss out what was happening. All those men gone, all in a month, and all of them seen leaving with Zeke's daughters. Zeke wasn't too subtle about it. He came into town with the preacher's ring. His wife recognized it and that was that. They had their proof.

The next time Zeke and his daughters entered the village, the people were ready. Zeke left his girls at the town square and entered the metal shop to get his knives sharpened. When he emerged, he saw his daughters bound and gagged. Villagers were holding daggers to their throats. They told Zeke they knew what he'd done. He had to give himself up. They told him to be peaceful about it and there'd be no trouble. They asked him to think about his children, to keep them safe. Nobody wanted a bloodbath. Zeke looked at his daughters and nodded. He ran into the woods.

Zeke stumbled through the forest. The villagers were breathing down his neck. He could feel their torches, their screeches, their venom. He knew these woods better than anyone. They'd never catch him. He darted past trees and over rotting logs. He could hear the running water. He tore through the bushes, breaking into the clearing. He'd made it.

He saw the river as the pitchfork burst through his chest.

Zeke kept going. He stumbled into the water, splashing forward. Villagers watched him thrash and scream. He reached the middle point and stopped. He floated downstream, leaving a trail of watery blood. His daughters shared his fate. The villagers burned his cabin. People tried to erase him from their minds. He became a legend, a bedtime story to frighten children.

Zeke was a madman. But something drew him to this river, something unknown. It pulled him in and swallowed him. It's the same thing that tugs on me.

I look upstream. The cavern looms above me. A small castle of rocks and jagged edges. An unwelcome blemish on the landscape. All the water flows from its mouth. It is the source.

This river calls to me, like it called to Zeke. It demands sacrifice and blood. It's part of our plan. It's the abyss we must plumb. The cavern is a hungry maw, and I will feed it.

CHAPTER FIVE

I can't see anything.

No shapes, no distance, nothing. I'm standing. I can feel the ground beneath my feet. I hop up and I hear an echo as I land. Where am I?

I start walking, holding out my hands, groping for anything. My footsteps sound far away. I lift my right leg forward and it lands in the same spot it left. My left leg does the same. They feel like jelly. There's something heavy on my chest. It wraps around my torso, squeezing it tight. It's massive. My knees sink to the floor. I can't support this weight. It's crushing me. I'm falling. I can see now. It's a sea of white. Lines and edges run upward and forward in the distance. Smooth walls stretch to a jagged ceiling. I'm in a box.

The floor rushes to meet me. I rotate in the air, turning toward the ceiling. Water specks splash on my face. I see a waterfall next to me. It's silent, plummeting to the bottom. I can't see its source. It just flows. I touch it. My hand passes through it. I'm completely dry. The waterfall yanks me down, hurtling me to the ground. I'm almost there. I want to look away, but my head is stuck. My eyes won't close. My nose is an inch from contact.

I'm standing again. The walls have fallen away. It's an empty field. A red orb hovers on the horizon. I walk to it. My legs are fine. I'm wearing a golden chest plate. I rap it with my knuckles and I hear a hollow echo. I hook my hands between the exposed armpits and pull. I push it away, separating it from my body. I can see my stomach. It's moving. The armour snaps back to my torso. I tug on it, but it doesn't budge. It's welded to my body. I can feel it burrowing beneath my skin. It doesn't hurt, but I can feel it. I keep walking.

I'm closer to the orb. It rests in the middle of the horizon. It pulses, emitting a halo of light. I can feel its warmth and I shield my face, squinting through my fingers. I've reached the horizon. I stretch my arm out to it. The orb's moving. It rises to the sky. It goes higher and higher, towering over me. I'll never touch it. But it hasn't left the horizon. It still straddles the halfway point, obscuring its bottom part. It hasn't moved at all. But still it rises.

No, it's not rising; I'm sinking. My legs have been absorbed by the ground. I grab the floor and I pull out large clumps of mud. The whole place is dissolving into goo. I pump my legs, trying to gain momentum. I'm so close to the horizon. If I can just touch, surely... I swing my arms as I scramble forward. I don't move. I'm trapped. The mud is already past my waist. It's going to consume me. The orb is right there...

There's a brush on my neck. Soft, gentle, like a kiss. I turn around and I see a flash of light. I cover my eyes, bracing against the heat. Something pokes my chest. I open my eyes and look down. Three prongs have pierced the armour, penetrating my skin. I'm skewered.

The prongs stay glued to my body. They extended out from the light. I watch my blood ooze onto them. The armour falls away, disappearing into the mud. I can see my stomach. Something twitches below the gaping wounds. I crane my neck to look. I couldn't...

A shape is standing over me. It's a distorted blur. No, it's a person. He's shaking my shoulders, talking quickly. I bat him away and rub my eyes. My mind fights through the fog. I swipe at the air. I have to stop. I have to...

I'm in my bed. What was that? There was a waterfall, and an... orb? Was that it? And I was wearing...a suit? It's slipping away. I saw something down there. What was it?

"Sir, we need to talk." A voice tears at my concentration.

It's gone. I've lost it, whatever it was. Time to wake up.

Greg is standing over me. He's chewing his lips. He's wearing his night robe. He's staring at the door. Moonlight beams through the window. I sit up.

"What's wrong?" I slap my cheek to focus.

Greg opens his mouth and winces. He paces in front of me, wiping his face and wheezing. He stops to speak, says nothing, and resumes pacing. He dashes to the window and scans the darkness.

"Greg, talk to me." My body tenses.

He looks at me and nods. He wrings his hands as he approaches me.

"Sir, there was a... God, I can't... There was... We found...Oh, God." Greg rubs his eyes and starts pacing again.

"Greg, tell me what's happened." I feel cold sweat gathering on the back of my neck.

Greg squeezes his chin as he stares at me. His eyes are watery. He grabs my hand and pulls me out of bed.

"Sir, you have to see this." He opens the door, letting in a cold breeze.

"See what? What's going on?" I grab my shoes under the bed and slip them on.

"I can't, I just can't. You have to..." Greg stumbles to the porch, grabs a lantern, and wanders into the compound.

I follow him, struggling to keep pace. He marches past the buildings, slamming his feet on the ground. The lantern wobbles in his hand. The light sways back and forth, half-illuminating his face. His lips are pursed, drained of colour. He doesn't spare a glance for me; he just stares ahead. I don't bother to ask what's going on. He can't hear me.

Silence surrounds us. No one else is outside. This place looks like a mausoleum. The buildings are reduced to shapeless black blobs looming in the distance. We can only see patches of grass spotlighted by the lantern. We're a speck traveling through a sea. I cross my arms against my chest. My heart is trying to climb out through my throat.

We reach the compound square. Greg stops, looks around, and pinches the bridge of his nose. He points towards Sandra's garden, biting his lip. Did something happen to her? No, he lowers his hand and tugs on his hair. He spins around, rapping his knuckles on his forehead. His body is shaking. His breath is short and shallow.

"Focus." I pat his shoulder, using it to steady my trembling hand.

Greg blinks. He takes a deep breath, resting his hands on his knees. He stands straight and picks up the lantern, holding it forward. He arcs his arm, searching through the beam of light. He stops, dangling the lantern as he stares at the shadows. He gestures at the cafeteria. He walks towards it, but I jog in front of him. Impatience is killing me.

Faint traces of light follow me as I approach the double doors. I wrap my fingers around the handle and curl my toes, grounding myself. I'm here, I'm ready. I pull on the doors and they don't move. I rattle them, but they don't budge. A chain is sealing them together. Greg's standing at my side, shaking his head.

"This way." He disappears around the corner of the building.

His lantern's glow bobs in the distance, dimly lighting the trees and bushes on the edge of the compound. I trace my hand on the building as I walk to the back. I hear whispers. I let out a shaky breath and rub my neck. I round the corner.

Greg is near the forest, standing on a pile of snapped twigs. Ken is standing next to him, dangling a lantern on his fingers, moving his lips. I can't hear him. He spots me and stops talking. I approach them, raising my eyebrows. Ken nods and Greg moves aside. Ken pulls back a bush. Greg holds his lantern over the ground as I look down.

It's a man. He's staring at the sky, his head resting on a tree stump. His back is curved, matching the natural dip in the ground. His arms rest on his stomach, his knuckles curled. His bare feet point to the cafeteria. His pants and shirt are covered in dirt and leaves. His beard obscures a red line running across his neck.

The cut doesn't look that deep. It doesn't reveal any of the inner workings. It's just a thin slice from ear to ear. One little nick and it all pours out. No more effort than opening a letter.

Blood is smeared all over his neck. His beard is a mix of red and black. His shirt is painted crimson. Lines run down his pants. His hands are covered in blood. He must have squeezed his neck tight, trying to keep it all in...

Plasma has formed a halo around his head. Roots and grass clumps are torn up beside him. He grabbed on to anything for support. Scratched and clawed for something to help him. Then he...stopped. Faded away. Alone in the woods.

Greg and Ken are making noises. They sound muffled. I can't understand them. Everything's distorted, garbled. It's like I'm underwater. I'm hunched over the man. I'm nearly on top of him. I can't look away from the cut. One small slice and that was it. His life, everything he did, everything he was, every memory, every love, every hate, every moment, it all led to this: Lying on the ground staring at stars. His thoughts, his feelings, everything he knew, it was all ended by a paper cut. A quick wrist flick. Nothing special, just a trace across the neck. Nothing could stop it...

Hands grab my shoulders and pull me away from the man. Ken is facing me. He's moving his lips. It sounds like a drone. I shut my eyes and focus on his voice. The distortion drifts away. I can hear Ken's words. I open my eyes.

"-esting us?" Ken's eyes are bloodshot. His cheeks are wet.

"What?" I stare at him. I can't look at the man. Not again. Not yet.

"Is this a test? Some sort of trial?" Ken tightens his grip on me. Greg leans in, raising the lantern to my face.

They're dead serious. They think I'd do anything to test their mettle. I'd laugh if I knew I'd be able to stop. I don't know what I'd do here. I'm not in full control of myself right now.

"No. Absolutely not." I peel Ken's hands off my shoulders.

Greg nods and scratches his chin. Ken clicks his jaw. They huddle together, whispering. I glance at the man and shudder. I step between Greg and Ken.

"Who found him?" I jerk my head at the man.

"I did." Ken raises his hand.

"How?" I inch towards the building.

"Couldn't get any sleep. Thought a walk would help. I came out of the forest here and noticed...something in the bush. So, I pulled it back and..." Ken's voice cracks.

"If you found it, why did you come to me?" I turn to Greg, who blinks.

"I was...out for a walk, too. Mind was racing. Tried to tire myself out. I was in the square when Ken saw me. He showed me...him, and told me to fetch you." Greg winces with each word.

"Did you see anyone around here? Anybody in the forest." I peer into the darkness, shining the lantern for any clues.

"No, no, I didn't see anyone. I just saw the...body. He was lying here. His throat was slashed, blood was everywhere, and I didn't know what to do. I didn't look for anyone. Maybe there was someone here. Maybe I missed them. I couldn't focus. I was just, just..." Ken keeps rubbing his head and pointing at the man. I squeeze his hand and stops speaking.

"We have to stay calm." Right. Like I can talk.

"Of course, sir. Sorry, sir." Ken sighs and cracks his knuckles.

I crouch beside the man. Something is poking out of his pocket. I grab it and bring it close. It's a ring. Small, silver, nothing fancy. I put it in my pocket.

I stare at the man's eyes. He didn't see it coming. It wasn't supposed to go like this. He deserved better. We'll figure this out.

"Ken, can you take him to the cafeteria basement?" I stand up.

"Basement, sir?" Ken shivers.

"Yes, the basement. We need to get him inside."

"Why?" Greg is staring at the man.

They didn't sign on for this. None of us did. Their brains are trying to catch up. But I need them now.

"We can't have this getting out. If people see him, they'll panic. We have to fix this ourselves. We have to keep it quiet." I let it sink in.

Ken looks at the man and wipes his eyes. He starts to nod and Greg follows suit. We're in it now. Ken leaves to get a tarp as Greg and I watch over the man.

"I want you to look into him. Learn everything you can. His friends, his enemies, what he ate for breakfast, all of it. Can you do that?" I glance at Greg. His eyes are glazed. He can't look away from the cut. I snap my fingers in his face.

"Can you do that?"

"Y-yes, yes, of course, sir. I don't know how long it'll—"

"Just get it done." I squeeze his arm.

I watch them wrap the man up in the tarp and carry him into the dark. Just like the crippled builder. Two bodies carted away in one day.

I'm alone now. Just me and the night. I look at the forest, holding my lantern like a shield. The woods stretch on forever. My chest tightens. Someone's out there.

CHAPTER SIX

Jason Neary licks his lips.

He can taste the staleness. The air always has the same odour. It's air conditioning mixed with dry-cleaned dress shirts mixed with homemade lunches. They swirl together into one giant, bland nothing. It doesn't change, or diminish, or leave; it just sits there. It surrounds him. From the moment he arrives until he leaves, it's all he can taste or smell.

When he got off the elevator today, he was eating a bagel with cream cheese. He slept in. No time for breakfast. He stopped by the bakery on the ground floor. The second he stepped on his level, the bagel changed. Its flavour and scent faded. They became part of the office. He was eating the same thing he did every day.

Jason is sitting at his desk. His shoulders are slouched over, his spine curved against his chair. His back is sore. He's been hunched over his desk for hours. He tilts his head to the side and feels a series of cracks. His body is stiff. He knows he's warping his bones. He knows this day, and every day here, will add up. He'll pay for it down the road. Twenty years, thirty years, forty years, it doesn't matter. His back will be withered, or his neck will be immovable, or his gut will reach past his feet. He'll mould around this chair, sinking into it. He knows he should stand up, run, stay on his feet all day. But he doesn't.

Jason looks up from the desk. His grey cubicle wall greets him. It stretches past his desk, reaching out to two other connecting walls. They run around him in a square, only broken up by a small gap, just enough for one man to pass through. His escape route. The greyness towers above him, extending to the tiled ceiling and constant fluorescents. The lights hum incessantly. They litter the space above him, each separated by a foot. They wash the office with a dull yellow. Three of them hang over Jason's cubicle, droning in unison, a monotone choir.

Jason rubs his eyes and drums his fingers. The desk echoes metallically. He leans back in his chair, one hand tugging on lint in his pocket, the other dragging a chain of paperclips across his leg. He's arranged them by colour. Neon pink and pitch-black bookend this trail of cheap plastic. He built this colour-coded train five weeks ago. It was a highlight.

Jason tosses the paper clips on the desk. They land on his stapler and day calendar, forming a limp bridge over a half-finished crossword. He pushes against the floor and spins in his chair, watching the grey rotate with him. With each spin he moves further from his desk. He faces the back wall in the middle of the cubicle. He scratches his crotch and stares directly at the fluorescents. His vision glazes over as his mind wanders. He could be anywhere. He sees ruins, towers, citadels, libraries, seas of towns and villages stretching out to meet him. He can be anywhere, be anyone...

Someone coughs. Jason jerks up and looks at his cubicle opening. He sees Jeremy walk by. He's slashing his clipboard with a pen. He disappears behind the grey. Back into the office rows. Jason peddles his feet on the floor and inches back to his desk.

He looks at the sheet in front of him. It screams at him, begging to be read and re-read. It needs edits, changes, corrections. Jason picks up his pencil and twirls it in his finger. He passes it over and under his knuckles. Just one skill he's picked up here.

Jason glances to his right, looking at the wall. There's a small section before the opening. It's grey at the top and bottom, but the middle is different. It's a pause. It's covered in postcards. Sunsets, tropical forests, villas, landmarks, ocean side views, all in obnoxious Technicolor. They're pinned to the wall in a tight collage, overlapping each other, fighting for attention.

Some images are lined with writing. Descriptions, greetings, and condolences written in uniform print, ink-blotched cursive, and everything in between. Small photos are clipped to these paragraphs, obscuring their own messages. Beaming faces of friends, family, and a few strangers who wrote the wrong address. They stare at Jason, beckoning to him.

Jason returns to the sheet. It's covered in columns and rows of numbers. Jason rubs his chin as he traces his pencil down the page. His eyes dart from number to number, doubling back to previous sections. He draws circles over certain groups, making a tally at the bottom. He punches the data into his calculator. He reads the answer and runs his pencil across the sheet again. He uses a blank page to extend his tally. He pours over each digit. He throws the numbers into the calculator and it spits out the same answer. He scrunches his nose and grabs another blank sheet. He prints out every number in small font, fitting them into one column. He goes up and down, adding each section to the total. He circles the answer. It's the same one.

Jason massages his temples. He tries to find some mistake he made, but he knows there's none. He looks at his phone. Its receiver is coated in a thin dust layer. He glances at the sheet, nearly illegible with pencil markings, and sighs; no choice. He dials the number.

"Hi, it's Jason...Jason Neary, fifth-floor review and inspection...Yeah, that's me...Could you connect me to accounting?...Thank you...Yes, I'll hold."

Jason hears the muzak creep into his ear. The same six notes grind gracelessly against each other. It blasts through the receiver, as if all the volume levels have been cranked to the maximum and robbed of their knobs. Jason can hum it on cue at this point. It's a solo piano accompanied by background noise and static. It loops over and over, slightly changing the pitch each time. It fades out and for three seconds, there's perfect silence. Then it barges through the receiver, drunkenly picking up where it left off. Jason just stares at the wall, wincing. His legs are bent, ready to bolt out of the cubicle, but he has to stay. The song repeats twice and threatens to start again when a ringing sound silences it. Jason holds the phone to his ear, cradling it with his shoulder.

"Hello? Hi, yes, is this accounting?...Perfect, I'm Jason, Jason Neary, fifth floor- Oh, hi, Sam. How are you? Good, good. Got any plans for-? Really? Whoa, the whole thing? Well, good luck...Me? Oh, not much. Maybe head to the vineyard. Thinking of doing some hiking before it gets too cold...Yeah, wouldn't want to freeze, that's for sure...Yeah, yeah, heard that..."

Jason passes the phone to his other hand. No more small talk. He grabs the sheet and clears his throat.

"Yeah, so, Sam, I'm calling about some numbers. I got a sheet today...Yes, that one. I picked it up this morning...Yes, right, so I went through it and I noticed a few...Sure, take a sec...You have a copy?...Yes, so I noticed a few inconsistencies with the totals...Well, I added them up and they didn't match the predictions from last week...Yes, the ones you sent me...Yes, I'm sure...I added it three times, same answer...Sure, go ahead."

Jason taps his pencil on the desk as he hears mutterings through the phone. Keyboard clacks and pencil scratches join Sam's mumblings. Jason draws a square on his sheet and overlays another, creating a cube. He sketches another one on the left side of the page. As Sam tallies up the numbers, Jason makes an additional column of cubes. He starts drawing on the right side as Sam clears his throat.

"...Right, right, I thought. Sorry about it, but it's just not...I see...Yeah, simple mistake. Not your fault...Yeah, exactly, could've happened to...Uh-huh, completely...Great, so when do you think you could send up the correct numbers?...Yeah, I'm going to need a new sheet...Uh-huh, uh-huh, I see...I'm going to need it before the end of the month...How long?...That's cutting it really close...I know it's a busy time, but...Yes, that makes sense...Everybody's plates' are...Huh...Alright, could you put this on the top of your list?...I just really need...Yes, yes,

yes...Alright, well, let me know when it's done...Okay, okay, bye now...Yeah, have a good weekend, too."

Jason puts the phone down. He scrunches his nose and flexes his fingers. He pushes the sheet away. He grabs his day planner near his stapler and flips to today. He scrolls down his to-do list, scratching out a row. He sees a whole column of crossed-out items. He closes the book and opens his desk drawers. He flicks past mounds of completed forms, papers, and requests. He can't find a blank sheet. He drums his fingers, glancing around the cubicle. He grabs his day planner and searches through older dates, finding a sea of pencil scratches. He rubs his cheeks.

He stares at the collage, zeroing in on a postcard in the middle. It's Erica, his high school valedictorian. They got high in the woods behind the gym a few times. She listened to him ramble about thought control in cereal, or whatever he talked about back then. They drifted apart for college, then met up the summer after undergrad back home. That final moment before the big plunge. They got drunk, tore through the town, and puked their guts out. She even let him crash on her couch. Now she's a humanitarian. In the postcard, she's sitting in a kayak. Fellow paddlers are floating behind her, out of focus and blurry. A green coast looms over her right side. "New Zealand" is emblazoned in bright-orange bubble font across the top. She's wearing sunglasses and a helmet. She's grinning, showing her perfect white teeth. Jason can't see her eyes past the shades, but he can feel her looking at him. He could send a letter, let her know how he's doing. Maybe he could call her. How much is it to call New Zealand? How much per minute? He doesn't really have that much for a long call...

Jason looks at the phone. His hand reaches for it. He could just check in. The company wouldn't mind, surely. They'd give a warning at most. Jason hovers his hand over the receiver. He pulls it back and rests it on his lap. He shifts away from the collage. The fluorescents are particularly grating now. He stands up and squeezes out through the escape route.

Jason walks along the carpet flooring. He runs his fingers across the cubicle walls. He peeks into offices through their small gaps. He sees Martha yelling into her phone, rapping her knuckles on her clear glass desk to emphasize every point. He sees Todd (or is it Rod?) propping his head up with his hand as he flips through a report packet. Poor bastard. He sees Hugh playing with his abacus, just sliding pieces back and forth. At fifty-eight, he can see the finish line and he's stopped caring. Nobody notices Jason as he strolls down the halls.

Jason rounds a corner and reaches the water cooler. He grabs a paper cup from the dispenser and holds it under the tap. Water flows out, immediately overflowing the cup. Every time. A bubble floats up in the jug as Jason sips his water. He drains the cup and bends down to refill it. As he stands up, he takes a swig of water and he sees her.

She's checking her wristwatch as she rounds the corner. Her flats crunch on the carpet flooring. The lanyard holding her work ID sashays across her button-up blouse. Her jacket, two sizes too big, is draped over her shoulders. She smiles at Jason and waves. Her teeth are a little crooked and her gum line is receding; still, it's a nice smile.

"Hi, Jason." She grabs a cup.

"Hi, Donna-augh." Water spills out of Jason's mouth as he speaks.

The liquid lands on his chest and a blotch spreads over his shirt. He covers his mouth, wiping water from his chin. Donna laughs it off as he turns away, dabbing at the stain with his hand. He quickly downs the rest of his drink.

"All good?" Donna peeks over his shoulder.

"Yeah, yeah, all fine. Slight mishap, that's all." He faces her and flashes a weak, self-effacing smile.

"Happens to the best of us." She chuckles. Jason laughs along with her.

Donna sips her water, looking up and down the hall. Jason fiddles with his cup. He goes to refill it but stops himself. The fluorescent buzz surrounds them.

"So, what are you weekend plans?" Donna tosses her cup in the nearby trash can.

"Oh, this and that." Jason raises his shoulders.

"Cool, cool." Donna nods.

More fluorescent buzz silence. Jason scratches his elbow as Donna fondles her earring. Jason shuffles through his brain for anything to say. Sports? Haven't seen any. Weather? Come on. Work? He doesn't quite know what she does…

"So, you're going to be pretty busy?" Donna steps closer.

"Maybe. I'll see." Jason flips his hand back and forth, trying to be coolly noncommittal.

"Well, I'm going to a concert on Saturday if you want to come. You know, if you're free." Donna words dangle like bait.

Jason's brain scrambles for words, assembling the perfect response. It ships the sentences off to do their work. Unfortunately, they have to pass through his mouth.

"Uh, yeah, yeah, I mean, maybe I could. I'd have to check. Saturday, you said? Yeah, I'd have to double-check that one. Where is it?" Jason's lips quiver and shake.

"The Pitstop. Just off Cranberry Street. Two floors under a diner. You heard of it?" Donna's eyes light up.

"Of course." He has no idea what she's talking about.

"Yeah, it's going to be great. The Purple Heart is the opener. They're like Skynyrd with twice the bass. And The Leftovers are headlining the whole thing. They're like the heaviest thing ever. Oh, and Jessy James is doing a set. She's amazing. Her voice…Wow. Have you heard her?" Donna's wearing a big grin.

"Oh, yeah. Just a few songs, but they're something else." Jason's never heard of any of these bands.

"Tell me about it. And the guitar work. God, I'd kill to play like that. They just dance on the fret board, y'know? It's next level stuff. And The Leftover's drums are pummelling. I saw them live once and I couldn't hear right for a week. It's awesome how they…" Donna rambles, animating every instrument with her hands. Jason watches, nodding at the appropriate cues. He doesn't know what's going on. Donna seems to be speaking in tongues. But he knows he has to smile and listen. He's not really here. He's in New Zealand, perched on a cliff, sitting next to Donna, naked...

"Sorry, went on a tangent. Got really excited." Donna brushes loose hair from her face.

"No worries." Jason snaps to attention, giving a quick smile

"So, you'll be there?" Donna leans against the water cooler.

"Yeah, I'll definitely try. I just have to check my schedule. I'll give you a call." Jason bobs his head up and down. It looks like a nod.

Donna smiles. The fluorescent buzz descends on them. Jason knows he should ask for details, or when they should meet up, or how her day is going. He knows he could say a dozen different things. They've got plenty of time to talk.

"Well, I'd better get back to work." Jason nods down the hallway.

"Slave to the grindstone, eh?" Donna's smile falls a bit, but she holds it up.

"That's me. Can't keep me away from that desk. I'd sleep there if I could." Jason lets out a gasp that's meant to be a laugh.

"I'll, uh, I'll give you a call tomorrow. Let you know what...my deal...is." Jason shuffles to the corner.

"Sure thing. I'll see you tomorrow, then." Donna waves her fingers.

Jason flicks up his hand as a goodbye and rounds the corner. He strides down the hall, keeping his head down, ignoring his coworkers as they ignore him. He squeezes into his cubicle and sits down.

His mind replays the entire conversation. Every awkward pause, every fumbled word, every nervous tick. He sees it all over and over again. What was he thinking? Why did he say that? Why did do that? Could she tell he was sweating? Why did he try to tell a joke? He's never been funny. She must think he's a complete idiot.

Jason winces as he watches his meeting with Donna in his head. His face feels warm. He fidgets in his chair, hearing the wheels and joints creak. He sees Donna's smile, her eyes, her body language. Did he weird her out? What did she think of him?

Jason sees the same flashes. Donna waving, grabbing a drink, smiling, asking about the concert, looking at him. He sees himself jerking his hand up, nodding vacantly, staring at her, mangling his words, laughing, slinking away like a coward. He's stuck in a loop of humiliation. He could have done this better, or this, or this, or this, or—

Jason seizes his knees. He shuts his eyes and purses his lips. He opens them both and looks at his phone. He's waiting for a call. Accounting might get back to him today. They could reach out at any moment. They're a heartbeat away. Jason stares at the phone, blocking out everything else, willing it to ring.

That's how he spends the rest of the day. He locks his gaze on the phone, distracting his brain. He doesn't think; he just stares. When the lights go off, he knows it's time to go home.

This is his job.

Jason is standing in a bus. His satchel is draped on his shoulder. He's holding onto a vertical metal bar. He's leaning against the window by the rear door. A man is sitting near him, holding his bag on a free seat beside him. Jason's grip tightens as the bus jerks to a stop. A few stragglers hop off as a swarm forces its way in. A woman lugs a stroller onto the entrance and stands there. People squirm past her, shooting dirty looks she pretends to ignore. A man bumps into the stroller and the kid starts bawling. The man retreats deep into the bus as the woman groans and mutters to her child, half-heartedly rocking the stroller. The baby keeps screaming.

No one in the front moves so the new passengers shuffle down the line. A gaggle of people surge towards Jason. They gather around him, seizing metal poles. A woman with a backpack grabs Jason's pole and turns her back to him. Her bag, stuffed to the brim with posters that poke out of an opening, slams into Jason. A fat man in a leather jacket is breathing down Jason's neck. He reeks of cigarettes, sausages, and scotch. Jason holds his satchel close. He can't move.

The bus lurches forward. The woman in front of Jason falls back, shoving her bag into his chest. Jason stumbles away from the pole, losing his grip. He mumbles an apology to the leather jacket man and reaches for the pole. Somehow, it's covered in hands. He can't find a spot to grab. Every pole is taken. He looks out the window and sees an upcoming stop. He widens his stance and clutches his satchel to his chest, bracing himself.

The bus sputters to a stop, tossing Jason back and forth. He bounces off passengers like a pinball. He mutters a dozen apologies. The bus starts again and he collects himself. His satchel's strap has snapped. His eyes dart around, looking for a seat, a pole, an opening, anything. He doesn't find a single space. He sees another stop rushing to meet the bus. He bends his knees, curling his toes for a grip. Baby screams, coughing, yelling, groaning, and inane chatter surround him. This is his ride home. He never finds a seat.

Jason reaches into his pocket, squirming his fingers past his wallet and old receipts. He pulls out a jumble of keys. He holds his satchel against his side as he flips through the shiny teeth. He picks out a silver one and shoves it in the doorknob. He jimmies it in the hole, but it doesn't budget. Jason sorts through the roll of keys. It's the silver one that has the longer teeth at the front, not the back. He always forgets that. He twists the knob and opens the door, falling into his basement apartment.

He turns the lock, slides the deadbolt, and drops the satchel next to his shoes. Its severed strap is a limp tail with frayed edges. Jason yanks off his tie and unbuttons his shirt. He unfurls his belt and throws it on the bed, letting out a sigh. A red line runs around his stomach, which sticks out with a slight paunch. A beer gut, at his age.

He turns on the dangling light bulb in the kitchen. His dishes are dry from their morning wash. Ready to be put away to make room for the next batch. How efficient.

He brushes aside crumbs on the floor as he opens the fridge. A few fresh vegetables, a box of leftover pizza, some uncooked chicken, and a container of milk. Plenty for the weekend. He grabs a beer bottle from the bottom shelf and closes the door.

Jason pops off the cap and throws it in the garbage can. He flops down in his leather chair, taking a long swig. He scratches his chest and stares at the wall. It's smooth and white. A bookshelf leans on it, but beside that it's bare.

Maybe he'll see Donna tomorrow. Maybe they'll dance and party and... who knows. Maybe he'll take that karate class, or finish that book, or call home, or go for a walk. He could do anything.

But right now, this is what he's doing: Staring at the wall and drinking a beer. This is all he wants at this moment. Quiet time for himself. There's time for everything else later.

This is his weekend.

CHAPTER SEVEN

There's a hole in the floor.

I could fit my hand down it. Probably just four fingers. No thumb. It's off centre in the aisle. Just enough out of the way. It's shaped like a jagged diamond. It runs lengthwise, the same direction as the aisle. Its ends point to the exit and to me.

I'm standing in front of the podium. I'm leaning over it, my fingers wrapped around the edges. Everyone's staring at me. I hear murmurs, titters, questions. They think it's part of the sermon. I know I should talk. I know I should speak to them, inspire them, lead them. I know today shouldn't be any different than any other day. I know, I know, I know. But I can't stop staring at this hole.

It's more than a hole. A web of cracks and splinters run away from it, spreading under chairs and the stage. Thin slits branch out from it, weaving through the hall.

I made this hole months ago. I was pacing onstage, talking about strength through pain. Or maybe it was pain as a path to strength. Or maybe it was about pain as a strength. Yes, that was it. Probably. That's something I would say.

I was holding a spear. Well, more like a staff with a sharp end. A builder gave it to me before the sermon. She said she's been working on it for week. I thanked her and held onto it all morning. I brought it with me as I passed through the curtains. I love a good prop. It was solid wood, shaved and finished. It was half as tall as me. It bent slightly in the middle, jutting out like a baby bump. I twirled it and tossed it back and forth. It almost slipped from my grip a few times, it was so smooth. A loop of feathers was tied to its top. They were dyed red with black streaks peaking out. They were secured with twine. Their tips swayed as the stick moved, creating a hypnotic effect. They made a swooshing sound as they spun. It had a certain...tribal quality, but I thought they added a ceremonial touch. The spear poked above the feathers. It was a jagged rock shaped into a sharp point. It could gut a woolly mammoth. I really liked that staff. I leaned on it, pointed at audience members with it, and stamped the stage with it. It became an extension of me.

The next part is hazy. I was gesturing with the staff, picking out members of the crowd, and asking them questions. Basic sermon stuff. I noticed that a few people weren't paying attention. They were whispering, or looking at their feet, or resting their eyes. They weren't here. And that pissed me off.

I was near the curtain at this point. I was holding the staff like a harpoon, pointing its sharp end down. I was talking about strength as more than a collection of moments and events. It's a totality, a continuation, an ethos. Something like that. I was frowning. I couldn't stop looking at the talkers. I was getting riled up. And then I was running across the stage.

I soared through the air. Well, not really. It barely lasted a second. But a few people gasped. It must have looked amazing.

I crashed to the ground, nearly falling over. I let the staff go. It was planted in the floor. The spear had stabbed through the wood, creating a hole. Splinters and wood chips surrounded the impact zone. The staff wobbled and vibrated, echoing in the room. A web of cracks started to spread away from it. The stick stood there, tilted to the side, a physical exclamation mark.

I was breathing with my mouth, shoulders hunched over, my face flushed and sweaty. I could taste the adrenaline. Everyone was staring at me. It was a perfect silence. I savoured it.

I pointed at the staff and opened my mouth. I said...something profound. I must have told them to be like the spear, or resist the spear, or maybe do both. I could barely hear myself think; I was making it up on the fly.

The crowd clapped, stomped, yelled, and whistled. I waded into the audience, shaking their hands, squeezing their shoulders, looking into their eyes. The whole place felt electric. We stormed out of the hall and went to the river. We swam together. It was autumn, but we didn't care.

At the next sermon, I removed the staff and returned it to the woman. In front of everyone, of course. I told her to keep it safe. I instructed everyone to not touch the hole. They weren't to repair it, fill it, or cover it. It would be a reminder of that moment. That one time everything made sense. Mostly, I thought it looked cool.

So that's how this hole came to be. This hole I can't stop staring at.

The air is getting stale. Anticipation is morphing into impatience. People are fidgeting and muttering. I flex my fingers and crack my jaw. I have to speak.

I am sitting at my desk. The sun is sliding across the floor, creeping up to my feet. Outside, a thin layer of fog fades away. Everything's waking up. I woke up in my robes. At least, I think I woke up. I went to bed and stared at the ceiling. I noticed a tiny red blot on a panel. A speck of paint from some art project. It reminded me of...him. I just looked at it. Then I noticed the sun rising and I rolled off the cot. My eyes felt heavy. They still do.

I went to the garden. Dew coated the plants. I walked the perimeter, trying to enjoy the silence. I felt itchy. I scratched and scratched, but it kept popping up over my body. The garden felt ominous. I looked around for...someone. I rubbed my eyes, willing myself awake. I went inside.

Greg is here, hunched over in his chair. He's pouring over medical records and member profiles, making notes on the fly. His face is an inch from the desk. He was there when I woke up. He didn't acknowledge me. He only pauses to crack his neck, sharpen his pencil, or throw another folder on the large stack at his feet.

Ken is searching through the forest. He's been out there all night. He'd come in a few times for food and to warm up. He found a few footprints, but nothing concrete. Greg told me Ken said he'd be out there until I needed him. I look at the dark circles clinging to Greg's eyes. They've been killing themselves for answers while I've been sleeping. Disgraceful.

I'm staring at a folder. I trace my fingers around its corners. There are blue splotches on the cover; someone spilled ink when they filed it away. It's just an average member profile folder. We have hundreds buried in the archive. I haven't bothered to look at most of them, but I have to read this one.

It's a file on the man we found. The man in the bush. Before they put him away, Greg and Ken found a driver's license in his pocket. Lucky break. Greg checked his name in the directory and pulled out his file.

I have the man's ring in my pocket. I pull it out and I roll it back and forth on the desk. It's something I can focus on. Something I can control.

I can see him lying on the ground. Blood pouring out his mouth and neck. Clothing stained, dirty, and torn. Eyes staring up at the sky, empty. Just another corpse waiting for—I stop rolling the ring. I'm rubbing my hand across my neck. I didn't even notice. Trying to protect it? Coward.

I put the ring aside and pick up the folder. It's light. A man's whole life summed up in a pamphlet. I flip the cover open and start reading.

I'm moving my mouth. I'm gesturing with my right hand, using the other one to lean on the podium. My throat is vibrating. My tongue and lips are flapping. I am speaking. My head feels heavy. Everything is moving slow motion. I just want to lie down and sleep.

I'm still speaking. I can hear the words, but they're distant. I'm detached from them. I'm an audience member watching from afar. I'm not in control. All I can do is listen to myself.

"We're all going to die. Each and every one of us. Not right now, not right here, but eventually. We know this, of course. I'm not blowing anyone's mind with this fact. But think about it, really picture it. Death, in all its forms. Every moment, every sensation, every good, bad, or average day, everything, all of it, gone. Poof. Snatched away. Packaged worm food."

My eyes drift to the hole again. It seems bigger. A wide black space. Something that could swallow you. I'm still talking.

"We're all sliding toward the void. This inescapable force tugs on us, never letting go. It beckons to us, implores us, demands us. It consumes and consumes and consumes, and it's never full. All that awaits us is that black space. That's all we're promised. Isn't that terrifying?"

I'm looking at the audience now. My eyes are glassy, but I can see their faces. They don't know where I'm going. Neither do I. I feel like I'm going to topple over.

I slump over the podium, wrapping my fingers around the microphone.

His name was Henry Spittal.

His photo is snapped to the top corner of the folder, held there with a red paperclip. It's a standard membership photograph. His body is cropped off at the shoulders. The top of his head is obscured by the border of the frame. He's standing off center, tilting to the right. His eyes are a lively green, even in this faded photo. He looks straight at me. He's smiling, showing off a crooked set of teeth. His neck looks...fine, considering what I've seen. I commit his face to memory. I want to remember him, not that...thing in the bush. I unclip the photo and dive into the papers.

He was born and raised in Kentucky. After high school, he moved to Minnesota to work odd jobs. He bopped around the state for a while, cashing cheques, drinking at bars, and getting arrested. He met a woman and settled down. Got a job as a postman. He made some friends, joined a sports club, collected stamps, even volunteered at the church. He had a regular route, a regular routine, a regular life. Kept it up for almost ten years. Then, thirty rolled around and something changed. He stopped going to church and sports meetings, he called his friends less and less, he threw out his stamps. They felt hollow to him, empty. He spent his time at the bars. When that didn't work, he started wandering around town looking for distractions. Nothing could stop this gnawing in the back of his head.

Everything fell apart. He lost his job (he never had the courage to quit) and his wife asked for a divorce. It was an amicable split, all things considered. She kept most of the furniture and valuables, and he got the house. She moved to Delaware with her mother. Spittal never saw her again. He watched her leave from the front window. He sat down in his empty house and stared at his wedding ring. He didn't cry or scream or break anything. He just sat there.

Greg made a side note. It reads: "Emotionally upfront. Quite earnest. Seems legit. High recommendation." I see what he means. Even for a new recruit, Spittal's crushingly honest.

Spittal stayed in the house. He didn't have anywhere else to go. He snagged a job as a removals man. It distracted him for a while. He worked all day, then walked around town at night. He was exhausted, but he couldn't sleep. Something was prodding him along.

This routine went on for months. A few friends reached out to him, but he didn't respond. He observed everything at a distance, detached from his surroundings. He was numb.

One night, Spittal was walking on the suburban outskirts when it started to rain. He ran into the nearby community centre to wait out the storm. Aside from the half-asleep receptionist, it was empty. Spittal wandered down the halls, peeking into rooms.

He came across the message board. It was covered in concert announcements, yard sale posters, and art class brochures. He saw a pamphlet pinned to the bottom corner. It was dark blue with a black line running down it diagonally. Spittal picked it up and started reading.

It all fell into place. He saw the big picture. He realized there was a higher calling waiting for him. He read it over and over, spending the whole night in the community centre. He studied every passage, every picture, every line. He knew this place was where he belonged. He was reading our pamphlet.

A few years back, Greg suggested we expand our reach. I was against it. I thought if people wanted to find us, really wanted to find us, they could do it on their own. No need for cheap advertisements. Greg insisted. He said we needed to ensure the widest possible breadth of audience, whatever that meant. I relented and he drew up a couple hundred copies. I wrote the inner text and signed off on them. He sent them out and I forgot about them. We never got the huge attendance spike Greg promised, but every few months we get someone walking through our gates, clutching a pamphlet. Spittal was one of them.

He made up his mind right away. He couldn't waste his time anymore. He sold his house, packed his bags, and hitchhiked down here. After the interview process, he got in. Simple as that.

There are a few more notes at the back. Greg updates the profiles now and then. Spittal worked as a builder. His supervisors had nothing but praise for his work. He helped with a series of renovations and construction projects. He was a model member. He attended every sermon, helped clean up after dinner, and always made himself available for chores. He even led some camping excursions into the woods. They were "enlightenment trips" meant to test people's resolve in the wild. Mostly they were glorified vacations, but Spittal ran them like clockwork. Greg noted Spittal's passion for everything. He was dedicated. I vaguely remember him asking me questions after a lecture. We had a good conversation, I think. He was the perfect follower.

Then, last night, he bled out in a bush.

I close the folder. That's it. The man's entire life summed up in one file too short to be a magazine article. I can feel my eyes watering.

I rip the microphone from the podium and start pacing the stage. I shoot quick glances at the audience. They fall silent. I sigh into the mic, letting my panting fill the room. I bang the mic on my forehead. I'm trying to wake myself up.

My mouth starts moving again. I'm in control of my body, but not the words. I hear them, I'm aware of them, I understand them, but I can't stop them. I listen.

"So, is that all there is? A black void and nothing else? Are we doomed to simply turn off? Is there no escape route, no bargaining chip, no alternative? Can we get away? Don't we deserve something more? At the end, haven't we earned a reward? Haven't we?"

I'm not speaking rhetorically.

I wipe my eyes and put down Spittal's folder. It feels obscene to confine a man's entire life to that paltry stack of papers. It's the ultimate reduction. Henry Spittal, studied, codified, and compressed into one easy-to-carry file.

I close my eyes and I see Spittal lying on the ground, but I'm not close up. I see everything in widescreen. I'm high above Spittal, high above the compound. It's dark, but I can still see him. Darkness surrounds him on all sides. No one's near him. The trees and buildings tower over him, obscuring his body. Nothing moves. One man, completely alone.

I run my fingers over the folder. Spittal's death was cheap and meaningless. There was no transcendence, no overture, no grand statement. He just lay there in the dark, leaking. No one was there to reaffirm him, to cherish him. He simply disappeared.

I was supposed to lead him forward. I was going to give his death meaning. I was going to give us all meaning. It would- It will be a glorious moment. But Spittal was robbed of it. All his work was leading to a great final sacrifice; instead it crumbled away. Spittal's work, his denial, his sacrifice, it all amounted to nothing. He pushed himself, he fought and struggled, and in the end, it added up to zero. He didn't achieve meaning. I didn't give him meaning. I failed...

I tug on a clump of my hair. Did he find purpose on his own? When the knife pressed against his neck, was he at peace? When the warm liquid started flowing, did he understand his fate? Did he accept his suffering? Did he fight or try to find a way out? Or did he lie down and let it happen? Did he wait for the reward I've promised him, and everyone else? Did he-?

What am I talking about? I saw the body, and the blood-soaked hands, and everything else. I know what he did: he panicked. He thrashed on the ground. He clawed at the earth. He tried to clog the wound, tried to keep his insides from spilling out. He scrambled, and fought, and squirmed until the end. That knife wound was the only thing on his mind.

His death wasn't glorious; it was hideous. It was senseless and depraved. It had no meaning, no grace. It was an empty act in a void. Not like ours...

What if we all die like Spittal? What if it's always the same, no matter how it's done? What if we can never accept it, no matter how much we've been trained or how hard we've tried? What if we're wrong?

I grip my shaking hand, hoping Greg doesn't notice. I look at my robes. They're hanging by the window. A breeze makes them flutter. In this light, they look like any other fabric.

God, what if I'm wrong?

"No."

I'm holding the microphone below my chin. My voice can barely be heard. I flex my fingers and look around the audience, licking my lips. I'm back in the driver's seat.

"No."

I hold the microphone close to my mouth. I'm breathing with my nose. It echoes through the speakers. I stride to the edge of the stage. I nearly slip off it. I stalk back and forth. I look the members in their eyes. I know what to do.

"No."

I widen my mouth, nearly swallowing the microphone. I shove my voice forward. People closest wince and cover their ears. My heart is pounding. I hold the microphone to my side like a dagger. I feel the current surging through my body Everyone's staring at me, dead quiet. I could destroy all of them. I bring the microphone back to my mouth.

"That's not the way it has to be. Not for us. We don't have to sink into the muck. We don't have to give up. That's not what we're here to do. Surrender is the choice for the weak, the hopeless, the enslaved. The people in the world we left behind, they submit. They accept all of it. They accept mediocre lives and mediocre deaths. We're more than them."

The crowd is buzzing. I toss the microphone to my other hand. My knees are shaking. I bounce on the balls of my feet, swinging my arms. I squeeze the microphone to steady myself.

"No, we're much more than them. We don't collapse in the face of death; we stand. We fight until the last moment. We challenge death. We don't let it rob us of meaning; we make it give us meaning. We turn the end into the climax. Our lives are leading up to this point, this grand apex. We sacrifice, and suffer, and struggle to shed our weaknesses. We give purpose to ourselves. Death doesn't stop this; it fulfills it. We are vindicated by death. We ascend."

I see rows and rows of smiles and nods. They feed me. My head feels light. I jump off the stage. I crash to the floor and stumble forward, nearly falling to my knees. I see the hole. Up close, it seems small, insignificant. I can see its insides: Just dust and wood chips. I place my foot over it.

"We're going to rise up. Death will be a grand finale, but only for this story. We're going to find another chapter, another moment. It will be our crowning achievement. We'll find a new purpose. Death is just the next step. Who's willing to take it with me?"

The cheers envelop me. I plunge into the crowd. I brush past hands as I wade through the mass. I pat shoulders and arms. I point at people and look into their eyes.

"I know I won't do this alone. I know you want to come with me. All of you do. You're willing to do what's necessary. There's something special out there and I'm going to find it. And you're going to join me. And you. And you. And you. And you…"

It's melting into a swirl. Faces spin around me, all staring, all smiling. I can feel my lips move and I can hear the words travel, but it's all blending together. My ears are pounding. I feel hot and sweaty. I'm in the vortex.

"No death is forgettable. Not for us"

I drop the microphone and shake hands. I let the cheers wash over me. I'm drunk. We won't be forgotten. None of us. We have a purpose.

I shove Spittal's folder into my desk drawer.

CHAPTER EIGHT

It's beautiful to see.

Five people are gathered in a semi-circle. They're half-naked, shirts stuffed in their pockets. Sweat glistens on their bodies in the noon sun. Their cheeks are flushed and red. Their bodies will start to burn soon and there's no shade in sight. They're standing elbow-to-elbow. They're not talking or moving. They're all looking down.

They're staring at man buried up to his neck in the ground.

The man is eye level with their shins. The ground is packed in around him, forming a tight seal. The dirt moves and shifts as he turns his neck but doesn't really budge. Passersby would think they're looking at a discarded, decapitated head. His goatee is pale and dirty, blanched by a thick layer of dust. He's developing a serious sunburn. He's trapped.

The man is looking up at the semi-circle. He locks eyes with each person. His face is still. The semi-circle is silent. Their faces are blank.

The man looks forward, staring through the semi-circle's legs. He's looking past them, past the moving feet of members, past the garden patches, past the woman drawing a bucket of water from the well. He gazes at the woods. Dark blotches loom out deep in the forest. Oblivion at our doorstep. The man nods.

He closes his eyes and starts rocking his head. He tilts to one side, brushing his ear on the ground, and rotates to the other side. He goes back and forth, jerking his head to the left and right. Cracks in the ground form around him. He opens his eyes and tilts his head back to look at the sky. His face is even messier and redder. His cheeks are smeared with grass stains and ground flecks. He's breathing through his mouth, coughing away a cloud of dirt. He's already exhausted. He looks like he could sink into the earth and rest underground. The semi-circle is quiet.

The man takes a deep breath and looks ahead to the forest. He tucks in his chin, forcing it between his chest and the ground. He yanks his chin forward, spewing out chunks of dirt and pebbles. He mashes his chin on the surrounding ground, digging away at his prison. He grinds his jaw line against the earth, tearing apart his coffin. His face is filthy now. His grunts and groans fill the air. The semi-circle is silent.

The man widens the gap around his neck. He can freely move his head. He starts bopping up and down. He extends his head to the sky and ducks back down, nearly disappearing beneath the ground. He pops up again, reaching further to the sky. He's a human mole, pounding away at his enclosure.

On his left, a finger emerges, clawing towards him. It's joined by four others, each blackened and grimy. His right side is a mirror copy. His fingers wriggle and flex, all stretching towards the sun.

The semi-circle backs away from the man. They surround him, forming a true circle. They're silent and motionless, but their eyes are electric.

The man shoots to the sky, straining his neck up. The tips of his shoulders join him. He falls back, smiling. He tears at the ground with his fingers, pulling out his hands and arms. He's no longer a decapitated head; now he's a severed torso.

The man drags himself forward, grabbing every clump of grass and every spare root. The ground clings to him, but he soldiers on. Mounds of dirt fall off him as he surges ahead, staring straight at the forest. He rotates his body, freeing it from the suction of the ground. He pulls his thrashing legs out of the hole as it falls in on itself. He scrambles away from the opening before laying flat face down. The circle peers at his body.

The man is still. There is no sound. Slowly, he turns over and stares at the sky. He's squinting his eyes and gulping for air. He wipes his face, tearing off his dirt mask, and blinks. He stretches his hands, which were still curled and flexed, and rests them on his stomach. He looks at the people staring at him, cupping his hand over his eyes to shield them from the sun. He lays his head down and drums his fingers on his belly. It's perfectly quiet. He starts to laugh. It begins as a chuckle, but it grows. His face contorts into a full-on smile as he lets out a maniacal cackle that shakes his body. His laugh echoes through the compound. His eyes are tearing up, but he's still laughing. He pounds his fist and covers his mouth, but he can't stop himself. He's euphoric.

The circle is laughing, too. They help the man to his feet and clap his shoulders, giving him the thumbs-up. They're all still laughing as a woman jumps in the hole. They push in the dirt, burying her up to her neck, giggling all the while. The form the semi-circle again, trying to compose themselves. The man is off to the side, laughing uncontrollably. He dusts himself off, shaking his head, snorting and grinning. He sits down and watches the woman settle into her hole. He holds himself tight. He'll never feel this happy again.

I drum my fingers on the window sill. My forehead is pressed against the pane, smearing it with sweat. I look through the dirty glass, watching the distorted figures circle around the hole. They'll be at this all day.   I look at the man. He's face is frozen in a deranged smile. He jolts his head and stares at me. I stand up straight to match his gaze. Still laughing, he nods and sticks his thumb up. I tilt my head and he walks over to the hole to watch the woman.

I pick up the knife lying on the window sill. I pull back the curtain at the edge of the sill, revealing the small corner covered with notches and scratches. The farthest ones from me are faded; the closest ones are coated in fresh splinters and chips. I look back at the man. He's crouching next to the woman as she stabs her chin into the ground. He's bouncing his body along with her head movements. His smile hasn't budged an inch. I press the knife against the sill and carve out a new notch. I move it up and down in a vertical line, digging in a deep groove. I blow on the mark and brush away stray chips. It merges with the collection.

I press the knife on my palm and gently twirl it. I look away from the burial and scan the compound's ebb and flow. Builders carrying logs, planters tending to the field, people popping in and out of buildings, etc. In all the movement, two people are standing still. One is a man, clearly a builder. He's holding a toolbox. The other one is smaller, maybe a woman. They're facing the man with their back to me. They're spinning their hands and pointing. The man frowns and shakes his head. He gestures to his toolbox and walks away. The person tugs at their hair and turns around. It's Sandra.

I stop moving the knife. Sandra's wearing a standard planter outfit. It's covered in dirt, but they're old stains. She hasn't worked today. Her face is pale. Bags cling to her eyes and her hair is frayed. She's holding a piece of paper. A woman walks past her and Sandra grabs her arm. The woman jerks back, but Sandra pulls her close. She points at her paper piece, pressing it to the woman's face. The woman takes the piece and studies it. Sandra's talking, wringing her hands behind her back. The woman says something and gestures to the cafeteria. Sandra shakes her head and takes back the paper. The woman shrugs, pats Sandra's shoulder, and disappears. Sandra massages her face and runs her fingers through her hair. She bites her lower lip and taps her foot. She scratches her neck as she looks around the compound. She's on the verge of a panic attack.

I force the window open and I lean out, gripping the sill. I can hear the burial group now. Lots of grunts and cheers. I see the woman breaking the ground with her hands. The smiling man is behind her, twitching his fingers like a puppet master. I look away and lock eyes with Sandra.

She's closer now. I can see the exhaustion and worry on her face. I freeze as she stares at me. She's begging me for something. I squeeze the sill, whitening my knuckles. I don't what to do. I shrug with my eyebrows. She looks away, pinching the bridge of her nose. Her whole body sighs. Sandra turns her back to me, massaging her wrists. She's clutching the paper to her side. Actually, up close, it looks like a photo. Can't tell of who...

Sandra wanders deeper into the compound. She weaves through the crowds, never letting go of her crumpled paper. I follow her until she rounds a building. Those eyes... What did she want? I should have gone out there, taken her aside, talked to her. But I just stood here. I need to find her, figure out what I can do. What's she looking for?

I'm staring at the spot where Sandra disappeared, resting my chin on my propped-up hand. My elbow is digging into the wood. It's annoying, but I ignore it. I see Sandra's eyes. They're two floating orbs in my hand, levitating pools that stare into me. They were desperate, lost, confused, and I did nothing to help. Goddammit.

Greg and Ken appear from behind a building. Greg's holding a bundle of papers against his chest, taking care not to bump into anyone. Ken is glaring at people who get too close. They're speed-walking, almost jogging, tearing up a small cloud of dust. They're coming to my office.

I pull back inside and slam the window down, blocking out the celebrations of another burial escapee. I tuck the knife behind the curtain. I stand in front of my robes. I could put them on. It might be an important discussion, after all. Gravitas would be—No, no, I'm making excuses. It's ceremonial, not a protection blanket. I walk to my desk and sit behind it. I fold my hands and wait.

Ken bursts through the door. He nods at me and circles the room. He dips his head under the desks. He dashes about the room, checking every nook and cranny. He covers the window with the curtain, darkening the office. He glances around the room. I don't bother to say hello. Greg is right behind him. He bolts into the office and slams the door. He readjusts his grip on the stacks papers and wipes his face. He breathes a hello and stares at Ken. There's a moment of silence.

"I think we're good." Ken steps away from the window, flexing his hands.

Greg approaches me, his face alive with twitches. I study his face (panicked) and Ken's (concerned, which is panicked for Ken). They've been digging into the case for days. They wouldn't come here like this with empty hands. This is going to be a long conversation. Greg opens his mouth, but I hold up my hand. I stand up and open the back door. I gesture to the garden. We need some privacy.

I grab my watering can and I walk to the edges. I face the sun, closing my eyes. A moment of calm. Ken and Greg join me, closing the door. Greg stands next to me, rustling his papers and clearing his throat. Ken walks to the center of the garden, tense and ready. I breathe in, collect myself, and breathe out. I nod to Greg.

"Okay, first things first: It's definitely a murder. No doubt there. I studied the...body and the neck wound. I looked up old medical books we had lying around, and the wound is consistent with a slashing cut. Probably a knife or a smooth blade. Very precise stuff. Couldn't be a wild animal attack. Not messy enough. We're dealing with a killer." Greg flips through several pages.

I cluck my tongue and squeeze the can handle. My chest tightens. I rub my eyes and blink. I'd hoped (prayed) it might've been a pack of wolves or a wildcat of some sort. I think I saw one of those in the woods once. Spittal could've come across an animal and agitated it. He could've run and startled it. Or froze and startled it. Or made a noise and startled it. Whatever it is that startles animals. The animal attacked and killed him. Maybe it was all just a freak accident. I knew it couldn't be, but I wanted it.

I move the can to a different flower bed. I watch the water splash and roll off the petals. Greg shuffles his feet. I put out my hand and he places a portion of his paper stack in my palm. I read.

It's a collection of medical photos. A series of different slashed throats greet me, all dried out and gaping wide. I wince and look at Greg through the corner of my eye. He sighs and looks away. The throats all have straight lines running from ear to ear. I turn the page and see Spittal. It's just his neck, but I've memorized it by now. It's cleaned up, spotless, really, but it still seems fresh. I can picture the blood. I grit my teeth and study the cut. I flip back to the other page, tracing my finger over the cuts. I return to Spittal. It's a match. He was murdered.

Fuck.

I turn to the last few pages. They're covered in photos and diagrams of knives. Hunting, surgical, kitchen, they're all here. Greg has dotted the images with measurements and side notes. There's a large knife in the middle. It has a wooden handle with rounded grooves at one end that serve as finger grips. Its blade is twice the length of the handle. Its bottom half is smooth, sharp enough to tear open skin. The top half is a row of jagged teeth, rough enough to dig into a bone. Its tip is a perfect point, the right size to perforate. This knife is probably what I'd use if I were...whoever did this. Slice the throat, carve into the chest, or poke the heart. You'd have plenty of options. It'd be a bit messy, for sure, but it'd get the job done. If I were to do it.

Greg's written out the math for several photos, trying to determine the dimensions. I don't pretend to understand what any of it means. I give him the papers and move to another flower bed.

"So, we know what and how, but we don't know why or who." I rock the can back and forth.

"No, no, we don't, sir." Greg shuffles the papers back into his stack.

"Did you see any weapons in the grass with Spittal?" I hold the can up, stopping the flow.

"No, I didn't see anything. Whoever did this must've taken it when he was finished. I'll look again, though." Greg looks exhausted.

"You've done good work. Thank you." I squeeze Greg's shoulder. He smiles weakly and pats my hand.

"What have you found?" I look over Greg to speak with Ken. He doesn't move.

"Not much, sir. I spotted a blood trail, but it led back to Spittal. It started a few feet into the woods." Ken keeps his eye on the back door.

"So, he was attacked in the woods and made it to the bush before he collapsed?" I drum my fingers on the can and tilt it down. This sounds like a lead.

"That's what we think." Greg raises his hand.

"Any luck?" Why can't they cut to chase?

"None. I've looked through every spot in that forest. If there's something there, I can't find it." Ken deflates me. If he can't find anything, it's a dead lead.

"I checked, too, sir. Couldn't find a scrap of evidence." Greg's search is less important, but I don't want to discourage him.

"We're dealing with a professional." Ken lets his words sink in.

A professional killer. Someone who's trained murder. That kind of person is stalking my compound, waiting. This is too heavy. We're a religious organization. We're peaceful. We're not prepared for this. I'm not prepared for this. We just want to be left alone. Why did they do this? Why is this happening? This wasn't—

My watering can is empty, swaying limply in my hand. I've drowned a flower. Its soil bed is submerged in water. Its stem sags and it droops over to the side, petals brushing on the dirt. I lost focus and killed it. I scowl and drop the can.

Ken and Greg are staring at me. Ken is calm, but there's fear in his gaze. He can't do this alone. Greg's eyes are wide and weary. They're stuck in the moment before the bullet hits. He'll fall apart by himself. I rub my temples. They need me as much as I need them. I have to lead. I pick up the watering can, stand up straight, and pull Greg close.

"Greg, keep looking into this. Do whatever you have to do. Work with Ken. Follow Spittal's friends, his enemies, anyone you suspect; pull up any file you need; if you think it's necessary, do it. We have to find this person." Even with Ken and Greg here, the garden feels vulnerable.

"Yes, sir, of course, sir." Greg's head bobs up and down. Ken slowly nods at me.

"And be discreet. You understand what's at stake here. We can't have people panicking. We can't let this affect them. This will just upset and disturb them. This is our problem and we'll fix it." I grip the back of Greg's neck as I talk.

"Absolutely, sir. We won't tell anyone. Don't worry." Greg's eyes turn to steel. I believe him.

"Good. I know you won't fail me." I pat his cheek and smile.

I fill up the watering can in the rain barrel. It sinks and I pull it out, spilling water on my feet. I go to water more beds, but Greg and Ken are staring at me, motionless.

"What?" I put the can down.

"Sir, we think we have a suspect." Greg scuttles towards me. Ken inches closer.

My chest tightens again. I rock forward and steady myself. Why couldn't they have started with this?

"Go on." I beckon Greg to come closer.

Greg scurries to me as Ken walks behind him, never looking away from the door. Greg digs into his stack and pulls out a square piece of paper. It's a photo of a man. He has olive skin. His hair is black and smooth, parted to the left. He's sporting a neatly trimmed goatee that forms a tight circle around his mouth. His smile reveals a gap tooth. There's a large mole on his upper cheek. His eyes are soft and grey. Just another member.

"His name is George Carr. He's been a member for a while now. Not as long as Spittal. About a year...yes, yes, just over a year. He came from the suburbs, wanted a little more, found us, same old story. Nothing special. He works in the fields. Used to be a builder, but an accident messed up his right hand. No reports or complaints against him. Average member by all accounts. Hasn't stood out from the pack. I couldn't find too much on him. He mostly..." Greg is tearing through page after page of notes.

"Why's he a suspect?" I put my hand over Greg's pages. I'll read the abridged version later.

"Ah, well, you see, I didn't find evidence in his file to suggest...much of anything, really. I'd actually touched up his notes not too long ago, so he was fresh in my mind. I thought of him, but nothing led me to...to think of him as dangerous. As a killer. But, but, you see, we..." Greg is flinging his hands everywhere. I hold my finger to his lips.

"Why...do you.... suspect...him?" I grit my teeth.

"I saw him fight with Spittal in the woods." Ken steps forward.

I tilt my head and stare at Ken. Greg moves back. Ken's chin is raised, almost defiant. He's been hiding something from me. I nod and he continues.

"It happened a few weeks ago. We were in the forest at night. Spittal and Carr were arguing over...something. I couldn't make out the details. Seemed serious. Carr shoved Spittal and one thing lead to another. They rolled on the ground and we gave them space. Let them work it out. Spittal clocked Carr with a mean right hook. He always had strong punch. Left Carr in the dirt. Few days later, I heard rumblings that Carr was looking to get even. I didn't think much of it until we found the body." Ken takes a deep breath.

"What were they doing in the woods? What were you doing there?" I hold my hands behind my back and pace.

"We'd been there for about an hour. We needed isolated space." Ken scratches the back of his ear.

"We? How many? Why did you need space?" I dig my heels in the dirt as I pivot.

"There were about seventeen of us. No, wait, it was sixteen. Margaret never showed up. It was a smaller crowd than usual. We needed the forest to blow off steam." Ken cracks his neck.

"Blow off steam?" I stop walking and raise my eyebrows.

"Yeah, relieve some stress. Talk, complain, argue, whatever we have to get off our chests. Some of them fight or wrestle. They just need a spot to unwind." Ken's lip twitches.

I watch Greg's face, but he seems as surprised with this as I am. I look at Ken and frown. A support group flying under my radar. All those people gathering in the woods to...what? Comfort each other? Lean on one another? Take a break? Escape? Unacceptable. We don't take vacations here. We don't get time off. We don't have reprieves. We sort through our problems and move on. We soldier through the pain. That's what we're founded on. I'm not running a spa; I'm running a revolution.

This knitting circle mocks our principles, mocks me. It's insubordination. They're taking the easy way out. They don't have to try when they can always run away to "blow off steam." Disgusting. Absolutely despicable. And my closest aide is a part of it. I've given Ken everything. He's respected, feared, even. He sees everything. He's in the inner circle. He has a front row seat to our ascension. I've shown him a better way, the right way, and this is how he shows gratitude. He slinks into the woods to unwind. To relax. To escape.

My hands are balled tight, fingers digging into my palms. I'm shaking, actually shaking. I stare at Ken, boring a hole into his face. He's sweaty and his eyes tremble, but he stands his ground. I can respect that, at least.

"How long has this...club been going on?" I lean in close.

"As long as I've been here. Probably before then." Ken clears his throat.

I bite my tongue and close my eyes. All this time I've been teaching people, there's been this group lurking in the shadows.

"Sir?" Greg raises his hand, but I ignore him.

"How many? I want names." I grind my teeth.

"Don't know them all off the top of my head." Ken sounds petulant.

"Sir."

"Think hard." I shoot a steady, angry stream of air from my nose.

"Sir."

"Is this entirely-?" Ken sighs.

"Yes, yes, it is entirely necessary. This...after-school special is operating without permission or consent. I want to know why—" I feel something tug on my sleeve.

"Sir." It's Greg.

"What?" I spin around.

"Shouldn't we focus on more pressing matters?" Greg's holding Carr and Spittal's photos.

I take the pictures. No matter how we heard about Carr, it's a lead. We need to deal with the bigger problem. Then I'll chop through that group one by one. I exhale and nod.

"Fine, fine, follow up on him. It's all we've got anyway." I rub my thumb over Carr's face. I memorize every blemish, every freckle, every feature. I need to know him when I see him.

"I don't think he's in here." I gesture to the door.

Greg glances at Ken and nods. He puts the papers under his arm and walks to the door. Ken turns to leave, but I grab his shoulder.

"Ken, I want you to know that when this is over, I'll demolish that group." Ken shudders. I feel the vibrations in my fingers. He nods without looking at me.

"I'm not the bad guy here. That group is dangerous. What if we all acted like that? What if we slacked off or took a break or ran away when things got too tough? Where would that leave us? We'd be the very thing we abandoned. I can't allow that. No matter the circumstance, no matter the person. No exceptions. You understand, don't you?"

Ken looks at the ground. He rubs his eyes and lets out a heavy sigh. He faces me and nods.

"Thank you. We'll talk about this more later. Oh, and it goes without saying you're not to attend these meetings anymore. Quit it cold turkey. And... discourage anyone else from going. Clear?" I let go of his shoulder and smile.

Ken offers a weak grin. His eyes seem hurt, betrayed. He should see how I feel. My lieutenant breaking my most stringent rules. But I'll let it go. He'll thank me later.

"Glad to hear it. Leave the door open on your way. Get some circulation in that stuffy office." I tussle his hair.

Ken walks away, clenching and unclenching his hands. His feet drag on the ground. I'll let him savour this temper tantrum. I pick up the watering can as he opens the door.

"Ken, what do you do in the woods? Personally?" I eye the inside of the can. Plenty left.

"Blow off steam." He doesn't look at me as he disappears into the office.

I let out a half-chuckle. Finally, a moment of peace. Perfect silence. I tilt the can over a flower bed. I picture Carr standing behind Spittal. He's holding a knife. He runs it across Spittal's throat, releasing a torrent of blood. Carr stands over Spittal as he fades away, clawing at the dirt. Carr blends into the woods as Spittal dies, choking and gurgling.

I tilt the can up. My mind won't stop racing. I need to focus. I close my eyes and try to clear my thoughts. I see the river. A perfect flowing system. Serene, calm, orde—

I see flashes of Carr and Spittal. Blood. Knives. Trees. Begging. Crying. Darkness. Silence.

I open my eyes and curse. I can't let this consume me. I have to think straight. I have to be a leader. I have to—

I hear shouting. Not regular compound chatter and conversation. Not builders grunting and planters digging. It's shouting. A yelling rumble. It leaps over the garden walls.

Greg appears in the door frame. His eyes are wide. I shake my head. I'm never going to water these plants.

"What is it?" I put down the can.
"Everyone's leaving."

CHAPTER NINE

I'm on the edge of a swarm.

I'm standing at the center square with Ken. A gaggle of members walk past us. Most of them keep their heads down. They mutter and shake their heads. Some are scowling, others are smiling. They all join the horde.

I'm looking at a sea of people. They're all facing the gate. Everyone from the compound must be here. I look at the fields and construction sites. Tools are strewn everywhere, some leaning on buildings or scarecrows. Doors are open, swinging in the air. When we left the office, the burial group was gone, leaving behind the half-filled hole. Looking away from the gate, this place resembles a ghost town. Everybody's concentrated here.

They're all shouting. Nothing concrete, really. A few "Watch its" and "Moves," but that's it. It's a constant wail of jeering, clapping, hissing, and laughing. They're riled up. Above the voices, I hear a consistent sound: Ringing. It's tinny and sharp, a solid metallic echo. It shoots through the compound. It keeps going and going, a never-ending stream of ringing. I've been here for three minutes and it's already pissing me off.

The crowd jostles and moves, looking for a better spot. Their eyes are locked on the gate. I can't see what they're looking at. I stand on my toes and arch my back and neck, craning my head over the mass. I see a glimpse of the iron gate. It looks open, but I can't tell. I pull myself up further, straining to rise above the rows of heads. It's no good. I fall back on my heels.

"See anything?" I look up at Ken.

He leans forwards, peering through the mob. He cups his hand above his eyes, shielding them from the sun. He shakes his head. I groan and kick a mound of dirt. I run my tongue over my gums. The crowd is unruly, wild, angry. It's like a sermon, but they're not looking at me. I have no idea where to start with them. I'm about to shrug at Ken when I spot Greg.

He broke off from us when we approached the crowd, circling the edges. He's leaning over a porch of a building, craning his neck like me. He spots us and jogs over.

"Anything?" I wave at him.

Greg shakes his head. I put my chin in my hand and stare at the mob. I could yell at them to turn around, listen to me… No, that wouldn't work, they're too loud. Maybe I could… No, no, that's terrible. Fuck. I have to go in there…

"Sir, did you organize this?" Greg taps my shoulder.

"Huh?" I blink.

"Is this an impromptu ceremony or something?" Greg gestures at the crowd, nervous.

"No, no, I didn't arrange this. No ceremonies without my consent and presence, you know that." I wave him off.

"Well, that's good to know, I guess." Greg sidesteps an incoming pair of members. They walk right past me as they join the mob. Unacceptable.

"So…who did?" Ken looks up and down the compound.

I move from side to side, analyzing the crowd. They're filling up the whole space. People are spilling out on the left and right. I won't be able to go around; I'll have to cut through. I see several openings in the middle. I'll have to be firm. God, what if he...she...the killer's in there? Waiting. No, no, can't think like that. Focus. Get to the gate.

"Time to find out." I sigh.

Greg is bouncing his head all over the place, trying to soak everything in. He's dealt with rowdy crowds before. He's always in the hall during a sermon in case things get out of control. He's got a plan for anything. Greg can go. But this is out in the open and he's had no prep time.

Ken just stares ahead. His eyes wander to some of the bigger members. He knows what they can all do. He arm wrestles in his spare time. He won't like it, but he's ready.

My soldiers. A manager, a bodyguard, and a fidgety leader. Let's dive in.

"Alright, I'm going to the gate. I think there are a few spaces I can squeeze past in the crowd. There shouldn't be any problems" I look at Greg and Ken, daring them to challenge me. Ken raises his eyebrows and Greg scrunches his face, but they're quiet. Loyal, if nothing else.

"Right, while I'm doing that I want you two out here. Greg, stay in this spot. See if you can talk to any stragglers. Try to figure what's going on. Keep it verbal, yeah?" Greg smiles and nods. This is something he can manage.

"Ken, I want you to circle them. Look for any rowdy members. If someone is getting too rough, yank them out of there and send them on their way. Basic crowd control. You know what to do." Ken doesn't look at me as he flashes a quick thumbs-up.

"Perfect. Alright, here I- wait, wait, before I go." I look up at Ken and cough. He gazes down at me. I point at my cheek. My finger is shaking. He smiles and puts his hand on my shoulder. He squeezes it, steadying me. He slaps me as hard as he can. I stagger back, massaging my cheek. Its sting wakes me up. I'm here. I nod my head as I plunge into the crowd.

I force my way through two people. They're both taller than me so I push my hands between their elbows and walk forward. The both yell, but stop when they see me. I jerk my thumb backwards and they retreat from the mob. I see Greg, holding his mini notebook and pen, stopping them to talk. I adjust my shirt and keep going. Just at the tip.

I fight through the crowd, pushing and pulling people away. Some members fall to the side, melting into another part of the group. Others turn to argue, but demur. I squeeze past every opening I can find, snaking deeper and deeper into the horde. The shouting is clearer. They're yelling names, shouting at "Chris," "Marcus," "Jonathan," and "Martin," telling them to stay or fuck off. These boys must be at the gate. What'd they do to piss everybody off? They've already pissed me off by assembling this crowd, and I haven't even met them yet. We're going to have a nice chat.

Fuck, that ringing bell is still going. It's splitting my ears.

People are shoving me. I trip forward, stumble backward, tilt to the side. I fall every direction but down. I slam my feet against the ground every time someone pushes me, keeping myself vertical. I want to punch everyone in the face. I want to shove them all to the ground and out of my way. But I don't have the time. I keep going. I find a small clearing in the mass. I catch my breath and look around. I can see the front of a building. The repair shop, I think. That's pretty close to the gate. I must be halfway through the crowd. Christ, only halfway. I plough forward. More people, more pushing, more fighting. I keep my head up, hoping people recognize me. Some do and make a path. I want to ask them what this is about, but it's hardly the time. I'll find out soon.

A man is front of me. I try to squirm past him, but both sides are jammed packed. I tap his shoulder, but he doesn't move. I clap my hand on his back, but he keeps his back to me. I push him, but he still faces forward. He just flips me his middle finger. An insubordinate hick. I grab both his shoulders and spin him around. It's George Carr.

He looks just like the photo. The slicked-back hair, the olive skin, the gap tooth, they're all there. His goatee is a little messier, but it's got the same shape. There's a thin cut above his mole.

Carr snarls as he faces me. His grey eyes are on fire. His fists are curled. But, when he sees me, he steps back and looks away.

"Sorry, sir. Didn't know it was you." He barely moves his lips as he talks.

Carr scratches his head, keeping his eyes on the ground. He goes to leave, muttering under his breath. He pushes past me, struggling to get past a pot-bellied woman. I grab his arm. This is an opportunity.

"George, how are you doing?" I raise my voice above the shouting and the goddamn ringing bell.

George looks at me. His eyes narrow, but he doesn't pull away.

"I'm fine." I can barely hear Carr's mumbling over the crowd's din.

I wrap my hand around the back of his neck, leaning my forearm on his shoulder. I lock eyes with him. He looks past me. He feels tense.

"George, how are you doing?" I can smell his sweat.

"...Could be better…" Carr shrugs. He's still not looking at me.

"George, do you want to talk? I'm always here." I flash a quick smile.

Carr glances around the crowd. People surge past us. Carr gestures at the noisy mob with a feeble hand wave. I nod.

"No, no, not here. Not the place. How about you meet me at the hall tonight? Around 11. Private one-on-one session. Could you do that?" I force him to look me in the eye.

"...Sure…" Carr gives another shrug.

"Wonderful. Good to hear. See you there." I clap his shoulder and let go of his neck.

Carr shirks away from me. I smile again, offering a thumbs-up. Carr jerks his head and vanishes into the crowd. I'll unpack that problem later. I return to the slog.

I've found a rhythm. Pull, push, eye contact, nod, go deeper. People behind me filter out of the crowd. The bottom half of the mob is scattered and divided. People to my side stay out of my way. People at the front still don't notice me. I dodge errant elbows, taking a few blows to the chest. I grunt and keep moving. Pain is good.

The jeering is still going strong. I can hear one voice over the fray. It seems to be directed at the crowd. It's shrill and hoarse. I can't make out the words, but it's annoying. Not quite as annoying as that bell, though. If I find that thing. I'm almost at the end. I can see a large section of the gate. Just a few more steps...

I touch a woman's shoulder and she stands aside. She doesn't look at me. I glance at her. It's Sandra. Her hair's a mess and her face is covered in sweat. Her body is twitchy and her eyes dart everywhere. This crowd is agitating her. I put a foot forward and stop myself. I hold my hand in the air and pat her back. She turns to me and her eyes light up a bit. I show her a row of my pearly whites. She returns with a faint smile and looks away. I let my face fall and think of something to say. Something encouraging, something supportive. I should say...anything, really. I give her back another pat and continue to the gate. I don't look back.

I'm in the home stretch. Only a few more people. About fucking time. I comb past members, pulling on their shoulders for momentum. I break through a couple holding hands. I stumble out, thrown off balance by my speed. I made it to the gate. I stretch my back crack my neck. A whisper ripples through the mob as it goes quiet. They all stare at me. I shake my head and glare at them. No time for lectures. I turn around. The bell ringing has stopped. Small miracles.

Four members stand before me. All men. Three builders and a planter, based on their clothing. The first three are wearing overalls and work boots. Their heads are bent to the ground. They won't make eye contact. Weak. The fourth one, the one on the far right, is wearing loose clothes covered in dirt. He's facing forward. Trouble.

A builder is behind them, standing at the center of the gate. He's holding a large stick. It's top heavy, smoothed out with a large clubbing orb. He's on guard duty for today. He switches his gaze from me, to the crowd, to the men. He has no idea what to do.

The three builders are quiet. The planter is talking. No, that's not it; he's sermonizing.

"...time for change. There's more out there than this woeful place. We were meant for more. We weren't meant to

wallow in misery. We were meant to indulge, to satiate, to rise.
We have to throw off our shackles. Join us, join us, join us..."
Oh, yes, he's definitely trouble.

I start clapping my hands. I raise them above my head. I
look at the planter (no, the dissenter). My claps echo around the
compound. The dissenter stops talking and stares at me. Insolent.
I hold my hands together and walk forward. I stop at the middle
point between the crowd and the four. The mediation spot.

"Well, this is quite the crowd. Can't say I approve.
What's happening here?" I nod at the guard.

"Well, uh, sir, these, these men are trying to leave the
compound, and I, uh, I'm trying to stop them." The guard grips
the stick against his chest.

"You're stopping them?" I approach the four. The
builders inch away. The dissenter stands his ground.

"Uh-huh." The guard rocks forward as he nods. I'm
dealing with a scholar.

I scan the four. The builders are easily broken; they've
given up already. They must have been talked into this farce.
They just want to disappear into the crowd. The dissenter
matches my gaze. I'll have to be creative with him. I look at the
crowd. They've stepped closer, narrowing the gap. They want to
rough up these boys. This is going to require the right touch.
Showtime.

"Well, that's absolutely ridiculous. If they want to leave,
let them." I shrug.

The guard stares at me. He twitches his fingers on his
stick. The three builders look up at me. I wink at them. They turn
to the dissenter. He squints at me. He was expecting a fight; I've
chopped his balls off. He's on his back foot. I savour the
uncertainty, smiling at the four's suspicious faces.

"Go on, open the gate. I won't have barriers for these
people. They're free to leave. Open it, open it." I spread my arms
wide.

The guard is still staring at me. He doesn't move. His
mouth hangs there. He's slowing me down. I rotate my hands,

motioning to the gate with my eyes. Everyone's watching him, except the dissenter. He's holding his gaze on me. I'll get to him.

The guard blinks. He holds the stick to his side and reaches into his pants pocket. He fishes around in it and pulls out a collection of keys. No one talks as he approaches the gate. He looks back at me. I nod. He flips through the key batch and inserts one into the lock. The gate creaks and moans as he pushes it open. The road stretches before me. Nothing but free space.

The four don't move. The builders look back and forth from the gate to the dissenter. Their feet are stuck in the ground. The dissenter chuckles. He heads to the gate and the builders follow suit. The crowd starts hissing. The guard glares at the four, thumping his stick on his open palm. The three keep their heads down, but the dissenter walks backwards, smiling at the mob. He looks surprised. They reach the edge of gate. Five more steps and they're completely free.

"Of course, I hope you'll permit a few closing words from yours truly." I raise my hand, wriggling my fingers.

The four stop. The dissenter stumbles over a rock. His sneer returns. The builders are shaking. They could keep going. They could hop over the line and run for it. They don't have to listen to me. But they turn around. I rub my hands together and I approach them. I inspect their clothes and faces. They avoid my gaze, except the dissenter, of course. I can see anger in those eyes. But there's doubt there, too. I can use that. I roll up my sleeves and stand at an angle, speaking to the four and the crowd. Intimate and theatrical.

"As I said, you are free to leave. I would never stop you from doing so. In fact, if you need to depart, I encourage it. It is your right and I would never take it from you." I put my hand to my heart.

"You, as always, are free. You're free to walk away from this place and all the progress you've made. You're free to abandon the people who depend upon you. You're free to erase the person you've become. You're free to wander back into those congested cities and deserted towns. You're free to return to your cramped apartment or your overpriced home or your parents' basement. You're free to crawl back to the job you hate or find a new job to despise or do nothing at all. You're free to have brain-dead conversations with empty husks obsessed with nonsense. You're free to go back to a world of compromise, lies, and regret. You're free to clamp the shackles back on your neck and wrists. You're free to numb yourselves and swallow gruel and pills until you fall into a hole in the ground. You're free to do all of those things. You are free."

The crowd whistles. The builders' heads are bent even lower. The dissenter's gaze seems to have dipped a bit. I stride in front of the four and stop at the left end.

"I want you to consider all of that. Before you cross the threshold, I want you to think about everything you're diving into. I want you to remember every empty, unfulfilled moment from your lives before coming here. I want you to accept all of them, because they're waiting for you past this gate. And I want you to look me in the eye as you tell me this is the right choice for you." I fold my hands in front of my chest. I stand in front of the builder on the left. I press my shoe on his foot and wait. I stare down at him, letting the silence weigh on him. Slowly, he looks at me.

"Are you ready to walk away from salvation? It's tempting to go back to that world. All those choices and pleasures. It's so easy out there. You find your niche and you stay there. But, ultimately, you'll fall into the same rut. And this time, we won't be there to pick you up. Is that what you want?" My voice is a low growl. I only want him to hear me.

The man's eyes are wet. His face is quivering. He opens his mouth and lets out a hiss. It sounds like air escaping a tire. He clears his throat, pounding his chest with his fist. He looks at my shoulder. He moves his lips. I lean close, pushing my ear forward with my fingers.

"...stay..." He whispers his words in one breath.

"I'm sorry, you'll have to speak up." I gesture to the crowd.

The man winces. He looks at me, begging for an excuse, an escape. I offer none. He sighs.

"I'll stay." The man's voice strains as he pushes it.

The crowd claps and cheers. The man glances at me for approval. I give a quick nod. He scurries away, disappearing into the mob, avoiding back slaps and shoves.

I move to the second builder. He pulls his head up to look at me. His face is steady. No tears, no quakes. But he's not firm.

"I won't blame you for leaving. I want you to know that. I won't resent you, truly. It will be your choice. You'll have to live with the consequences. All of them. Can you do that?" I poke my finger right below his chest. It's soft. The man sniffs and scratches his neck. He looks at the dissenter. The traitor scrunches his forehead, burning a hole into the builder's heart. The builder shrugs and approaches me. He gives a quick nod and walks away.

"Coward! Weak, pathetic coward!" The dissenter's voice breaks.

"Please, please, no need for histrionics. He made his choice." It's hard to suppress my smile.

The builder goes to the side of the crowd, hugging the wall of a building. A few members shout his name, but most stare forward. I stroll over to the third builder. He's a puddle of frayed nerves. He's hopping from foot to foot, stuffing his hands deep into his pockets. He shrinks away from me and the dissenter. I let him stew for a minute. Then he faces me. His eyes are wobbling. It looks like his brain wants to burst out of his head and streak away from his body as fast as possible. I lock his gaze, dissecting him. I don't quite know what to say. I don't want to completely destroy him. I open my mouth. The builder blurts out an apology and dashes into the crowd, keeping his head down. He's lost behind the sea of people. The crowd laughs with me.

I hold up three fingers and turn to the dissenter. He's staring at the ground. Always show your power; that breaks them. I learned that fact decades ago. My dad took me to a farm. They were taming a new batch of horses that day. One buck was causing some trouble; he kept tossing riders to the ground. A line of ranchers clutching their backs and necks led away from the pen. My dad volunteered. He climbed the horse and held on. He let it stomp, run, and buck across the field. He didn't fight or yell; he tightened his grip. My dad bore down on it. He brought it to heel and led it to the stable. That's the one thing he taught me: You let the horse tire itself out, then you flex your muscles. I let this dissenter burn himself out; then I broke him. I try not to gloat, I really do. I push down on an incoming smile. I have to be humble, gracious. I have to be the bigger man.

"Well, you're a one-man act now. Your friends changed their minds; will you? I'd hate to see you go. I'm sure we can work through any problems you might have. That's what we're about. What do you say?" I extend my hand.

This is a formality. I've already won. But it's a show of good faith. The dissenter tilts his head up and meets my gaze. He's smiling, but his eyes are resigned. He knows he's lost. He can't go out alone. He reaches for my hand. He shakes it and we're done. He pauses, freezing his hand in the air. Let's get going here. Wrap your limp fingers around mine and we can all move on. He unfreezes his hand, reaching towards mine. Almost there...

I barely register when he spits on my face.

I can see it happening. He slaps my hand away. He pulls his head back like he's retching. He launches a glob of phlegm. It lands on my cheek, splashing on my lips. A massive smile spreads across his face. He bares his teeth, letting out a throaty laugh.

I don't move. I touch my face and wipe off the spit. I stare at the dissenter and blink. He points at me and laughs even louder. He's talking.

"Fraud! Fraud! Fraud! You're following a liar!" The dissenter's voice splits my ears.

He's greeted by a chorus of boos. They surge forward but I hold up my hand. The dissenter gives us a middle-finger salute and runs past the gate, ducking a sharp swing from the guard, who tries to chase him.

"Let him go, let him go. He made his choice." I watch the dissenter sprint down the road, half-impressed and half-murderous. I rub the remaining spit from my cheek. My teeth are clenched. I turn to the crowd. They're waiting for a kill order. That's encouraging.

"I hope you all learned something here. It's not every day that you get a chance to see...stuff like this. We have to experience a, a...test up close and… not everybody follows the same...script. We have to understand them. And we can't be...belligerent or violent. We're better than that. If we weren't, we wouldn't…" I have no idea what I'm saying.

I shut my mouth, letting my words die in the air. I pinch the bridge of my nose. Most of the crowd is staring at me, but some are peeking past me to watch the dissenter. Others are glancing around the compound. They're losing focus. I need to wrap this up. But I don't have the words. It's all a jumble.

Fuck it.

"Alright, everybody, that's enough for today. Don't you people have work to do? This place won't run itself. We're done here. Get going." I wave my hand. The mob disperses. Some stick around to watch me. I watch the dissenter shrink into the distance.

The dissenter wobbles as he runs, staggering from side to side. His limbs shoot out like wet spaghetti. His arms flail up and down as his legs bend and stretch at weird angles. He trips over his feet, catching himself by shoving his hands on the ground. It's painful to watch him move. Weak genetics.

I hold my thumb and my pointer finger close to my eye, forming an incomplete rectangle. They tower over the dissenter, trapping him in a box. I could just press my finger down. He'd resist, propping up his feeble arms to halt the pressure. But it wouldn't stop. His knees would buckle, forcing him to the dirt.

He'd scream and beg and fight but that wouldn't halt the finger. It would only stop when it touched the thumb, leaving behind a red smear. If only.

I see Ken and Greg in my peripheral vision. Ken is keeping his distance, probably still searching for crowd problems. Greg is close, holding his arms tight across his chest. I ignore them. I keep my eyes trained on the dissenter. He's an undefined blob at this point. I can barely make out distinct parts of his body. He reaches the end of our path and stops running. The highway stretches out to his left and right. No chance he'll hitch a ride, not in that outfit. The nearest town is a few miles away. Hope his feet don't get sore.

Three robed figures are standing beside a dark blue car. Their robes are pure black with sharp gold stripes running around the sides. Their backs are blazoned with a bright yellow orb. How did I not notice them beforehand? Their outfits are disgustingly excessive.

The figures approach the dissenter. He extends his hand. They stare at him, their faces obscured by their hoods. The dissenter steps closer and pushes his hand out further. I can see them slapping his hand away, shoving him to the ground, denouncing him, and speeding away. He crawls to the compound, scrapping his head on the gravel. I stand over him, allowing him to grovel for forgiveness. I pick him up by the chin...

No. Not today. The figure in the middle removes his hood. Blonde hair, fair skin. The right and left ones reveal their faces. Black and olive skins. The middle one grabs the dissenter and pulls him into a hug. The other two wrap their arms around them. I can hear their laughter from here. The robes applaud the dissenter, patting his back. He shakes their hands repeatedly, bowing his head. He even kisses the blonde's robe hem. Disgraceful.

The dissenter spares one look at the compound, throwing up a pair of middle fingers. He piles into the car with the black and olive skinned people, disappearing beneath the tinted glass.

The blonde one wanders down the path. I approach the gate, trying to get a better look. I can't really see his face, but I know he's looking at me. He's holding something behind his back. I clutch the gate steel, leaning forward. The blonde stands there, surveying the compound. He pulls his hand away from his back; he's holding a bell. He swings his arm above his head. The ringing returns, more obnoxious and splitting than before. I want to run up there and shove that bell down his throat. I'm wringing my hands over the gate bar. The blonde dashes to the car and jumps into the driver's seat. The vehicle spins around, kicking up rocks, and hurries down the road.

I turn to Greg. Ken is standing behind him. Our brows are furrowed.

"Who was that?" I jerk my thumb to the road.

"Zaan, sir, that compound I mentioned. The one that's been poaching some members." Greg rubs his eyes.

"Looks like they've stepped up their recruitment." I drum my fingers on the gate.

A member theft, right in my compound. The nerve. The fucking gall. Who does that? How'd they do it? How are my members learning about them? We can't have this, not now. Not with...everything going on. This is a problem.

"Ken, get the car ready. We're paying Zaan a visit."

CHAPTER TEN

I can only smell eggs, bacon, and piss.

Ken is sitting in front of me. His face is obscured by the menu. He mutters as he flips through the pages. His coffee is untouched. The waitress approaches our table, holding a writing pad and a pitcher of water. A pencil is perched above her ear, caught in her tangled hair. She raises her eyebrows and reaches for her pencil. I glance at Ken, still engrossed in the food selection, and shake my head. She sighs and fills up my glass. She walks to another booth.

I sip my water and spin the knife on the table. It hits the spoon, bounces away, and stops moving. I grip an ice cube in my lips and pull it into my mouth. It stings my teeth. I rest the cube on my tongue. It burns as it melts. I swallow what's left of the cube and put the glass down. My menu is open on the brunch page. I run my finger down a column, as if I'm actually considering what to buy. I know what I'm getting: Scrambled eggs, sausages, toast, and hash browns. It's the only thing worth eating here, and it's within our budget.

I push the menu away and put my chin on my fist. I bore a hole into Ken's menu, willing him to put it down. He ignores me. He knows what he wants, but he has to study every meal on the list. I should make this a sermon trial: watching Ken order food. I'd have no more members. Anybody who stayed would be clinically insane and I'd have to ship them away for my own safety.

My eyes wander to the grimy window. The sun's retreated behind the clouds, giving everything a dull colour. A semi-circle gravel parking lot lies in front of the diner. A series of white paint lines are smeared along the edges, representing car spots. Two pickup trucks are parked together. One of them has a trailer. A brown station wagon is double-parked. A red convertible flies by without stopping. Slow day. My favourite.

Our car is parked under a dead tree. Its leaves are long gone and its branches are severed, shortened, or deformed. Our usual spot. The car is dark blue, mostly faded at this point. It has a dent on its passenger side (the result of a particularly wild sermon). Its headlights and windows are in good condition. The rear bumper is loose. It's a standard old car. And it's our only transportation to the outside world.

I prop my feet up in the booth seat and lean into the back cushion. I start spinning my knife again. I stare at Ken, waiting for his decision. We need this rest; we're going to war.

Ken brushed the twigs, leaves, and sticks off the car and yanked off its tarp. We were in the forest. A big empty clearing. Nobody comes here but Ken and I. Even Greg hasn't been to this spot. The clearing leads right out onto the highway. It's where we hide the car.

Ken dusted off remaining the tree scraps and pulled out his key. He hopped into the driver's seat and plugged it into the ignition. It stuttered and stopped. Ken turned the key again, banging on the steering wheel. The engine coughed and sputtered to life, pumping out gas. Ken popped open the passenger door. I slid in and we took off down the highway.

I don't like this thing. I think we should be independent and isolated. We should be able to sustain ourselves. A few months after we started, I decided to cut members off from the city. No more day trips or grocery shopping or distractions. Sink or swim. It worked. We're still alive.

But we can't be an island. Problems pop up. Emergencies we have to address. And, sometimes, we have to leave the compound to do so. This car is our lifeline. If something needs to be solved away from the compound, we have a remedy. We've had it for years, and aside from some nicks and bumps, it's served us well enough.

Ken drove in silence, staring dead ahead. When he's driving, he can only focus on the road. I shifted in my seat, listening to the leather groan. I rolled the window down and stuck my head out. I closed my eyes as the wind rushed past me. I swayed with the current, letting my neck roll back.

I pulled myself back in and rolled the window up, leaning against it. I watched the scenery zoom by. Trees, farms, yards, trailer parks, mailboxes, trees, yards, mailboxes, farms, billboards, trees, billboards, billboards, billboards. A sea of advertising. Signs pimping shaving gel that also serves as an aphrodisiac. Restaurants promoting their latest filth-as-food. A man in a chicken suit begging people to enter a dilapidated casino. A car passed us and I could hear the inane music celebrating vacant hedonism blaring from its radio. I wanted to ignore this pollution, but I had to witness it. I had to see the enemy in action. I had to experience cultural inebriation.

Rows upon rows of mediocrity and compromise greeted me. Nothing more than prostitution, exploitation, and misery. A valley of dead souls and scavengers. Wished I could burn it all down...

"Got it."

Ken is grinning with his hands crossed over the menu. I stop the spinning knife.

"Got what?" I blink.

The waitress returns. I remove my feet from the seat, bumping them on the table. I grimace as she pulls out her pencil.

"Made a decision?" She's pressing the pencil on the pad.

"Yes. I'll have the BLT with a side of fries, please." Ken hands her the menu. Unbelievable. The same thing every time.

I tell the waitress my order and she walks to the kitchen. Ken adjusts his cutlery and slurps his water. I run my fingers over the table. I wipe up the ring of perspiration at the base of my glass with a napkin. Ken and I look at each other. We have nothing to say. He excuses himself and slides out of the booth. He sidesteps a waiter and enters the bathroom.

Our waitress is talking with two men at the far end. They're both wearing baseball caps and flannel. Their jeans and boots are coated in dry mud. They're laughing and pointing at each other. The waitress smiles and shakes her head. The men pound their fists on the table, shaking their glasses. Mouth breathers.

A woman is sitting at the counter. A half-finished skillet is to her side. She's hunched over a newspaper, scribbling on it with a pen. She sips her coffee loudly. Her purse sits on the stool to her left and her jacket is draped over the right one. Greedy.

Ken emerges from the bathroom. He wanders to the far side of the diner and approaches the juke box. He inserts a quarter and flips through the records. This will take a while.

Who is this Zaan leader? Greg said his name is Smit. What kind of name is that? Did his parents forget the "h" on his birth certificate? They let him go through life thinking Smit was a real name? Told him it was completely normal?

No, it's probably a pseudonym. Which is worse, quite frankly. That means he chose to be called Smit. He wants people to know him as Smit. All the names he could have chosen and he went with Smit. What a moron. What a total—

Focus. Name-calling isn't going to get me anywhere. I have to be ready. Greg gave me a brief rundown before we left. What did he say, what did he say...?

Zaan popped up two years ago. Small-scale stuff. Seems to be centered around a form of hedonism. Revelation through the debauchery, those were the words Greg used. Broken people justifying their vices. They don't have convictions besides their own pleasure. That's nothing to build a following around.

Smit's been there since the beginning. Showed up one day and started building. Roped in a few fools and went from there. Greg didn't have much background information on the guy. I don't need to know where he's from; I know where he's going. I've heard of guys like these before. We've received some runaways over the years, stragglers from other compounds. They talk about groups that never stop growing. Their leaders are charismatic, faultless, impeccable. They have all the answers. Then, one day, without fail, they crack. They denounce everything, or they break down in front of everyone, or they never return from a long trip into the woods. The groups disintegrate and we get the scraps. Their leaders were charlatans who couldn't keep up their charade. The mask always slips. Smit's the same. It's no coincidence he set up shop so close to us. He's a leech sucking on our hard work. Of course he's centered on hedonism; it's easy. He thought he could jump on this bandwagon for a while. He's weak.

Two plates slide across our table. I feel the warmth of the eggs and sausages. Their smell rushes into my nostrils. The waitress fills our glasses and leaves. I lean out of the booth and snap my fingers. Ken turns to me and I motion to our food. He nods and puts on a record. A soft guitar chord chugs along as he sits down.

Ken bites into his sandwich, spilling tomato juice on his shirt. I pick up my fork and knife and stab a sausage, slicing off a piece. I tear into my eggs, gnashing on shredded chunks with my teeth. I scrape my knife on my plate as I cut.

I'll enter Smit's office. No, no, I'll already be there. I'll be sitting on his desk as he returns from a sermon or something. I'll shake his hand and tell him to sit down. I'll ask him about Zaan. Keep things light for a bit. I'll make him admit to stealing our members, to stealing from me. I'll run through his beliefs, tearing them apart. I'll reveal how empty his scam is. I'll make him cry. I'll break him down and cripple him. He'll never poach my members again. Maybe I'll have Ken drive the point home. We'll leave him in his office, curled up and weeping. God, I feel stiff.

My plate is empty. My mouth is stuffed. I just kept piling food in there as I daydreamed. I chew and push the plate away. That was too much, too fast. Ken's plate is empty, too. Only a toothpick's left. He's looking over his shoulder, watching the black-and-white television. There's no sound, but I can tell what it is: Professional wrestling. It's always playing in this diner. Two grown men circling each other in a square. A lot of punching, kicking, grabbing, and throwing. Sometimes they use a chair. Pathetic. A few dummies playing make-believe and thousands buy into it. Just another distraction. I snap my fingers in Ken's face. He snaps to attention.

"Fill it up. We're going soon." I jerk my thumb at the car.

Ken pulls out his keys and stands up. He steals one more look at the wrestling show (a man puts a woman through a table) and exits the diner. For a true devotee, Ken enjoys distractions. Odd.

I pick up a few crumbs on my plate. The waitress hands me the bill and I fish out some change from my pocket (no tip). I stretch as I stand. I'm greeted by the smell of garlic. I know who it is. I turn around.

"Hello, nutter." Sheriff Blume flashes a crooked grin and tips his hat.

"Blume." I try not to look fazed.

"Sheriff Blume." He taps the grimy badge on his jacket.

"Sheriff Blume. How are you?" My lips move into a faint smile.

"Damn knee's been acting up, but I can't complain. Still got my wits. What about you? How are the other fruitcakes?" Blume clears his throat, dislodging a wad of phlegm.

"I'm fine. We're all fine." I struggling to keep the smile up.

"Warped any new minds?" Blume adjusts his belt, tucking in his potbelly.

"We're not hurting anyone. We're a completely leg—"

"Yeah, yeah, I know. I've heard it before. Christ, you're boring. Lighten up." Blume pats my cheek. I resist the urge to punch him.

Blume peers over my table. He inspects the bill and the money I left. He shakes his head. He lifts my plate and tilts it, spilling crumbs on the floor.

"Good breakfast?" Blume pushes the plate to the window.

"Yeah. Eggs and sausages." I see Ken filling up the car. I need to get out of here.

"Always a good choice." Blume picks at his teeth with his pinky finger.

Blume looks me up and down. I match his gaze, refusing to blink. The waitress squeezes between us and grabs the money. Blume chuckles and makes room for her as she goes to the kitchen. His eyes follow her as she leaves. He licks his lips.

"Well, I really must be going. Good to see you, Sheriff, as always." I motion to the door.

Blume wraps his fingers over my shoulder, pressing down on it. I feel the sweat from his palm. Even his hand reeks of garlic.

"Always on the move. You never slow down. We were having a nice conversation. Let's continue it outside." Blume points to the back door next to the bathroom. I sigh, remove his hand, and walk. He follows me, right on my heels. I can feel his breath on my neck.

I can see into the kitchen. The cook is flipping an egg in a skillet while he watches bacon sizzle in another pan. He meets my eyes and returns to his food. The waitress grabs a plate and turns to us. She gives me a half-shrug and strolls into the diner. Blume shoves me. I grimace and open the door, stumbling out into the back lot. I always forget about the drop between the stoop and the ground. I stand up and face Blume as he hops down. This place reeks of cigarettes and grease.

"Now, what were you telling me about your looney bin?" Blume rubs his hands, flashing that shit-eating grin.

"As I said, we're fine. We're a fully—"

"Everyone's happy?" Blume circles me.

"Yes, we're all—"

"No problems with the food?" Blume pulls a lighter from his jacket pocket.

"No, we're well fed. I don't see why—"

"All ready for the winter? Going to be tough one from what I hear." Blume puts a cigarette in his mouth.

"Yes, yes, we're quite prepared. Thank you for your—"

"And you're all strictly above the board? Nothing...untoward?" Blume lights the cigarette, bathing his face in an orange glow.

My heart doubles its pace. I don't let it show in my face. Blume is watching it for the slightest twitch. He can't know about Spittal. He can't have the smallest inkling of what happened. No one knows but me, Greg, and Ken. He's just trying to provoke me. There's no way he has any evidence. No, he doesn't know about the body. Can't let him rattle me. Can't raise suspicion. Don't want him snooping around the compound. Play it cool.

"We're utterly legal, if that's what you're driving at. We haven't broken any laws and we don't intend to." I give the same answer every time we meet.

Blume takes a deep drag of his cigarette and blows a cloud into my face. I fan it away. He puffs on his stick for a while, keeping his eyes glued to me. I don't move. Blume drops the cigarette, grinding it into the dirt with the heel of his boot.

"Yeah, yeah, I know. Well within the law. My deputies tell me you don't hurt anybody. No reports, no charges. The judge tells me you're protected by the county charter. It's right there in black ink. Even the mayor tells me we have no proper recourse against you. You're one-hundred percent in the clear. But I don't care." Blume raises his hat as he leans into my face.

"I don't like you. I don't like your voice or your haircut or your face. I don't like that lollipop guild you've got in the woods. You freak me out. No one wants to drive up there anymore. They always take the long way around. They think you might split their heads open and drink their brains. Well, that's what Bill told me. Honestly, I don't think you'd do it. If you'd done anything, we'd know about it. I'd be there with an army. I don't think you're dangerous. You're a bunch of forest faggots. But I don't want you around here." Blume pokes my chest.

He's panting. Sweat beads dribble down his chin. He looks aroused.

"Sir, I respect that, but we've been here for years, and there's no reason—"

"Yes, you've been here for too long. You know what that area was before you moved in? A field, just an empty field. You could go up there and satisfy any itch. I popped my cherry up there, yessir, right on the hood of my daddy's car. Did it out in the open. That's a special place. Now, every time I drive by it, I don't think about Jessica Pleasen and our special night together. I think about what you're doing when no one's watching. You ruined my memory." Blume tugs on his pants. Definitely aroused.

"Sir, I... apologize for that, but it's our right to be—"

"Yes, absolutely, it's your right. You paid for that land, it's all yours. There's no legal reason to throw you off it. Which is why I'm working extra hard to find an excuse." Blume lights another cigarette.

I drop my plastic smile. I push my chest forward. I rub my chin with my knuckles, curling and uncurling my hand into a fist. My eyes are steel. I know the game.

"Oh, don't worry, I won't stomp over your freakshow without a warrant. I play fair. You won't see me there without a reason." Blume strokes his mustache, flicking out stray crumbs.

"That's good to know." My voice is a pure monotone. Don't show your hand.

"Of course, if someone filed a complaint, any complaint, I'd be there. Doesn't matter what it is, I'll come running. Guaranteed." Blume snaps his fingers.

"Now, when I'm there, I'll probably look around your compound. Look in some buildings, talk to some of your lemmings. Maybe something will fall out of my pocket. Maybe it'll be something...unsavoury. And if someone were to find it on your compound, well..." Blume spreads his hands and shrugs.

"You retarded pig." The words are out of my mouth before I can process them.

I seal my lips, biting on them. I don't look away from Blume; I can't. Blume's smile somehow gets wider. He lets out a harsh, smoky laugh. He puts his fingers to his ear and pushes it forward.

"That sounded good. That sounded real good. Could you repeat it? I want to make sure I heard it just right." He tugs on his earlobe.

I press my tongue against my cheek. I tilt my neck, cracking it. I clear my throat. I keep my eyes trained on Blume. I don't say a word.

"No? Damn, I really wanted to hear it again." Blume lets go of his ear.

Blume takes a long drag of his cigarette and circles me. I pivot, never turning my back to him. He stops halfway, leaving me looking at the highway. Just around the corner is the parking lot. It's only twenty steps away.

Blume doesn't say anything. He's not even paying attention to me. He's scrubbing at a yellow stain on his badge. I don't have to stay here. He's got no reason to detain me. He has no right to keep me in a filthy back lot. I'm a leader. I don't have to dignify this interrogation. I'll stride past him and walk to the car. I'll be off to Zaan in a few minutes.

I step forward. Blume doesn't look up from his badge. I smile. I start moving. Gravel scatters beneath my feet. Just need to round that corner. Blume's palm flattens across my chest, fingers digging into my shirt. Blume flicks his cigarette away and leans in close. I try not to gag.

"C'mon, say it again. I really want to hear it." Blume is right next to my ear.

"Sheriff, we've done nothing wrong. If you harass us, I'll be forced to pursue charges. Now, please, I must get going." I peel his hand off my body.

"Look, kid, I understand you're a big shot in your little pond. You want to keep everything running smooth. I respect that, in a way. But you're not welcome here. You never have been. And now it's getting crowded with that other dump, oh, what is it...?" Blume purses his lips, searching for the word.

"Zaan?" I narrow my eyes.

"That's it. You nutters must keep tabs on each other. Anyway, two cracker factories are intolerable. When it was just you, I could stomach it. I didn't like it, but I let it slide. Now that there's two, I've got to do something. Can't let this town get overrun. Have to maintain a stable balance." Blume holds his hand horizontally.

"So, it's us or them?" I raise my eyebrows.

"I knew you were a sharp one. Let's see if you can keep up: I need to get rid of one of you freak shows. I don't care which one goes, as long as it's soon. Since you're so informed about your friends across town, I'm sure you could point me in the right direction. Zaan gets shut down and you go back to fucking trees or whatever it is you do. Sound fair?" Blume extends his hand.

"I'm not a rat. Besides, I barely know more than you." I fold my arms.

"But you do know more. And do you think the other guy will be so noble? Cooperate." Blume leaves his hand in the air.

"If I don't?" I know the answer.

"Well, then, we'll probably find something on your compound and shut it down. Your members will be forced to leave or be arrested. Your property will be seized and sold. You'll be dragged to court, convicted, and sent to prison, where I'm sure you'll be very popular. You've got a nice face." Blume withdraws his hand.

I see everything shutting down. Every building closed, every item stolen, everyone sent running. All our work, all our plans, ruined. I see myself locked in jail, lost in a sea of inmates. No purpose, no plan. Just a face in the crowd. All because of this obese Napoleon.

"You wouldn't dare." My body tenses up.

"Touchy. And I would. In a heartbeat. Dragging you to jail, chained-up and bloody, ooh, that warms my heart." Blume taps his chest.

"Stay away from us, you fat fuck." I spit for emphasis.

"No, that's not what you said before." Blume wallops me in the stomach.

I double over, clutching my belly. I grunt, trying to suck in air. I claw at the gravel. Blume crouches next to me.

"Again: What did you say?" He taps my head. I can only wheeze.

"I thought so. Well, I've got to be off. Have fun down there. Think about our deal. Somebody's gotta bleed; doesn't have to be you." I watch Blume's feet as they disappear around the corner.

I stand up, still holding my stomach. I take short breaths. I touch the side of the building as I round the corner. I watch Blume's car pull out of the driveway. I walk to our spot, wincing. Ken is sitting on the car hood, staring at the sky. He jumps to his feet as he spots me. His eye light up. I shake my head and get in the car. He joins me.

I can breathe again. I sit there as Ken watches me. If Blume finds that body... Fuck. One thing at a time.

"Drive." I slap the steering wheel. Ken starts the engine.

CHAPTER ELEVEN

I want to vomit.

The sign hang above us, suspended with pristine steel. A dim glow surrounds it, a rectangle of lights. They're shining at full volume in the middle of the day. A perfect arrangement of waste. The words are thick and heavy. They're covered in pure white paint with smooth black outlines. I saw them as we turned down the driveway. Even from the highway I could read them.

"Zaan: Indulgence is Salvation."

The words are supported by a massive wire frame. Rows of poles run above and below them, forming a tight sandwich. The poles themselves are packed between two large beams embedded in the ground. There's an open space in the center of this cacophony of meta. It's the main entrance to Zaan.

It took us a while to find this place. Greg's directions led us to an abandoned minnow shop. I found a few non-rusted hooks. Might make for good sermon props. Ken tried to find Zaan, but he only brought us to a cul-de-sac. Twice. We asked the locals for directions. Most of them ignored us. The eighth one showed us the way.

I made Ken stop at the front of the gate. I needed to drink the sign in. I have to be ready for what lies ahead.

A path stretches away from the sign. Large bushes flock it on both sides. I can't see the compound from here. This gate is the only evidence that people live here. I nod at Ken and he shifts the gear out of park. We slide under the sign. The gate doors are painted yellow, almost gold. Glitter specks are coated into the paint. Seriously. The gate doors are pushed to the side, tied to the frame with chains. No one is stationed near the entrance. I guess security isn't a concern.

The car rumbles away from the gate. I peek out the window. The path is paved. Smooth, fresh black road greets me, reaching far down into the compound. I spit. Signs, gates, pavement: How do they afford this crap?

We weave through the woods, passing lampposts with unlit candles and signs that read "Zaan." I look past the trees, trying to find buildings or people, but nothing's there. So far, this is the most well-preserved nature tour I've ever seen.

Ken rides over the crest of a hill and we see it: Zaan. A small patch of buildings clumped together in a valley. The forest surrounds it on all sides. A thin river ropes around the compound like a noose. Its tail leads deeper into the woods. It's a naturally isolated location. The sun is at the right angle to give everything an ethereal glow. I hear Ken gasp, which he passes off as a yawn. It's the perfect spot for a compound. How did we miss it?

We roll down the hill, reaching a second gate. It's also wide open. The buildings are huge. They're twice the size of our largest structure. I can identify a cafeteria, a woodshed, and a bunkhouse, all bigger than they need to be. They're all built out of metal, built to last. This entire place is made of iron and steel. It's a metallic eyesore. It's unnatural and utterly—

"Decadent." I snort as we pass by a lawnmower.

Ken doesn't speak. His eyes drift from building to building, letting out a soft whistle. His eyes barely stay on the road. Not that he needs to pay attention; this place is deserted. I don't see anyone. Aside from our engine, it's completely quiet. Did a plague do my job for me?

We reach a large opening with a fountain in the centre. The buildings all face towards it, forming a rough circle. Ken parks next to a bicycle rack. We get out. I walk to the fountain, hearing my footsteps echo around the compound. Ken stays with the car, watching over his shoulder. I study the fountain. It's a wide oval with a deep base. A large spear shoots out from its middle. Water spews from its tip, tumbling back down the shaft. The bottom of the fountain constantly ripples from the stream of falling water. Beneath the surface I can see a faint shimmering glow. It's a coating of coins. More delusions.

I look around the compound. I still can't see anyone. Ken shrugs his shoulders after peeking through a window. I pinch the bridge of my nose. We're not driving back empty handed...

"Hel-loooo." I cup my hands around my mouth.

I listen to my voice fade away. I walk around the fountain. I clap my hands and whistle. Ken follows suit. I let out a few guttural shouts. Nothing. I'm about to return to the car when I hear footsteps.

Three people appear from behind a building (a butcher shop, based on the window contents). They're garbed in black robes with gold stripes, just like the men from earlier. Hell, they might be the same men. Their faces are all round, chubby, and flushed. Each one of them is sporting an insufferably smug smile. They're instantly punchable, but I resist the urge as they approach me.

"Can we help you, sir?" The middle one bows his head.

"Tell your boss Solomon Netty would like to speak with him." I puff my chest out.

"Yes, yes, he's been meaning to speak with you. Please, follow us." The middle one walks past me and heads down a slim roadway.

The other two brush past me. I gesture to Ken and we follow the robes. They're giggling. I see their jowls shake as they laugh. I can't tell which one is talking.

"But wait, but wait, after that, Jerry smeared it over his face, just rubbed it everywhere."

"Ahh, fuck, all of it?"

"Every last bit."

"Nasty fuck. Oh, what a—"

"And then, and then, oh, man, he went up to Smit—"

"Fuck me, no way."

"He went up to Smit—"

"Right up in his face."

"He went up to Smit and offered a piece."

"You gotta be joking."

"No lie, no lie."

"And, get this, and then, you know what Smit did?"

"It's crazy, crazy, man…"

"He just scooped out a chunk and ate it right there."

The robes break into a louder chorus of laughter. They keep chuckling as they lead us down the street. The left one looks at us and releases a high-pitch snicker. Ken frowns at him. The robe smirk, nodding at us. Ken gives a nervous laugh in response, flashing an uncertain smile. The robe looks away and I flick Ken's earlobe.

We get a better look at the buildings as we walk down the street. This area is dominated by well-ordered shops. I see an assortment of cameras, puzzles, clothing, toys, and other knick knacks. It looks like a tourist trap, not a religious compound. I don't see a single tool. It's pure consumerism.

The robes lead us to a large temple. It towers over every building, casting them in a heavy shade. It's made of smooth cobblestone. It's square-shaped with a small dome on its top. Its front side has four pillars that support its roof. The robes jog up the stairs and enter the building. Ken lets out another whistle as he admires the temple. I pinch his cheek and pull him close.

"United front. That's what we have to be. No more whistling, or ooh-ing, or ahh-ing, or sucking their goddamn dicks. You are stoic. Got it?" Ken nods and I let go of his cheek. Ken gives me a hangdog look. I turn away and hurry up the stairs. I push open the door and slide into the temple.

Rows upon rows of round people. I'm standing at the edge of a center aisle. Clumps of people are sitting on both sides of it. They're all wearing the black-gold robe ensemble, but each one has added a different colour. Red circles, green stripes, and pink diamonds all swirl together in a jarring miasma. There's coordination or order. It's a random collection of styles, all clashing against one another.

The temple hall is ornate. Pillars are planted by the walls, all of them draped in purple sashes. Speakers dangle on the ceiling, connected with a maze of wires. A sparkling chandelier hangs above the aisle. The whole room smells like a model home. I'm fighting to keep the vomit down. How, in the name of all that's holy, do they afford this?

I step behind a pillar and scan the room. Our guides have disappeared. Everyone is facing forward, ignoring us. I hear a voice coming from the army of speakers, reverberating in the temple. I follow the crowd's eye line and reach a stage. It's made of varnished wood with a blue curtain backdrop. On top of it, I see him.

He's wearing a purple and gold robe over his shoulders like a cape. It flows and weaves as he moves, never quite touching the ground. His perfectly shined black dress shoes gleam in the glare of the overhanging spotlights. He's wearing a dark bodysuit beneath the robe. His hands are covered in fingerless red driving gloves. He's holding a yellow baton, twirling and tapping it as he speaks. To top it all off, a gnarled crown sits on his head. Pure depravity.

So this is Smit: A mad king crossed with the sensibilities of a deranged homosexual. This is my competition, this child playing dress-up. He looks like a lost toy. I cross my arms and lean on the pillar. Might as well listen to his tripe while I'm here. Need a good laugh.

"...work was the same. Day in, day out. Everywhere I went, there it was. This, uh, this tension in my chest. You know what I'm saying?" Smit pats his ribs. The crowd nods.

"Right, right, of course you do. Well, I had to- You know, I'm sorry, I'm sorry. I must have told this story a dozen times. I know we have some new friends with us. Where are you? Could you stand up?" Smit spreads his baton over the crowd.

Five people stand up. They're leaner than the others. I recognize one. He used to be a planter. Vanished a week ago. I thought he'd turn up in the woods. He'll wish he did when I turn this place to cinders.

"Welcome, welcome. I've met you all, but I want to welcome you again. Now, this story I was telling, Christ, your new friends must have it memorized by now. I've yakked their ears off with it. Now, I don't want to bore most of my audience. I never want to do that. Nothing worse than a bore. Rob me, rape me, kill me, but do not ever bore me." The crowd echoes Smit's phrase.

"Exactly. So, maybe I shouldn't tell the story. We should just move on. It's not that important. Hell, it's not even that good. Do y'all want to hear the story again or should I stop wasting your time?" Smit looks...bashful. The crowd yells at him to finish the story. People in the front row pound on the stage. Smit reveals a quick grin. He's sees the strings and knows where to pull them. Not bad. For a fraud.

"Alright, alright, no need to shout. I'll get on with it. Now, where was I? Oh, yes, the tightness." Smit starts to pace.

Smit taps the microphone on his torso, rubbing it up and down. A dull scratching sound fills the temple. He pulls the cord away from his feet and sashays it.

"The tightness. It was right here." Smit pokes his chest with the microphone. The audience flinches from the harsh "pop" sound.

"Every day. It was latched onto me like a vise. Dead bolted to my ribcage. I could barely breathe. I had to fight just to move. It smothered me. I thought my heart was going to explode. I was drowning and I couldn't find a way up." Smit holds the baton over his breasts, his hand curled into a fist.

"I didn't try to break it; I ignored it. I thought it would fix itself. I went to work early and stayed late. I took projects home. I ate high-fiber breakfasts and low-fat dinners. Every moment was a chance to work. And I took them all. I drove myself to exhaustion. But the tightness was still here." Smit adjusts his crown.

"I would get home, dead on my feet. I could barely lift the key into the doorknob. It'd be pitch black out, not a single person awake in my apartment building. I'd shovel leftover chicken into my mouth, force myself to read the newspaper, clean up, and go to bed. I'd lie on my lumpy mattress and stare at the ceiling. I wanted to sleep. It was the only thing I wanted in the world. I could give up sex, food, and the use of my legs for a good night's rest. But I couldn't close my eyes. The tightness was still here. I couldn't weaken it or tire it out. The screws wouldn't loosen." Smith contorts his fingers and turns them clockwise.

"I decided to get proactive. This whole thing had to be a health problem. I gave up meat. Full-on vegetarian. I munched on kale during lunch breaks and always had a tofu stir fry waiting for me at home. I joined a football club, a soccer club, a basketball club, and an ultimate Frisbee club. I jogged, swam, hiked, biked, lifted, and climbed. I walked to work every day and sat on an exercise ball at my desk. I purged every possible poison from my body. I was completely clean. But the tightness...was still...here." Smit jabs his thumb into his chest. He hasn't looked at the crowd in a while. Amateur.

"I knew this was serious. I couldn't ignore it anymore. I went to doctors and specialists. I needed to find out what was wrong with me. They gave me diagnoses, and prescriptions, and diets. They said it was normal and typical and temporary. They told me it would pass. So I took their pills and followed their instructions. I trusted them. For months I waited, scoffing down mounds of medication. But, you know what? The tightness was still here." The crowd repeats the phrase as Smit says it.

"I was lost. Utterly lost. I had no idea what to do or who to talk to or where to go. I skipped work. I avoided the gym. I stayed away from friends. I slept all day and wandered the city at night. I retreated into myself." Smit's shoulders are hunched and he's facing the floor.

"I walked the streets, looking for distractions. I watched late movies and strip teases and diner room conversations.

Anything to keep my mind of this fucking tightness. One night, I found myself inside a fast-food restaurant at three in the morning. In front of me sat a double-cheeseburger, a side of fries, and cigarette. I have no idea how they got there or how I found them." Smit is still curled up.

"I stared at the burger. This chunk of meat was everything I had avoided for the last year. Fat, slimy, and delicious. It was a poison I'd ejected from my life. Wasn't it the cause of my problems? It just sat there, taunting me. It was an affront to what I believed was right and healthy. I was better without it. But I'd tried everything else. And I still had the tightness. I was a walking corpse. This burger was all that was left. It couldn't hurt. I picked it up, peeled off the pickles and took a bite." Smit uncurls and faces the audience. He's wearing a massive grin.

"I devoured that burger in thirty seconds. It was fucking perfection. The fries were gone in a minute. I rushed the counter and ordered three more meals. I ate until I was bloated, until I was stuffed, until I was satisfied. I picked up the cigarette, went outside, bummed a match from a woman, and lit it. I inhaled my first smoke in ten years. I savoured every puff, surrounding myself in a haze of nicotine. In that heady moment on the sidewalk in the dead of night, holding a cigarette and patting my enlarged belly, I noticed something: The tightness was gone." Smit drops his baton.

"My chest was loose. Free. Nothing was pushing down on it. I took a deep breath and let it out, easy as you like. I couldn't believe it. I waited for it to return. I stood on that street for hours, expecting its resurgence at any moment. As the sun rose over the office buildings, I knew it was gone. And I knew what had loosened it." Smit picks up the baton and twirls it.

"I hadn't been unlocking the vise on my chest; I'd been fastening the screws. All my cures were killers. My diets, my regimens, my work, my schedules, every attempt to order and organize my life, they were bleeding me dry. All that suppression smothered me. I'd built the vise and I'd sealed it tighter and tighter every day I denied myself. I was dying." Smit is pacing the stage again.

"I denied myself again and again, day after day, trying to bury every desire under a wave of structure. All that denial, and for what? Why did I do it? Why do any of us do it? Why do we torture and deny ourselves? To feel good? Absolutely not. No one enjoys dieting or waking up early or working overtime. We refuse to indulge ourselves because we're made to feel that it's 'bad.' You can lie to yourself. and say hard work and persistence are their own reward. Feel free to press your nose deep into that grindstone. I'll be enjoying another burger. And I won't be alone." Smit is met with a surge of wild applause. I'm appalled.

"Some say there's more to regimens than false pleasure. Every sacrifice is rewarded at the end. There is something greater waiting for those who temper themselves. There's more than all of this. Well, you know what I think about that." Smit makes a jerking-off motion with the baton. The audience laughs.

"There's nothing waiting for us. There's no great beyond or happy afterlife where you meet all your friends and frolic in the field like pixies. This is it. This is all we get. We're not going above; we're going below. When it's all said and done, you'll be roommates with worms. Everything we'll ever have is right here." Smit slams his baton on the stage.

"I know that can be depressing. Hell, it scared the hell out of me. But I saw this revelation for what it really is: Freedom. We don't have to be shackled to repression, or fear, or morality. We have the entire horizon in front of us. Anything can be ours; we only need to reach out and grab it. Impulse is our guide. I've let it rule me and it's led me here, led me to all of you. I count you as my dearest friends, because you aren't afraid to ask for more. That's the ultimate pursuit: More, more, more. We can have it all, friends. If you want it, take it. Take it all." Smit raises his arms in a "V" shape, closing his eyes.

The crowd leaps to their feet, stomping and hollering. It's deafening. I haven't heard anything like this at... No, no, my sermons have been louder before. It's the acoustics in this place.

Makes everything seem bigger. They're just riled up sheep. They'd cheer for anything. If I went up there, I'd bring this building to its knees. I'd show them the truth. Not that they'd want to hear it. The applause is still going. Of course it is. Smit told them what they wanted to hear. No confrontation, no reality, no grit. That speech was tailored for them.

What a garbage speech. Smit's a deranged orgy conductor, nothing more. He's leading a bonfire rave on a cliff, leading the dancers closer and closer to the edge. There's nothing behind what he said. It was hollow pleasure praise masquerading as truth. It was a cavalcade of easy answers. Why think or try, when you can just indulge yourself? Smit ran away from society only to create a miniature one on steroids. It's got all the trappings and obsessions squeezed into a one-mile radius. Impressive, if it wasn't so pathetic.

Christ, they're still clapping. Smit hasn't moved. What's wrong with these people? Can't they spot a con man? This is a celebration of cowardice. I spit on the floor.

The applause dies down. People return to their seats as Smit opens his eyes. He chucks the baton to stage left.

"Alright, alright, that's enough about me. Thank you for indulging me. It's always good to know I'm not alone. If I'm going crazy, I'm glad I'm doing it with you." Smit runs his fingers through his sweaty hair as he lets out a high-pitched giggle.

"But, seriously, seriously, I have something special for you. I want you to meet the new member of our family. He's like all of you: Sick, tired, and ready for change. He left a desert for our oasis. Now, let's not disappoint him. Give him your warmest reception. Carl, get out here." Smit points to the stage curtain.

A man steps out from behind the fabric. The crowds cheers and stomps their feet, whistling and shouting. A spotlight bathes him in sharp light. I pull myself off the pillar. It's the man who left the compound.

I look at Ken. He's too busy admiring a pillar to pay attention. I ball my fist. I want to jump onstage and drag Carl back to the compound by his ear. And slap him every step of the way. But I wouldn't make it past the first row. Carl waves at the crowd. He's wearing the standard black and gold robe combo. He's face is a lot cleaner and he got a haircut. A complete sellout in a half a day. Christ.

"Welcome, Carl, welcome. I'm so glad you could be here with us. It really is a pleasure to meet you." Smit wraps his arm over Carl's shoulders.

"Now, you'll get to know me and everyone else very soon. But before that, we have a little rite of passage here." Smit winks at the crowd.

"Carl, you're here because you want to snap off your shackles. You want to follow your impulse. So, I have to ask: What's your favourite food?" Smit shoves the mic into Carl's face.

"Um, well, uh...l-lasagna. It'd have to be lasagna." Carl bites his lip.

"Damn fine choice. Damn fine. We've got a treat for you, Carl." Smit snaps his fingers. Two cultists wheel a table onstage. It's cloaked in a white tablecloth. A large bump protrudes from the middle. Smit yanks off the cloth to reveal a round dinner plate cover. Smit gestures to Carl, who removes the cover. It's a mountain of lasagna.

"Freshly made just for you, Carl. Dig in." Smit slaps Carl's back.

"H-here?" Carl fidgets.

"Of course. You wanted lasagna, so we brought it to you. Go for it." Smit pushes Carl closer to the plate.

Carl scratches his arm and glances at the crowd. I move closer to the aisle, staring right at him. He doesn't notice me. He looks at Smit, who nods. Carl takes two fingers, pierces the lasagna, and pulls out a small piece. He eats it and smiles. The crowd laughs.

"No, no, no, c'mon, now, that's no way to eat. Dig in." Smit raps his knuckles on the table.

Carl looks uncomfortable. Good. He presses four fingers into the meat dish and tears out a medium chunk. He bites into it, rubbing sauce over his cheeks. He wipes it off. The crowd laughs again.

Carl looks at Smit, who has his arms crossed. He's tapping his foot. He points his head at the lasagna. Carl takes out another medium scoop. And another. And another. And another. Each time, he looks to Smit for approval. Each time, Smit grows more impatient. As Carl polishes off his sixth bite, Smit pulls him close.

"Carl, you came here for a reason, yes? You wanted to follow your impulse? You wanted to be free? Tell me I'm right." Smit wraps his fingers around Carl's neck.

"Y-yes, yes, absolutely, yes, I do, I do." Carl can't stop nodding.

"Then act like it." Smit grabs a huge chunk of lasagna and stuffs it in Carl's mouth.

Carl staggers back. His cheeks are swollen like a chipmunk. Everyone is silent as he chews. His bulging mouth recedes. He swallows. His face is coated in sauce. He doesn't try to clean it. He stares at the plate.

"How did that feel?" Smit holds the mic below Carl's chin.

"...Amazing." Carl is panting. Pig.

The crowd applauds yet again. They'll cheer if someone wipes their ass. Carl tears into his food, piling scraps into his mouth. He's lost. Smit pats his back and grins.

"Indulgence is salvation." Smit drops the mic as the crowd repeats his mantra.

People swarm the stage, shaking Smit's hand and hugging Carl. I feel a rush of bile in my throat. This is regulated, normalized madness. They're mindless. I look to the stage. Smit meets my gaze. The little bastard smirks. He disappears behind the crowd.

Two robes are standing next to me. They point to the door. They say I'll have a private meeting with Smit. I can't really hear them; there's a pounding in my ears. I want to incinerate this place. I want to dance on its ashes.

I grab Ken and we push past the door. I leave them to their orgy of opulence.

CHAPTER TWELVE

His office is an insult wrapped in an obscenity.

The robes led us here. We walked down a series of alleyways and followed a path away from the buildings. We came to a clearing that brushed against the side of a hill. A small cottage was perched on the bank of the river. The robes let us inside and left, saying Smit would join us in a moment.

We're sitting in plush leather chairs. They each have cup holders and throw pillows. My pillow is squished beneath my feet. Ken has propped his pillow on his back. His hands are splayed over the armrests. He sinks into the seat and sighs. I cough. He looks at me as I roll my shoulders, straighten my back, and push my chest out. He pulls himself up. His hands still dangle to the side. I wiggle away from the back rest, resting on the edge of the chair. I clasp my hands on my lap, squeezing my knuckles together. I grind the pillow under my feet. I'm ready.

We're surrounded by monuments to Smit's ego. A red chair sits before us. The light shines off its polished wood. Its red cushions bulge out from the frame, sealed in with gold buttons. Its back obscures the wall behind it. A pattern of carved roses and swords runs around the outline, climaxing at the top with a blade plunging into the bud of a flower, a mess of petals surrounding them. Its armrests curve down at the end to form small claws. The left one has a plastic cup holder attached to it.

A desk rests in front of the chair. Its body is pure glass. Not a smudge on it. I hold my hand above and see a near-perfect reflection. Its steel legs stand on the shag carpet. I want to lob a hammer into its heart. The desk itself is fairly empty. A stack of papers is on one side, sloppily arranged. A pen is on top of them, its tip exposed. A crossword puzzle is in the middle, half completed. On the right a photo of Smit faces us. He's flashing that smug grin, two thumbs-up pressed to his cheeks. This isn't a work area; it's another distraction.

His walls are covered in trivialities. Posters, newspaper clippings, photos, all centered on him and Zaan. There are promotional materials ("Join Zaan and Grow!"), news stories, and random pictures of the compound. Smit is dead center in all of them, a vortex of egoism. Nauseating.

A trophy case stands to our left. Its glass is spotless (naturally). It contains three shelves. The bottom one holds medals. Gold, silver, bronze, red, yellow, every colour and shade. They're piled onto each other, wrapped in striped ribbons. They're thrown together in a mesh of melted metal. The middle shelf holds two things. On the far right rests a grey statue of a man running forward, his feet melded to the base. Another statue of a man sits on the far left. His lower body is still, but his top half is twisted. His right hand is curled next to his face, his elbow tucked into his stomach. His left hand stretches out, shaped into a fist, bumping against the glass. Two figures caught in endless motion. The top shelf is full of photos, all of Smit. It's a sea of Smit. My personal Hell. Smit climbing a mountain, leaning over a walking stick. Smit perched over a diving board, endless water stretched before him. Smit riding a dirt bike, clearing a road bump. Smit holding a guitar, his foot resting on an amplifier. Smit shoving hot dogs into his mouth, surrounded by competitors. In every shot, without fail, Smit is looking at the camera. He's always wearing that smile, even as he shovels fatty food down his gullet. Arrogance in stereo. I look away.

He's ambitious. He found his calling and seized it. What a waste. All that energy, all that verve, blown away on mindless hedonism. He could have done anything, anything at all. He could have made a difference. Instead, he jumps, climbs, and pigs out in front of a camera. He's a self-aware trained monkey; ready to do a trick if you're paying attention.

I shift in my chair. I massage the back of my neck and rotate my shoulders. I look back to the door. Any second now, Smit will walk through it. He'll come in, reeking of sweat and

desperation, and see us...sitting here, facing away from him.
He'll spot us before we see him. He'll be ready.

I stand up and turn around. I stare at the door, looking at
its dead center. I step back and I brush against the desk,
wrapping my fingers over its edges. I lean into it, letting the
weight off my feet. The glass tilts towards me, bumping on my
legs. I step off the desk and the glass slams down on the frame.
The papers jostle and the pen rolls off the table. Ken looks at me
and I scowl. He shrugs and looks at the trophy case.

Okay, so, the glass isn't attached to the table. No
problem. I face the door again and, keeping my feet planted, lay
my palms on the glass, taking care not to lean into it.

Smit will enter the room. He'll be adjusting his robe or
checking his watch. He'll look up and see me staring right at
him, standing over his desk in the middle of his office. I'll be
looking straight into his eyes. There'll be a pause, the briefest
pause, as he tries to think of something. That's when I'll pounce.
I'll tell him to sit and—

"Do you think it's real?"

I blink and look away from the door. Ken is staring up at
me, his eyebrows raised. I tilt my head.

"That. Do you think it's real?" Ken jerks his arm up,
pointing.

I follow his finger, reaching the top shelf. I look back at
him and shrug. He sighs and stands up. He presses his finger on
the glass.

"This one." He taps the frame.

I step away from the desk and, giving a quick look to the
door, lean close to his hand. He's pointing at a photo of Smit
with a black man. They're facing each other, bodies hunched and
knees bent. They're wearing boxing gloves. The black man's
right fist brushes on Smit's chin. They're smiling.

"What about it?" I give the door another glance.

"This guy, this guy right here." Ken smudges the glass
as he points at the black man.

"Ken, get to the point." I take my eyes off the door.

"He's the state heavyweight champ. Saw him fight a few times. Mean left hook." Ken mimes a punch.

"Okay…" My gaze is split between Ken and the door.

"Do you think this photo is real?" Ken raps his knuckles on the glass.

"What?" I can hear something beyond the door…

"Do you think Smit met the champ? That'd be something. I mean, it looks real…" Ken presses his face on the case.

I release a short sigh. I grab Ken's elbow, pulling him away from the case. We both look at the photo. It seems real. Why would Smit fake it? How would he—?

The door opens.

Laughter fills the room. I spin around, twisting my foot and stumbling over Ken's chair. I grab onto the armrest and pull myself up, jerking forward. Smit is standing in front of me.

He's wearing his purple robe, although it's barely attached, held up by his bent elbows. His crown is askew, resting on the nook between his temple and ear. He beams as he looks down at me.

We don't say anything. He matches my gaze and doesn't look away. Christ, even his eyes are laughing. They're bright and bouncy, almost like they want to burst out of their sockets. They seem endlessly delighted by a joke they won't tell anyone. But there's something behind them, something steady. It studies me. There's cunning there.

I rise to Smit's level, never breaking eye contact. I match his smile and extend my hand. He lets out another giggle and nods at his hands. They're covered in lasagna.

"Give me a second, would you? Have a seat, have a seat." Smit licks his finger as he passes me.

I stand there, watching him saunter around his desk. I raise my hand to speak, but...I don't have anything to say. I don't *know* what to say. A minute ago, I was sitting on the desk. I had a plan. Then the door opened and...I'm here.

Ken sits down, puffing up his throw pillow. I scowl at him, but I follow suit. I press down hard on my floor pillow as I sit. Smit is standing next to a poster of him pointing to the sky in front of a purple background ("Zaan: You Worshipping You"). He's hunched over a water basin. He whistles as he scrubs sauce and meat off his fingertips. He turns off the taps, flicks his hands, wipes them on his pants, and faces us.

"Now, how about a proper introduction?" Smit walks behind his desk and extends his hand.

"Solomon Netty. Charmed." I lean off the chair and clasp his hand. I give it a tight squeeze. Strong grip.

"Smit Norstrom. Shaking your hand." Smit flashes his teeth.

"Sorry, sorry, terrible joke. Couldn't resist. Got it from my dad. And you are?" Smit turns to Ken, who's still staring at the photo.

"Uh, Ken."

"Admiring my photos?" Smit smiles.

"Yeah, um, actually, I have to ask: Is this photo real?" Ken points at the boxing picture.

"Oh, yes, completely genuine. Met him on a road trip. Saw the card and I had to buy a ticket. Man, he did not disappoint." Smit walks to the trophy case. He's not even looking at me.

"Really?" Ken sounds like a salivating dog.

"Ooh, what a left hook. Never seen anything like it. Knew I had to meet him. My buddy worked with the crew. We went backstage and grabbed this pic. He was a class act all the way. Even let me spar with him." Smit leans on the case.

Ken whistles. They both stare at the photo, wrapped up in their circular egoism. I cough.

"Well, enough reminiscing: What can I do for you?" Smit holds his hands open.

I place my right leg over my left knee and lean into the chair. I clasp my hands together on my lap, twiddling my thumbs. I let a smile tug on my face. No need to rush; let's take it slow.

"We were in the neighbourhood and we thought we'd check out the competition. I always want to see how the other half live. I can't believe you've been here for...oh, how long is it?" I snap my fingers, searching for the number.

"One year, two months, and five days." Smit's smile becomes more plastic.

"Very nice. As I was saying, I can't believe you've been here for so long and we've never met."

"It's been too long, hasn't it? I've been meaning to drop by, but I've been too dang busy. This place can run you ragged" Smit sits down.

"Oh, you don't have to tell me. I remember those early days. Up at dawn, asleep after midnight. Trying to find tools, food, and God knows what else. Every time you solve one problem, three more pop up. It's exhausting." I wipe the mock sweat from my brow.

"Exhausting, yes, that's exactly it. You've hit the nail right on the head." Smit slaps his desk.

"It got so bad, one time, and this is true, I fell asleep during a sermon." I let out a fake laugh.

"No!" Smit clutches his chest. Overactor.

"Right there on the podium. I was talking about our crops and I collapsed over my notes. Nobody said anything until I started snoring. This one had to carry me to bed." I pat Ken's arm.

"Well, I hope that doesn't happen to me. I don't think we've got anyone strong enough to carry me. Not like you, eh?" Smit winks at Ken.

"You've got to rest. That's the one thing I've learned. You're no good to anyone if you pass out. Want to hear a trick I learned?" I lean over the desk.

"More than anything." Smit puts his chin in his hand.

"Standing naps." I snap my fingers.

"Like a horse?" Smit narrows his eyes.

"Exactly. I found it in a book once. Tried it during a sermon. Whenever I paused, I closed my eyes. Added a little drama. I did it eight times. When it was over, I was better rested than when I started. True story." I put my hand over my heart.

"Huh. I'll have to try it." Smit leans back in his chair.

"Oh, you must. It's a lifesaver. You'll age ten years in one if you let this place walk over you. It's a killer. You can't run yourself ragged, even when your group is so small." I let that last sentence linger.

Smit's smirk twitches. He cracks his neck and stares at me. I don't blink, still wearing my smile. He puts his feet up on his desk and crosses his arms.

"Well, I wouldn't say we're small. We've had quite the expansion in the last year. Went from this-" Smit holds his hands next to each other. "-to this." Smit's hands stretch to the ends of the desk.

He winks at me. My jaw clicks as I rotate it. I keep smiling.

"Oh, it doesn't seem too overwhelming. I counted a few dozen at your sermon. A very manageable size." I hold my thumb and forefinger next to each other.

"Hmm." Smit's hands fall away.

I've had enough foreplay. Time for the—

"What was it like?" Ken scoots to the desk.

"What was what like?" Smit looks bemused.

"Sparring with the champ. How was it? Did he try his left hook? Did he—? Sorry, sorry, I didn't mean to interrupt. I've just been thinking about it. I'll let you get back to it." Ken doesn't look at me, but he must sense my mile-long glare.

"No, no, it's perfectly fine. We always encourage curiosity here. The champ was...how do I describe him? He was perfection. Every move was flawless, it was..." I tune Smit out.

Ken and Smit prattle on about punches and stances and other nonsense. I drum my fingers on my lap, darting my eyes around the office, which gets more obscene every minute. I keep finding new posters, new photos, new monuments of ego. It's like I'm drowning in Smit's vapidity. This place is squeezing me like a vise. Everywhere I look, I see Smit's face. In competitions, in advertisements, in news stories, in the flesh. He leans in close to Ken, miming a jab. Ken can't stop smiling. He even laughs. Next he'll be clapping and calling for an encore. I have to get out of this place. I have to—

"Can we get back to business?" I'm surprised at how loud I am.

Ken and Smit stop mid-conversation. Ken retreats deep into his chair. Smit snorts and pats his knee. He returns behind his desk and smirks. Again with the fucking smirk. I stick my tongue between my teeth to prevent them from grinding together.

"I didn't know we were conducting business. I thought this was a friendly visit." Smit acts hurt. Audience of two and he's a first-rate ham.

Damn it. Why'd I snap? I could have eased into this, brought it up naturally. I had all the cards; now I've set them on fire.

"You know why we're here, Smit." My smile is gone; his won't leave.

"Can't say I do. Borrow some sugar, perhaps? I'm your neighbour, after all." Smit is unrepressed smugness.

"Our members, Smit. We're here about our members." I plant my hand on the desk.

"Hmm, well, I can't help you there. Haven't met any of your members. We've only got our members here. That's how it works. They're here, so they're ours. When they're with you, they're yours. That's how membership works, right? I think I covered the basics." Smit speaks like an elementary school teacher.

"You've stolen our members." I feel the bile rising.

"Really? That's horrible? Of course, we have so many new members I can't keep track of them all. But that's awful, truly. I would never authorize something like that. Do you know who stole them? Do you have their names?" Smit grabs a pen.

"What?"

"The men who stole your members. Did you see who did it? How many did they take? Did they do it at night or while you were away? Did anybody get hurt? Oh, please, tell me nobody got hurt. Please, give me details. I want to help." Smit's pen hovers above a pad of paper.

"They didn't, they didn't...physically steal our members, they, they..." I close my eyes, searching for the words.

"They what? They brainwashed them? They hypnotized them? What? What?" Smit clicks the pen, in and out, in and out, in and out...

"They recruited them. Your men recruited our members." I shove the desk.

Smit is smiling. It's different from before; it's real. He's been told the punchline to the perfect joke. His notepad is covered in doodles. He crumples it and tosses it to the floor. He's fucking with us.

I kick my chair back, letting it crash to the floor. Ken rubs his knuckles and flexes his arms. I tower over Smit and put my fists on the desk. He's still smiling. I don't grab his throat and squeeze. I don't smash his face through the glass. I don't throw him into his trophy case. I keep my voice steady.

"You fucking thief." I'm dripping with venom.

Smit clears his throat. His eyes are narrowed and fiery. The smile drops.

"No, no, I'm not. Don't call me that. I'm a businessman and I saw a business opportunity. So I took it." Smit grabs the air.

"You stole our members, you little prick." The sneak past my clenched teeth.

"I would remind you that you're a guest. That is a privilege I can easily revoke. Be gracious." Smit shoves his finger in my face. I grunt.

"And, no, we did not 'steal' your members. We don't steal people. Blume would have us in a four-by-four cell if we did that. We've just done a little 'aggressive targeting' and your former members are the beneficiaries." Smit treats me like an idiot.

"You stole them." I can't think of anything else to say.

"Who did we take? Name one person we stuffed in a bag, dragged across the city, and locked in a basement here. Name one. Give me one name and I'll shut down immediately. I won't tolerate that. Give me one." Smit holds up his finger.

"You encouraged them to—"

"Give me one."

"You told them—"

"One."

The bile is boiling in my throat. Smit is twirling his finger. I pound my brain against my skull, looking for the words. They don't come. I look away.

"Well, there you have it." Smit curls his finger down.

"You're still a thief." I feel the glass straining under my weight.

"Give me one—"

"Shut up. These people don't wander here on their own. It's not a coincidence and you're not clueless. You come to my compound and you preach your poison. You colonize their minds and lead them astray. You're trash." I wipe the spit from my mouth.

"One more and you go out that door head first." Smit's face darkens. "You know, when I found this town, you were all anyone talked about. 'So dangerous, so scary, so blah blah blah.' These hicks couldn't stop thinking about you. They thought you were a witch or the devil or something. My curiosity was piqued. So, I snuck into your compound." Smit's eyebrows shoot up. I blink. Smit's face is a caricature of bland innocence. I turn to Ken, who offers a confused shrug. I shake my head. "All those background checks and files and tallies, but it's still so easy to be a face in the crowd." Smit savours every word.

"I walked through the centre square, I wandered into the barracks, I talked with members, I even caught one of your sermons. Something about continual struggle. Decent speech. A little plain for my tastes, but fine. It was disappointing, though, after all the buildup, to see that you were just a man in a cheap robe. "I didn't stay long. Didn't want to overextend my welcome. As I drove down the road, after seeing it all, after seeing you, the devil himself, I only had one thought: 'This would be so much better if it were mine.'

"So, that's what I did. I told my men to target your group. We wrote up brochures, scripted speeches, everything we could do. We set the bait and now they're taking a bite. Your people know there's more out there and they'll come to me. They're better off here."

I drill Smit's head through the desk. Glass shatters everywhere, throwing shards at my arms and chest. Ken shields his face and bolts to his feet. Smit lies on the floor in the middle of the table, screaming and clutching his face. I turn him over. Glass fragments jut out his cheeks and forehead. Blood coats his face. The plasma pools in his gaping mouth, darkening his teeth. A large glass piece is embedded in his eye. I tear it out. His screams get louder.

"Laugh. C'mon, laugh. Smile, tell a joke, shrug it off. Laugh, you fucker."

Smit thrashes on the floor, grasping for the desk, trying to stand. Ken winces and looks away. I kneel on Smit's chest. He punches my leg. I grab his wrists and smash them to the ground. They fall to his side, limp and worthless. He's mine.

"They're better with you? With you? You can't lead them. You can't protect them. You can't protect yourself. You're an ant. You're the gunk between my toes. You're nothing."

My fist runs across Smit's face. A stream of saliva and blood spews from his lips. Tears stream down his cheeks. He's sobbing, gasping for air. There's no trace of a smile. He's begging me, apologizing. I can't hear him. I wrap my fingers around his neck.

"You stepped into the wrong world. You interfered with me. You could have stayed away. You could have medicated yourself into oblivion. But you fucked with me. You understand?

You fucked with me. This is bigger than you. I'm bigger than you. You do not fuck with me. You. Do not. Fuck. With me."

I squeeze. Smit tries to pry my hands away, but they're too slippery, slick with gore. His breathing slows. The light fades from his eyes. I don't let go. I can see him leave. I can—

No.

I'm still standing over the desk. Smit's undamaged face smirks at me. Ken is seated in his chair. Nothing has changed. I sigh.

Smit's smile has consumed his face. He's more toad than man. He has no scruples. He's a corporate stooge acting as a spiritual leader. He thinks in marketing solutions and strategies. He picks a destination and plots a route. He doesn't care how he gets there, as long as he gets there first. I thought I was dealing with a hedonist, a rank amateur. But Smit's more than that; he's a Suit. For a Suit, the world is a briefcase waiting for the right key. Maybe he buys into all this, but above all, he's a Suit. He's dangerous.

"Face it: I have a better product." Smit's voice invades my thoughts.

"I'm not selling a product. I'm showing people the way out of this hell. I'm trying to help them. This isn't a popularity contest." My fists turn into open palms.

"It is, and I'm winning." Smit inspects his fingernails.

"You're playing with people's lives. You're confusing them, taking them down the wrong path. You have to—"

"Oh, save the drama for the pulpit." Smit dismissively waves.

I don't know how to engage a Suit, not yet. I can't debate him here. I'm suffocating in this office. It's stifling my thoughts. Yes, that's it.

"Stay away from my compound. They're my members, not yours. If I see your men there again..." I let him fill in the rest.

"If someone comes here, I won't turn them away. Now, I think it's time you hit the trail." Smit snaps his fingers at the door.

I nod at Ken, casts one last look at the trophy case. I grab the door handle.

"Solomon, how big is your compound?" Smit's voice is a cheese grater to my ears.

"Why?" I don't look at him.

"Just curious. Never know when I'm going to need some extra space."

Smit's laugh follows me as I walk through the compound. We don't see anyone. Ken doesn't say a word as we pile into the car.

I stare at the buildings. So, this is the enemy. Decadent, depraved, and utterly assured. Ready to cross any line for success. A challenge, no doubt. I embarrassed myself here. I underestimated him. I filled my gun with blanks. But I've seen his weapons. I know his strategy, his mind. This is going to be a fight, but, in the end, I'll walk away. He won't get up.

"So, do you think he fought the champ?" Ken taps the steering wheel.

"Oh, just fucking drive."

CHAPTER THIRTEEN

Jason Neary clears his throat.

He sticks his finger between his collar and his neck, letting out some heat. He scratches the back of his ear. Another itch pops up on the top of his head, but he ignores it. He adjusts his sleeves and presses his black-and-white tie against his chest. He grabs a knife and traces its dull edge on the tablecloth.

Music surrounds him. It's soft and light, full of strings, horns, and baritone voices. Men and women in black uniforms rush past him, weaving through halls and past each other. People sit around him, illuminated by candles, lost in their worlds. Jason is an island in an ocean.

He pulls a piece of bread from a basket and slathers it in butter. He scarfs it down, crumbs falling on his lap. He brushes them away and checks his watch. Twenty minutes late. He'll give it another ten. No more. He takes a drink of water. Ice rushes to his teeth, shocking them. He grimaces and puts the glass down. He drums his fingers. The music stops, leaving the room with only idle chatter. It picks up again, right from the beginning. This is the third time it's done this. No one notices.

Jason pushes away from the table. He fishes in his pocket for his car keys. His watch gets caught in the stitching. He curses and tears it free. He's ready to leave.

"Hi. Sorry I'm late. Parking was a nightmare."

Donna is standing before him. She's wearing a blue dress that kisses the floor. Her hair is frazzled and her lipstick is smeared. Her purse hangs loosely from her shoulder, worn and beaten. Her face is flushed and her breathing is loud. But she's smiling.

Jason mirrors her, pushing his mouth up. He stands and kisses her cheek. He gestures to her seat, sweeping his hand across the table. He knocks his glass over, spilling water to the floor. His face turns red as he grabs a wad of napkins, muttering apologies. She laughs and sits down. A waiter touches Jason's shoulder and points to his chair. He sits as she dries the mess with a towel. She refills his glass and disappears into the crowd.

"Sorry about that." Jason cleans his hand.

Donna giggles and waves her hand. She apologizes for being late. Says she got stuck behind a bus. Had to park between to two pickup trucks. Practically crawled out of her window. She giggles again. Jason does the same.

They look over their menus, mouthing the ingredients. Donna closes her menu. Jason flits his eyes from the steak to the linguine. He wants the linguine, but he's making a batch of pasta tomorrow. It's in his schedule. He bites his lip. He sees Donna staring at him. He shuts his menu and gives his order to a waiter.

Jason wraps his fingers around his glass, brings it to his mouth, and puts it back on the table, all in slow motion. There's silence. They both speak. They laugh. They trip over each other's words. Jason nods to Donna. She smiles and takes a breath.

She's from the mid-West. Bopped around trailer parks. Went wherever her dad could find work. He was busy, but he always made time for her. Every night. Until her mother threw him out when she was fourteen. Never saw him again. She clears her throat.

She finished high school with decent grades. Almost became prom queen. Lost by three votes. Worked as a waitress and a store clerk for a year. Saved up. Went to college to study...something. Dropped out after two years. Wandered around for a while, odd jobs here and there. Landed an office job. Only temporary, something to support her while she writes. She'll head out West soon.

Jason nods and smiles. His eyes glaze over. He's looking past her, watching a couple leaning in close, merged into one face. People who found each other. Donna wraps up her story; she asks Jason for his. He opens his mouth. Their food arrives.

They fall silent as they unfold their cutlery from their
napkins. Jason tears a chunk off his steak. Donna lifts the top
bread slice of her sandwich. She scrunches up her face.

"Every time with the fucking pickles."

Donna's hand shoots into the air. She flags down a
waiter. She shoves the pickles under his nose, waving them back
and forth. The waiter nods, his eyes drifting away. Jason doesn't
say anything. Donna gets a new sandwich. She inspects it and
takes a bite. She complains about the first sandwich all night.
She can't let it go. All over a pickle. Jason knows he should
change the topic. Or challenge her. Or tell her to shut up. Or he
should walk out the door. But he doesn't say a word. He chews
his steak.

Jason is on top of Donna. They're in her bed. The lights
are off. There's a teddy bear on her nightstand. It's black with
yellow stripes. It's turned away from the bed. Jason moves up
and down. He clutches the bed sheets and grunts. Donna arches
her back and moans someone's name. Jason wipes the sweat
from his face. He looks into Donna's eyes. He sees two black
pools. He finishes.

Donna is asleep. Jason, naked, pours a glass of water
from the sink. He stubs his toe on the coffee table. He spills
water on the floor. He swears. He wipes it up with his foot. He
walks to the window. The lights from the buildings are smeared
by fog, out of focus like a bad photo. Car blobs float below,
vanishing into the darkness. Horns and shouts waft through the
air. The buildings and streets are stacked on each other, layers of
concrete and steel. They stretch out forever, the perfect cage.

Jason sees a road that leads out. It snakes away from the
city. It's right there, easy as you like. He'd just have to take it.
Simple.

Jason leans his head against the window and closes his
eyes.

CHAPTER FOURTEEN

My footsteps surround me.

I tap my feet on the floor. I lean over the stage, dangling above the abyss. I retreat to the center, facing the curtains. I feel them waiting. I find the words. I spin around and open my mouth. Empty chairs greet me. The room is dark. The chairs are shapeless blobs in endless rows. Moonlight trickles through the windows, painting the floor with pale white patches. A spotlight washes the stage. Darkness consumes it on all sides. I am alone.

I spit and watch it vanish off the stage. I take a step and hear its echo bounce around the room. It reverberates for an absent audience. I feel like a zoo animal for a ghost crowd. I keep expecting to see the audience. I'll close my eyes, open them, and they'll all be here. Rows of eager faces, ready to learn, ready to listen. Electricity in the air. But I'm only confronted with dim silence.

It's wrong to see these chairs empty and unused. It's like a plague has wiped out everyone and I'm all that's left, the last performer onstage. An actor without an audience. It's too horrible for words. I should be lecturing for hundreds; instead, I'm waiting for one. I check my watch. I've been here in the dark for thirty-seven minutes. He's twenty minutes late. I'll give him ten more.

I sit on the lip of the stage. My legs dangle above the floor, half-absorbed by the darkness. I feel exposed. Something could rise up from there and could drag me beneath the murk, pulling me down, down, down. I'd be gone, not a trace left. I crisscross my legs. Focus. I have to know what to say when he walks through those doors. I need the answers. I can picture him. He'll see me dead-centre stage, bathed in light. I'll beckon him forward. He'll slink down the aisle, looking at me for—

Spittal is hung up at the centre square. He's propped against a makeshift cross. He's covered in cuts and gashes. Blood oozes from every pore. His ribs are exposed. His head rolls to the side. He locks eyes with me. He says—No. I slam my eyes shut and slap my forehead. Focus, dammit. He's gone. I can't fix that. Deal with the now.

He'll reach the stage and I'll pull him up. He'll be trembling. I'll touch his shoulder and nod. He'll lie down. I'll go backstage to retrieve the—

Spittal is lying on my desk. His limbs dangle in the air. He's staring at the ceiling, unblinking. There's a hole in his chest. A man is tearing out organs from the wound. He looks up at me and smirks. It's Smit. He grabs a—For fuck's sake. I stand up and walk in a circle. I massage my temples and grind my teeth. I stare at the spot on the floor where the man will be. I'll stand over him, carrying—

Spittal is face down in the mud. It's raining. I'm alone in the woods. I turn him over. He has Smit's face. The smile is gone. He never saw it coming. I smile, but I slap myself, bringing myself back to the stage. He'll be here soon. I have to—

I'm shoving Smit down the aisle, forcing him to trip over his feet. He stumbles into members, who push him away. They spit and jeer at him. Even the people he stole from me are here. They're holding their black and gold robes in the air, punctured and torn by spears. I—I clamp my teeth on my thumb. I wrap a lock on my mind, stopping it from wandering. I need to be here. I've got to—

Smit is slapped and kicked as he walks. He crawls onto the stage and I jump up next to him. I hold my fist above my head and the crowd falls silent. Smit whimpers. Everyone is staring at me. I'm the centerpiece. I'm in control. I raise my hands and—What the fuck is wrong with me? I've got a one-on-one meeting with a member and I'm indulging a power fantasy. I'm mentally masturbating when I should be steeling myself. Where's my discipline? Where's my—?

My blows are raining down on Smit. I scream at him to repent. The crowd joins me, chanting and clapping and stomping. I reduce him to tenderized meat. He shrinks to the floor. I grab his hair and force his head into the light. He repents. The crowd explodes. I leave Smit at my feet. My arms form a "V." I soak it all in. It's—

"Sir?"

I snap my hands to my sides. I clear my throat and move away from the spotlight. I peer through the darkness, looking for the voice. I see a shape lurking in front of the door. I beckon to it and it enters the moonlight. George Carr.

"Is this a bad time? I can come back…" Carr glances back at the door.

"No, no, this is perfect, c'mon down. I've been waiting for you." I hop off the stage.

Carr keeps peeking at the door as he makes his way down the aisle. His hair is ruffled and his clothes are wrinkled. He looks half-dead.

"Sorry I didn't see you there. I was doing, uh…victory stretches. Something I picked up in, uh, Seattle. They're supposed to strengthen blood flow or something. I try 'em out now and then. Y'know, just to see…" I lean against the stage, trying to look natural.

Carr nods and smiles. At least, I think it's a smile. His lips curve up, but his eyes are shifty and cold, weighed down with heavy bags. He winces as he walks, as if every step is agony. He's the physical embodiment of a prolonged sigh.

"Why don't you have a seat?" I pat the stage.

Carr shrugs and sits down. There's a gulf between us. I shrink it, bumping into him. He stiffens. I hold my hand above him, unsure if I should give his shoulder a squeeze or rub his back. Something to reassure him. I retreat, clasping my hands over my lap. He looks brittle. I have to ease into it.

A dozen thoughts jostle to get out. Demand a confession? Grab him and throw him onstage, raining down fists? Poke and prod him with endless question? Let the silence

envelop him until he falls apart and talks? So many options. I
pick the practical one.

"How was your day?"

"...eh, y'know, not bad, I guess." The words trickle out
of Carr's mouth.

I rub my eyes and I inch closer.

"What'd you do? You're a...planter, yes?"

"Mm-hmm. Did a few chores. This and that. Got pretty
tired. Had to lie down." Carr scratches his neck and turns further
away.

"Yeah? Why was that?" I strain my voice to sound
interested.

"Happens a lot. No energy. Don't know why. Been
going on a few months." Carr raises and lowers his shoulders.

"Have you tried meditating? That always works for me.
A few minutes every day to clear the head. It does wonders. I
could show you a few techniques if you like." I place my open
hand on Carr's knee. He just needs to take it...

"Maybe. Worth a shot." Carr shifts his weight. My hand
falls away.

Silence descends. I bore my eyes into the back of Carr's
head. He doesn't move. He only looks ahead, his neck craned
forward. I flex my fingers and rotate my wrists. Going to take the
forceful route here. He'll talk, whether he wants to or not. I
position my hands below his armpits, ready to grab and pull. I
bring my arms back to build momentum. I'm about to launch...

I follow his gaze. He's not looking around the room.
He's staring straight at the pillar near the stage. It's etched with
names of builders. I recognize one of them. I lower my hands. I
smile.

I hop off the stage. Carr doesn't spare me a second
glance. I wander into his face and wave. He's forced to look at
me. I nod and backpedal. I reach the pillar and lean on it.

"You know, I see these pillars every day, but I never
stop to appreciate them. They're quite impressive, wouldn't you
agree?" I run my hand up and down the wood.

Carr's eyes light up, just a bit. He nods, straightening his posture. I've found the bait.

"It's really marvelous. I couldn't dream of something this good. And the texture, my God, the texture. You wouldn't know it used to be a collection of bark and twigs, it's so smooth. Have you touched it before?" I beckon to him.

Carr slides off the stage. He walks to the opposite side of the pillar and rests his hand on it. He guides his palm through its patterns and lines, running over the faded names.

"I can't believe men built this thing. It's almost too perfect. It's something we could never achieve. But of course we can. We've got the proof. It's inspiring, wouldn't you agree?" I peek around the pillar to look at Carr.

"Yeah. It's amazing. I wish I could..." Carr touches his right hand, which is covered in scars.

"I know. Sometimes it's enough to just appreciate good work, I think." I pat his shoulder.

"Hmm." Carr digs his fingers into the grooves on the pillar.

"You know, I've had the pleasure of meeting every one of these men. Phillips, Marson, Garrison, Kent. Good, hardworking people. The kind of folks you can trust. I'm sure they'd build a hundred of these pillars if I asked them to. Have you met any of them?" I creep closer to Carr.

"Oh, yeah, a few. Haven't talked to them much. Nice guys." Carr nods absentmindedly. He's barely here.

"Have you met him?" I point at a name near Carr's face. It's Henry Spittal.

Carr blinks. He traces his fingers over Spittal's name, resting on the "S." He stares at it, picking on its edges.

"Yeah. Yeah, I knew him. Know him. Good guy. I thought so." Carr withdraws his hand.

Silence again. Carr's transfixed by Spittal's name. Time to push the knife in deeper. I prop myself against the pillar, arms folded.

"Yeah, I heard the same. Dedicated member. No complaints from anyone. Model worker. You know him well?" I jab my thumb at Spittal's inscription.

"Mm-hmm. We, uh, hung out a bit. Just a few times. He's usually busy. Don't see him too often. He's always doing something. Hard to keep up. But he's a good one, that's for sure." Carr shirks away from me.

"You think so?" I look at Spittal's carving. It's clean and smooth.

"One of the best." Carr's voice wavers.

"That's not what I heard." I face him.

"Oh?" Carr sounds sharp.

"I heard you two had a falling out a few weeks ago. Out in the woods." I shove off the pillar and tower over Carr.

Carr fidgets and shuffles his feet. He hunches his shoulders and looks at the ground. I hold his chin and tilt his head up. His eyes are watery.

"George, you can talk to me." I hold my hand over my chest.

Carr's face twitches. His lips tremble and wobble. His mouth moves up and down. No sound comes out. He rubs his temples and grunts. He stamps his feet. Still nothing.

"Just say what's on your mind. This is a safe place. No one else is here. Just the two of us." I'm very close to him now.

"I, um, I need to, jeez, um, well, I, how do I…?" Carr's arms flail at his sides.

"George, do you want to confess?"

Carr stops squirming. He lets out a big gulp of air, like a deflated balloon. He nods and opens his mouth. I place my finger in front of it.

"No, not here. There." I gesture to the stage.

The spotlight stands before us, an angelic tower of gold. The only light in an ocean of darkness. A tight circle of confession. It couldn't look any better. Like something out of a movie. Carr will be too overwhelmed to think straight; I'll have him dancing in my palm. Damn, I wish a crowd was here. It would be—Carr grimaces. It's only for a moment, a brief flash on his face, but it's there. Annoyance, irritation, anger. As if confession is some unbearable chore, some tedious roadblock. As if my olive branch is an inconvenience. The bile rises in my throat.

Carr climbs onstage and walks to the spotlight. He doesn't complain or moan; he does what he's told. Let it go, let it go. It was a split second, that's all. I hop on the stage. Carr puts one foot in the spotlight, divided between visible and blackness. I take his hand and pull him forward. We spin for a moment, two dancers in the dark. Carr plants his feet.

"George, I feel this is no ordinary confession. This room, at this time, with the two of us alone onstage, it all feels...special. I don't think I've ever done something quite like this before." I've done this dozens of times before. Night is always the best period to draw out confessions. The isolation, the silence, the encroaching shadows, they all add pressure. Night is the perfect vise to clamp onto someone's mind. "Yes, this whole thing seems unique. I feel a current in the air. Do you?" I wriggle my fingers, feeling for the unseen energy.

"Yeah, I guess, I mean, it's different, for sure." Carr's words are aimed at the floor.

"Different, exactly right. Out of the ordinary. We're venturing into uncharted waters. And I think your confession is no small order. I don't think it's a run-of-the-mill sin you need to release. You're carrying a burden, something you can't shake off no matter how hard you try. And I'm sure you've tried. I can see it in your eyes; it's suffocating you. Am I right?" My words seep into the darkness, echoing throughout the room. I am everywhere.

"...yes..." Carr's voice is below a whisper.

"Yes, yes, I can tell. Heavy baggage is pressing down on you. Something you need to get off your chest. Now, I normally only do this on big occasions, but I think this is important. I think it's something we're duty-bound to do. George, will you take the Weight?" I spread my hand over his stomach, pushing it.

Carr's eyes widen. His body shudders. No grimace this time.

"Are, are you sure? Do you, do you think I'm ready for that, that, that..." Carr chews on his thumb nail.

"Anyone's ready if they truly want to confess. It's a very particular type of person, no doubt. But I think you're that person, George. Do you?" I push harder on his stomach.

Carr stares at my hand. He takes it and squeezes it between his palms. He moves his head up and down. He opens his mouth. "Yes" trickles out.

I slide my hand out of Carr's grip, wiping off the sweat. I smile at him and nod. He's still dazed. Time to go to work. I tell Carr to lie down and stare at the ceiling. I'll do the rest. Couldn't be simpler. He crouches down and tumbles onto his ass. He flattens his body, stretching his limbs far from his centre. He looks at the lights and squints. It looks all wrong. His legs are completely out of the spotlight circle, consumed by darkness. His arms are bent, forming a W-shape with his head.

I rub my eyes. Calm, calm. Minor hiccup. I push his feet, bringing his full body to the circle. He goes to move, but I stop him, telling him not to worry. He'll just make it worse. I kneel beside him and grip his left side, shoving him into the centre. I ask him to fold his arms on his chest. I stand up and smile. Perfect. Like a portrait.

"Alright, George, I need you to wait here, exactly like this. Don't move an inch. I'll be right back. No, no, don't adjust anything; it looks fine. Don't fidget. Lay back and relax." I disappear behind the curtains.

I slam my shin on a chair. I wince and stumble over to the floor. I can't see a goddamn thing. I let out a stream of curses. I flip over the chair. Carr asks if I'm okay. I tell him to stay there. I prop myself up, nursing the bruise. I tug open the curtains, letting a sliver of light into the backstage. I see a lamp on a desk. I walk toward it, avoiding boxes and crates, and flick it on.

Wires and cords are strewn everywhere, bunched up and tangled together. Chairs are loosely stacked on top of each other, many resting sideways. The desk is covered in old sermon notes and reminders. I see countless props stored in boxes and leaning on the wall. Staffs, knives, goggles, firecrackers, stuff I never even used. They're all here. One wrong step could lead to a decapitation. Ken and Greg need to clean this place up first thing tomorrow.

I tiptoe through the wreckage, keeping my elbows tucked in so as to not knock anything over. I reach the far end of the backstage, catching my foot on a cable pile and crashing into the wall. Thank God no one's back here with me. I move a file cabinet away from a door, smashing it into a pile of white masks. I force the door open. I venture into the closest, brushing aside streamers and a scarlet cloth. There it is: The Weight.

I found it years ago. I was swimming in the river, seeing where it would take me. I'd finished a particularly powerful sermon and I was feeling exuberant. I swam until the current pushed me to the bank. I crawled out, grasping at grass and roots, anything for leverage. My hand landed on something rough and hard. I wiped my eyes and climbed ashore. I was standing at the mouth of a cave. It was filled with abandoned hammocks, tents, and sleeping bags, all rotted and shredded. A hobo camp in the woods. I didn't find anyone. I'd never seen it before. I've never returned.

I looked down at what I had grabbed. It was magnificent. A near-flawless circle in a mountain of rubble. Jagged and chipped at the edges, but a circle nonetheless. Wider than my chest and twice as thick. I ran my hands over its smooth surface, feeling the occasional bump and crack. You could prop it up on steel bars and use it as a dinner table. It was a discus for a giant.

I had to have it. I knew it would be perfect for our compound. I flipped it on its side and started rolling it. I immediately ran over my toes. I let out the appropriate response. I dragged it along the bank, following the river back to my clothes. It was dark when I got there. I should have gone home and come back for the circle in the morning with five men. But I couldn't wait. I stumbled through the forest, circle by my side. It bumped into logs, stumps, and trees, falling flat on its face. I hauled it up and kept going, grasping in the dark, looking to the moon for light. I reached the edge of the compound and collapsed, resting in a ball on top of the circle.

Ken found me in the morning. He helped me push the circle into the compound. We planted it in the centre square. I called out for builders. They came running. By afternoon, they'd carved and smoothed it into perfection. I dragged it into the sermon hall and tucked it behind the curtains. We had our Weight.

I haul it past the curtains and drop it near Carr's head. He flinches, but doesn't move away. I can smell his sweat from here. Hopefully the Weight doesn't slip off him. I raise my hand up to silence the crowd that isn't here. Force of habit. Doesn't feel natural doing this for an audience of no one. There should be hushed pauses and thunderous applause. Instead we have empty seats and Carr's sighs. It's off-putting. Still, it has to be done. Only way I'm going to find out about Carr and Spittal...

"George, I commend you for doing this, I truly do. You've shown real character. Are you ready?" I stand on the Weight, peering down at Carr.

"Wonderful. Let's begin. Hold your hands up flat and brace yourself. It's going to be quite heavy, but it's nothing you can't manage." I lift the Weight up and place it on Carr's chest.

Carr wheezes as the Weight presses on him. He snorts as he wraps his hands around the Weight's edges and holds it up. It's barely off his body, just enough for him to breathe. I place my hand on it and push ever so slightly.

"Now, George Carr, you are here to confess. You have come looking for absolution. What are your sins?" My voice booms throughout the hall.

"...eh, lots, many, lots to confess, eh, lazy, hah, don't do enough, ooh, can't help it, ugh, just want to, eh, want to relax, urgh, do it too much, fuck, don't listen much, ooh, zone out, phew, zone out when you talk sometimes, urr, don't know why, goddamn..."

Carr prattles off a list of basic transgressions as he struggles with the Weight. Sleeps in too much, goes to work late, leaves early, blah, blah, blah. I don't have time for the appetizers; I need the meat. I push down harder.

"Yes, yes, those are all reprehensible sins. We will address them in full, I promise. But I want to talk about a big one, the biggest in your life, the one that's eating you alive. I want to talk about Henry Spittal." I nod at the pillar.

"Sp-Spittal…?" Carr sprays saliva all over the Weight and my face. I wipe it away and resist the urge to crush him.

"Yes, Henry Spittal, the man who built that pillar, the man who carved his name on it, the name you couldn't stop staring at. I know you want to say something about him. I know you have a sin to confess. Speak." I ease off the Weight.

"Y-you're right...I need to tell you...everything about him...what I did...Christ…" Carr's face is turning red.

"Start from the beginning. I'm patient." I crouch over Carr and grab the Weight, pulling it an inch away from him. Just enough for him to talk.

"I was a builder with Henry. He was here before me. He took me under his wing. Showed me how everything worked. Kept me out of trouble. Someone I could trust, someone I could rely on. Then I crushed my hand." The spotlight shines off the sweat pooling on Carr's forehead. I raise the Weight up a little more.

"I got moved to the planters. Decent work. Took care of my garden. Enjoyed it. Didn't talk with Henry anymore. He was too busy. Couldn't make time for me. Lived in a different world. Saw him from the other side. Saw the real him for the first time. Hated him." Carr lets out a blast of air from his mouth and bares his teeth. I flick the sweat off his brow. The Weight rises further up.

"He was arrogant. Only talked about himself. Only concerned with himself. Made sure he was the focus of every conversation. Steamrolled people. Never shut up. Swollen head. Unbearable." Carr rubs his eye with one hand and returns it beneath the Weight. I'm practically carrying it at this point. We're getting somewhere...

"He bragged about everything. Bragged about the things he's built. Bragged about his woman. Bragged about his camping trips. Bragged about those fucking pillars every goddamn day. Pointed to his name on them every chance he could. Pure ego." Carr shakes his head; I mirror him. I picture Spittal's opened throat and, for once, don't feel pity. If he was this self-obsessed, this arrogant, he was no follower of mine. Maybe he deserved it...

"I heard him every day. In my garden I could hear his voice from the construction site. When I walked around the compound I could hear it bouncing off the buildings. I'd sit at the far end of the lunchroom and I could still hear his voice. I had to listen to him drone on and on. One boast after another, stacked to the sky. It never stopped. I'd hear his voice and my toes would curl. I hated him. I wanted him to be quiet. I had to..." Carr bites his lip and darts his eyes.

"Go on. I'm listening." I bring the Weight down slightly, peering over it. Almost there...

"I had to do something. But I didn't know what. Didn't know how. So I just listened. I had a hole in my head. And the more I listened, the bigger it got. I burned into me. I couldn't sleep. I couldn't think. All I had was the hole and Henry's voice in my head. He was all I could focus on. I needed an out. Ken showed me one." Carr fidgets as he feels more pressure from the Weight. Ken...

"We went to the woods. Everyone goes there. Everyone who needs...release. We did...things. Sorted ourselves. I went every night. Went in deeper and deeper, away from the crowd. Didn't want to talk. Wanted to clear myself. But I couldn't. The hole was still there. Henry's voice was still there." Carr clears his throat. Where's he going with this?

"Then, one night, Henry was there. I'd never seen him in the woods. Didn't think he needed it. Watched him from behind a tree. Listened to him. Had to know why. He was talking with someone. No, talking *at* someone. He was bragging again. But it was different this time. He was excited, jittery. He was bragging about leaving the compound for...somewhere. I'd never heard of it before. He called it Zaan." Carr coughs as the full force of the Weight falls on him.

I'm gripping the Weight with my white knuckles. My nose is nearly touching Carr's face. My whole body is tense. That son of a bitch. All this time we've wasted on a traitor. Some wishy-washy turncoat. How dare he walk away from us. Is that why Carr killed him? Loyalty? Moral outrage? I should give him a medal for that. No, don't rush it. Push deeper.

"Keep. Going." My nails scrape on the Weight.

"He said, ugh, he said it was better. Said it offered more. Said this place was a, oh, was a dead end. Said we're wasting our time. Said we'd been lied to." Carr grits his teeth to keep the Weight up. I want to resurrect Spittal just to kill him all over again.

"I'd heard enough. Watching him in the forest, in my place, spreading his...filth, I snapped. Wanted the hole gone. Wanted his voice gone. I stepped away from the tree. I walked behind Henry. Shoved him to the ground. Watched him slam on a rock. Heard him yell. Pushed his friend away. Stood over him. Told him to shut up. Called him a traitor. Called him a liar. Felt good. Felt right." There's a hint of a smile on Carr's face.

"He stood up. Wiped blood from his mouth. Glared at me. His face was...scary. I froze. Felt his fist ram into my stomach. Fell to my knees. Tried to breathe. Watched everyone look away and melt into the woods. It was just me and Henry. No one could see us. No one would know..." The Weight surges up, throwing me off balance. Carr's eyes are steel.

"I scrambled to my feet. I tripped over leaves and roots. Henry shoved me down. Landed on my ass. I reached out and grabbed his shirt and belt buckle. Pulled them down. Henry slapped my hands away. I went to my knees. I was going to tackle Henry to the ground, shove dirt in his face, pummel him. Didn't get a chance. Henry took my head and slammed it into the earth. Tasted soil and grass. Couldn't see straight. Could feel Henry on top of me. Could feel his punches." Carr's face is beet red.

"Henry yelled at me. Didn't hear him. Tried to get up, but he pinned me down. Went to slap him, but he blocked it. I apologized, I guess, but he didn't listen. I was trapped. Closed my eyes. Guarded my face with my arms. Henry's punches rocked me. He hit my face, my stomach, my legs, everywhere. Went on for ages. Couldn't stop him. Had to take it.

"The punches stopped. I could hear Henry's breathing. Could feel his weight. I opened my eyes. Henry was sitting on me. His knuckles were red. He looked at me with...pity? I'm not sure. He slapped me and shook his head. He walked away. Left me in the woods. Alone." Carr looks past me. He's back in the forest.

"Don't know how long I laid there. Minutes, hours. Curled up in my blood. Crawled to my knees. Cleaned my face. Held my ribs as I stood up. Limped home in the dark. Could barely walk. Went to bed. Couldn't sleep. Miserable. But I was glad. I remembered your sermons. I knew every failure was an opportunity. Pain is a path. I'd seen the real Henry. He was a fraud, a wolf in the flock. I thought about you and I knew I had to do something. I had to take care of Henry." My heart flutters with pride. At least someone has been paying attention. Carr suffered and learned from it. Can't ask for more than that. But what'd he do about it?

"Healed up. Covered my bruises. No one seemed to care. Suited me fine. Watched Henry's every move. I studied him. I wanted to know everything I could. The more I watched him, the sicker I got. This...imposter in our compound. This snake plotting to leave, laughing and eating in our meal hall. Working alongside the men he planned to betray. Probably trying to convince them to join him. Ready to throw it away, to walk out.

The hole in my head grew. And something started gnawing at my stomach. This pit tearing at my insides. This, this, anger, this hatred. I wanted to destroy Henry. I wanted to pulverize his pretty face in front of everyone. I wanted to bring him to you and have him confess, have you humiliate him." I suppress my flattered ego.

"But I didn't. I didn't do anything. Just watched him. He was all I could think about. He filled up my mind and wouldn't leave. I knew I had to do something, but I didn't know what. I'd lay in bed at night, trying to find a solution. But I couldn't. And the pit kept getting bigger. It ate me alive. Had to act. One night..." Carr squirms and adjusts the Weight in his hands. I'm close enough to taste his breath.

"One night, I went outside. Don't know why. No one was around. Could barely see. Walked in circles for hours. Opened a door. It was a cabin. Sleeping quarters. Henry's sleeping quarters. I had a knife in my pocket. I don't know where it came from. Think I stole it from meal hall. I put it in my hand. I walked past the beds. No one heard me. I made it to the window. Saw light from the moon. Saw Henry's bed." My feet are barely on the floor. I'm teetering over the Weight. Carr can barely breathe. So close...

"I knew what I wanted to do. But I stood there. I, ugh, didn't move a muscle. Just, ahh, listened to the snores and mumbles. Held the knife up. My palm was sweaty. I could feel it slipping. Had to do it now. I pulled back Henry's sheets and saw...saw..." Carr takes a big gulp of air.

"What? What did you see? What did you do? What? What was it? Talk." I slap Carr. I'm fully on the Weight now, nearly crushing its edges in my grip. Carr could buckle under all this pressure. I could crush him. I can't ease off.

"I saw...he was...the truth...laughing at me...he was...gone...can't breathe...please." Carr slaps the Weight, tapping out.

"...What?" My body shifts to the side, giving Carr relief.

"He was...gone. Henry, he'd...left. Walked out. Must've fled...in the night. Please...too heavy"

I roll off the Weight. Carr wheezes. I sit beside him, head near my knees. My face is cold with sweat. I rub my eyes. All that buildup, all that pressure, all that work...for a non-confession. Carr just missed Spittal. Probably arrived right after the real killer dragged Spittal into the woods. He was too late to see anything. Useless. A whole night thrown away on a...sniveling toad. I bite my knuckles to stop myself from screaming.

I stand up and pace. I clasp my hands together and shake them. Fuck. I thought I was close. Carr seemed like the perfect fit. Right motive, right time, right personality. But I'm still nowhere. What a waste. What a complete—

I hear sobbing. I see tears streaming down Carr's face. They pool around his ears and mouth. He gasps and snorts. He lets out a high-pitched warble that fills the room. His face looks like it's melting. The Weight heaves up and down, nearly falling off. I place my foot on it, keeping it in place. His cries are like a squealing pig's screeches. They make my head ache. He wastes my time and now he's annoying me. I can feel the bile rising in my throat.

"Stop that." I snap my fingers at Carr.

Carr doesn't look me. His head rolls from side to side. His hands slap the Weight, impotent and helpless. His moans and tears keep flowing. My headache grows. I bite my lip.

"Stop it." I clap my hands.

Nothing. A constant stream of water and whining. He doesn't even know I'm here.

"Stop it. What's wrong with you?" I stomp on the Weight. Carr grunts and pushes back. The tears and moans end. Peace.

Carr rubs his head on the Weight, trying to wipe the tears away. He succeeds at smearing them on his cheek and grinding dust over his face. The Weight stops bouncing beneath my foot. He opens his mouth, but only sighs and sobs come out. I roll my eyes.

"Talk. Now." I apply more pressure.

"Henry, ugh, Henry...Henry left...He went to Zaan...He escaped...Got out... Found a new way...Went to Zaan..." Every time I hear that name, the bile crawls further up my throat.

"We've been over this. Move on." I shift my foot down the Weight, pressing hard on his stomach.

"I...envied Henry. He had everything. The woman...the friends...the drive...the body...he had it all. I wanted it. Wanted to be him. So I hated him. Wanted to destroy him. Prove...I was better. I was going to do it. I was going to...expose him. Show everyone who he...really is. But he beat me to it. Went to Zaan. Proved he was..." Carr chokes on his words and clears his throat.

"Proved he was...better. Better than us. Better than...me. He did what I wanted...He did...He did..." Carr's eyes dart everywhere. I lean in close, simplifying his worldview.

"He did what? What did he do that you couldn't?" My foot nearly slides off the Weight.

"He left. He did what I wanted to do. He got out."

I step off the Weight. I stare at Carr. I hold my hands close to my chest, shaping them into fists. A deserter lying at my feet. One more defector for the pile.

"He's better than me. Did what I couldn't. Walked away. Wasn't afraid. Freed himself. No doubt, no second-guessing. I couldn't do it. Can't do it. Should do it. Not right, not right, not right..." Carr rambles into the darkness.

I watch Carr's lips move up and down. I feel my blood boiling and bubbling. There's a ringing in ears. Another traitor, right in front of me. I black out. I'm on top of Carr. My body is spread across the Weight. My knees are curled into my stomach. I plant my hands on the floor next to Carr's head, one on each side. I'm looking straight into his eyes. He can't escape me.

"Explain. Yourself." The words slither out of my mouth. I can taste the venom.

"Sir...ugh...sir...I can't...fuck...can't breathe..." Carr's face turns even redder. All this pressure could crush him. He could pop like a tomato, flattened on the stage. But I don't move. I can't.

"Explain. Why. Do you. Want. To leave?" I speak without moving my teeth. Carr knows he can't get away. He's mine. He only has one option.

"I'm...Christ...I don't know...what I'm doing here...Ugh, hurts...Used to know...what I wanted...Believed...Something happened...Lost my way...Lost my belief...Can't get it back...I sit in your...sermons...and I want to believe...I follow your words...I want them to matter...I want them to...ahh...want them to mean something...But they don't...They're empty...I'm empty...Don't know...what I'm doing here...Fuck, fuck, fuck...Maybe I belong in Zaan...I don't don't...I'm afraid...Please, sir...I'm afraid..." Carr's eyes are fresh with tears.

I gaze over Carr's face. I can smell the fear on him. He's unmoored in the world. He came here for solace, for a purpose. I gave it to him. I showed him a way. I showed him *the* way. And he... And he...

He threw it in my face. All my work, my attention, my sacrifice; it meant nothing to this...slime. He wants to flush it away and run to Zaan. Run to mediocrity and compromise. Run into Smit's waiting arms. He's slapping my face and expecting pity for it. Hell, I bet he wants me to pardon him. Give him my full blessings to stab me in the back and skip down the road.

They're all against me. Smit. Spittal. Carr. All these schemers, liars, and whores. Doing whatever they can to fuck me. Dragging me down into the mud. Smashing what I've built. I'm surrounded by vultures.

"Sir...the Weight...too much...please...sir...breathe..." Carr's eyes flutter.

I don't deserve these attacks. I'm trying to help people, trying to save them. I'm providing shelter, guidance, meaning. I've built a world with two hands and a voice. And now they're sinking their blades into me. They're trying to bleed me out and leave me to die. My own people are turning against me. Ungrateful bastards. They're all like Spittal. Spoiled, vain, fickle. Ready to run when things get too hard. No, no, they're not like him. He died before he could flee. These people lurk in the shadows, looking for an excuse to leave, praying I pardon them. They're all like Carr.

"Sir...the Weight...please...Christ...Sir…" Carr's hands fall to his sides.

I feel his shallow breath. I watch his eyes close. I could end him. Just apply a little more pressure. The slightest push. The same force used to crush a fly. I could cover his mouth. Watch him spasm trying to escape. Watch him beg for mercy, for forgiveness. I'd have none. I could snuff him out. Eliminate a traitor before he can twist the knife. Drag him to the center square. Leave him as a message. Let everyone know the stakes. Let them see my power. Force them to kneel. It would be so easy. I have to wait for one more minute. I'll be rid of him. I'll be…

I jump to my feet and shove the Weight off of Carr. He rolls to his side, clutching his chest and fighting to breathe. I cover my mouth with my trembling hand. I smear the sweat off my brow. My heart has plunged into my stomach and it hasn't reached the bottom. My legs are jelly. I seize my knees to stop myself from collapsing.

I almost did it. I wanted to do it. I wanted to squeeze the life out of Carr. I wanted to turn him into paste on the stage. I wanted to hear him beg and wheeze and choke. I wanted to feel his bones crunch beneath me. I wanted to kill Carr.

Christ, my body can't stop shaking. When I looked at Carr's face and I realized I could end him, when I understood I held his life in my hand, it petrified me. I flinched from death. I'm a fraud. I preach sacrifice and punishment and the honour of dying, but my words couldn't prop me up. I confronted death, real, actual death, and I blinked. I let go. I couldn't take that step into the darkness. I shrank back into the light.

I'm a liar. All my sermons, all my commandments, all my words, they meant nothing. I couldn't back them up. I shriveled and wilted. I found a limit and I didn't smash it; I bowed to it. This traitor lying on the floor, growling for air, showed me what I really am: A fake. He exposed me. I'm nothing but some pretty words and hollow convictions. I'm not a leader. I should—

No. Stop it. What am I saying? Throw in the towel over one minute of doubt? I slap my cheek. Ridiculous. This night has beaten me, exhausted me, worn me down. I'm not thinking straight. I belong here. This is my place. I built it. I breathe it. It's my salvation. I belong here, I belong here, I belong here...

I'm not afraid of death. And I'm not afraid to kill. But it has to be for the right reasons. I'd destroy Smit in a heartbeat. I'd squeeze the life out of him with piano wire. I'd do anything to stop him. I'd make sure he couldn't hurt us. I'll fight any invaders, any barbarians at the gate. I'll kill as many enemies as I have to in order to secure and defend our ideals. I'd do it with a smile on my face.

But I won't kill my people. I'll help them transcend, but only with their permission. I need their consent to release them. They have to make the decision to free themselves; I'm just the errand boy filling out his order. I will not kill my people without reason, even this curled ball of agony on the floor.

Carr has crawled to his knees. He shrinks away from the Weight. I compose myself and walk over to him. I put my hand on his shoulder. He looks up at me. His eyes are bloodshot.

"You've had quite a night. Thank you for sharing so much with me. I'm sure you must feel relieved. I'm sorry it got so...intense, but it was necessary. I had to be sure you weren't holding anything back. It was for your own sake, you see. I wanted you to be completely honest and you were. You'll have a lot to think about on your way home." My lips form I smile, I think.

Carr blinks. His mouth twitches. I crouch down and lock eyes. My face is stone. I want there to be no ambiguity.

"Pack your bags." I stand and turn my back to Carr. I hear him gasp and sob. I hear him stumble to his feet. I hear him jump off the stage. I hear him walk down the aisle. I hear him open the door. I hear nothing.

I won't kill, but I'm not stupid. I can't have a traitor in my midst, no matter how impotent and useless he may be. Carr's doubt would have curdled into defiance. He could've dragged others down with him. Best to cut off the infected finger before it spreads to the body.

I sit on the edge of the stage. I lean back with my head in my hands. Spittal, Carr, that lasagna man; does anyone want to stay here? It's probably going to be just me, Ken, and Greg at the end. What a sight: Three rejects trying to find transcendence. I'd laugh if I wasn't so—

"Hello?"

Christ, will this night ever end? I squint my eyes, shielding them from the spotlight. There's a figure standing in the aisle. For fuck's sake. Carr, how did you not get the message? He'd better leave before—

No, it's not Carr. They walk with more assurance, not stumbling over their feet. They're not gasping for air or nursing their bruised chest. Can't tell who it is. They're close to the light now. It's Sandra.

I haven't seen her since the exodus earlier today. Heavy bags are under her eyes, black and thick. Her hair is tied in a sloppy ponytail. Her shoulders are slouched, tired of carrying their weight. She's been through a wringer. Her photograph is crumpled in her hand.

"I just saw the lights on..." Sandra jerks her thumb at the spotlight. I'm staring at her photo. I can see a few wisps of brown hair and white skin. Nothing concrete. Who the hell is it?

"Sir? Are you alright?" Sandra waves her hand, tucking the photo into her pocket. I look at her and nod. I spring to my feet and smile.

"Yes, yes, I'm perfectly fine. How are you? Sandra, wasn't it?" I snap my fingers, pretending to search for her name.

"Yes, that's right, sir. Is this a bad time? I can always come back…" Sandra inches away from the stage.

"It's a perfect time. Why do you say that?" I adjust my sleeves and tuck my shirt into my pants, hiding the sweat stains.

"George bumped into me on his way out. He looked upset." Sandra looks around the room for…what? Evidence? Another rat in my—Stop. For fuck's sake, just stop.

"We had a late night confessional, that's all. Strictly one-on-one. It got pretty…emotional and George took it hard. I can't disclose the details with you. It's a private matter, you understand. Don't worry about George. He's just a little shook up. He'll be fine in the morning…" I clap my hands for punctuation. That's the last time I want to talk about George Carr.

"Oh, I see." Sandra is staring at the Weight.

"Now, how can I help you?" I slide the Weight out of the spotlight.

Sandra strides to the stage, then backs away. She starts to speak, but trails off. Her hands fidget close to her chest. She bites her lip and gives me an awkward smile. She rubs her forehead and sighs. It takes all my energy not to yell at her. This night has been far too long.

"Um, well, I'm actually here for a confession, too." Sandra leans over the stage, looking up at me.

"Is that so?" I stop a sigh from escaping my lips. I need a break. Power through, power through…

"Yeah, I, uh, I've had something…gnawing on me all day and I… I need to talk. I know it's late but do you have a minute?" She clasps her hands together. She's tired, desperate, and dedicated. She wandered into the hall on the hope that I would be here. Her eyes are exhausted and expectant. I'm her last resort, her answer. This is what I live for. I nod.

"Thank you. I, uh, where do I begin? I've been—"

"I can't hear you down there." I bend over and offer my hand. Sandra smiles and takes it.

"Thank you. Um, anyway, I've been looking for my boyfriend, Henry, and I, whoa—" Sandra nearly falls to the floor.

My grip loosened for a second when I heard that name. Surely she didn't mean Spittal? I seize Sandra's wrist before she tumbles off the stage. She stumbles forward, landing on her knees.

"Sorry about that. Lost my grip. You slipped." I move to help her up but stop myself. She can handle herself. Don't need to make this more awkward.

"Right, right." She massages her legs as she stands up, wincing. I can feel my face getting red. We're off to a great start.

"Um, yeah, so, my boyfriend, Henry, uh, Henry Spittal, you know him? Tall builder, leads the camping trips, really defined biceps?" Sandra flexes her muscles and puffs out her chest.

Fuck. Of all the people, she has to date the murder victim. She couldn't make it easy on me. Spittal couldn't have been some loner no one would've missed. Oh, no, he had to have a girlfriend who'll probably snoop around looking for him, exposing his death, and...

I'll be fine. She won't notice anything. I'm certainly not going to tell her. Answer a few questions and she'll be on her way. Just keep a straight face, keep a straight face...

"I've seen him around." I push the image of his corpse out of my head.

"Right, of course you have. Um, yeah, well, he's my boyfriend. Sort of. We don't like labels. Or, well, he doesn't. We kept it...I don't know. We were definitely...together. I mean, I knew he had others. He always told me. Sorry, you don't need to know that. I'm just trying to...I don't know." Sandra's arms are spinning like windmills, keeping pace with her mouth.

"No need for a novel. Let's get to the point." I give a wry smile. At least, that's what I'm aiming for. Probably looked pissed off more than anything.

"Gotcha. Well, uh, I haven't seen Henry for a while. His roommates don't know where he went. I wasn't surprised. Henry goes on random camping trips all the time. He just didn't tell me, that's all. He'd left behind a lot gear, but I thought he might be roughing it. He's probably sleeping in a tree. That sounds like something he'd do. He'll be back in a few days with pines in his hair and a big shit-eating grin. I was sure of it." Sandra paces inside the spotlight.

"I didn't see him for days. I talked to his coworkers, his friends, his ex-girlfriends, his current girlfriends, everybody. They hadn't seen in for a while. He hadn't been to work, he hadn't been to lunch, he hadn't been sermons, he hadn't been anywhere. He'd vanished. It's like an eraser came down from the sky and rubbed him out." Sandra makes a scrubbing motion with her arm.

"I've spoken with everyone in this compound. No one has a clue. They don't want to talk about it. I can see it in their eyes. They all think he ran away, ditched us for something better. They want to forget about him. I knew they were wrong. I thought I did..." Sandra stands on the spotlight's edge, staring at the darkness.

"Thought?" I touch her elbow. She flinches and falls back to the center.

"Yeah. I've been looking around all day. Asked everybody at that big brouhaha by the gates. Bad idea. Nobody could hear me. I squeezed out of the crowd. Didn't know what to do. I decided to check out Henry's bunk again. Maybe I'd missed something. I looked in the pillow and under the mattress and between the sheets. I found something." Sandra pulls a piece of paper from her back pocket and throws it on the floor.

It's a Zaan pamphlet. I can see Smit's plastic smile from here. It consumes the page, stretched to hideous proportions. His face is plastered with "Escape!" and "Freedom!" and "Your Decision!" Images of food, pornography, and sports trace the borders. The font is bubble-shaped and red, while the photos are glossy and bright. Smit's face looks extra-shiny. It's an advertisement as shallow and glossy as the man's religion.

So Carr was telling the truth. Spittal was going to abandon us for Zaan. Dirty fucker. Sandra's shaking, her arms folded. I should comfort her.

"I'm...sorry. It's never easy when someone betrays you. It can feel...awful." I put my hand on Sandra's shoulder. She brushes it off.

"I don't feel awful. I don't feel betrayed. I don't feel...anything." Sandra's eyes well up.

"When I saw that pamphlet, I knew Henry was gone. I knew he'd run off to Zaan and he'd left me behind. He didn't spare me a second thought. We've been together for three years, on and off, and he walked away. He didn't even say goodbye. I looked at that pamphlet and I knew I was looking at the death certificate for our relationship. And I didn't feel a thing. I felt bothered, like I'd found out my milk soured or my car got a ticket. It was a mild inconvenience. All that time with him and I felt...nothing. That scares me." Sandra shakes her head.

I stare at her. She's biting her lip and fidgeting. She's afraid of something she can never control: Herself. This is true despair, knowing there's something wrong with you, but unable to fight it. Feeling broken with no tools. This is true hollowness. I haven't seen it since...

I bite my knuckle. I need reach out. I should speak about courage and sacrifice in the face of despair. I should say that this is a moment for real change, real growth. I should say that this is a phase, a passing darkness. But those words seem shallow and false. I can't speak them.

"If you need to talk, I'm always here." I lift her chin and smile, trying to make it look natural.

Sandra forces her head into my chest, hugging me. My arms are frozen beside her. I force them to pat her back. I mumble nonsensical reassurances. It's quiet. Just two people in the light.

Sandra breaks away from me. She looks into my eyes. She seems...worried.

"T-thanks. I'll, uh, talk to you later. Thanks again." Sandra hops off the stage and disappears into the darkness. I hear the door swing open and shut.

What did she see? Did I show too much? Oh, Christ, why'd I hug her? Why'd I get close? I should have been firm. I should have told her to soldier through. Fuck, what did she see?

I stand there in the spotlight, alone with the darkness and my doubts.

CHAPTER FIFTEEN

Jason Neary runs his thumb over his lips.

He can feel cracks forming on them. He licks them, rubbing his tongue on his blisters. The cuts are fresh. The bus was thirty minutes late today. He stood on the curb, shin-deep in snow, chin tucked into jacket. Snow whipped at his cheeks, sneaking down his collar. The bus shelter was full of businessmen staring at their newspapers. They didn't let Jason in. He stood there, shuddering and feeling his lips chap. He didn't want to call a cab. He didn't want to spend the money. He might need it down the road. You never know.

Jason coughs and feels phlegm rumble in his throat. He blows his nose into a tissue. His eyes are puffy and sore. He should have stayed home, but he didn't want to use up his sick day. He might really need it down the road. You never know.

Jason tosses his sticky tissue at the garbage bin. It bounces off the rim. Jason grabs a stack of papers on his desk and flips through them. An ad for a new pizzeria with free delivery. An electricity bill. An offer from a cable company. A heating bill. Car insurance. Penis enlargement. Better teeth. Better hair. Better life. On and on they go.

Jason tosses the pile away. Not even a postcard or a letter. Jason rubs his eyes and sniffs. He looks at the clock. The hour hand ticks past ten. Jason opens his notebook, flipping past pages of statistics, charts, and doodles. He parses through today's data. His reads rows and rows of numbers. He makes notes on the margins. Numbers recur over and over, always in the same order. Only on his eighth read-through does he realize he's been analyzing the same row.

Jason groans and wipes his nose. He shoves his pencil under the first number, digging into the paper. He focuses on it, zeroing in on the lead point. He slides it to the right, stopping at each digit, leaving behind a grey trail. It's his guide. He makes it down six columns when he has to look away, just for a moment, to rub his eyes. He looks back at the sheet. The numbers are blurred together, warped and distorted. He moved his pencil to the side without thinking. He's lost his place.

Jason pushes the notebook away and leans back in his chair, staring at the fluorescents. He fishes in his pocket and pulls out a bottle of pills. He reaches for his glass, but it's empty. Jason grumbles as he walks out of his cubicle with it. Jason walks by the aimless chatter. He hears mentions of "sales" and "figures" and "bottom lines." He doesn't peek into cubicles and or talk with passersby. He keeps his head down, pressing his glass close to his chest. He just wants to return to his cocoon.

A familiar voice greets his ears. He looks up. He's standing at a four-hallway intersection. The water cooler is right around the corner. Across from him is a cubicle. Its opening faces the intersection. Jason can see into the cubicle. He sees Donna. She's on the phone, smiling. Her hand is fluttering next to her face, exploding and contracting over and over. She's laughing. Jason can't pick out words; only a steady hum.

She doesn't notice him. He pictures her looking at him, tugging on his belt. He sees her dress fall to the floor. He sees her lying on her bed. He sees her smile, her hair, her eyes. He sees the things that sparked that flame, that primordial attraction. But these images are swallowed up by one thing, one sensation. Jason looks at Donna and all he can see are those two black pools.

Jason rounds the corner, fills up his glass, and retreats to his cubicle. He sits down, his face flushed. He sees those pools everywhere. He can't shake them. They consume him. He grabs a pill and downs it with a swig of water. He leans over his armrest, rubbing his temples. He can feel a headache starting to gestate. Another malfunction to add to the growing list. He's falling apart.

He shifts in his seat and hears something crumple. He looks down and sees the edge of a white paper sticking out from under his shoe. He moves his foot and squints. It's another letter. Must've fallen from the stack. It says, "Winner."

Jason feels a pang of excitement. He grabs the letter and tears it open with his teeth. He throws the envelope away and reads. It says he's a guaranteed winner. A week-long stay in Hawaii, a new car, a fresh batch of spending money, the whole meal deal. It's all his for the taking. He just has to mail in his credit information. They'll send him copies of this letter and he'll send them to his friends. That'll improve his chances of— Jason drops the letter on his desk. More junk. Nothing but scrap. And it excited him. It got his heart pumping. This cheap piece of advertising thrilled him. Jason stares at the letter. This gaudy chunk of merchandising exhilarated him. He hasn't felt a rush like it in weeks. This written scam woke him up. He felt...good, for at least a moment. He was present. All because of a disposable money trap. Reading it is a highlight of his week. Jason is terrified.

He throws the letter in the trash. He shrinks away from it. He grabs his notebook and pours over the numbers. He calls departments and asks for estimations. He writes and writes and writes. He keeps his eyes glued to his desk. He pushes the letter from his mind. He can't think about it. He ignores it. He focuses on his work. He loses himself in it. He drifts away. He forgets the letter. He doesn't even—He's staring at the letter. He rubs his knees and bites his lip. He holds his arms close to his chest. He feels something cold running up and down his spine. His stomach is queasy. Something's squeezing his head. He paces in a circle. He scratches his neck and cracks his fingers. He presses his head against the cubicle wall, moving it against the green fabric. He stares at the fluorescents, listening to the oppressive buzz. He stares down at the letter, feeling it gnaw away at him.

It's a meaningless slip of gibberish and Jason ate it up. He latched onto the smallest sliver of excitement. He scrambled for the tiniest sensation. Jason wants to vomit. He's been reduced to empty gratification. It's all he has left. Jason flicks his wrists and twiddles his fingers. His heart is plunging into his stomach.

He's getting woozy. He wants to leap out of his body. He wants to escape from it. He wants to escape…

He blinks. He glances at the letter and nods. His headache has faded. He has a moment of clarity. He knows what he has to do. It feels right. His hands are trembling. He can hear the buzz ringing in his ears. His heart is pounding. He has to do it.

Jason grabs his knapsack and jacket and runs out of the cubicle. He runs past the rows of offices and endless conversations. He runs past Mark readjusting his calendar. He runs past Sarah shoving a folder into her file cabinet. He runs past Paul loosening his tie and reaching for his medicine. None of them notice him. Jason stumbles over a bump in the carpet. He careens forward, landing on his jacket. Rug burn forms on his wrists. Someone pokes their head out of their cubicle. They offer to help. Their voice sounds familiar. Harold, maybe? Always a nice guy. Jason doesn't look at him. He scrambles to his feet and bolts down the hall.

He's about to round the corner when he notices Donna again. She's hunched over a folder, scribbling notes. She's humming a formless song. She brushes a strand of hair out of her face and parts her lips. Beautiful. Jason clutches his bag close and considers knocking on her cubicle. He steps forward. Jason could ask her to…

The phone rings. Donna answers it and unleashes a whirlwind of words. She's back in her own world. Jason watches her, hoping she'll hang up. She doesn't. He can't wait. He gives her a smile she doesn't see and he shoots around the corner.

Jason's bag and jacket slap against his pants, creating a fluttering noise, like a helicopter preparing to lift off. He reaches the elevator and jams the "down" button. An automated bell chimes. A light above him illuminates the number "3," then moves to "4." Jason's on the eighteenth floor. He hops from one foot to another, watching the light slowly crawl to his number before it stops at "16." It doesn't move. Jason dashes to the left and bursts through a door and into the stairwell.

He tears down flight after flight, watching windows and modern art pieces whirl past him. His footsteps echo around him. His legs wobble and buckle but he keeps going. He unbuttons his collar and loosens his tie. He emerges at the ground floor, coated in sweat. He rushes past the lobby security guard before he can finish saying "hello." He grabs the door handle and pauses. His body is tense. He could walk back...

Jason shoves the door open and walks into the harsh light. Sun reflects off mounds of snow, glaring into Jason's eyes. He shields them and looks around for...something. He darts his head around, bracing against the cold. He slips his jacket on and looks up and down the street. It's pretty quiet; most people are at work. It's alien without the bustling crowds.

Jason slides his knapsack over his shoulders. Every part of him is trembling. His stomach is doing somersaults. He has no idea where he's going.

Jason turns to the right and starts running.

CHAPTER SIXTEEN

I wipe the back of my neck, soaking my palm in sweat.

Dark stains have formed at my armpits and knees, growing larger and wetter with every minute. I'm drenched. Ken is even worse. Sweat drips from every part of his body. It looks like he's going to collapse into a cream-coloured puddle.

We shouldn't be out here. He should be inside, studying case notes with Greg or following leads. I should be in the garden, perched under some shade, meditating and planning for our future, sipping a cool glass of ice water. Instead we're walking around the compound. I have to be out here. People need to see me, need to be reassured. And I have to see them, have to connect with them. Gazing around the compound, I'm confronted with one inescapable fact:

I am surrounded by sloth.

Five builders are hauling a wooden log across the compound. They grunt and curse and shout. Their muscles and veins bulge as they hold the enormous weight. They inch along, readjusting their grip as the log slips from their sweaty hands. They glisten in the sun like bronze Greek gods. It's enough to make my heart swell. On a day this unbearably hot, they haven't forgotten their duties. They have a job to do and they're going to do it. On a day when I can barely walk around the compound without looking like a drenched mop, they're carrying enough weight to punch through a man's chest. It's inspiring, really. Despite Smit and the departures and everything else, I know my message still resonates. These men are the ideal.

Two men are trailing behind the log carriers. They're builders, clearly; I can tell from their clothes. But they're not carrying anything. Their hands are stuffed in their pockets. They move their in legs wide arcs, kicking away pebbles. They're strolling. While their co-workers are heaving a log that could

178

break their backs, these two jokers are lingering in the background. They're doing nothing to help. Worse than that: They're *laughing*. They're having a friendly little chat. The one on the right is moving his hands as if he's grabbing something while the one on the left is howling to the sky. They both clap and chuckle, slapping each other's backs. They bump into a planter, causing her to drop her bucket. They keep on walking. It's a parody to have these two loafers trail behind these Adonises. I feel ill.

I recognize these men. They're the ones who nearly decapitated me with that wooden board. I suppose I should be grateful they're not holding the log; they'd probably drop it on someone. They might be better off amusing their miniscule minds than helping anyone. But everyone has to pull their weight.

I step close to the men and cough. The men freeze, their faces stuck in mid-laugh. I walk between them, looking up and down. I grab their shoulders, forcing them to lean down. I bring my mouth close to their ears.

"Get to work." I feel their bodies quaking.

I shove them forward. They bump into each other and nearly tumble to the ground. Pathetic. I stab my finger at the lifters. The loafers nod and rush to help, seizing the back end. The group erupts into cheers.

I rub my temples. Baseline competence. That's all I ask for, at the end of the day. Self-sacrifice is a process, one we may never finish. I accept that. But I expect a little effort, a minimal display of competence. That's beyond these two yahoos. It's beyond a lot of people.

I study the compound. I see builders holding up beams with one hand while they yak it up with their co-workers. I see planters sitting at wells, feet propped on their buckets, enjoying the sun. I see people drifting from building to building when they should be moving like bullets. I see three people sitting in the grass, resting on each other's stomachs. These people move in slow motion, eclipsed by the actual workers. There's a gap

between the dedicated majority and the indolent minority.
They've forgotten where they are. I've noticed this behaviour in
the last few weeks. Ever since Smit stepped up his campaigns...

I'm grinding my teeth. My hands are white-knuckled. I
close my eyes and breathe, releasing the pressure. My mouth
droops open and my fingers unfurl. These tension attacks started
a few days ago. I was standing on the pulpit and I felt my body
go rigid. I had to crash my lecture mid-sentence just to get a hold
of myself. Ruined the flow. I've been seizing up daily. Every
time I think of Smit, it washes over me. Breathe. Just breathe.

I sit on the bench at the center square. Ken looms behind
me, casting a large shadow. I see more people talking and
laughing while their co-workers struggle. I see members darting
into the woods, looking for privacy. I see two planters leaning
against a building, whispering to each, glancing at a crumpled
piece of paper. Zaan propaganda? They spot me and disappear
around a corner. Traitors. Backstabbers who haven't summoned
the courage to flee. I'll have Greg keep tabs on them.

I put my head in my hands. The serpents are everywhere.
Zaan recruiters sit on the edge of our compound, ringing their
bells and hugging deserters. Ken chases them off but they always
return. Trespassers. I should ask the police to arrest them. Yeah,
that'll happen. I'll get Sheriff Blume to personally handle our
problem. He'd love to help. He's itching to lend a hand. Sure.

We're alone. No one's coming to stop the barbarians
pounding at our gate. Smit isn't going to have a change of heart
and reel back. He'll keep wailing on us until we crumple to the
floor or he passes out from exhaustion. But if we make the
slightest move to hit back, to land a big blow, to shut Smit up,
Blume will descend on us with his locust horde of trigger-happy
cops. We'll be carted off and Smit will swoop in to pick the
carcass clean. He knows we can't retaliate physically, nor do we
have the resources for an equally aggressive recruitment
strategy, so he's just going to jab our nose until we make a
mistake. We're stuck and he knows it.

Fuck, I want to smash his face beneath my shoe. I'd kick out his teeth and crush them as he watches. I'd- Breathe. Just breathe.

Patience. That's all we need. Wait for our next move. That's all we can do. We've got to take the punches and stay on our feet. Lean on the ropes until we can formulate a plan. "We." I'm talking like we're a tight-knit group of ragtag rebels. I can't discuss this with the compound; they'll panic. Or doubt. Or leave. This "we" is me, Ken, and Greg. We're all that's holding this place together.

Ken's picking dirt out of his fingernails. He's distracted. If something were to happen right now, something bad, he'd need a second to react. One whole second. In that second, the killer could sneak up and stab my chest. Or Blume could have us in handcuffs on trumped up charges. Or some traitor could pass out Zaan flyers like free condoms. Anything could happen, all because Ken is staring at his nails. I cough.

"We." There is no "we," no really. I can't depend on Ken and Greg. My trusted aides, my right and left hands, and I can't fully trust them. How can I? All the time they've had, all the resources they've had at their disposal, and they're nowhere near catching the killer. They've solved nothing. They can achieve any minute task, but when I need them, when everything's on the line, they shrug and twiddle their thumbs. Greg constantly questions my final plan. Ken embarrassed me in front of the devil incarnate (Smit). I'm alone. I'm the only one who can fix our problems. I have to stay afloat with all these weights dragging me to the seabed. They're all shackles on my body: Smit, Blume, Ken, Greg, and my followers.

My followers... What followers? This morning's sermon was anemic. I saw a dozen empty chairs. A dozen! One guy had free space on his right and left. He propped his feet up and lay on them like a couch. Insolence begets sloth. That's what I screamed as I dragged him onstage for a series of slaps. I made him confess to something trivial; I don't remember what. He slunk out of the hall afterwards, glaring at me. I probably made an enemy today. I wasn't even mad at him, not really. I was mad at those empty chairs. But I couldn't very well take my aggression out on sculpted wood. Even I would have a hard time selling that to my followers. I just needed to hit something.

A dozen followers. A dozen people spat in my face and walked away. These missing members weren't late, or helping in the field, or on a spiritual camping trip. Hell, I'd settle for them simply being lazy. I checked the sheets with Greg and inspected the bunks with Ken: They were gone. I found a flyer of Smit's smug face stuffed under one of their pillows.

The sermon crowd could feel the lack of attendance. Their clapping was shorter and their chants were quieter. Their enthusiasm was a dim echo of better speeches. A month ago they were stomping their feet and braying for blood. Now, when they notice a couple rats leaving the ship, they shrink into themselves. That's not what I've taught them. They need to rise above this mutiny. I should tailor my next few speeches around commitment. That should send the right message...

I drag my hands down my face. It's not supposed to be like this. I'm surrounded doubt. It's all wrong. I should be preparing for the final step, the great leap above. Instead, I'm fretting over petty betrayals and an invisible murderer.

Everything feels...off, like it's a step out of tune. We could see the finish line and our legs snapped. Now we're crawling to the end, trying to return to our feet. This disorder was not what I was promised, what we were promised. Is it a sign? Am I being told something? Am I just wro—

Sandra.

She's standing in the slim shade of a building, pressed against its wall. She's fanning her face with her hand, blowing hair out of her face. She arcs her back, pushing her chest forward. She stands on her toes and cranes her neck. She holds this pose, frozen in a perfect stretch, every muscle tensed. She's a statue. It's perfection.

There's only the two of us. The compound is background noise. Ken slides away. I lean back, admiring

Sandra. Muscles without bulk. Attractive but not glamorous. Loyal while still able to think. Dedicated, not reckless. The ideal follower, captured in the right moment. It's an image only I can see, only I can appreciate.

She falls to the balls of her feet and wipes her face. The compound comes roaring back. I hear Ken cough. I cling to the image in my mind.

Sandra rotates her wrists and flexes her fingers. She bends down and picks up a crate filled with soil. She props it on her thigh and grips it close to her waist. A builder stops in front of her and strikes up a conversation. He's laughing. She smiles and nods, moving away from the building. The builder holds up a piece of paper and waves it in Sandra's face. Her smile drops. She brushes past him, elbowing him in the gut. He slides the paper on top of her soil and strolls away. She storms across the compound. She rounds a corner and disappears.

I should check in on her. See how she's dealing with the whole Spittal...thing. And I need her to know last night was a...mistake. I was off. That hug was unbecoming of me. She needs to know that. She needs to not tell anyone about it. I have to make sure she doesn't. Safety first.

I stand up and dust my pants. Ken snaps to alert. I shake my head and point across the compound.

"I'm going to talk with a member. Alone." I hold up one finger.

"You sure? I should be with you. Because of...everything going on. You shouldn't be alone. You might run into...him." Ken leans forward and makes a stabbing motion. It's the middle of the day, we're in the centre of a crowded town, and he's too afraid to even say "killer." I'm a dead man.

"The killer?" Ken flinches and scans the compound. Oh, I'm definitely a dead man.

"I very much doubt he'll strike during the day. He's probably in the woods masturbating over murder fantasies. That's where you're needed: In there, looking for him." I spread my arms over the forest.

"What if this member is the...killer? He could be anybody. You could be walking into a trap." Ken wrings his hands. He's making me anxious.

"Then she'll put me out of my misery. No more worries." I throw my hands up. Ken looks horrified.

"I'm joking, I'm joking. I'll be fine, I promise. Don't worry. If anyone attacks me, I'll come running to find you." I squeeze Ken's shoulder and offer a forced smile.

"I'm coming with you. It's too risky." Ken shakes his head.

"No, you're staying here. Better yet, go help Greg with his leads. Or do another search in the woods." I put my hands on Ken's chest and push him back. I barely move him.

"Are you sure? I could—" Ken approaches me with his palms up, practically begging.

"Yes, I'm positive. Get to work with something else. I'll see you later." I'm striding across the compound before Ken can respond. I hear him kick the dirt. He doesn't follow me. Loyal, at least.

I reach the corner Sandra rounded and stop. I part my hair from my face and smooth out my shirt. I wipe the sweat from my cheeks. I clear my throat. After last night, I can't look...foolish. I turn the corner.

Sandra' is surrounded by empty water cans. Her crate of soil is nearby, half full. A miniature windmill make a small creaking sound as it spins. The air is thick with the smell of dirt and bugs. Sandra is kneeling in a soil patch. She's tugging at the ground, grunting and cursing. I move closer. Her hair's bunched up. Her clothes are filthy. Her arms bulge as the pull up and down, trying to lift something from the dirt. She's the picture of perseverance. A solitary figure toiling in the ground, bending it to her will. Struggling to achieve her goal. She's the image of—

Something hits my face.

I stagger backwards, letting out a yelp I immediately suppress. I touch my face and feel a lump. My palm is covered in

dirt. There's a mangled collection of weeds lying on the ground.
I look at the sky. Is it a sign? Am I—

"Oh, fuck, I'm sorry." Sandra's wiping her pants clean
and walks to me, wincing.

I blink. She reaches at my face. Her hands are coated in
dirt and grime. I step back, rubbing the soil off my face. I see it
fall to the ground, but I can still feel it clinging on to me.

"No, you didn't get all of it. Let me…" Sandra points at
my chin.

"I got it, I got it." I run my hand down my face, picking
at dirt flecks with my fingers.

"Here, try this." Sandra pulls out a cloth from her
pocket, dunks it in a water bucket, wrings it out, and holds it in
front of me.

I smear the cloth on my cheeks and rub it under my chin.
I swipe it on my nose and around my eyes. It's a dark swirl of
brown now. I toss it back to Sandra. She pockets it.

"I'm so sorry. I didn't see you. I was pulling so hard on
that weed, when it got loose it just flew out of my hand. I'm
sorry. I'm really sorry." She's grimacing.

"Worse things have happened. I'm grateful you weren't
weeding coconuts." I wave my hand and fake laugh at my
terrible joke. Sandra doesn't join me, but she looks relieved.

She's covered head to toe in soil. I know I still have dirt
patches on my face. I can picture the whole thing from Sandra's
perspective. Looking up and seeing your leader, the man who's
promised you salvation, get smacked in the face with a bundle of
weeds. This figure from the pulpit, this larger-than-life person,
standing before you looking like he just took a mud bath.

I laugh. A real laugh this time. Sandra raises her
eyebrows. I can't speak through my chuckles, so I simply point
at my face. My laughter grows and Sandra joins me. Two people
standing in a garden, laughing at a dirt slap.

Our laughter trails off. Sandra smiles and I mirror her.
We stare at each other. There's only the sound of buzzing flies. I

have this feeling in my gut, but I can't translate it through my mouth. I just stand there. Sandra rubs her neck and looks away.

"Well, again, I'm sorry. Next time I'll watch where I'm throwing." Sandra closes one eye, holds her arm to her face, and looks down it like the barrel of a gun.

"Yeah, and I'll try to have faster reflexes." I grab an invisible weed from the air and clutch it close to my stomach. We chuckle.

"I'd better get back to work..." Sandra jabs her thumb at the garden.

"Can I help?" The words are out of my mouth before I think about them. Something about her makes me want to stay,

"Are you sure? Don't you have...leadership duties or something?" Sandra nods to the compound.

"We won't fall apart if I take a few minutes off. Besides, I haven't gotten my hands dirty in a while. I should earn my keep." I roll up my sleeves. What am I doing?

"Well, I could always use some help. But are you sure they don't need you out there?" Sandra kneels down in the garden.

"Tell you what: If we hear an explosion and screams accompanied by hellfire in the sky, I'll drop the weeds and get to work." I approach Sandra, wearing a big smile.

"Sounds good. Alright, take a knee." Sandra moves to the side and pats the ground. I join her in the garden.

"You've weeded before?" Sandra brushes dirt away from a weed's base.

"I've dabbled." I scan the garden for a good starting point.

"Then bon appétit." Sandra seizes a weed and pulls.

I put my legs behind me for a stronger stance. I hunch over a swath of weeds, searching for weak-looking ones. I see feeble strand poking through the ground. I wriggle my fingers and loom over the weed. I grab it and yank.

It slips out of my hand. I jerk back, landing on my ass on my feet. Leaves and weed flecks stick to my palm. The weed is barely out of the ground. Sandra giggles. My face reddens.

I lunge forward, burrowing deep into the weed's roots. I wrap my fingers around it, feeling my nails gather dirt. I pull. My muscles tense and flex. It's stuck hard in the earth. I grunt and snort. I tear through the ground. I press my free hand on the top soil for support. I raise the root up inch by inch. Its roots snap and break in my hand. The surrounding soil tumbles away as I drag it up like a stubborn newborn. I give one final yank and feel its ties give way. I hold this evil fucking weed in my dirt-covered hand, panting and smiling. I turn to Sandra. She's moved ahead of me. A pile of five weeds rests beside her.

I drop my smile and wipe my forehead. I toss the weed on the stack and move on to the next one. It surrenders faster than the first. I throw it away and crawl forward. I plunge my hand into the earth, grab a root, pull, toss, and move on. Over and over and over. It's therapeutic. A simple solution to a simple problem.

I mow through the weeds, throwing them over my shoulder as I advance down the garden. Grab, tear, toss, move, grab, tear, toss, move. My hand is stained with soil. My pants have brown streaks running down them. I don't think they'll ever wash off. My sweaty face attracts endless flies. The sun bears down on me. I should be miserable. But I'm fine. I feel...calm.

It's just me, Sandra, and an army of weeds. I don't have to fight for meaning or purpose; I see a weed, I destroy it. End of story. No one's breathing down my neck or sinking a knife into my back; it's all simple. No thinking, no doubt, just work. I yank out a particularly tough weed and survey the garden. This place is what I've always preached about: Pure work. No bullshit, no distractions, no temptations; there's only you and a job. You're not bogged down with a television set or sex or prescription drugs. You're finally you, no strings attached, no additional description. You boil your life to its raw essentials and you're left with something...perfect. This garden is what everyone should strive for.

I've missed this feeling. I've let myself slip away. I've spoken the words but I haven't lived them. I've tumbled into disarray. That's why everything's been so off balance; I've been out of sorts. I needed to re-center myself. I needed this garden. I'm ready to—

"I'm sorry."

I look up from the weeds. Sandra's kneeling at the end of the garden. Her row is a massacre of tangled roots and gaping holes. She's staring at me. I tilt my head.

"What for?" I wipe a layer of dirt from my hands.

"For last night. It was...inappropriate." Sandra bites her lip.

"Inappropriate?" I inch closer.

"Yeah. Coming to you in the middle of the night, right after your big session with George. Rambling on about my life. Giving you a, a..." The word is stuck in Sandra's mouth.

"A hug?" I offer a smile. Sandra gives a curt nod.

"Yeah, that. And then I just fucked off. I wasted your time and I...crossed a line when I touched you. I don't know why I did it. It was... I'm sorry." Sandra bows her head.

She truly is the ideal follower. She's repentant over a hug. She believes she's violated something sacred, something holy. I'm flattered. Reverence tinged with fear. It's beautiful. And yet...I'm not proud. I see a true believer crippled by fear. She's overwhelmed by it, smothered in it. She's trembling, unable to look me in the eye. Other members need a firmer hand, a strong reminder of their position. But Sandra knows her place. She needs a break. She's had enough of the stick; she deserves the carrot.

"There's nothing to apologize for. I fucked up." I sit down, leaning back on my hands.

Sandra looks up at me and squints. I give her a smirk and shrug. I gaze at the sky, watching a cloud drift into another.

"I was exhausted last night. I had just finished a long session with Mr. Carr. I was on my last nerve. I was ready to collapse in my bed. Then you showed up." The clouds merge together.

"You had a problem, a genuine problem. You needed someone who could listen. Someone who could give you real advice. That wasn't me, not last night. I was useless." The clouds are now one. I look at Sandra. She's crawled next to me.

"I should apologize. You needed something real last night and I gave you bland platitudes. You reached out and I let you down. I screwed up. I—" Stop. Don't go into your life story. You're still her superior. That's enough carrot for one day.

"I just want to apologize. And I want you to know I'm always here to talk." I put my hand on Sandra's thigh.

"Thank you. That means...a lot." Sandra pats my hand.

I feel my fingers sink into the soft ground. I could fall backwards and let it swallow me whole. A good way to go. When I die, I want them to bury me in a garden. I want them to dig a hole and throw my naked corpse in it. I want the earth to consume me.

"Move over." Sandra brushes past me and starts pulling out weeds from another row.

I finish my row, letting the final weed roll into the grass. Roots, soil, and rocks cling to my clothes. I look at my trail of carnage and smile. I stretch my back and put my hands on my hips. I see a small stone at the end of my row. It's no bigger than my fist. There's some writing on it. The words are jagged and scratched. I lean in close. It says, "Henry Spittal: A man."

"You found my tribute." Sandra is standing over me.

I raise my eyebrows. She's tearing the roots off a weed. She tosses it aside and crouches beside me. She licks her thumb and rubs it over the engraving. She's silent as she stares at it.

"For Mr. Spittal?" I tap the top of the stone.

Sandra nods. More silence. She looks into the forest. I straighten my back, adjust my shirt, and twiddle my fingers. The stone is slightly off kilter. I nudge it to the side, centering it. Sandra turns to me.

"When I left you last night, I didn't sleep. I just at in my bed and looked at that flyer. I read it over and over and over. I finally accepted it: Henry's gone. I need to move on. But I still had this hole in my gut. I still didn't feel anything about him. I wanted that to change." Sandra picks up the stone and rotates it.

"I went down to the river and found this beauty. Grabbed a chisel and carved out Henry's tombstone. I know he's alive, but not to me. He's a ghost. This marker is all that's left of him here. Every time I work here, I'll see this stone and I'll remember him. Maybe I'll reflect, or ignore it, or get angry. Maybe I'll feel something. A rock memento. Who knows, it might make me nostalgic." Sandra plants the stone back in the ground.

"Does that make any sense?" She looks at me.

"Whatever helps." I grip her shoulder.

Sandra smiles. I let my hand fall away. She stands up. I stay in the dirt.

"Sorry for the melodrama. Had to tell someone, you know? Don't really have anyone to..." Sandra glances at a path leading to rest of compound.

"We all need some melodrama now and then. Keeps things interesting. Hell, I've made a career out of melodrama." I close my mouth. I've revealed too much. Again.

Sandra grabs a root protruding from the ground. I look at the stone. It's leaning backwards, its writing facing the sky. I notice something white sticking out beneath it. I glance over my shoulder. Sandra's still engrossed with her weed. I raise the stone and grab the white object. Paper.

I pull it out and put the stone back. I hunch over so Sandra can't see me. The paper is dirty and torn, folded into oblivion. I carefully unravel it, watching it expand. It's blank. I turn it over. It's a Zaan poster. There's a red "X" drawn over it. It's covered in puncture marks. Smit's eyes have been stabbed out.

Sandra's coping; she's not forgiving.

CHAPTER SEVENTEEN

The goddamn dirt won't come out of my fingernails.

I hold my hands in the basin. Hot water circles down the drain. I stretch the skin under my nails, exposing the soil to the liquid. I pick away at the grime, but small bits are firmly stuck beneath my nails. They won't budge. I've been standing here for ten minutes. Steam rises from the basin. My skin is turning bright red. My fingertips are prunes. And the fucking dirt still won't come out. Next time I work in the garden, I'm wearing gloves.

I turn the water off and flick my hands dry. I look in the mirror. The face I see is exhausted, bleary, and worn out, but those eyes could cut steel. I part my hair to the side and adjust my collar. This is the face people see every morning. This is the face that's leading them to salvation. A few hints of grey hair, and those bags under the eyes have to go, but this face has still got it. It's a face you could slap on a poster or put on a podium. It's the face of a leader. I'd follow it to Hell.

I pluck loose strands from my eyebrows and tilt my head up to inspect my neck. I open my mouth and bare my teeth, looking for stains and food flecks. Somewhere in the background, Greg is talking.

"...Ken asked around, without raising suspicion, of course, and he didn't find anything. I found nothing new on Spittal. It's been a nightmare trying..."

Same old story. We've got nothing to go on. We're stumbling in the dark looking for a candle while we hope we don't stumble off the cliff. Maybe we'll get a lucky break. Maybe our killer was a one-timer. He could be halfway across the country now, praying for forgiveness in a flea-motel. One can dream.

It doesn't matter. Right now, we've got more pressing concerns. I run my tongue over my top teeth, rub my cheeks, and give myself a wink. I face Greg.

"What about our preparations?" I grip the basin and lean back.

Greg looks up from the folders on his desk. I don't think he's gotten more than three hours of sleep at a time in the last week. He's always hunched over his files or talking with Ken or inspecting Spittal's corpse for the umpteenth time. He barely eats and never attends sermons. He wouldn't waste time breathing if he didn't need it to live.

Greg takes his glasses off and pulls a new folder from underneath the desk. He stands up, cracking his neck and back. He stares at me, considering his words. Not a good sign.

"Sir, I think we should reconsider this...event." Greg steps forward.

I rub my eyes. Again with this shit. All these knives embedded in our gut and he wants to wait while we bleed out.

"Greg, we've been over this..." I try to keep the edge out of my voice. I don't succeed.

"I know, I know, you're absolutely right. I'm not doubting you this time, I promise. I want to go through with it. But..." Greg holds his finger in the air.

"Incredible how a thousand excuses can come from that one word." I roll my eyes.

"But it's the timing, sir. The timing's all wrong." Greg shakes his head.

I push off the basin and walk to Greg. He's crushing that folder in his hand. I can almost hear him trembling. But he's staring me straight in the eyes. I should listen to what he has to say before I chew him out, at least.

"What's wrong with the timing?" I tap the watch on his wrist.

Greg steps back and rubs his temples. He paces in front of me, never looking away. He grimaces and sighs. His skull looks like it's trying to escape its skin. I cough. He snaps his fingers and opens the folder, shoving it under my nose.

It's incomprehensible. There are drawings and charts and pages and pages of writing. There are photos of Spittal, Smit, the Zaan compound, Sheriff Blume, ex-members, and me on the pulpit. Greg flips the pages too fast for me to absorb anything.

"I've been compiling a, a...a list of everything that's been going on. Ever since Spittal died. I've kept track of everything. It's all here, all in this folder, all of it." Greg keeps stabbing the folder with his finger, nodding at me.

"What's all there?" I resist the urge to grab him by the shoulders.

"I didn't think it was so bad at first. I wrote down every event and put it in the back of my mind. I just focused on the killer and the ceremony. That's all I cared about. But I went through this folder yesterday and I can't put it down. I see everything laid out. It's clear as day. I can't believed I missed it. But I see it now. I see it all." Greg's eyelids and fingers won't stop moving.

"See what?" I'm using all my willpower to restrain myself.

"We can't go through with the ceremony." Greg stands still.

He lets the words linger in the air. I shake my head. Can I go one day with doubters hounding me? Can I not even have that from my right-hand man?

"We have to go through with it. That's why we're here. It's the whole point." Each word crawls out of my mouth.

"I know, of course it is. I'm not saying we should never do it. I'm all for it. I'll be the first in line when it happens. But I think we should postpone the ceremony. At least until—" Greg pulls out a sheet from his folder.

"No, we can't wait. We're not going to postpone anything. We picked out this date years ago. It's important. The ceremony has to happen on that day. We can't change it." I slash my hand through the air.

"Does it have to be on that day? I mean, whenever it happens, the results are the same, right? We're all going to get there, no matter when we do it. We could wait for ideal circumstances. We have to be patient. It's not the right time. What's wrong with holding off on it until we—" Greg approaches me, and I hold my hand up.

"We're. Not. Changing. Anything. I chose this date for a reason. It's not some throwaway third-tier holiday; it's everything. It's what we've been building towards all these years. It's the punctuation mark. I will not turn it into a comma because you're uncomfortable. We have a deadline and we will meet it. I don't care if there's a storm, a police raid, or thunderbolts from Zeus himself; the ceremony is happening on that day. Am I clear?" I loom over Greg.

He backpedals, nodding and looking at the ground. His hands are limp at his sides. I cross my arms and puff out my chest. I suppress a grin. Another bomb defused. Now back to—

Greg mutters something. He flexes his fingers and jerks his head up. His eyes are burning. I open my mouth but he beats me to it.

"Sir, I understand all of that, and I respect it. Believe me, I absolutely agree. We should be allowed to go forward on that day. But, please, hear me out." Greg puts the folder back in my hands.

I grunt and open it up again. More images of Smit's smirking face and Blume's mustachioed scowl and Spittal's gory neck. An endless barrage of quickly-jotted reports packed into the margins. I flip through it, pretending to read. I try to close the folder, but Greg stops me.

"Please, sir, just look at this part." Greg runs through folder and stops at a double-spread.

It's a diagram. Actually, that's a generous description. It's a fifth-grade collage with arrows. Photos of Smit, Blume, Henry's body, former members, and a blank face with a question mark over it are glued to the paper. All the pictures have lines directed at the page's heart. Right in the middle, there's a photo of our compound. And right in the center of that photo, there's me.

"What is this?" I raise my eyebrows at Greg.

"A powder keg." He comes to my side, looking at the folder from over my shoulder.

I can feel his breath on my neck. He reaches under my arm to hold the folder. He licks his lips, spraying spit on my cheek. I feel the bile rising in my throat.

"Okay, okay, I know this whole thing doesn't make a lot of sense on its own. I get that. But let's think this through. Let's really think about this. Let's start with him." Greg presses his thumb over the question-mark face.

"We have no idea where he is or who he is. We don't even know if he is a "he." He's a ghost. He could be anyone. We don't know when he's going to strike again. He's got all the cards.

"So, let's say we go through the ceremony and we haven't found him. We decide to let him go. We're done with him. But what if he's not done with us? What if he shows up at the ceremony? What if he tries to ruin it? What if he...taints it somehow? He could hack us at the knees. All our hard work, all our effort, all our sacrifice, and he could destroy it like—" Greg snaps his fingers.

"I doubt he could do much damage. One man, even one we can't see coming, doesn't stand much of a chance against hundreds of people. If he appears at the ceremony, Ken will snap him in half before he touches anyone. That's why we keep him around, right? Hell, it might even make for some good drama." I scratch at the question mark.

"But what if he isn't so blunt? What he tries to burn us alive? Or plant landmines around us? Or—?" Greg's breathing is very rapid.

"If he could do any of that, he would have done so already. I'm certain he lacks the budget for landmines or flamethrowers. He's strictly small scale. We can handle him." I flick the question mark.

"But what if he—?" Greg is yelling in my ear.

"Then we'll cross that bridge when we get there. Christ." I jerk away from Greg and he stumbles forward, clutching the folder.

I collect myself, masking my anger. All these questions, all this paranoia; he's only stirring himself up. He's even put me on edge. He's wrong. The killer won't spoil our day. It's too important for him to sully. We'll be fine. I'm certain.

"Alright, alright, I understand. Fair enough. Let's say the killer doesn't bother us during the ceremony and we go through with it. When they find us, they'll see our message and be inspired. They'll see the truth. And then they'll find Spittal's body. Or maybe the killer will come forward with a confession. And they'll ask a lot of questions. Wrong questions. Questions that will dirty our name. Questions that will muddy our message." Greg's eyes are widened like a saucers.

I see the scene he's painting. Police tape. Flashing bulbs and sirens. Reporters and citizens jostling at barriers around the compound. Detectives finding us. Beat cops uncovering Spittal's corpse, uncovering evidence of the killer. Everyone drawing the same conclusion, wiping over us with one brush. Everyone walking away, sliding us into the criminal file. Our compound abandoned. Our message obscured. Our efforts forgotten. All because of one man.

"...Keep going." I nod at Greg.

"If people find us, they think we're martyrs. We're inspirational. If people find Spittal's body, if they find out a killer stalked the compound, we're murder victims. People will look down on us and forget we existed. No one will learn from us. We'll be dust." Greg whistles.

I see my body being examined by a coroner. Spittal is lying next to me. They think we died for the same reason. They tag me and stuff me in a freezer with me. No one reads my words. They think I was one victim of many.

"And that's assuming we get any media attention. What if Blume finds us first?" Greg taps on the punch-able face of our dogged Sheriff.

"What if he discovers us in the cave? What if he learns about Spittal and the killer? We'll be lucky to reach the coroner. No one will hear about us. He'll tell his boys not to bother the town about us. He'll ship us off to the cemetery and throw us in the ground. No fanfare, just a dirt nap. Then he'll put our home up for auction. The real vultures will come out. And you know which one has the biggest appetite." Greg points to Smit.

I picture Smit strolling through our compound. He'll walk into my office and take my robe. He'll have his goons go door-to-door, swiping whatever souvenirs they can carry. They'll walk to the compound edges and watch a bulldozer crush everything we've built. Smit will smile. Bile is churning in my throat.

"If we go through with the ceremony now, with all our enemies holding knives to our neck, we'll be eviscerated. They'll erase us." Greg snaps his folder shut.

He's right. We're stranded on a cliff with wolves salivating all around us. If we throw ourselves off the cliff, we'll still be torn to shreds. We'll be a forgotten stain on the rocks.

Greg steps aside as I walk past him. I can smell the confidence on him. He knows he's convinced me. He knows he's kept us away from the slaughterhouse. He's probably got alternate plans written up. I'd be irritated if he wasn't right.

I approach my robe. It's hanging on the wall next to the door. It's damp and cold, with drops of water trickling down its lines. It was coated in sweat after the sermon today. Even with a mediocre crowd, I threw myself around the stage, screaming and jumping. Someone had to raise the energy in the room. I rinsed the robe in the river, wrung it dry, and hung it here. I squeeze one of its sleeves, feeling water seep onto my hand. Dry patches are spreading on its chest and shoulders. It looks... presentable. I could wear it outside and no one would know I drenched it my body fluids this morning. They'd see a clean robe. But that's not what I see.

I see every sweat stain from an hour-long sermon in the boiling summer heat. I see the dark circles that look like swimming pools around the armpits and stomach. I see the flecks of blood on the collar and sleeves from the time I knelt over a follower as he jerked his head up and smashed my nose. I see other blood marks on the cuffs, leftovers from followers whose faces opened up when they received the Honour, spraying themselves over my knuckles and clothes. I rubbed the blood off on their shoulders. They thanked me.

I turn the robe over and see a large blood stain that stretches across the shoulders and leaks down the spine. I was swimming in the river and lost track of the current. It pushed me against the shore, dragging my back along the rocks, slicing open my skin. I crawled my way to my robe and slipped it on. My back was aching, but I powered through. I walked around the compound, greeting people, talking with them. It wasn't until I reached the fields that someone pointed out the crimson blotch growing on my robe. I soaked the clothes and patched up the wound. I had no idea it was so deep. While I walked, I could my robe getting damp, but I kept going.

I let the robe fall back to the wall. I see the spit residue from overwhelmed followers as they blubbered all over me. I see dirt and grass stains from when I helped the builders haul a boulder up a hill and into the center square, all so I could deliver a sermon on top of it. I see the wrinkles and tears made by the grubby hands of anxious followers. I see every mark, every spot, every imprint of this robe.

I stand back. It's magnificent. More than that; it's a reminder. People have devoted their lives to this place. They've given everything to a higher cause. I can't let any outside threats derail us. We have a schedule to keep.

Greg's rifling through his desk, probably searching for his backup plans. He's barely suppressing a grin. I almost hate to deflate him. Almost.

"Greg, thank you for your concerns, but we're going through with the ceremony on time." I clap my hands and walk to the sink, reaching for a glass. I fill it up and drink it down. I wipe my face and slam the glass on the counter. I look at Greg. His mouth is agape and his eyes narrowed. A file is in his hand, halfway in a desk drawer.

"My decision is final, Greg. We're going through with it, no matter what's happening out there." I point at the door.

"B-but, but, sir, the message, our message, no one will hear it. The killer, Smit, Blume, all that noise. We'll get lost in the, in the shuffle. No one will..." Greg scrambles for his original folder.

"I can't let anyone interfere with our destiny. No matter how distasteful I find all three of those...cretins, I can't dedicate our resources to making sure they can never hurt us. I have to focus on our plan. I have to bring the people what they want." I sit behind my desk.

"I, I understand that, sir, but what about our message? No one will hear it. It'll be white noise. We'll be..." Greg thumbs through the folder.

"I don't care about our message." I shrug.

"...What?" Greg blinks.

"I'm here to save everyone in this compound. You, Ken, the followers; those are my concerns. I want to save as many people as I can, without a doubt. The more the merrier. But I'm not sacrificing our hard work so the public can understand us. If they wanted to find the truth, they'd be here. When we're gone, anyone who wants to hear us, really hear us, will cut through the noise. They'll pick up the cause. And I wish them the best. But I will not postpone our ceremony so people will be more receptive. I'm concerned with now, not then." I rap my knuckles on the desk.

"I, I see, sir. That makes...sense. We need to worry about the present. But you still want to send a message, yes?" Greg's eyelids flutter.

"Of course. It's a secondary goal, but it's still an important one. We need to continue our work after we're gone." I nod, giving up an inch of ground.

"Then shouldn't we make sure it resonates the clearest to even the smallest audience? I know you don't want to postpone the ceremony. But if we could...adjust the timetable and make...exceptions for our current circumstance, we could broadcast ourselves to the world. We could—" Greg clenches and unclenches his fists, grasping at invisible straws. Time to rein him in.

"If we want to make our message ring out, we'll have to catch the killer before our ceremony. Maybe you and Ken could have done it by now if you weren't wasting time finding excuses to postpone our event." I scrape my nails on the desk.

"Sir, we're trying our best. We've never dealt with something like this before..." Greg winces.

"I know that, Greg. I don't mean to insult you. But there is one simple solution to all our problems: We catch the son of a bitch. If we...dispose of the killer, the police won't assume we were killed, the media will hear our message loud and clear, and Smit won't be able to swoop in on such a venerated site. We'll have a clean slate." I spread my arms over the desk.

"You're right, sir, absolutely correct. But I don't know if we can catch him in time. We don't have any leads. We're stumbling in the dark. I don't know if we..." Greg bites his lip. His eyes are watering.

I resist the urge to roll my eyes. I drum my fingers, watching Greg fidget and moan. I put my hands on his shoulders and squeeze them.

"Greg, I wouldn't want anyone else working on this case but you and Ken. I have complete faith that you'll find this slime under whatever rock he's hiding. This whole debacle will be just another notch in your belt. You'll bring him to face our justice and we'll be on our way. You'll be a hero, I'm sure of it. I'm know you'll..." I lather on the compliments for a few more minutes. I don't really hear myself.

"Thank you, sir. We won't let you down." Greg nods, rubbing the corners of his eyes.

"I'm sure you won't." I pat his cheek.

Greg returns to his desk and rearranges the folders. He drops one and ducks below a drawer. I crack my neck and stretch my back. I need some fresh air. After that debate, I have to recharge my brain. It's always mentally draining to debunk Greg's research.

"I'll be in the garden if you need me." I tap Greg's desk.

I push the door open and stagger into the sunlight. It's a cloudless day. I can't hear any workers or gossipers or doubters. It's just me and the plants.

I let the warmth wash over me, tilting my head to sky. I spread my arms wide. I can already feel my muscles loosening up. I take a deep breath, swallowing every smell, every taste, from this moment. I feel the heat flowing through me. I exhale and open my eyes. Peace.

I walk to the center of the garden, brushing my hands over plants and flowers. I'll water them in a moment. I want to savour this feeling a little bit longer. I look at the ground for a spot to meditate.

Two bodies are lying at my feet.

They're two men, both builders. One has a beard, the other is clean-shaven. I've seen them in sermons before. Their clothes are smeared with dirt and mud. Their eyes are closed. Maybe they're taking a nap. Yes, that must be it…

I clap my hands. They don't budge. I slam my hands again, holding them above the men's faces. Nothing. Deep sleepers, that's all. A couple of narcoleptics. I crouch down. I'm shaking. Stop it. They're fine. I poke the bearded man's face, pressing my finger into his cheek. Cold. He doesn't move.

My heart is speeding away from me. I lick my lips and steady my hands. I reach out to the clean-shaven one, putting my thumbs on his eyelids. Chilled. I pull the lids up. His eyes are staring at the sky. They don't move.

No. No, no, no, no, no. I scramble to the bearded one
and open his eyes. They look past me, hollow and distant, gazing
into the clouds. I fall back into the ground.

My mouth is hanging open. No words come out, no
screams, no shouts; just a thin rasp. I cover it anyway. I squeeze
my hand around my jaw, trying to contain...something. I'm
going to explode. My body is convulsing. I'm going to sink into
the dirt. My hand won't let air escape my mouth. The back of my
brain is yelling at me to let go, but it's muffled behind static. I
can only hear one thought: Don't move your hand.

Red streams out from the bodies, pooling around their
necks and backs. It creeps towards me. I backpedal, kicking dirt
and rocks away. The blood flows out in every direction, forming
a circle around the bodies. It keeps going, touching the plants,
tainting them. It's rushing at me…

No. Focus. The blood's not moving. It's dry and crusted.
It never reached me or the plants. It created a crimson outline
around the bodies. It's not devouring me. Focus.

My hand doesn't budge from my mouth.

The bodies form an "X." The bearded one is splayed
over the clean-shaven one's stomach, his back curved into a
deformed arc. The bearded one's arms are stretched towards a
pot of flowers. His hands are clasped together. His legs are
straight, positioned over a clump of weeds. His shoes are
missing. His chipped toenails are pointing at me. I move to the
side.

The clean-shaven one is laid out in the exact same way.
His hands lead into a decimated flower bed while his shoeless
feet gesture down a path. Nobody dies like this. This was
deliberate. These men were killed somewhere else and dragged
in here. It's not murder; it's a deranged art piece.

I rise to my feet. I pry my hand from my face and wipe
the sweat from my palm and mouth. I stare at the bodies, and the
blood, and the clothes, and the limbs, and the faces. I stare at the
eyes. Empty pools lost in the sky. I'm watching myself look at
them. I'm above the garden for a moment, a detached observer.

It hasn't hit me yet. My brain is still trying to process everything. I know what's happened, but I can't accept it. I'm removed.

I know it can't last. I can feel the horror seeping into my head. I'm falling from the sky, inching closer back into the moment. I can't fight it. I take one step forward, just to get a good look at the bodies, and reality wallops me like a freight train.

Holy fucking shit, holy fucking shit, two bodies, two fucking bodies in my garden. Oh, fuck, oh, fuck, oh, fuck. How'd they get in here? I didn't hear anything last night. Did they get in when I was out today? Christ, did they sneak in here in broad daylight? Nobody saw anything? No, no, no way, they had to have come in here last night. That must be it. I have been in here for... Oh, fuck, I haven't been here for a week. No goddamn time for it. They could've been here for days and I didn't notice. Two corpses in my backyard and I didn't have a clue. Fuck me. Who did it? Who could've-? Oh, shit, it had to have been... Oh, fuck, no.

I spin around, holding my arms up in defense. I pivot my neck in every direction, scanning the tall plants for...him. I press my hand over my beating heart and tear through the garden, shoving aside flowers and greenery. I brace for a knife through the ribs that never comes. I run around the garden, looking for any hint of him. I strain my ears for the faintest hiccup. I return to the bodies and lean over my knees, catching my breath. No killer here.

I wipe my forehead and examine the bodies. The killer slaughtered them, dragged them into my backyard, put them in a pose, and sauntered away with no one seeing him. How the fuck did he do it?

I chew on my thumb and walk to the fence. The forest looms over me, its shadows heightened by the beaming sun. It seems to stretch on forever, endless corridors of darkness. He murdered these men in there and threw them in here. It wouldn't have taken more than five minutes. He could slink out of there at any moment. He could force the door open and enter my office.

He could stroll into my bedroom and stand over me. He could wrap his hands around my throat...

I back away from the fence. My mind is stretching to a million different possibilities. I can't think straight. Who is he? How can he do this? How can he get close enough to two people to butcher them? How can he leave no trace? He's like fucking vapour. Who is—?

Greg.

His face flashes in my mind. I see a web of everything. The murders, the locations, the timing, the confusion. They're all tied together in a knot. All these loose threads lead to Greg.

I grab onto a plant stalk for balance. My head is spinning. The heat is affecting the corpses, filling the air with the smell of rotting flesh. Their eyes seem to be following me. Silence envelops me, trapping me in cocoon. Everything is tilted, as if I'm sinking into the earth. I'm tumbling down a hole and I can't see the bottom. I can only cling onto one thought, one flash of clarity: Greg did this.

It's the only thing that makes sense. Who knows every nook and cranny of the compound? Who knows the best spots to hide in before an attack? Who knows every member that walks through our gates? Who knows all of our habits and routines? Greg. It has to be Greg.

I crush the plant in my hand. It's him. He has the opportunity, skill, and knowledge a killer would need. He's in the perfect position. Powerful enough to do whatever he wants and close enough to me to be above suspicion. He has every tool at his disposal and he knows how to use them. He's a surgeon and this whole compound is his operating room.

I'm grinding the plant between my fingers. My body is frozen, trapped by the thoughts hurling through my brain. My heart is pounding on my ribs, fighting to burst free, crawl up my throat, and escape out of my mouth. I'm coated in cold sweat. It can't be true. Even if he's studied all of us, even if he knows exactly when and how to strike, why would he do it? He's a glorified secretary, for fuck's sake. I've never seen him cut in line, let only assault someone. He's a...nerd. Why would he—?

I see him in the office, holding that massive folder in his arms. I see him unpacking it, spreading page after page over my desk. I see him laying out his points, telling me why we should cancel the ceremony, telling me it's too risky. I see him explaining how the killer has made everything too uncertain. I see that smug smile, pretending to clean our mess while he adds to it.

I snap the plant from its stem. My hands are bulging rocks. Every part of me is shaking. I have to find him. I have to grab him. I have to...

I face the door. Just a turn of a knob and I'll see him. He'll know exactly what I'm thinking. He'll know I've smoked him out. He'll try to run or talk his way out of it. Or he'll attack me, finish his job right there. When I open that door, I'll have one moment of surprise, only one. In that instance, before he gets his bearings, before he formulates a plan, before he can move an inch, I'll have to make my move.

I squeeze my fists even tighter to steady myself. I shift my feet and bend my legs, tensing them up. I swallow a deep gulp of air and release it in a steady stream. I glance at the bodies. Bugs crawl over their faces. They're really dead. This is really happening. I close my eyes, picturing how this will unfold, how I'll make this right. I start sprinting.

I burst through the door, nearly toppling over from my momentum. Greg jerks up from his desk, sending a file skittering to the floor. His face is scrunched in confusion, but there's a hint of a smile tugging on his lips. He thinks this is a funny, some random joke I'm pulling off. He can't read my face. He opens his mouth. I don't give him the chance.

I rush to Greg and grab him by the shoulders, trying to crush them in my hands. His smile evaporates, swallowed by surprise. I pull him forward, knocking over folders, sharpeners, and his favourite mug. I slam his back onto the desk and loom over him, bunching his shirt up in my hands.

"Sir, sir, sir, sir, sir, it's me, it's Greg, it's Greg. Sir, what's going on? It's me, it's Greg. What's going on? Sir?" Greg frantically taps me with his palms. I can barely hear him. There's a pounding drum in my ears.

"I know it's you." Our noses are touching. I cover his face with spit as I talk.

Greg's eyes widen. He tries to hide it by contorting his face, but I see the truth. I see the recognition in his eyes. I've got him cornered.

"Sir, what are you talking about? You know what? What did I—? Sir, sir, please, get off me. Sir..." Greg tries to shove my elbow off his chest. I don't budge.

"You're the killer." My voice is hoarse.

Greg stares at me. He squirms under my weight. He's searching his brain for an excuse, for a deflection, for anything. He needs a moment to catch his breath and formulate a plan. I won't give him one.

"You're the killer." I bark the words into Greg's ear. I'm practically smothering him.

"Sir...what...are you...I'm not...the killer...please...sir...can't breathe...sir...please." Greg's face is flushed. He's banging his hands on my sides, scraping and clawing for a sliver of air.

I pull up, only slightly. I keep my arm planted on his chest, pinning his arms to the desk. I shift my weight off his stomach. He gasps and huffs back a big gulp of air.

"Sir, why did you—?" Greg tries to sit up. My arm encourages him to stay down.

"You're the killer." I jab my finger at him.

"...what? Sir, are you...are you accusing me of...Oh, God, no, no, no, sir, no, you're not...Oh, fuck, no..." Greg's eyes swell with water. Crocodile tears.

"Yes, I am. I've figured it out. You overplayed your hand. I got you." I slam my free hand on the desk next to Greg's face. He flinches.

"Sir, I'm not the killer. I'm not. I swear to you. I swear on my mother. Please, sir, you have to believe me. Please, sir, please." Greg's voice cracks. He's in agony. It's a put-on…

"You were too obvious. You tried to convince me to cancel the ceremony, tried to get me to compromise. You pushed your agenda right before I found them." I nod at the door.

"Them? Who? Who did you find? Please, sir, I don't understand." Greg's voice is shrill. He's a trapped rat.

"Trying to make me betray myself. Leaving those two out there for me to find, posing them like dolls. Were you taunting me? Mocking me? You're sick, Greg. You're a sick man." I push my elbow down with every word.

"Two? What poses? I haven't done anything. Sir, please, I'm lost. Help me. Just let me up and I'll—" Greg tries to sit up again. I fall down on him.

"I should have known it was you. All the clues were there. You're a doubter. You always have been. You're trying to destroy us." I'm growling through my teeth.

"Sir...air...air...please...off me...sir...please..." Greg punches my ribs. Feeble.

"You've doubted me every step of the way. Every time I make a decision, you try to undermine me. You're always there with your smirk and your stammer and your fucking files, ready to tear apart anything we come up with." My shouting fills the room.

"Sir...I'm...loyal...completely...loyal...I'd never...do what...you're saying...I'm on...your side...sir...please...believe me...sir...I can't..." Greg's feet pound the desk, sending papers flying.

"You're the killer. You want to annihilate what we've built. You can't believe, so you won't let anyone else. You got close to me, as close as you could get, and you made your move. You waited until you had everything you needed and you struck. You fucking viper. You're the killer, aren't you? You have to be. Say it. Say it now." My throat is filled with bile.

Greg gurgles in response. I remove my elbow, giving him one second to catch his breath. I place my knees at his side, crouching over the desk. His hands reach up to me, pleading, and I slap them away. I take his head in my hands and bring it close to my face.

"Confess. Tell me everything. Tell me why. Tell me and I'll..." I shake my head. I have no idea what I'll do if he confesses. Throw him to the police? Imprison him? Send him away?

"I...didn't do it, sir. Please...believe me. I'm...innocent. I'm not a...killer." Greg licks his lips and coughs. I slap him.

"Confess. Explain yourself. Why'd you betray us? Why'd you kill Spittal? Why'd you massacre those poor men? Were you trying to get to me, trying to hurt me? Tell me. Confess." I tighten my grip around his skull.

"I didn't kill anyone, sir. I swear to you. I'd never betray this place. This is my home. I'd die for us. I'd never hurt you, sir. I'd do anything for you. Please, let me go. I didn't do it, I didn't do it, I didn't do it." Greg is choking on his sobs. Tears are flowing down his face and spilling onto my hands.

I loosen my grip. I study this blubbering mess before me. No one could fake this, could they? Maybe he's not the... No, no, I can't stop now. I have to find out. I need answers.

"Confess, confess, confess, confess, confess." I chant over and over, shaking Greg's head. My hands slide to his neck, fitting neatly around his neck. If it is him, if he's really the killer, I'd have to do it; I'd have to administer justice. It wouldn't take much pressure; no more than squeezing a lemon. All our problems would be solved. It'd be so—

I'm flying through the air. I tumble off the desk and land on my back, letting out a thunderous grunt. I roll to the side and blink. He must have stunned me. He might have a weapon. I bolt to my feet, fists at the ready.

Ken stands over me. He's pulling Greg off the desk, patting his shoulder and looking over his face. Ken's confused. I can't let Greg sway him. I've got to keep him on my side. If he isn't Greg's accomplice...

"Sir, what the hell is going on?" Ken holds his hands up.

I wipe the sweat from my face and part my hair to the side. I adjust my rumpled shirt and breathe. Greg is sitting over the desk, clutching his stomach, weeping. My face is flushed and my knuckles are bruised. Stay calm. Speak clearly. Don't let Greg talk.

"He's the killer. I was trying to get him to confess." I hold my voice at a steady tone.

Greg breaks into louder sobs. Ken steps back. He looks at Greg and I, lost. Okay, I know where he stands. No way he's acting; he can't stop his emotions from erupting on his face. So, he's not on Greg's side. I can persuade him.

"What? How do you...? When did...? What? No, that's impossible. He can't... What?" Ken shuffles his feet, unable to find his words.

"He killed Spittal. He murdered two men out back. He's got all the resources, all the patience, everything a killer needs. He did it. I'll make him talk." I move to grab Greg. He flinches. Ken stands in my way, uncertain.

"Which men? I thought there was only Spittal. Where are they?" Ken pushes me away from Greg.

I lock eyes with Ken. There's a glimmer of doubt there. He doesn't want to believe me. Fine. I'll give him proof.

"I'll show you his handiwork." I put my hand on Ken's chest.

Greg's curled his knees into his stomach. He looks at Ken, desperate. He whispers that he's innocent. Ken bites his lip and exhales. He nods at me and moves away, staring at the floor. I pat his back and grab Greg by the neck.

Greg falls to the floor, letting out a pathetic groan. I stick my arm under his armpit and haul him to his feet. He struggles in my grasp. Ken is right behind us. I drag Greg across the office, holding him tight as he trips and stumbles. I open the back door and toss him through it.

Greg careens into the ground, landing on his side. I seize him by the shirt and I pull him through the dirt. We reach the bodies. I push him into the bearded one.

We're silent. Greg stares at the bearded man and gags. Ken stumbles towards the bodies, cupping his hands over his head. I wait for them to speak. The bodies seem even worse than when I saw them a few minutes ago. Their skins are grey and clammy, coated with insects. I breathe through my mouth to stop myself from retching.

Greg lets out a high-pitched wail and crawls away from the bodies. Ken bends over them, covering his mouth and shaking his head. His head jerks forward and he turns away. He clears his throat and spits into a bush. My knees feel weak. I'm more nauseated than before. It's grotesque. Only a monster could slaughter these men and prop them up like mannequins. This is...beyond the pale.

I'm back in the driver's seat. I was running on passion, on anger, on a single purpose. I let the bowels of my brain, the primordial ooze, take over. I thought I was filled with righteous justice. Looking at the corpses, I know I was surrendering to fear. I shut myself off to thought and reason. I wanted an immediate answer and I gave myself an easy one. Only now, here in the garden with Ken and Greg, staring at these bodies, do I take back my mind.

I look at the blubbering mess at my feet. Greg is wiping a never-ending stream of tears from his eyes, unable to look at the corpses. He's more disgusted than Ken or I. This can't be a performance. This file clerk isn't a killer. He couldn't handle a paper cut.

"I didn't do this. I swear. Oh, God, no, I didn't touch these men. Ken, you have to believe me. I didn't do it. Oh, fuck..." Greg holds his head in his hands, rocking back and forth.

"I...I'm...I thought...he was the killer...he might be...I don't...he could've..." Shame stalls my tongue.

"You think Greg did this?" Ken grimaces as he points at the bodies.

"He's, he's...had every opportunity. He knows everything...about all of us. He could've snuck up and..." The words sound ridiculous as I stutter them out.

"What opportunities? Why would he do this?" Ken sounds more angry than confused.

"He...he doubted me. He said we should...postpone our ceremony. He's always looking for excuses." I rub the back of my neck, humiliated. What the hell was I thinking?

"Doubt?" Greg looks up at me, wiping the tears and drool from his chin. His fear is merging with fury.

"You always question me. You're a...doubter. You try to make me...rethink everything. You want us to slow down. You doubt..." I inch away from Greg.

Greg stares at the ground, his body heaving. His breath shoots out it short bursts. He digs his fingers into the ground, pulling pebbles and dirt into his palms. His whole body is shaking. What have I done?

"Sir, I don't even... What are you saying? Greg's been here longer than me. He's put everything into this place. He's bled for this place. How could you say that?" Ken moves himself between Greg and I.

"I'm not...I'm not sure. He told me... He tried to tell me what to do about the ceremony. He tried to... And then I saw these bodies and I... It all felt connected, like it was... I don't know. I thought he had a chance to..." I swallow.

Sweat is forming on my neck. Ken's eyebrows are raised in disbelief. Greg is shuddering with rage. Maybe it's a show. Maybe he's letting Ken fight his battle while he pretends to be innocent. He's got me on my back foot. No, no, that's not it. He didn't do it. I mean, I don't know for sure... I can't climb out of this hole; might as well dig deeper.

"I mean, he could have done it. He, he might have had an opportunity. We don't know where he goes. He could... He knows every inch of the compound. He knows everything about us. He could isolate someone and... We don't know where he was last night. He could've killed these men and, and stuffed them in the garden. It could've happened. It could've..." I'm begging. I want this to be true. I need this to be true. I can't be wrong. I can't have attacked Greg for no reason. I can't have...

"Sir, that's insane. It's Greg, for fuck's sake. He couldn't... You're wrong." Ken shakes his head.

"Last night, he could've—" I desperately point at the bodies.

"No, he couldn't have." Ken crouches down and whispers something into Greg's ear.

"How do you—?"

"He was with me. All night." Ken helps Greg up.

Of course.

Greg leans against Ken, wincing. Ken takes Greg's chin in his hand and turns it side to side, studying his wounds. A dark bruise has formed on his cheek. Ken frowns and touches it. Greg pulls away. Ken sighs. They turn to me, shell-shocked.

My assistants. My comrades. My left and right hands. My true believers. What have I done?

I cracked. I've been keeping all this anger and confusion bottled up. I processed my experiences with Smit, Blume, the killer, the exodus of members, and everything else, and I smothered them. I had to stay focused. I let all this stress and anxiety fester and gestate. When I saw the bodies in my garden, in my sacred spot, I erupted. The ooze spewed out, consuming me. I couldn't turn on myself, so I needed something to hit. Greg was the first person in my way.

I'm sick. I pounded my most loyal soldier into a fleshy pulp at the drop of a dime. I was sure, I was beyond certain, that he was the killer, that he was the source of my agony. I leapt on an excuse to beat him. I let my gut shove my brain into the backseat. I wasn't a man; I was a pair of fists and a scream.

It wasn't supposed to be this way. We're meant to be striding towards the finish line, not crawling on our hands and knees. We're supposed to be climbing the mountain, not tumbling off the edge. We're so close to our destiny, and instead of celebrating and preparing ourselves, we're grabbing at each other's throats. This isn't what I was promised...

I've got to be better. I have to be the example, the standard. I can't be devoured by my own fury. We have to collect ourselves and get back to work. We have to catch a killer, keep Smit away, and complete our ceremony on time. We can't be torn apart by my paranoia. This compound is bigger than me.

"Greg... I, I don't know what to say. I'm not sure why I did...that. It was...appalling. I shouldn't have doubted you, not for a second. No one deserves that, especially you. I'm...sorry." I extend my hand.

Greg steps away from Ken, who moves to walk with him. Greg holds up his hand and Ken stands still. Greg approaches me, sliding his feet across the dirt. His gaze never wavers. He reaches my hand and slaps it away. I don't retaliate; I deserve whatever's coming.

"How could...? How could you think for a minute that I would do something like...? I've done everything for this place, for you, and you turn around and... Sir, how fucking dare you." Greg's fists are curled, but he can't bring himself to strike me.

"C'mon, take a step back." Ken touches Greg's shoulder.

"I can't give you a good answer. I don't know what came over me. I saw those bodies and all signs pointed to you. I can't explain why. I can only apologize." I shrug.

Greg's fist slams into my stomach. I double over.

"Apologize? After what you did? That's what you're giving me? How can you even...?" Greg storms away, fumbling for words.

I straighten up, nursing my gut. Ken has his arm over Greg's shoulders. I clear my throat.

"I had that coming. You deserve to be angry. But we can't fall apart. Not now. Not when we're so close." I catch my breath from the punch.

Greg breaks free from Ken. He marches towards me, ready for a second punch. I nod at him to stand down. He stops right in front of me, biting his lip and uncurling his hands.

"Fall apart? Sir, you tore us apart." Greg rubs a fresh batch of tears from his eyes. He still calls me sir.

"I know that, Greg. It was absolutely disgusting. But we've got bigger problems. We have to stay united." I reach out to Greg. He moves away.

"How can we after…?" Greg touches his bruise and glares at me.

"We don't have a choice. I apologize to you, to both of you, from the bottom of my heart. I'll do everything I can to make it up to you. But we can't collapse, not now. We're the only people who can hold this place together. If we disintegrate, everyone will be lost. Blume will win. Smit will win. That...monster will win. We have to rise above this. Together." I hold my palm up, stretching it to Greg.

"I… I know we…. No. No, I can't…. I don't think I could… After that… No." Greg shakes his head and turns to leave.

"Did I train you to be a coward?" I grab his elbow and spin him around.

"...what?" Greg's too startled to be angry.

"I haven't spent the last six years teaching you to quit, have I?" I squeeze his arm.

"N-no." Greg squirms out of my grasp.

"Ken, what have I always taught you? Stand your ground and fight or run and hope someone else deals with your problem?" I raise my fists in the air to symbolize the two choices.

"I, uh, sir, I don't know what—" Ken cautiously steps forward.

"Pick an option, Ken. Fight or flee?" I shake my hands.

"Fight. Always. No matter what. Stand and fight." Ken nods and looks at the ground.

"Good to know." I lower my fists.

Greg and Ken stare at me. They can feel a lesson coming on. Greg looks like he wants to dash for the door, but his legs are rigid. Ken won't leave without Greg, not that he would if he could; he loves a good speech. I've got a captive audience.

"I've drilled this idea into your skulls day after day, week after week, month after fucking month: Stand your ground. Take the punishment. Run headlong into it. Be ready to sacrifice. Hell, relish the sacrifice. It's the reason we're here. Sacrifice is the core of this place. We don't quit and we don't surrender. We have to suffer." My voice fills the garden.

"We know." Greg is about to roll his eyes. I shoot daggers at him and his face falls.

"Do you? Do you really know that? Oh, yeah, you've heard the sermons. You've listened to my words, clapped your hands, and followed along with everyone else. You've helped me and defended me and kept me informed. You've accomplished every superficial milestone and hallmark I could wish for. But have you internalized what I've preached? Because you're filling me with doubt at the moment." I almost lean over an imaginary podium.

"Why?" Ken sounds nearly as concerned as when he saw me pummelling Greg.

"Right now, you're presented with a golden opportunity. You have an actual, real-life chance to overcome something. I'm asking you to overcome your anger for a greater cause. You can surrender your petty emotions to the altar of sacrifice. You can prove you don't just parrot my teachings; you are my teachings. This isn't a game or an exercise with a safety net. This is reality. This is what I've trained you for. This is something you have to overcome in yourselves. This moment could be your finest hour, your chance to shine. But instead you're submitting to your tiny gripes and complaints." I thump on my swelled chest.

"Gripes? Are you kidding? You almost—" Greg points his finger in my face. I swat it down.

"Oh, I know what I did, Greg. I'll make sure I pay for it. I'll have my penance. But this sacrifice isn't about me; it's about you two. You can climb to the top and prove you belong here, or you can wallow in your misery. You can be like everyone else: petty. Plenty of people have been where you are and done no different. They've moaned and cried and pounded sand. They've nursed grudges, letting them fester in their gut. They've descended into a pit and decided to live there. They've chosen to be average. But you two can overcome that. You can shed your anger and help me. I'm not asking you to hug and kiss me; I'm asking you free yourselves from a prison. You can be better. Or you can throw a permanent pity party for yourselves. Watch everything we've built float away while you luxuriate in your misery. It's your choice." My posture slackens, letting them know the speech is over.

Ken's nodding; he knows where he stands. I didn't really need to convince him anyway. He'd swim through a sea of glass shards if I told him it would prove his faith. I just had to stop Greg from turning him against me. He was on the edge for a moment. When he saw me on top of Greg, when he heard my raving accusations, when he touched Greg's bruise, he paused. He doubted me. He stepped back. I only needed a few words to reel him in. He won't leave this place. He might not trust me now, but he'll toe the line. He knows he belongs here.

Greg. His eyes are shaky. He purses his lips as he looks at the ground. I need him. I've fucked up bad, but I need him. This place will fall apart without his organization. I won't know my head from my ass. It's absurd for me to ask him to stay. I know it is. I beat him, I accused him, I humiliated him, and now I want him to let it all slide. Shrug it off and get back to work. It's ridiculous. But I can't afford to lose him, not now, not when we're teetering over a cliff. I can guilt him, threaten him, beg him, but in the end, it's his decision. He has to want to be here. Christ, why'd I fuck this up so much?

Greg scratches the back of his head. His body is twitchy. He glances at the bodies and shudders. He shuffles from one foot to another. He moves forward and retreats. He clears his throat and mumbles. I lean in close. He kicks a mound of dirt and looks back at the corpses. He stares at them. He wipes his mouth and sighs. He looks at me. No, he looks through me. He's searching for something. I don't blink. Greg's eyes soften. He nods.

I exhale, releasing all the tension in my chest. I smile at Greg and he gives a faint mirror reply. I open my mouth, ready to congratulate them. We can finally move on. We can—

"Paging Reverend Cuckoo."

The voice comes from inside my office. The door is still open a crack.

I can picture this entire scene from the doorway. Three men, one covered in bruises, standing over two corpses in a secluded garden. Oh, fuck.

"Move them behind the plants." I snap my fingers at the corpses.

Ken and Greg stare at me, appalled. I glare at them, shooting down any debate. I don't have time for their moral quandaries. We can't leave two bodies rotting in the sun.

"Stay with them until I get back." My voice doesn't rise above a harsh whisper.

Greg and Ken nod, warily eyeing the door. They grab the bearded man by his arms and legs. I remove a layer of sweat from my face and turn to the office. I straighten my shirt and inhale, steadying my body. Get in, meet the person, move them out of the room, and get back to the garden. Easy and clean. Don't waste time. I open the door.

Papers and pencils are strewn on the floor. Greg's desk looks like a warzone. The shades are drawn, coating the room in muted shadows. Ken must have closed them before he followed me to the garden. Wouldn't want to attract any attention. Smart move.

The office is a picture of chaos, violence, and doubt. I was here only twenty minutes ago and it feels like a lifetime. I've gone from pulse-pounding righteous fury to sheepish humiliation to desperate reconciliation in less time than it takes to boil water. I've crammed a week's worth of emotions into a

lunch break. The darkened room matches my mood; I'm
exhausted.

A single stream of sunlight runs across the room and
shines in my eye. I step to the side. One of the curtains is half
closed, letting in the stray beam. No one can see through it.
They're too busy with their work. They didn't see me attack
Greg. I'm fine. Surely…

My robe is hanging next to the sunlight, pale and limp.
A man is standing in front of it, obscured by the shadows. He's
heavy-set with dark jeans and a wide brimmed hat. He's
humming to himself, shaking his head. He touches my robe,
tracing his fingers over the chest. He grabs a sleeve and tugs on
it. He yanks on it, jerking it around. He yanks on my robe. My
robe. I feel a boiling anger rise in my stomach. I step forward
and clear my throat. The man lets my robe fall away and turns
around. He's sporty a dirty moustache, a grimy badge, and a shit-
eating grin.

Sheriff Blume.

"There's the nutcase." Blume winks.

Oh, fuck, oh, fuck, oh, fuck. Why him? Why now?
Those dead men are everything Blume's dreamed about: The
perfect excuse to lock us up and seal down the compound. I'm
the only thing standing between him and a mass arrest warrant.
Don't let him get outside, don't let get outside, don't let him get
outside…

"Sheriff Blume. How unexpected. What can I do for
you?" I force my anxiety and fear deep into my gut, stopping
them from bubbling onto my face.

"So formal, so formal. You're always so tense around
me. It hurts my feelings. You can't be this uptight all the time,
right? I mean, you don't live this bullshit 24/7. Even nutjobs
need a break. How do you unwind, Solly? Long walks at night?
Driving through the countryside? Midnight orgies with your
zombies? It's gotta be one of those, yeah?" Blume picks up a
pencil from Greg's desk and twirls it in his fingers.

"I take care of myself." I stretch my mouth into something resembling a smile.

I stand directly in front of the door. I puff up my chest to make it look like I'm being defiant. Blume chortles and tosses the pencil away. He looks at the robe and rubs his nose with his thumb.

"Y'know, a couple years back we had a guy who wore a nightgown just like that." Blume spits on the floor.

"Did you?" I don't rise for the bait. I can't.

"Oh, yeah. I remember him. He set up shop right on main street. Had a little soapbox, megaphone, posters, the whole deal. He'd spend all day walking up and down that street, preaching about...I don't know what. Something about mind expansion and tunnels through the earth. It was a little out there. I'm sure you could relate." Blume peeks around a curtain.

Blume stares at a pair of female builders. I hear him licking his lips. Letch. I slide Greg's notes under his desk. They're mostly incomprehensible, but they might have something on the killer. Blume turns around, adjusting his pants.

"Anyway, we all thought he was a riot. People would ask him questions just to get a laugh. A few times, me and the boys went up on Darryl's drugstore roof with a couple of beers and listened to him. Funny shit. We thought he was harmless. Just another crackpot. Good for a chuckle. Perfectly safe." Blume stares at the ground.

I try not to panic. There are a lot of papers on the floor, but I think I hid the incriminating ones. I can't read the papers from here. Fuck, is he reading them? Blume clears his throat, spits on the floor, and looks at me.

"Course, we didn't think it was so funny when he broke into the drugstore and blew half of Darryl's face off with a shotgun. He was still screaming about those lizard men and those fucking tunnels when we hauled him out in front of everyone. Nobody was laughing. He kept screaming when we threw him into the dirtiest cell we had. He screamed all night. But after three hours with me, he didn't scream about anything." Blume massages his knuckles.

"Interesting." My voice cracks. Fuck.

"Yeah, I thought you'd like that. He opened my eyes. Nowadays, I keep my streets clean. I keep my town clean." Blume drums his fingers on his holstered gun.

"Why are you here, Sheriff?" Stay calm, stay calm, stay calm. Don't let him through the door...

"All business I see. Fair enough. I didn't come to fight. I just need one thing from you and I'll be on my way." Blume takes a seat behind my desk.

"What can I do for you?" I flex my fingers behind my back.

"What? Couldn't make you out." Blume cups his hand to his ear.

I bite my lower lip. I can't stand here. If I have a conversation with Blume from here, he'll get suspicious. But if I move away from the door, he might… What? He might what? Notice a door in an office? I doubt he'll think it's strange. No, no, I'll be fine. Just talk to him, make him happy, and he'll be on his way. No problem.

"What can I do for you?" I stand at the opposite side of the desk and stare down at Blume, squeezing my mouth into a tight line.

"Ah, service with a smile. I knew you could be polite if you wanted to." Blume puts his feet on my desk. I resist the urge to scream.

"Sheriff, what do you need?" Irritation creeps on the edge of my voice. Couldn't help it.

"I'd like a list of all your members. Every knuckle-dragger, every tree-fucker, and brain-dead moron. I want a copy of your files. And don't bother denying you have them. No one has a place this big without records. You're crazy; not stupid." Blume tips his hat to me as if he just paid a compliment.

"Why would you need my files?" I brush off a pile of dirt from my desk that fell from Blume's shoes.

"Police business." Blume waves his hand.

"I'm going to need more than that to hand over my files, Sir." Shut up, idiot. Just give him what he wants. Get him out of here.

Blume glares at me. I meet his gaze, refusing to blink. Keep him focused on me. Don't let him wander.

"What the hell, I'll throw you a bone. We got a new series of wanted lists from the state. It's part of their new search and capture program. I've got a big pile of names and photos burning a hole in my desk and I'm going to cross-check them with your files. Make sure you're not harbouring any fugitives. Strictly a formality, you see. I'm sure you're clean. Of course, if you're not, that'd be grounds to close this little prayer group." Blume winks at me.

"And if I don't hand over the files?" The words are out before I can stop them. Stupid.

Blume runs his finger down his moustache, plucking out a stray hair. I don't move. Why couldn't I keep my mouth shut? I speak every minute of every goddamn day; why couldn't I be quiet for once? I should have nodded and smiled. But I couldn't help myself. The idea of this...cretin rifling through our files, rubbing his stubby thumbs over our photos, underlining our names with his chewed-up pencil; it was too much for me. It's revolting. I let my pride beat me,

I swallow and scratch my nose. I keep my face neutral, calm, unreadable. He can't get mad if I don't look insolent. Blume takes his hat off and holds it on his finger. He parts his hair to the side.

"You know what'll happen if you don't." Blume raps his knuckle on the desk.

I nod and look submissive, trying to hide my relief. I grunt in acknowledgement and walk to Greg's desk, fishing through his drawers. Blume whistles while I search, tapping his feet on the desk.

I give Blume a file of copies. Greg makes sure we have duplicates of every sheet. This file has all of our names, photos, and information. All of us boiled down to ink and paper. Blume flips through it, nods, and stands up. He heads to the door. I lean against the desk as he turns around.

"I hope your buddy across town is as accommodating." Blume jerks his thumb over his shoulder.

"Smit?" I narrow my eyes.

"That's his name? I thought I'd get acquainted. Doesn't seem like he's going anywhere. Town's getting full of crazies. I wonder who'll crack first." Blume strokes his chin.

"Crack?" It's a question I know the answer to.

"Can't have two idiot compounds in town. I'm gonna have to bring one down. Who'll it be? Personally, I'm rooting for him. I feel the two of us have built up a relationship." Blume gestures at himself and me.

"Clearly." I rub the back of my neck. Christ, when will this conversation end?

"Say, what do you do out there?" Blume points at the back door.

"Gardening. Meditation. Basic stuff." My heart is jack hammering into my ribs.

"Didn't think that'd be for you. Figured you were more of a walk on a mile of nails, 40 lashes before bed kind of guy." Blume chuckles at his own joke.

"Yeah, no, I've, uh, I've a-always done it around he-here. It's, uh, my thing. Yup. It's mine." I cap off this word vomit with a forced laugh.

Blume looks past me, studying the door. I never laugh around him. I look like I'm hiding something. I'd suspect me if I were him. Oh, fuck, what if he asks to go back there? I can't refuse, that'll be too obvious. Do I let him go? Hope Greg and Ken have moved the bodies? Hope he doesn't see them? Shit, shit, shit. Is there anything heavy nearby? I might have to—

"Mmm. Weird. Well, I've got to run. Don't do anything I wouldn't do. Which, I suppose, would be all of this. Next time, nutter." Blume checks his wristwatch, tucks the folder under his arm, and walks out the door.

I scurry to the window and peek through the curtain. I watch Blume stride out of the compound, sidestepping planters and builders. He manoeuvres around two people carrying a barrel, shaking his head. He disappears behind a building. I let the minutes tick by until I'm sure he's gone.

I let my breath out. I lean on the window to stand up. I want to sink into the river and float away. But I can't.

Blume wants one of us gone, Smit or me. He's going to squeeze us both and see who pops. We've got to plug up our holes and bail out this ship now.

I burst into the garden. Greg and Ken emerge from behind the plants. They hurry to me, armed with a dozen questions. I hold up my hand.

"I want everything put on the backburner. If it's not essential to the ceremony, drop it. We are going to find the killer and we have to do it now. We have a deadline."

CHAPTER EIGHTEEN

"There was a shepherd in a village. And he mattered."

I'm gripping the sides of the podium, nearly lifting it off the floor. The spotlight seals me in a cocoon of yellow. The bristles on my face brush against the microphone, sending scratching sounds around the auditorium. My shoulders are hunched and crooked as I lean forward. My body is tucked behind the podium, knees locked together. I must look like a severed head resting on a mantel piece.

The crowd stares at me. They're hanging onto every word. They're dying for the next part, the next drop of wisdom. They're covered in sweat, dirt, and grime, but they're still here, still focused, still believers. I barely notice them. I'm looking at the empty row in the back. The bloodletting hasn't stopped. Smit keeps roping in new members on a weekly basis. I'll catch a few trying to leave in the day and convince them to stay, but most people sneak off in the dead of night. Cowards, all of them. They don't have to the courage to face me and they don't have the fortitude to remain with us. They're weaklings searching for a quick fix. We're better off without them. But we look vulnerable. We have to bandage the wound.

I look away from the gaping hole and return to my notes. Greg helped me write my speech. We want a specific effect. I run my finger over the lines and find my spot.

"This shepherd knew he mattered. Everyone told him so. Everyone depended on him. They needed his wool and his meat. He kept the village alive. He endured bitter weather and long nights and roving wolves. He suffered and sacrificed for his people. He was a pillar." I turn a page.

I'm not speaking to the crowd. I'm speaking to the killer.

Greg is holding a list in front of my face. It's covered with names and faces. Greg is jabbing his finger at each person, explaining them to me. Ken is standing behind me. He's spinning a small baseball bat in his hands, stopping every few seconds to swing it. He cracks his knuckles and peers out the window. The sun is falling.

I'm sitting at my desk, idly stroking my robe on my lap. I've found it relaxes me lately. It reminds me who I am and what I'm doing. It lets me make the decisions I have to make. My chin is resting on my free hand, bobbing up and down as I chew the inside of my mouth. My legs are bumping on the desk. I've been sitting here for hours, waiting.

Greg keeps talking, describing each person in rich detail. I only catch snippets of his colourful language. He knows how to make some unassuming shoplifter sound like a bastard son of the devil. It'd be entertaining if it weren't so grim. Greg has poured through our archives, pulling out files even he doesn't remember. He's spent the last three days locked in his office putting together this list. He agreed to put aside our...dispute until this problem is solved. I think he's grateful to be back in the inner circle after his momentary exile, honestly.

This morning, Greg burst into my office and said he'd finished the list. Then he collapsed on his desk. He woke up twenty minutes ago. He fished the list out of his pocket and started talking. It's a list of every member with the slightest hint of a criminal record. This piece of paper is our checklist. We're going to run through every name. We're going to put these people through the ringer. We're going to find answers.

Greg puts the list back in his pocket. He asks me if I'm sure about this. We're about to violate our own members' trust. We're crossing a line. Ken and Greg stare at me. They need to know this is okay. It's not.

I nod.

"One day, the shepherd found himself in the desert."

Fuck me, we're in a desert. My face is flushed already. I wipe the sweat from my neck. I can taste the heat in the air. Any other day, I'd probably lead my group outside to the river, give a speech in the water as a reward for our hard work. A small carrot after all those sticks. But we have to be in here.

"He had to be in the desert. He had to stay there for months. He wasn't sure why, but he knew he needed to be there. The people depended on him. They relied on him. He answered the call." A drop of sweat splashes on the page.

"So he lived in the desert. He only had his sheep for company. He had water and bread and fruit. He had everything he needed. So, he sat on a rock and waited. "He waited and waited and waited. He watched his sheep and he wandered around. He kept waiting and waiting. The days crawled by. The sun bore down on him. The sheep were irritable. There was nothing to do. He became bored.

"One day, he stood on his rock and looked over his sheep. It was a particularly hot day and his rations were running short. He still had enough to last him until the end, but he was hungry. Hungry and bored. He had nothing to distract him, nothing to occupy his mind. He only had his resolve and his desire. 'What would be wrong,' he asked, 'with having one sheep?'

"He convinced himself that no one would miss one measly sheep. So he waded into the herd and picked out the scrawniest, puniest, most insignificant sheep he could find. He moved it behind the rock and slit its throat. He ate well that night, and damned himself." I slam the paper down as I turn it. The crowd flinches.

He's in there, somewhere. He has to be...

Ken and Greg stand next to me in the garden.

We form a triangle, touching shoulder-to-shoulder. We're positioned over the ground where we found the bodies. We're standing on them. I can still see them staring at me. The dirt seems to have soaked in their blood. We're talking in a graveyard.

This garden has been perverted. I haven't been able to meditate in here since the...discovery. I walk in here, close my eyes, and see them. I try to water the flowers and I see their cold faces. I feel like someone watching me from behind the plants, ready to pounce. I have to run to my office before I have a panic attack. I can still meditate at the river, but this place, my garden, my secluded spot, it's been...corrupted.

I don't want to be here. Even with Greg and Ken, I'm on edge. My eyes dart to every dark shadow and open space, looking for the glint of a knife. But this garden is the only place with any privacy. No one will hear us. Except for the killer. He could be lurking anywhere, listening to us, studying us...

No, no, Ken swept the garden. Nobody's here. Nobody can hear us. I pluck a loose hair from my cheek and focus.

Greg is talking. He's parsing through Ken's report. Ken keeps his eyes locked on the door. The report is the result of a week of surveillance. We followed everyone on Greg's list. We studied, tracked, and kept notes on them. Ken and Greg stalked them while I watched them from afar. I invited a couple of them to late-night confessions. They didn't say much between the blubbering and the tears.

Greg flips through the pages, reading off the litany of minor offenses. Some of them skipped sermons, preferring to sleep in. Others took long breaks or let their co-workers carry the load. A few insulted me, said I was losing my grip. One or two even slinked away to Zaan. They all failed in some way, but none of them are the killer.

I kick the dirt and swipe the file from Greg's hands. I wave it in front of Ken's face. I tell them it's not enough. A week of nose-to-the-grindstone research for a bunch of rulebreakers. We're looking for a killer, not a truant. We have to do better.

I toss the file on the ground. Greg says we've exhausted this approach. Ken says surveillance will only get us so far. I say we have to go deeper. Greg asks me how.

I turn away from them and rub my chin. I'm afraid to say it. I'm afraid where this will lead us. I say it.

"The shepherd ate and ate and ate."

The crowd is fidgeting. I keep talking, eyeing the empty seats.

"He couldn't stop with one sheep. No, he'd had a taste of something better than bread and water. He wanted more. He wanted a reward for his sacrifice. He looked at his herd and he didn't see responsibility or duty or the greater good; he saw food.

"The shepherd led his flock away from the rock. He took them to a tall tree next to a small lake. It was surrounded by plants and shade. He slaughtered his sheep.

"The shepherd ate for months. He lolled in the shade and swam in the lake. He grew soft and fat. He tore into his sheep, tossing their bones into a pile in the sand. He gorged himself.

"Eventually, the feast ended. He threw the last sheep away, packed up, and headed home. He knew his people would be mad, but they'd understand. They'd know why he deserved a reward. He'd survive it their scorn and disappointment. They needed him.

"He comforted himself with these thoughts as he marched through the desert. He saw his village on the horizon and started running. He ran to the center square and yelled out. He screamed his confession, begging for mercy and forgiveness. He threw himself on their compassion. But no one approached him.

"He wandered through the town, looking for his fellow citizens. He checked in homes and churches and taverns and schools. He saw no one. He only found scraps of clothing and abandoned carts. Everyone was gone.

"He stood in the center of the town and let the silence wash over him. People had depended on him and he had deserted them. They waited and waited, starving. When they could wait no longer, when their hunger was greatest, they left the village for food. They faced certain death. The shepherd was alone. He'd killed his home. He was the architect of his isolation."

I lean against a barracks building, listening to Ken rummaging through the crates inside.

Something slams on the ground. Ken swears. I peek my head through the door. Ken is holding his thumb and shaking his head. A dumbbell is lying on the floor. I let out a short chuckle. Ken notices me. I tell him to hurry up and I walk off the barracks porch.

I close my eyes and soak in the silence. It's just me and Ken. Two men breaking into members' private property. I'd feel sick with myself, but this is our ninth barrack today. I beat myself up enough during the first three. I just want to finish it.

I look down the main path of the compound. No builders hammering on wood, no planters hauling gardening tools, no one standing at the center square discussing today's sermon, not a soul around. It's a pure ghost town. It's like the first day we opened this place. Fewer buildings and younger skin, but it feels the same. All that energy packed into one place. Joseph and I, ready to spread the word...

I haven't wiped out my followers. They're in the woods with Greg. Deep in the woods. It's a weekend-long excursion into themselves. An exploration of their faith, strength, and character. A spiritual retreat. I'd planned it for a while, of course. I simply moved it up the schedule when I realized we had to be more...thorough in our research. I believe in the retreat. I wish I could be there. But we need answers. Ken emerges from the barracks, shaking his head. I slide against the barracks' wooden pillar, bumping my head on the wooden surface.

I want to sink into the pillar. Ken asks me what we should do. I don't say anything. The compound's silence engulfs us.

"The shepherd ran from the village."

People are murmuring to each other. Confusion is running through the room. I scan the crowd. A few members are staring at me, unblinking. Some are looking at the ground. Guilty consciences? I make a mental note of where they're sitting and return to the story.

"He couldn't bear the silence and guilt. Every empty building and street reminded him of his failure. He didn't want to stay sheltered in these haunted memories. He wanted to escape his remorse. He wanted to escape the accusations of his vanished friends. He wanted to wash the blood from his hands. He wanted to escape himself. So he ran into the desert.

"He had no sheep, no food, no water, no home. He was exposed to the whirling sands and crushing heat. He didn't care about the pain or the hunger; his only focus was dulling his shame. He thought the desert would let him forget his crimes. But his mind wouldn't let them go.

"He wandered for days. His lips dried up and cracked. His body became red and burnt. His bones screamed and moaned. Every step was a hundred tiny agonies. But the thoughts would not leave.

"Finally, he returned to the rock where he made his decision. He lay down on it and stared at the sun, watching it give way to the night sky. He was starving, dehydrated, and beaten. He knew he was going to die. It was inevitable. He had dug his way into Hell. But as he gazed at the moon, a smile crept over his face. Tears welled in his eyes. At last, alone in the desert, he saw the truth."

I'm surrounded by lies.

I'm standing in the center of the compound. Greg is in the office, buried under mounds of files and member data. I'm sure his fifth time through them will yield results. Only a matter of time. Sure. Ken's deep in the woods, following a series of snapped twigs and branches he's convinced himself is a trail. He's certain the killer's somewhere in the forest. He's seeing patterns even I don't pick up on. It's his fourth straight day in the woods. He never eats or shaves, and no one can stand to be near him and his smell for long. At least he's trying.

I'm alone for the first time in a while. No lead to follow up on. No barrack to investigate. No folder to pore over. It's me and the crowd.

People move past me, hauling their soil and lumber and tools. Some nod at me. I return the favour. Others avoid my gaze, finding something interesting to stare at on the ground. I bore my eyes into their heads, trying to force them to look up. A few members look right at me, stone-faced. They don't blink. I don't break eye contact with them as they walk by. Who are they? Spies from Zaan? I burn their faces into my mind.

Everyone's talking. They're always talking. Whispering and murmuring. People huddle in groups, heads lowered. Voices swirl around me. I can't pick out any words, but they sound...off. Wrong. The compound is off-balance, like it's sinking sideways into the ground. No one seems to notice.

Liars. I'm being smothered by liars. These cowards have to hide their words behind hushed voices and tight-knit cliques. They don't have the courage to speak in the open. They don't have the conviction to talk right to my face. They can't bear to confront me. Who are these people? I didn't teach them to sulk in the shadows. What are they hiding from me? Christ, any of them could be the killer...

I pinch the bridge of my nose. I've never hated my followers before. I've never suspected them this much. But I can't trust them. They could planning their next attack. They could be hiding knives behind their backs. No, no, I can't think like this. They're my people. I have to lead them. I can't suspect them. I have to—

Two men are talking near a barracks building. One of them gives the other a piece of paper. I recognize the design. I could spot it anywhere. I've got it pinned to my office wall, a pencil buried in its center. I see this paper in my dreams. It's a Zaan pamphlet.

The second man takes the pamphlet and stuffs it in his pocket. He nods at the first one and smiles. My teeth are grinding. They're betraying me right in the open and they couldn't care less. They're pissing in my face. They both notice me and turn pale. They separate, disappearing into the crowd.

Traitors. I'm surrounded by traitors. If they're not planning to kill me, they're looking for ways to jump ship. All these snakes trying to gouge out my throat.

I look at the sky. A batch of clouds begin to blot out the sun. What the fuck am I going to do?

"The shepherd knew what he had to do."

A haze has fallen over the crowd. They're drifting away. They're waiting for me to bring it home. They want the moral, not the story. Fair enough. I slam my hand near the microphone. People snap to attention.

"He'd failed. He'd failed as badly as anyone can fail." I pull the mic from its stand and move away from the podium.

"And how did he fail? Not through a naive mistake, or malice, or even simple incompetence. No, he failed his people through his sheer sloth. He indulged himself. He succumbed to his base desires. He feasted when he should have fasted. He relaxed when he should have worked. He sat when he should have stood. He slept through the decimation of his village. He reclined in the shade while his people roasted in the sun. He indulged when he had to sacrifice. He failed.

"He saw his disgrace stretching out for eternity. He looked at the sky and felt his total insignificance. He thought the earth was going to open up and swallow him. He thought his shame would crush him into paste. He stayed on the rock, waiting for the supreme judgment. But nothing happened. He was left alone with his agony. He had to live with it.

"He lay there and confessed his crimes. He told his sins to the stars. He spoke for hours, until his throat went dry, until his back was sore, until he was frozen to the bone, until he had listed each one of his faults. When he closed his mouth, when the sky had devoured his words, when he was barely awake, he felt a weight lift off his chest. He felt clean. He felt absolved.

"The shepherd never saw his fellow villagers again. The ones who lived founded a new home miles away. They thrived there, but he didn't join them. He never left his rock. He spent his days staring at the sky and confessing. His people didn't forgive him, but he did. He found freedom in confession. He saved himself." I toss the papers away.

"Friends, we are that shepherd. We fail from time to time. We slip and stumble. We stray from the path. We allow ourselves to sink into the muck. We submit to our urges. We indulge. It can be demoralizing, heartbreaking, spirit-shattering. But it doesn't have to be the end. We don't have to quit just because we fail. We can confess our sins and find forgiveness. Even the most wretched among us aren't lost. Even a murderer could find his way back to the light. If you feel you've fallen away, if you've lost the plot, if you feel you're irredeemable, I urge you to confess. Lift the weight from your chest and save yourself. Don't hide anymore; confess." I hold my hands out wide.

Everyone's leaning forward in their chairs. Their faces are glowing. They're on the verge of applauding; they just want to make sure I'm finished. No one rushes to the stage to confess being the killer.

My arms falter. There are no guilty or remorseful faces. No one is fidgeting in their chairs or avoiding my gaze. There is no nervous twitching or gnashing of teeth. Nobody is collapsing in a heap, begging for forgiveness, spilling their guts. The killer isn't here, or he's a very good actor, or they missed the entire message.

Why did I think this would work? A thinly veiled metaphor to coax the killer out of hiding; what did I think would happen? Would the killer be so moved they'd throw themselves at my mercy? What was I thinking? That was one of my worst speeches. Only an idiot would be moved by it.

Nothing's happening. All that planning, all of those rewrites, all for rapt silence. I've accomplished nothing. I've been reduced to pleading with the killer through a parable. Fuck me.

I lower my hands and nod. The crowd bursts into applause. I savour it for a while; it's all I've got.

I'm out of ideas.

CHAPTER NINETEEN

Darkness envelops me.

Ken and Greg are long gone. We had a debrief as the sun was setting. The moon's high, half obscured by clouds. Everyone's in their barracks. There are no footsteps, shouting, or conversations from the compound. I haven't seen anyone in hours. Hell, I can barely see five feet in front of me. My flickering lamp is the only source of light. If I closed my eyes, I could convince myself I'm deep underground, far from sign of life. I snap my fingers next to my ears every few minutes to make sure I'm not going deaf. I'm submerged and alone.

Greg and Ken wore their exhaustion on their faces when they left. A solid month of nonstop investigations with no results is bearing down on them. I've seen their eyes light up when they grasp at the slimmest chance, only to see it fade and die, dozens of times. Anxiety hangs over them. They can't escape it, so they're forced to live with it. They've never had to deal with it before, not like this. They're used to quick answers. Even here in the compound, even when I've pushed them to their extremes, they were able to stand tall because they could see a finish line. They can endure anything when they know the ceremony is the endgame. But this killer is something different. We're stuck in a maze digging after crumbs. They prepared for a sprint; this is a marathon.

They couldn't suppress their disappointment as they debriefed me this evening. After three solid days of surveillance, they've crossed Michael Crosby off their list. He's a cipher who works, eats, and sleeps. Nothing dangerous. There were a few arrests for drunken disorderly conduct on his file. Greg thought it was worth following up on. We've whittled our way to the bottom of the barrel. We have no more suspects.

There've been no new killings since we found the garden bodies. That's something. But it's only a matter of time. He's waiting, that's all. He's sharpening his knives and picking out a new target. We don't have a whiff. He's standing outside our grasp, laughing.

Ken and Greg don't have any new avenues. I have no suggestions. We sat around spit balling theories for which we'll never find answers. Ken said we could recruit members to spy on each other, but the words died in his mouth as he said them. Greg posited running through the entire database again for any possible loose ends, but the very idea drained all the colour from his face. He could see all the papers lying before him and his eyes went distant and cold. I reclined in my chair, letting our situation sink in. We have nothing.

I thanked Ken and Greg for their service. I told them to take the night off. We're not giving up, of course, we're simply taking a break. We're re-charging our batteries. I told them we'd dive back into this problem headfirst tomorrow. This killer wasn't going to get away. We'd find him some way. Their efforts weren't in vain. Now isn't the time to give up.

I pounded my desk and raised my voice and gestured at the compound as I spoke, trying to inspire them, trying to inspire myself. Ken and Greg nodded and mumbled as they walked out the door. They leaned on each other. They've got themselves; I've got myself.

I put my feet on my desk. My robe is draped over Greg's chair. Towels are placed on the floor beneath it. They're soaked, still absorbing stray drops of water that fall from the cloth. My robe reeks of the river. In the darkness it looks like a puffy drunk splayed over the arms of a stern friend, limbs dangling loosely in the air, head turned to the ground, ready to release a torrent from its guts.

I washed my robe after the shepherd speech. I've been washing it a lot lately. When Greg and Ken are chasing leads, when the members are busy with work, when I'm tired of staring around the compound, I'll grab my robe and disappear into the forest. It's something to do. It's something I can control. For a few minutes, while I hold my robe under the water, the world makes sense.

I needed that peace after today's speech. What a train wreck. "He confessed his sins to the stars." Fuck me, that's turgid even by my standards. Who could be moved by that? Who could hear those words and decide they needed to confess? Why would a killer surrender after hearing that story? Thank fuck I didn't go with my first draft: "He saw the truth in the moon." Ugh.

I've never delivered a sermon that terrible before. I must have looked like a lunatic, rambling about a shepherd and confession and sheep and the stars. What a disaster.

I chuckle as I remember every tortured metaphor and phrase in that speech. My laugh bounces off the walls. It makes my skin crawl. I take my feet off the desk and open a drawer. I push past the papers, pencils, and photos and pull out a shot glass and a bottle of whiskey.

No, it's not an escape. If anything, whiskey makes me more miserable. It lets me focus on my agony. I can zero in on my pain and wallow in it. Whiskey brings out the worst in me. It gives me another obstacle to overcome.

I've kept this bottle under my desk for months. I grabbed it from a liquor store when Ken and I were making a supply run. I've burned through about five bottles in all my time here. I save whiskey for special occasions. It drags me into the gutter. It lets me see something with fresh eyes. And it also takes the fucking edge off.

I break the seal and pour the whiskey into the glass. Some of it splashes on the desk. I wipe it up and lick my fingers. I down the shot and blink, feeling my eyes pooling with water. I let out a hiss. The drink lands in my stomach with a thud, like an anvil crashing in an empty pit. The taste burns on my tongue. I hate whiskey. I pour another shot.

Everything's fucked. My sermons are a mess. Today wasn't an exception. I haven't knocked it out of a park in a while. I'll ramble about the same three topics over and over until I get bored. Then I'll invite someone onstage for the Honour and I'll slap the taste out of their mouth. I'll thank the crowd and watch them file out. Rinse and repeat. I don't have the time to prepare original speeches. The shepherd story was the first script I've used in weeks. I can't focus on my sermons. My mind always circles back to one topic: The killer. Even when I'm hammering home an important point, I remember that somewhere in that crowd, the murderer could be staring at me. My brain refuses to think of anything else. I'll trail off and mumble out a conclusion.

If I'm not thinking about the killer, I'm focused on Smit. Every day I watch for those black cars and hooded men. I see them inch closer and closer to the gate with every visit, getting bolder with each member theft. I want to stick their heads into the car and repeatedly slam the door. But I can't. One aggravated assault and Blume will lock us up.

In my mind, I can see Smit's head looming over our compound like a setting sun, flashing down his smirk. All we can do is fling rocks and sticks up at him. I pour another shot.

It feels like we're in free fall, just trying to grab onto the cliff. I swallow the whiskey and sigh. These problems are part of one big test. A test we will overcome. We always do. We're going to find a way out. We'll be stronger for it. We'll be fine. I know we will…

The door moves.

Time stops.

Faint moonlight streams through the door. The hinges creak and groan. Cold air blows against my face. The door stops midway. It's a big enough opening for a person to slide past. No one comes in. I can hear breathing.

I grab the bottle, spin on the cap, and hold it by its neck like a club. I curl my free hand into a fist. I push away from the desk, giving myself some room to bolt upright. I draw quick, controlled breaths. My entire body braces itself.

I've been waiting for this moment. It's like being blindfolded in front of a firing squad; you know the bullets are coming, you just don't know when. You can only wait. I've been expecting this bullet. It's been loaded in the chamber, prepped to splatter the target painted on my head. The bullet is screaming towards my skull.

The killer's standing behind that door. He's here to give me a red scarf. I knew I was his target, his final target. Those other members were warm-ups. He always wanted me; that was his end game. Cut the tail off a lizard and it'll grow back; cut the head off a lizard and it'll wind up as your mantelpiece. He's going to murder me and watch this place crumble to dust.

I've planned for this. Well, not this particular scenario. I thought I'd be sober. And near people. And in broad daylight. Okay, maybe I didn't plan for everything, but I've got this. I can handle him. He's only a man.

I'll smash the bottle over his head. While he's scraping glass shards from his face, I'll tackle him to the ground. A few punches to the chest and throat should do the trick. I'll grab Ken and we'll take this psycho to the river for an... interview. I've got this. Oh, fuck, the door's widening. Here we go, here we—

"Sir? Are you in?"

I've heard that voice around the compound. So he is a member. No, the voice is feminine. The killer's a woman? Doesn't matter.

It's Sandra.

She's standing in the doorway, hands behind her hips. She's peering through the darkness. Her eyes light up when she sees me. She smiles and nods. I put the bottle onto the desk. My whole body unclenches. I sink into my chair. It's only Sandra. The bullet didn't come tonight. I'm fine, I'm fine, I'm fine...

"Sir, is this a bad time? Because I can..." Sandra gestures to the door.

"What? No, no, no, now's fine. I've got no plans tonight. Please, take a seat." I point at Greg's chair.

Sandra nods and grabs it, dragging it in front of me. She sits down and straightens her clothes. She glances around the room, biting her lip. Her knee is bouncing.

"Sorry for bothering you. I'm sure you've got better things to do." Sandra hangs her head.

"I assure you, I have nothing going on tonight. You've caught me during one of the dullest evenings of my life. Now, what can I do for you?" I relax in my chair. Looks like she's got something to confess. Good, that's in my wheelhouse.

"Thank you. I… I didn't know who to talk to. I was going to tell Marsha. She's my bunkmate. I tell her everything, I guess. But … I couldn't tell her. I don't think she'd… You're the only one who… Oh, damn, I'm rambling…" Sandra nibbles her thumb nail.

"Start from the beginning." I move the lamp closer to Sandra.

"Fuck, it's so…" Sandra rotates her hands as if she's juggling.

"Take your time. Deep breath. You know where to start." I flash a reassuring smile.

"Right. Okay." Sandra inhales, letting her eyelids fall down.

She sits still, her hands resting on her legs. I take the moment to tuck the bottle and glasses under the desk. I wipe my chin of any remaining whiskey and straighten my hair. Sandra exhales and opens her eyes. She reaches into her pocket. She pulls out a small black box and puts it on the desk. She doesn't say a word.

I reach for it, keeping my eyes on Sandra. I take the box and hold it under the lamp. It's about the size of my palm. It has a latch on its front. I pop it open. The interior is covered in red velvet. There's an empty groove in the center, barely bigger than my pinky finger. I snap it shut.

It's an engagement ring box.

I slide the box back to Sandra. She scoops it up and clasps it between her hands.

"I found it in Henry's trunk." Sandra flips the lid open and stares at the empty groove.

My fingers scrape the desk as by hand tenses up. I glance at my drawer. There's a ring in there, buried under the papers, photos, and pencils. It's grey with a circular pattern running around its edges. It wouldn't be out of place at a flea market. I've kept it hidden for weeks. I bring it out now and then, spinning it on the desk. It's calming.

We found it a month ago. Seems like a lifetime. We found it in the bushes. It was stained with blood and dirt. I pocketed it without thinking.

I've got Henry Spittal's ring in my desk.

I swallow and relax my hand. Sandra's still staring at the box. I sit up straight and roll my shoulders. I did nothing wrong. Spittal's ring is evidence, that's all. I have every reason to keep this ring. Sandra doesn't know about it. She doesn't suspect me. There's no reason she should. I'll be fine. Stay calm. Sandra plants the box on the desk.

"I haven't thought about him in weeks. I've just focused on work. I figured if I was going to feel bad about him, it would happen. But I needed my hair brush. I couldn't find it anywhere. I must have left it with Henry after a...sleep over. So I snuck into his barracks during lunch and opened his trunk. I didn't find my brush. But I found that box. I know what it means." Sandra jabs her finger at the square.

"Which is…?" I scoot my chair closer to the desk.

"He didn't leave for Zaan. He left for a woman." Sandra clears her throat and looks away.

Relief flushes my gut. For a moment, I thought she might be piecing the clues together. Maybe she connected Spittal's disappearance and the two garden bodies. Maybe she noticed our investigation. Maybe the ring clicked everything together in her brain. But she doesn't have a thing. We're alright.

Sandra's crying. I can see the water pooling in her eyes. She brushes hair from her face. I rub the back of my neck. I pull

the box across the desk, pressing my finger on the empty groove.
I listen to Sandra stifle her tears.

"Why should it matter to you?" I can picture the ring in
the groove. A perfect match.

Sandra's cheeks are flushed. Her eyes are shiny. Her
mouth is slightly agape. She's challenging me to continue. I
shrug.

"I don't want to sound harsh, but you didn't seem to care
much for our wayward bachelor. It was a strictly...physical
affair. Not exactly a romance for the ages. You couldn't summon
a shrug when you found out he'd left. I've seen people more
upset over losing their spot in a book. Am I wrong?" I lean
forward. Sandra squints, but doesn't respond.

"You had to impale a rock in your garden as a reminder
he's gone. You had to force yourself to feel bad, and even then
you couldn't do it. Mr. Spittal might as well have been a
paperboy who changed his route; a mild inconvenience, nothing
more. But you find an engagement box in his trunk and you're
getting all misty eyed?" I cross my arms.

Sandra raises one eyebrow. Her eyes are dry. She shakes
her head and chuckles. She takes the box from me and tosses it
between her hands.

"You're right. I didn't care when Henry left. I mean, I
felt a little bad. I liked Henry. He was fun to hang out with and
he was a decent lay. He was a nice guy. When I heard he'd left, I
tried to figure out where he went. When I found out he went to
Zaan, I was relieved. I didn't have to pretend I was sad; I could
just write him off. Another traitor who couldn't hack it. I was
happy with that. I knew where I stood with Henry. He chose
Zaan over all of us. I was a small part of it. I doubt I came into
his decision at all. I moved on. But then I found this bad boy.
And I knew why he really left." Sandra squeezes the box, her
fingers turning white.

"He left for a woman. Not for a cause, or a religion, or
even a mental breakdown; a woman. He bolted out of here to get
hitched. He grabbed his stuff, pocketed his ring, and poof. He

chose someone else over me. I don't have any barrier with this time. No larger reason. Henry fell in love and ditched me. Cut and dry. And that pisses me off." Sandra flicks the box onto the desk.

"So, a man you didn't really care about left you for someone he loves and you're upset over it? I didn't miss anything, did I?" I scratch my chin, suppressing a smile.

Sandra sees the amusement in my eyes and she flashes me a grin, showing off a row of pearly whites. The gates of heaven.

"Don't say it like that. It makes me sound shallow." Sandra dismissively waves her hand.

"How should I describe it?" I put my chin in my hand.

"...I'm jealous he chose someone over me. I guess that does make me completely shallow. Happy?" Sandra lets out a sharp laugh.

"No, not particularly. Why are you jealous?" I inch closer.

"I… I don't know. I… No, that's not true. I know why: I can't stand any attacks on my ego. Henry found someone better and I can't accept that. I can't let it slide. It's a personal insult. I know I'm supposed to say I'm not perfect, but…can I be honest?" Sandra looks around the room.

"I wouldn't have it any other way." I nod.

"Deep down, in my heart of hearts, I know I'm better than most people. I'm a harder worker than any of the planters. I'm proud of myself. I thought Henry saw that same person. But when I found that ring, I…" Sandra scrunches her face.

"Your self-perception took a beating." I slap my fist into my open palm.

"Exactly. I was offended. How dare he leave me for some...random bimbo. I was the best he's ever had. I know I should be humble and all that other stuff. But I can't do it. I'm just bitter." Sandra shrugs.

"Ego is hard to beat. I struggle with it daily. I mean, look at me." I puff out my chest. We laugh.

"Ahhh, damn, I was crying about him. I can barely remember what Henry looks like and I was tearing up over him. If he were back in the compound right now, I wouldn't care. If we got back together or never spoke again, I wouldn't mind either way. But now that he's gone, I can't stop thinking about him. Fuck me." Sandra mimes shooting herself in the head.

"Do you know who he left with?" I walk two fingers across my open palm.

"No idea. I can't even picture her stupid face. I've got nothing concrete to hate. Nobody around the compound knows who she is. She's probably some builder. They could talk about lumber all day or whatever." Sandra rolls her eyes.

"Well, that's for the best. It gives you less to cling onto. Henry will fade in time, I'm sure. You'll be fine." I lean back into my chair.

"Yeah, yeah, you're probably right." Sandra nods as she gazes at the box.

"You're lucky, in a way. Not many people reflect on their ego. You've seen the parts of yourself you dislike. Now you can form a plan of attack." I inwardly cringe as I speak. Terrible advice.

"That's one way of looking at it." Sandra gives me a wry smile.

Sandra shifts in her seat as I drum my fingers. She's still upset. She's trying to hide it, trying to move on. She wants to accept my advice. I just need one more phrase to bring it home, one more aphorism to nail it, one more—

"Sorry to bother you like this, barging in your office in the middle of the night. You must think I'm crazy." Sandra runs her fingers through her hair. God, it looks smooth...

"No, no, it's very normal to talk about unrequited love at one in the morning." I offer a forced chuckle. Sandra looks away. Idiot. A joke? Now? She's reaching out to you. Drop the—

"I'd better get to bed. Early morning tomorrow. Every morning's an early one, actually. Anyway, sorry again for bothering you." Sandra stands and gives me a curt bow.

I watch her walk away. Her shoulders are hunched over. Her feet drag on the floor. She holds her arms close to her chest. But her head is held high. I didn't say anything to improve her mood. She's the same person who crept into my office twenty minutes ago. But she's trying to drag herself up. She's trying to force herself out of the shadows. Say something, dammit. Something real. Talk to her.

"Sandra." I rap my knuckles on the desk.

"Yeah?" She rests her hand on the doorway as she turns around.

"Thank you for talking to me. I appreciate it. It took a lot of courage. And if you need to talk about anything, I'm always free. I don't have much to do at night." I smile, for real this time.

"Thanks. I'll remember that." Sandra winks.

I open my drawer and spot the bottle of whiskey peeking out. Sandra's opened the door, staring out into the darkness. She shudders, bracing against a sharp breeze. We're just two people at the end of the day. Strip away the titles, the ranks, the boundaries, and all you're left with is two bags of meat. We're both looking for answers. We're two people in the dark. We're trying to find someone.

"Sandra, how do you feel about a nightcap?" I plonk the bottle on the desk.

Sandra looks at me and the bottle. She bites her lip. She closes the door.

CHAPTER TWENTY

Jason Neary is walking down the road.

His shoes are torn. His shirt has a mustard stain he can't wash off. He's tied a rag to his head that droops over his eyes. His thighs ache with every step. The sun bears down on him. His face is flushed. He keeps walking.

Highways and city streets merge together. Pavements fade into boardwalks, which give way to gravel, which morph into dirt, which return to pavement, over and over and over. Trees become buildings. He passes by businessmen, panhandlers, roadside merchants, bible thumpers, and other faceless people. Dead leaves and budding flowers swarm around his feet. The horizon swirls into an endless distance. He keeps walking.

He's a roofer. He's nailing down a board with his nameless coworkers. His hat does little to stop his skin from burning. He stands up and stretches his back. He takes a swig from his water bottle. He loses his footing and tumbles off the roof, spraining his arm. He puts it in a sling and climbs back up.

He lies his head on a filthy motel pillow, keeping one eye on the door. He crashes on a friendly stranger's couch, clutching his bag close to his chest. He wanders deep into the woods and huddles under a bush. He keeps walking.

He's painting a room. He moves the roller up and down, staining the wall white. He feels dizzy. There's no ventilation.

He rides shotgun in a corvette with generous leg room. A minivan littered with receipts and fast food wrappers. A pickup truck with feisty chickens in the back. They drop him off. He keeps walking.

He's standing on a street corner. The neon signs hum and crackle. A black car pulls up to him. The driver opens the door and asks for the price. Jason tells her. She nods and Jason climbs in. She applies a fresh batch of lipstick. Jason adjusts his shirt and tries to smile.

He keeps walking.

Jason smothers his scrambled eggs in ketchup. The red velvet booth seat sinks beneath him. The fan above him stutters and shakes. His knife is stained with remnants of the last meal. He cuts off a chunk of egg and takes a bite.

The waitress eyes him as she pours a cup of coffee for another customer. She paused when he walked in the diner, balking at his shaggy beard and faded clothes. She led him to the booth closest to kitchen. The line cook is watching him as he flips pancakes.

Jason sips his coffee and looks out the grimy window, watching a man fill up his dump truck at the gas station. The waitress swipes his empty plate. She returns with the bill. Jason nods, not asking for a refill. He tosses a pair of bills on the table.

He grabs his bag and walks to the door, avoiding the patrons' gaze. He steps into the afternoon sun. He wanders away from the diner, counting the bills in his wallet. He doesn't see much green. It's been a while since his painting gig. He checks his coin purse and finds one quarter. He spots a payphone.

Months of travel. Millions of steps. Sleepless nights and exhausting days. Odd jobs with low pay. Gnawing hunger and stabbing thirst. Not a single clue what he's doing out here. He could end it all by sliding the quarter into the phone slot. One call and he'd be back in civilization. He'd be back in his apartment, back to clean clothes, back to regular meals, back to a comfortable bed, back to steady pay, back to familiar faces, back to four walls...

Jason clenches the quarter and hits the road.

Flies are feasting on a wolf's corpse in a ditch.

Jason winces and sticks out his thumb, walking backwards. Cars zoom past him. A group of twenty-somethings packed into a jeep, all wearing tie-dye shirts and long hair, shouting over pounding music, leaving behind the smell of weed. A family bickering in an R/V, a road map splayed over the front window. A couple in a convertible, lost in each other's eyes, a collection of cans jangling behind them. No one sees him.

The sun inches closer to the horizon. Jason rubs his arms and looks around for a shelter. A rock formation looks promising. He sets out for it when a black car stops beside him. The door opens. Jason leans in.

"Need a lift?" A clean-cut man with sunglasses smiles at Jason.

Jason climbs in. The car speeds down the road. Jason leans his head on the glass, watching a day's journey pass by in minutes.

"Thanks for the ride..." Jason extends his hand.

"Joseph. Good to meet you, good to meet you." The man jerks Jason's hand up and down without looking away from the road.

Jason studies his driver. His hair is shaped like a mushroom cloud. A scar runs from his chin to his throat. He's wearing an unbuttoned dress shirt and jeans. Jewellery covers his fingers and neck. The car is neat and orderly. There's a map on the dashboard covered in red "Xs."

"Where ya headed, amigo?" Joseph tilts down his sunglasses and glances at Jason.

Jason watches the yellow line stretch on into the setting sun. He shrugs.

"I like that." Joseph presses his foot down.

CHAPTER TWENTY-ONE

My ceiling is filthy.

A large brown spot is splayed on the wood, spread out like a deformed continent. Tiny brown dots surround it like island nations. It all looks like the aftermath of a shit-loaded shotgun blast. Small clumps of green cling between the ceiling holes, threatening to fall on my face. The ceiling looks like the remnants of an abandoned abattoir. How'd I let it get so bad?

The ceiling is the only thing I can see through the haze. My vision is crowded at the edges, dark and blurred. I focus on the mess looming over me, zeroing in on every fissure and blemish. I catalogue them, making a mental checklist of problems to fix. I'll clean it up as soon as I get out of bed. As soon as I can think straight.

The edges recede. I blink, adjusting to the brightness. Sunlight streams into the room. It shoots through my eyes and stabs my brain. Christ, it stings. I raise my head.

Ow.

My head falls back on the pillow. It's a bowling ball attached to my neck. It feels like an extra twenty pounds has been stuffed into my forehead. I raise my head again and feel my brain scream. I get the hint. I let myself sink into the bed, trying to get comfortable.

My body is limp. I bring my hand to my head and it's like someone cranked up the gravity dial. My arm is de-boned jelly, flopping onto my stomach. I tense my fingers and force my hand into the air, letting it fall next to my head. I shove it under my head, massaging my neck. It's like all the blood migrated to my skull, leaving my body a depleted husk. I twitch my toes and rock my hips, bringing sensation back to them. I'll be up in a moment. I just have to wait for my body to reboot. I've dealt with atrophy before. Back in the old days. But it's not the old days. It shouldn't be.

I wrestle with my tongue, pushing it away from the back of my throat. I squeeze it out of my mouth, a pink diving board beneath my nose. I pull my free hand close and pinch my tongue between my fingers, turning it from side to side. I sigh and rest my hand on my chest. My tongue retreats to its cave, lolling backwards. It's pure sandpaper. I summon a lob of spit from my throat. I coat my tongue with my saliva, thrashing it about around my gums. I bring it back to life.

I run my tongue over my lips, feeling the dried cracks. I pull my lips into my mouth, wetting them. I feel the rush of a familiar taste: Whiskey. Well, there's the answer for my head. And my body. And my vision. I didn't have a nightcap last night; I leaped into oblivion.

Drunkenness was the first thing we banned from the compound. When Joseph and I sat down on that long night, it was the top taboo on our list. We knew we couldn't forbid alcohol. It would be too radical, too extreme, for the newcomers. They'd naturally cling to their old ways. So we let them have their end-of-day bottles. But we made sure no one approached their limit. They went to bed relaxed, not obliterated. We had a few drunks at the start, but we showed them that wouldn't be tolerated. When they went for that extra glass, they'd think about their knuckles, or their knees, or their necks, and they'd sip water instead. We weeded it out of them. Nowadays, barely anyone touches the bottle, even the newbies. We're a dry town. We should be.

I was an alcoholic. I didn't even think about it. I needed it when I came home, when I went to bed, when I was bored. It was as normal as breathing. It wasn't until I was walking on that road in the middle of the afternoon with the sun beating down on me that I realized how much I needed a drink. I'd be covered in sweat, throwing up in bushes, and constantly twitching my fingers. I'd waste my coins on a stiff drink in every two-bit bar I stumbled across. I saw the problem. I could feel it in my body.

But I didn't want to accept it. I shoved it away, trying to suffocate it. It didn't budge. It stared at me, mocking every one of my deep gulps.

It wasn't until Joseph, until the drive, until that long night in the desert, that I saw myself. I wanted to scream, to cry, to hurl. I poured out every bottle we had in the trunk.

I'm not a hypocrite. I haven't lost myself to the bottle since we planted the first stake in this land. Sure, I've had a celebratory drink with my followers, on special occasions. Whenever we've completed a building or finished an exhausting sermon, I've indulged in a small glass. It's not for me; it's for my people. I want to join their celebrations so they can see me as a real person. I take one drink, only one, and I restrain myself. I don't let the liquid rule me. I show everyone they can be like me. They can control themselves. They can be better.

I kept that whiskey bottle as a reminder. A memento from a past life. It was there to keep me grounded. It showed me how far I've come and how I've barely changed at all. It was a prop, more than anything, something to reaffirm my goals. I wasn't supposed to drink it. But…

I bite my knuckles. Idiot. I drank the whole bottle. I can't see last night, not the full picture. I can only grab small moments, broken snippets. I wasn't grounding myself; I was a drunk.

Get up. I can't wallow in bed all day. I need to repent for this. I'll work in the fields or help with the buildings or pick up garbage. I need to punish myself. I was a coward. I retreated into the bottle. I escaped. I need to pay my penance. I roll to my side. Sandra is lying next to me. Asleep. Naked.

A strand of hair is draped over her face. A loose piece dangling from the middle of her head. It moves from side to side, brushing her nose and lips. She's mumbling. I move the hair away, pinning it behind her ear.

Oh, no. No. I didn't. I wouldn't. Even if I drank three bottles of whiskey, I wouldn't let it… Maybe I'd kiss her. It's normal. We get caught up in the drinks, we're friendly, we share a quick peck. That's it. I'd stop it before we'd fall into bed. She'd understand.

It was cold last night. Chilly. We must have been up late talking. Yeah, we lost track of time. We were tired and it was too dark for her to walk back to her bunk. She could've gotten hurt or...something, so I let her stay. I only have one bed, and she couldn't sleep on the floor, so she crashed next to me. That's why she's here right now. Naked.

She rolls to her back. I can't look away. Her lips and nose are in profile, looking like lumpy mountains. She sighs. It sounds familiar.

I need to get out of here. I need to crawl out of bed, put my clothes on, and run out the door. I need some space to think about...this. I can't have to wake her up. I have to stand up and walk to the door. Get up. Get up. Get up.

I don't budge.

Nothing seems to move. It's like someone hit the pause button. I don't hear anything but the blood pounding in my head. My brain screams at me to move. I can't even bend my fingers. I'm trapped in this moment. I can only stare at Sandra, seeing new snippets from last night...

Two glasses. A steady pour of whiskey. A hand passing a glass, another hand clasping over it. A look. Two lips. The bed. Falling, falling, falling...

Enough. I bite my tongue, forcing myself into the present. I'm in control. I'm in charge. I'm leaving this room. Now.

My left leg slides under the bed sheets and lands on the floor. I keep my eyes on Sandra. She snores. I guide my right leg off the bed, slowly turning my hips. I grip the end of the bed and pull myself up. My neck and back are stiff. I push the sheets off of me. I'm still wearing my underwear, thank fuck. My shirt and pants are huddled at my feet. The door is ten footsteps away. I just need to get outside and I can sort this out. Get to the river and think. Easy money. I reach down and—

"Hey, you."

Fuck.

Sandra's propped up on her elbow. She's running her hand through her hair, scratching the back of her head. She lets out a massive yawn, expanding her mouth like a black hole. She smiles up at me. I try to return the favour.

"Morning." Sandra arches her back to stretch.

I stare at her, a weak grin plastered on my face. A hundred phrases and words jostle in my head. From the simple ("Good morning to you, too"), to the loaded ("What did we do last night?"), to the aggressive ("Get the fuck out"), to the desperate ("Please don't tell anyone"), and everything in between. Images of her naked body fight for attention, too. There are a million sentences that would work right now. Not one of them escapes my mouth. I smile and nod.

She chuckles and pushes her hair away from her face. She pulls the blanket close, covering her chest. She bites her lower lip. She scooches towards me, rising to a sitting position. She leans forward. She smells like sex. She puts her hand on my shoulder. She kisses me.

She has a cut on her bottom lip. I never noticed it before. I've never been this close before. I feel a slight bump running across the rim. It's biggest in the middle, a solid protrusion in the dead center. It's scarred over and faint, years old. As my tongue traces over it, I wonder if it'll open up and spill her blood over my mouth. I wonder if she's clean. I wonder if she'll give me an infection that'll stop me from sitting down properly. I wonder a lot of things. But I don't move away.

My body has shut down again. My hands sit limply at my side. My legs dangle awkwardly above the floor as Sandra pulls me closer. My lips and tongue move lamely along with hers. I'm on autopilot.

Her teeth routinely knock into mine. She sticks her tongue into my mouth, then retreats. She breathes through her nose, blowing hot air over my cheek. Her eyes are closed, crumbs of sleep sand grouped on her lids. She makes a loud smacking sound. I've had better. She needs to work on her approach. I could—

What the hell am I doing? My follower is slobbering over me and I'm analyzing her technique? My heart's pounding. My palms are sweaty. I can feel a twitch below my waist. I'm acting like a seventh grader at an after-school dance. I'm...excited. I need to stop. Now.

My hands clasp Sandra's shoulders and I lean away. She kisses the air for a moment, chewing at nothing. She opens her eyes and gives me another grin. I struggle to keep mine upright. I clear my throat as she traces her fingers down my arm. She chuckles and pinches my elbow. Her eyes are hungry.

"Good for you?" Sandra drums her fingers on the bed.

My room is a mess. The door is wide open. The wall next to my dresser has a dent on it. Sandra's clothes form a messy trail to the bed. The sheets are crumpled and sweat-stained. My groin feels damp. Yeah, I think I had a good time. But I can't say that. I won't say that. I keep my smile frozen to my face.

"Me, too. Been a while." Sandra stretches her arm. I hear it crack.

I look at my clothes, disregarded on the floor. I put them away every night, no matter what. At the end of the day, when I'm dead on my feet, when I just want to sink into my bed, I put them away. I make the time. Every night I fold my shirt and place it in the hamper. My pants follow suit after I turn them out and bend them at the crease. Socks and underwear go to the top of the pile. I have a structure. I give myself order.

But last night, my clothes wound up on the floor. I didn't take the time to perform my final ritual. I let my order fall away. I just wanted to get laid. I only cared about my satisfaction. I let my penis rule me. And my clothes fell to the floor.

Something wraps around my wrist. I bolt to my feet, pulling my arm away. My right foot nearly slips on my shirt. Sandra's eyebrows are raised. Her hand is suspended in the air, fingers wrapped around my phantom limb.

"You okay?" Her voice is soft.

I nod, but it's not enough. She moves across the bed, nearing the edge. Her hand reaches out to me. She's trying to comfort me, listen to me, care for me, suck me in…

"I'm fine. I'm all good." I croak out the words.

"You sure?" She's not stopping. She stretches her hand for my forehead.

"Yup. Yeah, I'm great. No worries. I'm just, uh, just a little… Well, it's a bit late, you know?" I inch away from the bed.

"Shit, is that the time?" Sandra squints her eyes as she faces the sun. She doesn't notice me creeping towards the door.

"Yeah, we overslept. Must be nearly noon. I guess we really tied one off last night." I chuckle. It sounds like I'm being held at gunpoint.

"No doubt." She winks at me. Don't ask, don't ask, don't ask, just get out.

"Hahahaha, yeah, right. Well, I gotta run. So, I'll see you later." I fumble my hand over the door handle.

"You're leaving?" Sandra starts to slide out of the bed.

"Yeah, I've got a lot to do today. Inspections, paperwork, all that...stuff. And I'm running late, so…" Why can't I get a grip on this goddamn handle?

"You have to go right now? I mean, do you have five minutes? Could we talk…?" Sandra walks towards me. Oh, fuck, not again.

"Uh, sure, yeah, some other time. I'll, uh, I'll let you know when I'm free." I force the door open.

"Okay, I'll see you la—"

I've already shut the door.

CHAPTER TWENTY-TWO

My feet are cold.

My shoes are piled on top of my shirt. They're resting on the bank, obscured by the overgrown grass. My pants are splayed on the ground, sloping towards the water. My underwear is balled up at the base of a tree. I am exposed.

No one saw me enter the forest. Everyone was heading off to lunch when I burst out of my office. I could hear Sandra behind the door. She was pacing and sighing. I stumbled off the porch and made a beeline through the compound.

I forced my legs to walk when they wanted to run. Someone could've been watching. I had to stay calm. I nodded at a pair of builders carrying a wooden crate. They looked away. I stopped. Did they know something? Did they see me and Sandra? I studied them, trying to keep a steady face. They gave me weak smiles and scurried off. I breathed. They were the idiots who nearly decapitated me with that plank weeks ago. They thought I was going to punish them. I laughed. I must've looked mad.

I made it deep into the forest, far from prying eyes, when I started to run. I tore over bushes and ripped branches. My thoughts hounded me, taunting me with flashes of last night. I gripped trees and hurled myself forward, nearly careening into rotting logs. I gritted my teeth and barreled towards the river. I tried to push everything out of my head. I listened to the crunch of leaves beneath my feet. But I couldn't escape myself. More moments crept into my mind. More holes were filled. I kept seeing last night. I kept seeing her. When I tripped over a rock and crashed onto the river clearing, I had the full picture.

Now I'm standing in the river. My body is vulnerable, a fleshy outlier in the woods. I've put on flab in the last month. My stomach has a paunch. My hair is a mess. I rub my arms as a breeze blows past me, sending water ripples into my shins. My hangover is seeping into the water. I feel drained, tired, and miserable, but I'm here. I have my brain again. The organ that caused all this trouble is dangling near my thigh, shriveled and useless. It's a microcosm of me.

My feet look warped and bloated under the water. They seem discoloured, a mix of brown and yellow. I curl my toes, shoving pebbles beneath my arches. Dust erupts from the movement, surrounding my feet. The rocks and sand brush on my skin. I scratch my feet, moving the debris away. I flex my toes, ready to pull at the dirt again. I dig in and—

I've been staring at the water for an hour now. My feet are bloated and cold. They're bunched-up and pruny... I'm not waiting for inspiration. I'm not putting myself through some mild torture. I'm just staring at my feet.

It's all I can do. I can't think. I have to stand here like a deflated husk, lost in the water. I can't focus on anything for too long. I have to let my mind get swept along with the current. I've buried my thoughts under layers of numbness. I can't let myself concentrate, because if I do, I'll remember.

I can feel it happening. I'm not trying to think, but it's happening. When I bent down to scratch my foot, I had to focus. I had to think. My brain had to tell my body to bend down and rub my toes. I had to be a person again, just for a moment. Now my brain is awake.

I tilt forward, boring my eyes into the water. I stare at the pebbles floating near my feet, watching them drift away. I create a blank slate in my mind. I try to slow my heart rate. I become a statue. I can't let my thoughts get away from me. I'm in control, I'm in control, I'm in cont—

Sandra is beneath me, squirming on the bed. Her hands are running up and down my back. She's whispering my name. She reaches up to me and—

Fuck. The floodgates are open.

I close my eyes. Everything stretches before me like a desecrated highway. The fog melts away. I can see last night. I can see her. I can see what I did. I can't run from it. I have to face it. I sit down on the river bank. I can see it all playing out on the water, a movie projected from my mind to the screen. I don't have a choice. I watch.

I filled my glass with whiskey. It splashed on the desk. Sandra wiped it away with her hand before I could get a towel. She laughed. I laughed, too. This wasn't our first drink. She held out her glass with both hands, fluttering her eyelashes. I filled it up. She took a long swig.

I sat down, nearly falling out of the chair. She started talking. I listened. She lived out west. Grew up in the middle of nowhere. Moved out. Worked odd jobs up and down the coast. Partied. Drank. Learned how to make half a dozen cocktails. Had a good time.

Filled the glasses.

She woke up one morning and saw she was twenty-five. She looked in the mirror and saw that half a decade of drinking had caught up with her. She needed to escape. She sold her boyfriend's stuff (he deserved it, apparently) and went to college. She had a plan. She was going to be a veterinarian. She always liked animals. She ran a dog-walking business to earn some extra cash. She got her degree. It all fit.

Filled the glasses.

It was good work. She had her regulars. A man who took his cat for monthly checkups. A woman who fed her dog potato chips and wondered why he was overweight. A couple who were more interested in their parrot than each other. Sandra looked after them all. She delivered kittens and put family dogs to sleep and recommended diets for countless hamsters. She helped her boss with surgeries. The animals that woke up got a chew toy when they went out the front door; the ones that didn't rode a cart through the back door. She drank at the local bar and went to concerts with her co-workers and dated Phil, a cop from the station across from her apartment. She woke up, punched in, looked after animals, punched out, and went home. She went on road trips and vacations and workshops. She stayed busy. Her life orbited around her job. It grounded her. It was reliable. She knew where she stood. She hated it.

Filled the glasses. The bottle was getting light.

She wasn't struck dumb by some revelation. She didn't stand over the opened cadaver of a once-proud terrier and wonder what it all meant. She laughed at that idea, dribbling whiskey over her chin. She mostly felt nauseous when she saw the insides of an animal, not enlightened. No, there wasn't a thunderclap moment; it was a gnawing sensation. It tickled the back of her brain. She got the sense that she was wasting her time. She hadn't found the thing that lit the fire in her stomach. She was on autopilot. She was lost. But she didn't know where to go. Even if she got a new job, a new town, a new life, this feeling would follow her. Then she saw our pamphlet. It was hanging outside her yoga studio. She took it home and read it until morning came. When she greeted the sun, she knew where she belonged.

Filled the glasses. Our fingers touched as I passed her drink.

She quit, packed her bags, and hit the road. She didn't tell anyone where she was going. She found the compound, passed the interview, and slid into her role. It was second-nature. She'd found her calling. It was perfect.   Sandra paused to drink. My face was flushed. Sandra smiled at me. Our eyes locked. I cleared my throat and returned to my drink. She started talking again.

She met Spittal a year ago. I felt my face twitch when she said his name. I could smell the blood from his body. Sandra didn't notice. She probably chalked it up to the whiskey. We were both making weird faces.

She was working in her garden one afternoon. She was watering a cucumber when a toolbox fell on it. Green guts splattered on Sandra's shoes. She looked up. It was Spittal.

Filled the glasses.

She yelled at him. He apologized. She kept yelling at him. He kept apologizing. She ran out of breath. He was smirking. He always smirked. He made a joke. Sandra refused to smile. He promised to help. She glared at him as he walked away. She didn't expect to see him again.

But she saw him every day. He helped with the garden. He carried the soil bags and wheelbarrows. He never stopped talking. Sandra tuned him out, but he kept going. She thought he'd lose interest eventually, turn to someone else. But he stayed. He persisted. She relented.

He took her to the river at night. They brought kindling for a fire and meats they smuggled out of the kitchen. They swam in the water, gripping onto the bank to resist the current. They curled up on a blanket he brought. It was a decent first date, all things considered.

My head is swirling. More drinks. More talking. More quick glances and too-long stares... I try to follow the thread.

Spittal knew how to make her laugh. That was his best quality. When he saw her from across the compound, he'd grab a hammer and pretend to nail his hand to a building. Sandra giggled, letting whiskey leak out of her mouth. God, she's a slob.

Filled the glasses. Fuck, she's beautiful.

Sandra trailed off. She traced her finger over the rim of her glass. I wiped the sweat from my forehead. I drummed my fingers. Sandra polished off her drink, slamming it down. She grimaced and ran her finger over her top teeth. She darted her eyes at the door. She was ready to leave. Good. I'd finish my drink, walk her to the porch, thank her for the lovely evening, and say goodbye. I'd be in bed nursing my drunken headache in thirty minutes. I just had to swallow this last bit of whiskey. I just had to control myself. I just had to—

I started talking.

I offered my condolences about Spittal. I said I know how hard it can be to lose someone. Sandra nodded, biting her lip. I said I've been in her shoes before. Oh, no, oh, no, oh, no. I told her about Jason.

Fuck me. I wouldn't be that stupid. No matter how much I drank, no matter if I was completed annihilated, I wouldn't tell a follower about my past life. I wouldn't exposed myself... Sure, I've given a few... anecdotes about my life to juice up a sermon, but nothing concrete. People can't pin me down. I need to be an enigma. I wouldn't betray myself to her, would I?

No, no, I didn't. I told how I used to love a woman. Her name was...Tiffany. Oh, good, it was the Tiffany story. I wrote that one up years ago. It's a solid piece to fall back on. Easy to remember and just enough details to sound convincing. I told Sandra about Tiffany. I said she worked in human resources. I worked in a cubicle down the hall from her. We saw each other every day. We talked a lot. We hung out at the bar after work. We checked out the local theatre scene. We ate at the cheapest restaurants. We stayed indoors and read poetry. We went on a vacation to Rome. I met her parents. We moved in together. It was all going fine. I paused to wipe my eyes.

Sandra asked what happened next. I told her I started to feel that gnawing sensation she talked about. I felt unfulfilled. I had to find something...more. One night, I looked into Tiffany's eyes and I just saw two black pools. I ran. I ran from my work, from my life, from her. I had to get away.

Wait, wait, no, that's not how it's supposed to go. I'm supposed to dump Tiffany after she reveals her hidden hedonism. "Black pools?" Where did that come from? That sounds too...real.

I finished my drink. I told Sandra how I found my true calling and built this place. I told her I always had to look for the next mountain to climb. I knew I wouldn't have time for romance. Sandra chuckled. She held out her hand like she was holding a skull. She put her hand to her forehead and swooned. I laughed. We agreed; a bit too melodramatic.

I put the whiskey away. Sandra squeezed my arm. She said she was tired. I looked out the window. It was pitch black. I told her she could stay here. I had spare blankets in my closet. She could have the bed. I wouldn't mind the floor. I turned back to her. She put her lips on mine.

I grabbed her waist. My mouth was on her neck, she gasped. I clawed her back. It had been so long…

No, no, no.

I knocked everything off my desk and pulled her closed. She whispered in my ear. We stumbled to our feet. I forced my room door open. I tore off her shirt as she unbuckled my pants. Our lips stayed locked.

Stop. Walk away. Please. Just walk away.

We stood in front of one another, exposed. I ran my fingers over her shoulders and chest. She guided me forward. I pulled her close. We fell into bed and—

Fuck.

I smash my foot into the river. Water splashes in my eyes. I rub it away as I stumble forward. Rocks slide beneath my feet. I fall onto the bank and crash on my hip. More water lands on my chest and face. My lap is submerged in the river. I scramble up, grabbing onto grass for support. I dig my fingers deep into the earth, pulling myself to the shore. I yank on a root. It flies out of my hands, soaring halfway across the river. I tumble back into the water. I'm panting. I look up at the bank. It's covered in scratches and claw marks. I lift my hands but they fall to my sides. I look as impotent as I feel.

I sit there in my shallow throne and stew. I let my anger and disgust consume me. I sink deeper into the muck, leaning against the river side. My damp clothes cling to my body, chilling me. The sun shines just ahead of me, obscured by the trees that tower above me. This is where I belong, stuck in muddy water, coated in dirt and sweat and shame. This is all I deserve.

I reach up and grab another root. I rip it from its place, spewing out pebbles and dirt. I flick it across the river, watching it crash. I do it again and again and again. My hands are filthy. Grime is wedged beneath my fingernails. The ripples from the roots' crash landings lap at my chest. I keep going until I can't grab anything else. When they're gone, all I'm left with are my thoughts.

You absolute moron. How could you be so stupid? You fucked one of your followers. One of the people you're supposed to lead. You got your rocks off with your subordinate. Slime.

I want to disappear into the mud. I want to dissolve into dust and float away in the river. I want to escape myself. But I can't. I'm stuck here in the water. I have to face what I did.

Why? Why did you do it? Why'd you put your hands on her? For two minutes of pleasure? For a brief release? For a break from the murders and Blume and Smit? You acted like a horny teenager because you wanted a reprieve from the pressure. You took the easy way out. You drank and screwed because it distracted you from what you need to do. You betrayed yourself so you could stain your bed sheets. You're not just a degenerate; you're a hypocrite.

I clutch a ball of muck in my hand. I can see the mouth of the cavern past the river bank. That's where I'll transcend. That's where I'll take everyone to Paradise. That's what I've always thought. But maybe I'm wrong. Maybe I'm not meant to go higher. Maybe this is where I'm meant to stay, down in the mud.

I failed. I crossed the line: I lay with a follower. I let my stress overwhelm me. I used my fear and my...loneliness as a justification to spiralling down with Sandra. I was weak.

I see Sandra lying next to me after we'd finished. We were staring at each other. She was falling asleep. We were both smiling. She kissed my nose and turned to her side. She grabbed my arm and draped it over her chest. I closed my eyes. My problems were worlds away.

I'm not a prude. I know we're animals, at the end of the day. I don't deny what we are. I don't forbid...physical relationships here. I'm not a tyrant. People need time to overcome their urges. I don't try to stamp them out; I coax them away. I let the old fade so the new can flourish. Everyone's allowed to make a mistake.

Why not me? Why can't I be allowed to falter? What did I do, really? I slept with someone, that's it. A follower, certainly, but a consenting adult. Two people found each other, simple as that. Sometimes people need to let go. A wrongheaded move, of course, but not unpardonable. Who did it hurt? It could've happened to anyone. What's so bad about it?

I raise the dirt in my hand above me and drop it. I splatters of my chest, throwing chunks in my face. I flinch. My body brings my mind back to reality. I leave my fantasies behind.

I'm not anyone. I'm the leader of the compound. I can't make mistakes like this. I'm supposed to be the example. I'm meant to be the standard everyone should measure themselves by. Instead, I sank to the standards of the masses. I was typical. I was average.

I look at myself. I really look at myself. A frail man huddled in the mud on the shores of a river. A man ruined by his insecurities and failures. A man who let his urges overwhelm him. A man who turned his back on his principles. A man who can't climb onto a riverbank.

Maybe I had it wrong. Maybe I wasn't meant to be a leader. Maybe I was just supposed to provide the spark, kickstart the compound, but nothing more. If I can't overcome myself, how can I lead everyone? What if my destiny isn't at the top? What if I already achieved what I needed to do and everything else is...filler? Am I just running out the clock at this point, coasting on momentum? I'm a...fraud.

I could walk away. I could sneak off into the night, just like the people who've fled to Smit's compound. Maybe it'll be better for everyone if they don't know what happened to me, if it's open to interpretation, if they don't see me exposed as a liar. If I self-destruct in front of everyone, if my followers found out my...indiscretion, it could damage what I've built. It might be best for me to leave and try to find what I'm really meant for. Leave the compound to Greg and Ken. They'd know how to handle the place. They're real believers; I'm a pretender.

I look back at the mouth of the cavern. The sun hits it at just the right angle, revealing its unexplored depths. All that potential, all that promise, lying in wait. The spot where we'd all become more. The symbol of what we've worked towards. Our final resting place.

I found that cave. Not Greg. Not Ken. Not even Joseph. I climbed the hill and I entered the mouth with a flashlight. I found the chamber. I heard the booming echoes as I spoke. I saw the future. It came in a flash. I knew this place would be the perfect theatre for our ceremony. I realized we were meant to be here. I gave us the right place for closure.

I was even weaker back then. I had only begun to purge myself of the poison coursing through my veins. Poison that still clings to me. My weaknesses gripped me like a vise. I was blind. But I could still see the cavern, really see it for what is: Paradise. In the depths of my ignorance, I saw the truth. I wasn't completely lost. I could redeem myself. I could ascend.

I scramble to my knees. I pull myself onto the bank, resting my chin and arms on the grass. I see the full cavern. It towers over me, beckoning to me. I can see the way. It's not too late. I'm down in a pit I threw myself into, but I'm not stuck. I can get out. I don't have to leave. I can redeem myself. I can still be a leader. I can fulfill my destiny.

I failed. Clearly. I crossed the line. I damaged myself and my follower. I let Sandra and me be corrupted. I'm despicable.

But this place is about second chances. How many broken, confused people have walked through our gates? How many sinners and liars and crooks have I absolved? How many times have my followers strayed from the path, how many times have they let themselves down, how many times have they stumbled, only to be met with forgiveness? I pardoned each and every one of my people, because I knew they could transcend. I knew they simply needed an opportunity to prove they were better than their urges. It's never too late. It's not too late for me.

I'm not past the veil. I've let myself down, but it's not unforgivable. I don't deserve to be cast out. This compound was built on redemption. We fail every day here; that's the point. I deserve a second chance. After all my hard work, after all the people I've helped and supported and forgiven, I've earned a break. One mistake shouldn't mar my legacy. It shouldn't erase what I've created. I'm entitled to a pardon. After my endless patience, I deserve a stay of execution.

I'm not giving myself an easy way out. I'm not skirting the system and avoiding my punishment. I'm merely allowing myself to find redemption. I'll put myself through the grinder for what I've done. I will lash my back until it's painted red. I'll fast until my stomach screams and contracts. I'll stay awake until my eyelids sag and my body goes limp. I will pummel myself as penance.

But I won't leave. I can't, not now, not when everyone needs me. The killer, Smit, Blume, they're tearing at us from all angles. We're in the snake pit. This place needs strong leadership. I can't let my indiscretion hurt the whole compound. I will stay. I will command. I will get better.

Sandra's face flashes in my mind. I grimace. Being with her is relaxing, simple, easy. But I'll cut it off. Next time I see her, I tell her everything. I let her know that last night was a mistake we can't repeat. I'll tell her we shouldn't be around each other anymore. I won't force her to leave, of course, but I'll hold her at arm's length. I won't talk to her, I won't engage with her, I won't think about her. Cold turkey. I know it'll be hard for her to accept. But she'll soldier through. She'll find someone else. And if she can't let it go, if she feels she can't stay here with me...well, that's too bad. But it's better this way. It's best if we stay apart.

I curl my hand into a fist and rhythmically pound it on the ground. I bob my head along to the beat. My heart rate rises. I can see it all playing out in my head. My rejection of Sandra. My self-punishment and flagellation. My dreary isolation and contemplation. My journey into the cave for further meditation. My emergence, stronger and wiser, ready to lead once again. It's perfect. This might be my best mistake. I've fallen only to rise even higher.

I smile as I look at the cavern, feeling my feet get cold in the water.

CHAPTER TWENTY-THREE

"It's understandable to have cold feet. This is a big decision. A terrible decision. One you'll live with for a long time. It's not too late to step away from the edge."

Three followers are standing before me. Soon-to-be ex-followers. They're clad in dust-covered overalls. Their brows are sloped and furrowed as they concentrate on the ground. The gate looms behind them, wide open. A group of Zaan recruiters stands beyond it. They're cheering and dancing, blasting music from a car radio. Bastards.

A small group is behind me. Intrigued spectators. Ken is standing between them and me in case they try to interfere. He needn't bother. The crowd is made up of builders on a lunch break. They're tittering amongst themselves as they eat their sandwiches. They're only half-paying attention. A few passersby stop to watch, but the majority keep on walking. Most people stick to their jobs. The exodus has become routine. There's nothing salacious about it now; it's dull.

I'm tired. I can hear it in my voice. I can barely muster the energy to make it loud. I don't have time for this nonsense. Another batch of cowards too weak to face their own demons. I'm scraping and crawling my way to redemption while they're sneaking out the back door. I don't have patience for them, or any of the other deserters. I have to focus on the believers, my real followers. If these pretenders want to flee, I should let them. Wash my hands and be done with it.

I eye the Zaan lunatics celebrating in their golden robes, a swirling mass of piss. More of them are here each time. They're getting bigger, bolder, more belligerent. I can't suffer any more losses. I need to hold onto what I have, even if it's a bunch of traitors. We have to stop the bleeding. I need these builders. I keep talking.

"Consider the consequences. The real, honest consequences. This isn't a minor choice you're making. When you walk past that gate, you'll be locking yourself out of our compound. You'll be condemning yourself to a lifetime of waste. You'll be denying yourself paradise. Think, gentlemen. Think before you damn yourselves." I study their faces.

They can't look me in the eye. One rubs his nose while another coughs. The man on the right picks at a scab on his elbow. He seems to shirk away from me more than the other two. I step towards him.

"This isn't a matter of bodily pleasure or momentary satisfaction. This is a battle for your very souls. Beware of the sellers of simple balms to your worries. They'll coax out the worst in you. They'll let you indulge in every delight you can think of. They'll smile and laugh and pat your back. All the while they'll fasten the weights to your souls that will drag you into the dirt. They are not your friends. They are snake oil salesmen in cheap robes. They are not to be trusted." I fix my eyes on the Zaan members. They notice me and wave, cranking their music even louder.

I want to shove their heads into their car trunks and smash the lid until it breaks. I want to stain the road with their teeth. But if I even touch them, they'll run off to Blume and he'll pull out the warrant. That fucker's waiting for whoever steps in shit first. So I stick with words.

"Don't be seduced by these liars. Don't take the easy way. Your decision will impact the rest of your lives. Remember what I've taught you. Remember everything you've accomplished here. Don't throw everything away. Stay the course. Stay with us." I spread my arms.

Someone in the crowd cheers. A few people clap their hands. Ken hollers something encouraging. The deserters' mouths twitch and their eyes narrow. There's doubt there. The one on the right shuffles his feet forward before stepping back. He looks at the others, but they don't meet his gaze. He's ready to crack. Time to bring the hammer down.

"Son, you don't want to do this. It's not you. You're not cowardly like those hedonists. You're a soldier. You've fought through things most people can't imagine. You don't want to leave it all behind. You want to fight for it. You want to be better. Am I right?" I put my hand on the man's shoulder. He flinches.

The man slowly raises his head to look at me. His face is controlled. He's not chewing his lips or scrunching his nose. But there's guilt in his eyes. He didn't think he'd have to confront me. He thought he'd be able to crawl away unseen. I won't let him.

"Am I right? You're a strong person, yes?" I give his shoulder a hard squeeze.

He nods. A grunt escapes his lips. I feel his arm flex in my grip. He's trying to intimidate me. Or impress me. I suppress a smirk.

"Then you know the right thing to do. You know where you really belong. You know what you have to do." I let my hand fall away.

"I... I think I do... I'm not sure... but we... we all thought..." The man's compatriots inch away from him.

"Look how frazzled he is. Here is a man who knew his place in the world. He had certainty. But after listening to that poison from those frauds, he's switched around. He can't even find the right words to speak their nonsense. He's lost. We have to help him, yes?" I gesture at the crowd. Ken cheers on cue. The people copy him.

"And we will. We will help each one of these confused souls. We will return them to structure. We will fix them. We will bring them back into the fold. If they step back from the edge." I hold my finger in the air.

I savour the silence. Even with the small crowd, even with my low energy, even with Zaan lurking in the background, there's electricity in the air. A sense that something important is going to happen. I return to the man on the right.

"I've said my piece. I know what's right. I want to hear from you. I want you to explain yourself. I want you to tell us why you want to walk away from your hard work. Please. Speak." I move to the side of the man, exposing him to the crowd.

The man grimaces and steps forward. He glances at his friends, who nod. He glances at the Zaan members, seeing them stumble around like golden idiots. He looks at me. I've got him. He's ready to relent. He's going to show people how empty Zaan truly is. Then he'll crawl back into the compound along with his buddies, begging for forgiveness. And I'll grant it. Oh, it will come with a heavy price, but I'll grant it nonetheless. I lick my lips. He opens his mouth.

"We're bored."

I blink. The guilt in the man's eyes is gone. His chest is puffed out. His chin is cocked up. He's challenging me in front of everyone.

"...what?" The word croaks out of my mouth.

"We're bored. All we do is build, eat, sleep, and listen to you. Once we're done building something, we move on. It's the same crap. We want something different. We're bored." The man shrugs. He shrugs when he's talking to me. Me.

"You're...bored?" I blink again.

"Yeah, we want more. We're sick of this." The middle one's voice cracks as he speaks.

Christ, even the cowards are talking against me. I run my hand through my hair. The crowd is tittering. Ken shushes them. I'm losing control. I take a deep breath and zero in on the one on the right.

"How… how can you be bored here? How can you be sick of the routine? It's making you better, stronger. Every day is a new mountain to overcome. We're fighting here to save ourselves. This is not boring." I try to keep the knee-jerk anger out of my voice.

"It is to us." He shrugs again. Fucking hell.

"You didn't come here to be entertained. This compound isn't a full-time distraction. It's work. It's hard, back-breaking work. You came here because you wanted something more out of life. You wanted to evolve. You wanted something meaningful." Slight applause behind me. Probably all Ken.

"Eh, it's not for us. We want something else." The man on the right turns his head to the Zaan members.

"How could you want anything else? We have everything you need. Shelter. Work. Support. Purpose. A sense of-" I stop as the man coughs.

"Can you promise we won't be bored?" He raises his eyebrows.

"What?"

"Can you promise we won't be bored? If you can, we'll stay."

He's trying to negotiate with me. I can see a smile tugging at his lips. He thinks this is a buyer's market. I feel the blood surging to my face. I bite the inside of my mouth to contain myself.

"I'm sorry this compound doesn't meet your criteria for...excitement. This isn't a resort. If you want to roll up your sleeves and accomplish something, you should stay here. But if you want to wallow in your own filth, you should—"

"Thought so." He turns away from me.

The other two glance at me before slinking behind him. They pass the iron bars and shrink as they follow the dirt path. They hug the Zaan members, slip into their golden robes, hop in the cars, and peel down the road. I've lost three followers.

I turn to the crowd, wiping the surprise from my face. Everyone's staring at me. They want an explanation. I look like an idiot. People are muttering. They're shaking their heads. I blink. My mouth is frozen open. I can't connect my brain to my lips. Say something. Speak, for fuck's sake.

"Uh, as, uh, as you can see, our enemies', tentacles can reach far and pull hard. They can, they can drag the strongest of us down to the, uh, depths of our...depths. I mean, depths of our weakness. Yes, yes, yes. They can lead the best of us down the wrong path. Those three men, no, those three lost souls are a warning. We can't be like them. Right?" I wipe my forehead and nod at the audience. A pair of planters clap their hands.

"No, no, of course not. We can't be like them. We can't be like them. We can't be like them…" I stop myself from pacing. Wrap this up.

"And we won't be like them. We're better than them. We won't be misled. We won't be distracted. We won't be dragged into the muck. We're going to stay the course. We're going to send those tentacles back to their sewer." I jerk my thumb to where the cars were parked.

I clear my voice. My neck itches but I don't scratch it. I hope my face doesn't betray my confusion. I want to run into my office, barrel into my garden, and meditate. I want to put as much distance between me and this gate as possible. But I can't. Everyone's watching me. They're listening. I need to reassure them. I need to guide them away from temptation. This place is a raw nerve. I have to massage it.

"These are trying times, my friends. Make no mistake. We're being tested every day. They want to see us falter and fail. They want us to be like them, wallowing in mediocrity. They want us to suffer. But we won't give them the satisfaction." My raised voice startles the crowd.

"We won't. We're going to shove our successes down their throats. Friends, I know you've given everything to this compound. I'm proud of each and every one of you. I only asked you to do exactly what you've been doing. Stick to your path. Don't let these jackals splinter us. Stay united. Stay strong." I bump my fist on my chest.

"Be a rock. Stay with me and you'll be fine. Don't give in. Focus." I've run out of words.

I stand there and nod. Seconds tick away. The crowd titters and whispers. Members drift back to their jobs. The moment's passed. Some people applaud. Ken is slamming his palms together. I raise my hand in... victory, I guess. I spare one last look at the open road, grimacing.

I don't let my feet get away from me. I control myself as I move into the crowd. I shove my screaming brain into the background. I'm on autopilot. I'm patting shoulders and shaking hands, smiling at the remaining members. I repeat "stay strong" over and over, like a mantra. If I say it enough, it'll stick. I work my way through the group, watching them fade into the compound. I take it one step at a time. Don't panic. Stay calm, stay calm, stay...

Somehow, I'm standing at the center square. My foot is planted on the bench as I lean over my knee. I'm staring at the laces on my shoe. They're tied in a sloppy knot. One loop dwarfs the other, dropping to the left. I reach down and tug on the lace. I shrink the loop until it matches its twin. Neat and ordered.

Ken and Greg are standing next to me. Greg is flipping through his clipboard. Ken's arms are crossed and flexed. Members walk past us, giving us a wide berth. I see the gate in the distance, wide open. I see the road where my members slide on their new gold robes. Autopilot switches off. I'm awake. And I'm livid. I grab Ken and Greg by the back of their necks and pull them close.

"This is unacceptable. We're bleeding members every day." My spit lands on their faces. Greg wipes his glasses. Ken doesn't move.

"I understand that, sir." Greg tries to weasel out of my grasp. I don't let go.

"Do you? Do you really? Because I just had to embarrass myself out there when those Zaan shits stole three members right in front of us. They turned their backs on me. On us. And everybody saw it. I was humiliated because we can't plug a leak. Do you understand that?" I'm pressing my fingers onto his neck muscles.

"I do, sir." Ken raises his hand. Christ, he's like an abused puppy.

Greg slips out of my grip, massaging his neck. I glare at him and he returns the favour. Ever since the accusation, he's been...less obedient. Can't blame him, but I need him to listen. Ken stays bent over, still in my grasp. I sigh and let him go.

"We have to stop this. Now." I'm close to tearing my hair out.

"We're trying everything we—" Greg points at his clipboard.

"Everything? I had to beg those members not to leave while those Zaan lunatics watched. You haven't done anything. We're dying here." I fight to keep my voice low. Can't panic the members.

"Well, in between trying to solve a murder and arrange the ceremony, I don't have a lot of time to worry about member retention." Greg's glare deepens.

I step toward him, fists balled. He moves forward, too. A month ago, he wouldn't dream of challenging me. Now... Ken comes between us, putting his hands on our chests.

"We're all under a lot of stress. We're doing our best." Ken attempts a smile.

"Fine, fine. What have we done?" I brush his hand away.

"I've told everyone not to bother with Zaan. When I see someone talking about it, I pull them aside and set 'em straight. If any of those Zaan fuckers get near the gate, I chase 'em out." Ken juts out his chin. He really thinks he's making a difference. Maybe he is.

"Great. Greg?" I raise my eyebrows.

"Like Ken said, we're physically keeping Zaan members out of the compound. We hear someone talking about it, we change the topic. We're keeping our eyes peeled. But..." Greg kicks a mound of dirt.

"Always a but."

"But we can't be everywhere. And those damn pamphlets keep pouring in. We destroy the ones we find, but they're everywhere. I can't stop the flow. As long as they're here, we're going to lose people."

I rub my temples. We're being beaten by paper. Ludicrous.

"Sir, there's something else." Greg taps his clipboard.

"What is it?" Judging by his face, I really don't want to know.

"We've only gained ten members in the last four weeks. At this pace, if the leaks continue, we're going to be below half our top number in a month." Greg shakes his head.

Fuck, fuck, fucking fuck, fuck. Less than half? In a month? Motherfucking fuck shit fuck.

"Anything on Smit?" I'm desperate.

"Nothing yet. He's clean. Independent businessman who started a compound. Vanilla background. He's squeaky. We're not going to take down Zaan through him." Greg shrugs.

I look around the compound. A pair of builders walk past me, hauling a large barrel. Huge black bags sag beneath their eyes. Their arms tremble as they balance the awkward weight. They're nearly crippled with exhaustion. They want to take a break. But they don't. They're here. They're working. They're making the effort.

Other workers stream around me. A swirl of plants, wood, buckets, and ropes. A perfectly ordered web. Everybody working together for one common goal. It looks like a functioning system. But I can see the virus. There are slow walkers, people who drag their feet as they move from building to building. The diligent ones manoeuvre around them, offering apologies that are met with rolled eyes. Four people are huddled together, propped against the cafeteria wall. They're laughing and slapping each others' backs. A builder approaches them and points to the construction site. They keep on chuckling. The builder grabs a slacker by the shirt and pushes him off the wall. His buddies groan and follow suit, shambling to the site. I see someone sitting under a tree. His eyes are closed. His body is limp. He's sleeping in front of all of us. He's sleeping in front of me.

The poison runs deeper. A collection of women cross the square. They're carrying bags of dirt. Some are talking, but most are silent. They're staring down at the ground. I clear my throat. They meet my gaze. I offer an encouraging smile. The three women closest to me return the favour. They bow their heads and mutter thanks to me. Even as they break their backs, they have reverence. There's a spark buried beneath the exhaustion. They're awake. The two women in the back stare at me. Their lips are separated into the smallest of smiles. Their eyes are narrowed. Challengers. They look at me the same way Greg does. The group disappears behind a building.

This infection is spreading. I can hear the whispers. They're questioning me. They don't think I can deliver the goods. They're wondering if they should jump ship. They're turning on me. I need to cut this serpent's head off. My fingers twitch. My heart rate quickens. My head is getting light. An energy is gripping me, pushing me forward, showing me what to do. I have to act. Now.

"What time is it?" I pivot to Greg.

"Uh, 11:30...no, 11:31." Greg taps his wristwatch.

"Get the car." I pat Ken's shoulder.

"Long trip or short trip?" Ken holds his hand up.

"What does that matter?" I shrug.

"Well, the tank's a little low, so if we're going to be on the road for a while, I'll have to fill it up, and that means I'll need to grab a gas can from the shed, and that means I'll have to grab the shed key, and—" Ken stops as I put my finger over his mouth.

"The tank'll be full enough. Go start the car." I wave him away.

"You sure? If we run out—"

"We'll hitchhike home. Start the fucking car." I gnash my teeth, throwing spit in his face.

Ken flinches and bows his head. He wipes his cheek and strides towards the woods. I think to apologize for snapping at him, but he's already gone. I don't have time to make sure everybody's okay. I can't let this energy slip away.

"I need you to hold down the fort. You good with that?" I walk back and forth in front of Greg. I need to move.

"I'll manage." Greg gives me a withering glare. Sarcasm is dripping from his voice.

"Ken and I will be back in a few hours. If Zaan comes back, lock the gate and direct everybody to the river. Say it's for...meditation or something. Or take them to the cafeteria. Ooh, actually, the main hall, that's where you should take people. Plenty of distractions there. Stay there until Zaan buggers off. But they shouldn't come back today. They're done for the day, right? Right, yeah, they'll stay away. Just go to the hall and you'll be fine. " I flick my hands.

"Gotcha." Greg's not writing any of my ideas down.

"Yeah, yeah, I'm sure you'll be fine. Just carry on as normal. I've noticed a few slackers today, so get them back in order. Check with the cafeteria for today's dinner. I think they're making a—" I stop when I see Greg shaking his head.

"I've run this compound by myself before. I'll be fine." Greg tucks his clipboard under his armpit.

I consider him. There's a shell around him. He's harder, colder. When I called him a killer as he stared at those corpses, something in him broke. He saw the world one way, through one lens. I pushed him to see everything another way. He's still a believer; I don't think anyone could beat the faith out of him. He's keeps it buried now; you couldn't break in with a jackhammer. He knows this is where he belongs. He'll be here to the bitter end.

But he's a step removed, as if he's viewing everything from a distance. He moves like a prolonged sigh. And he looks at me as if I'm a liar he's barely tolerating. He thinks he saw the real me back in the garden and he's disgusted. I built a bridge between us. I don't know how to cross it.

I wouldn't let anyone else disrespect me like he's doing. He's undermining me. I need absolute loyalty. But I won't touch him. I'll let him burn through this hatred. He doesn't want to stay out on the edge for too long. He'll lower his walls eventually and I'll be there. I'll let him stew. I owe him that much.

"Greg... Thank you. We'd be lost without you." I flash an encouraging smile.

"...yes, sir. See you when you get back." Greg jerks his head in a quick bow and walks away.

I stretch my arms and legs while I flex my fingers. I crack my neck. I bounce on the balls of my feet, throwing out boxing jabs. I picture what's going to happen. I see myself emerging from the car, Ken flanking my side. I enter the building and sit down. My opponent is smiling. I unleash a torrent, tearing him to shreds. He tries to defend himself, tries to distract me, but I persist. I pick him apart word by word. I leave him shell-shocked. He concedes. Applause.

I open my eyes. It won't go like that, not completely. Maybe I'll only get ninety percent of what I want. But I can envision my success. I can see my path. I have a roadmap.

I'm ready for lunch.

I reach the edge of the compound when I see Sandra.

I freeze. She's bent over, yanking on weeds poking out beneath the living quarters. I didn't spot her until she was right next to me. I was too focused on the forest, on getting into the car, on hurling down the highway. I was lost in my world.

Sandra continues rips at the earth, letting out the odd grunt or curse. Dirt and grass fly over her shoulder, landing at my feet. Her muscles tense as she pulls on a weed, tearing it from its home. Her neck glistens with sweat. I can smell her from here. It's a mix of—

Stop. No more of that. She's a member, nothing else. She's just a worker like everyone here. Nothing special about her. Nothing at all.

I turn to leave, but I don't move. My waist twists, but my legs stay still. I'm going to sneak past her. No need to bother her. She's busy. Look at her tear into those weeds. I don't want to throw off her concentration. She probably doesn't have the time to talk. She's a workhorse. She's got a lot to do. I shouldn't bother her.

I'm burning daylight standing here. I've got to get on the road and fix our outmigration problem pronto. Then I need to hurry back here and prepare tomorrow's sermon, look over Greg's ceremony estimates, do a perimeter sweep with Ken… Hell, I don't know how I'm going to fit it all in. I'm wasting time here twiddling my thumbs. Every second counts. Get a move on. No need to talk with Sandra. We're both busy. Let's get going.

But my feet don't move. Something's nudging the back of my mind. A niggling thought. I can't let go. I sigh and rub my eyes.

I owe her something, don't I? I took advantage of her. I used her. I brought her into the muck. And then I shut her out. I haven't spoken to her in over a week. I've deliberately avoided her. I've kept my head on swivel, ready to dart around a corner or grab an unsuspecting member for a spontaneous conversation if Sandra pops up.

Immature? Probably. Cowardly? Absolutely. An overreaction? Almost certainly. I've been a spineless toad, but how else am I supposed to separate myself from her? This is my detox. That's the only way to beat your problem: Stuff it in a box and don't think about. That's what I'm doing with Sandra. I'm simply following my own prescription.

I know, I know, I know, that's not the way it's supposed to go. Every night, my brain keeps me awake by replaying my revelation at the river. It shows my desperation, my desolation, and my declaration. I've stayed true to my words. I've punished myself like never before. My back looks like a red road map of middle America. And I'm not done. I have another month of penance planned out. I've stayed the course. I'm sticking it out. I'm a man of my word. Mostly.

But my brain doesn't care about all of that. It doesn't care about my repentance or my renewed focus. It only cares about one little, tiny, insignificant thing I said at the river. It keeps telling me I said I'd break it off with Sandra to her face. And I haven't.

I've tried. I've seen her around the compound a few times...from a distance. I've wanted to talk to her, to take her to one side, to tell her everything. I've wanted to let her know I'm sorry and it won't happen again and I'm here for her as a leader. I started walking towards her once. I had the speech ready in my head. She was sitting on a bench overlooking the field. The sun was setting and she was drinking a cup of tea. I could see the steam rising from it. It seemed like the right time. Someone tapped my shoulder. It was Greg. He wanted to talk about supplies. I let him lead me to the cafeteria. I told myself I had to speak with him, that it was my responsibility, that I couldn't talk with Sandra at that moment. But I felt the weight lift off my chest. I'd found a way out.

Every night I've pounded my head on the pillow and bunched up the sheets in my fists. I've said that tomorrow will be the day I finally do it. Tomorrow becomes today and I step back. I pass the buck to a tomorrow I don't want to come.

Now I have a golden opportunity to talk with Sandra. No members around. Silence surrounds us. It might not be that hard...

No, I don't have time for it. I'm falling behind schedule. I should be watching the pavement race beneath me by now. If I leave Ken alone with that car for too long, he'll probably drain the battery. Yeah, that's it. I should get moving.

"Oh, hey, you. Didn't see you there."

I blink. Sandra is looking at me. She's wiping dirt off her palms. She's walking towards me. The decision's been made.

"Oh, hello. I didn't see you, either. How are you?" I slap a smile on my face.

"I'm good, I'm good. No complaints." She flicks the last layer of dust from her hand.

"That's good, that's good…" I stretch my smile up higher.

We look at each other. Sandra pushes her hair away from her face. I shift from one foot to another. She clears her throat. We widen our awkward smiles.

"What have—?"

"How are—?"

We close our mouths. We laugh. Silence. Sandra gestures at me. I shake my head and point at her. She waves it off and nods at me. I sigh through my nose.

"How are… I mean, how's work going?" I kick the weed pile at my feet.

"Oh, it's fine. Hard stuff today. These fuckers won't cooperate. But someone's gotta do it. And that someone's usually me." She grinds her heel into a loose weed on the ground.

"Mmm. True, true. You're a…hard worker, that's for sure. And, uh, how are…things?" I rub at a stubborn itch below my chin.

"Things? Things are good. Eat, sleep, work, sermon. You know the routine." Sandra steps closer.

"Oh, I do, I do." My muscles to stop my legs from moving away from her.

"Right, of course you do. So how's the whole…leadership thing going?" Sandra jerks her head at the rest of the compound.

"It's good, it's really good. Lots to do. Keeping everything above board. Few rough spots, but it's under control. You know how it goes." What the fuck am I saying? We're not co-workers chatting at the office water cooler. You're her superior, dammit; act like it.

"Yeah, nonstop work, right? You must be pretty busy these days. I never see you around the compound. I mean, I see you during the sermons, of course. That last one was great, by the way. Really made me think. But you disappeared as soon as you were done. I didn't have a chance to talk to you. I pushed my way to the front. Nearly caved somebody's face in. I'm kidding. But you were already gone. Must've had something important to do, I guess…" Sandra gives a hangdog shrug. Oh, she's good at the guilt game. A real pro.

"Yeah, yeah, it's been a busy week. I've, uh, been going from one thing to the other. I haven't gotten a sliver of sleep. It's been nuts." I give an exaggerated sigh.

"I'll bet." She bites on her fingernails.

More silence. We glance at the ground and the sky. I stretch my arms and make a popping sound with my mouth. Sandra bobs her head. I go to speak, but nothing comes out. The speech is unfurled in my head, full-written and ready to go. Everything I need to say is right there. But it doesn't want to travel to my tongue. It doesn't want to pass through my lips. It doesn't want to hurl itself into her ears. I just stand there with my plastered-on smile, feeling the seconds tick away.

I can't do this. Not now. I've got too much on my mind. I can't give her my full attention. I'm sparing us both the embarrassment, really. This conversation deserves more breathing room. I'll get to eventually. I swear I will. We'll talk. Just not right now.

"Well, duty calls. I've got to get going. A million things to do and only so many hours. Slave to the schedule. Good to see you. We'll, uh, we'll talk again sometime." I backpedal as I point to the forest. I keep my smile stuck in place.

Sandra opens her mouth, but she stays quiet. She gives me a short wave. I reply with a salute as I turn around. I see my destination dead ahead. Just a few short steps and I'll be in the forest and climbing into the passenger's seat. My plan returns to my head, showing me flashes of what I have to do. It's going to be good. Great, even. Everyone's going to talk about it. Maybe I'll work it into a sermon. I'm going to—

"Could we talk?" Fuck.

I nearly trip over my feet. I face Sandra. She's folded her arms. Her nose is scrunched up.

"Can we talk about...the other night?" She coughs the words out.

No more getting around it, no more stalling, no more excuses. It's going to happen. But not right now.

"Of course. I've been meaning to talk to you about...it. It's important. We should definitely...discuss it. But I really do have to run. This errand can't wait." I jerk my thumb at the forest.

"But I think we should talk abou—" She steps towards me and I raise my hand.

"And we will, we absolutely will. It's the top thing on my mind. But if I don't deal with this now, it'll never get done. It concerns the whole compound. You understand?" I'm using the compound as a defense. Shameless.

Sandra exhales and nods. She furls and unfurls her hands into fists. Defuse the situation. Now.

"I'm taking this...thing seriously. Look, let's talk tonight. Around...midnight, let's say. Meet me in the sermon hall. Plenty of privacy. We can talk until the morning if we have to. Sound good?" I flash a thumbs-up.

Sandra's hands are on her hips. She glances at the compound. She can see the corner of the sermon hall from here. She presses her tongue against her cheek. She nods.

"Midnight works for me. Looking forward to it." She returns my thumbs-up and smiles.

"Excellent, excellent, me too. Now, I've really got to run. See you tonight." I take off for the forest before she says anything else.

It's really happening. A chance to fix my mistake. And in the sermon hall, no less. I couldn't have planned it any better. It's the perfect spot to reject her.

CHAPTER TWENTY-FOUR

Farms melt away, transformed into rows of suburban decay.

My head leans over the dashboard. Ken holds the steering wheel with one hand while he scratches his crotch with the other. The compound is a distant blip in the rear-view mirror. The radio is tuned to some local garbage belting out homogenized ballads and guitar solos. It helps me focus.

I rub my eyes. I've finished mapping out my speech. I know what I have to do. Now I just need to do it. No need to dwell on it; I'll second-guess myself. Enjoy the ride.

A pickup truck is pulled over on the side of the road. A trailer is hitched behind it, weighed down with suitcases. A silo looms over the truck. A man in a plaid shirt is standing in the back of the truck. He's surrounded by furniture and tools. He's securing fasteners to everything, pulling on the ropes, making sure they don't move. A woman is leaning over the side of the truck, pointing at different items in the back. Two kids are sitting on the grass next to the truck. They're staring at the silo. None of them notice us as we drive by.

There's a barn on our right. A homestead is next to it. An empty pen with splintered wood rests on a small hill. The ground looks tired and beaten. There's a faded sign in front of the gravel driveway. A woman in a power suit is smiling on it, half-obscured by a red sticker that reads, "Sold."

I look back at the family. They're already reduced to a barely-visible blob. I rub my arms. I feel cold.

We continue down the highway. More farms pop up on the left and right. Some are full of people. They keep their heads down, darting from one task to the next. They're moving in fast motion. Most properties are empty. Barn doors are open and troughs are overturned. A construction crew is tearing a house down, ripping the door off its hinges.

We see more developed buildings. Newly minted cul-de-sacs with above ground pools. Modern flats with artificial grass. Frameworks for future mansions, teeming with workers and planners. Realtors are crawling everywhere, shaking hands with new owners, nodding sympathetically with old ones, and slapping their gleaming faces on driveway signs. They're reclaiming this road one house at a time, stretching out the city limits further and further. The champions of progress, drunk on success.

"Are you still going to go through with it?"

I turn to Ken. His jaw is clenched and he's staying focused on the road. He glances at me for a moment. I raise my hands and shrug; I need more information.

"With the ceremony. You still going to go through with it?" Ken drums his fingers on the steering wheel.

"Of course." What a stupid question.

"Even with everybody leaving?" Ken clicks his teeth.

I stare at him. Ken, my most loyal member, my foot soldier, my bodyguard, my champion; even he doubts. He's been rocked. He's watched everything we've built slowly crumble. He's waited for answers, for solutions, but nothing's happened. Now he's questioning me. Ken, my lapdog, is questioning me. Fucking hell.

"We're going to get them back, Ken. We're going to rebuild. This won't last. It's just a passing storm. We're going to endure. Things will be back to normal before you know it." I give his arm a good squeeze.

"I...I know, sir. But—" He turns to me. I snap my fingers so he focuses on the road.

"But nothing. We've overcome worse things than a little leakage. I'm going to plug the hole and then we'll be back on course. Simple as that." I wipe my hands for effect.

"Simple as that." Ken nods vigorously.

"Ken, don't worry yourself with this stuff. It's well at hand. Why did you join the compound in the first place?" I tap my finger on the dashboard.

Ken raises his eyebrows. He can't believe I asked him that. I stay nonplussed, offering a short shrug.

"I...I joined because I wanted to...I wanted to make a difference. I wanted to save myself. I wanted to find if there was something I was missing. I wanted to be part of something more. There's nothing like our compound. I wanted to be here more than anything. And I wanted to do whatever I could to help." His words would look perfect on a brochure.

"Exactly. You wanted to help. You wanted to do your part and carry some of the weight. You wanted to do what you're best at to lift us up. And, Ken, what are you best at?" I trace my finger slowly towards him on the dashboard.

"Protecting people. Making sure everyone stays in line. Keeping my ear to the ground. Other stuff." He shrugs. How humble.

"'Some other stuff.' You do about a million things at our compound, all of them vital. You hold things together. But, Ken, you're not a logistics guy, are you?" I flick the steering wheel.

"Uh, no, no, I guess not." Ken furrows his brow, trying to determine what "logistics" mean.

"No, you're not. You don't have a head for numbers or planning or any of that boring stuff. You're a hands-on guy. You're an elbow grease guy. So stick with what you know. And leave the logistics stuff to me and Greg, okay? No need to muddy things up, right?" I pat his shoulder.

Ken frowns. He flexes his fingers, squeaking the rubber on the steering wheel. He nods. I lean back in my chair. It's good to dismantle a weak argument before a big debate. Keeps the mind sharp.

I roll down my window. Winds whips past my hair and slams into my eyes. We're close. Just a few more minutes.

"Sir? I'm sorry, but what will you do if everyone's gone? Will the ceremony still happen?" Ken's voice just barely rises above the outside noise.

I'm not going to debate him again. There's no need to argue, not after I won, not when I'm so close. I don't face him as I speak.

"Yes." The wind swallows my words.

The gravel crunches under the tires as Ken brings the car to a stop. We lurch forward as he shifts the gear into park. He removes the key from the ignition and turns to me, waiting. Silence.

I'm staring through the front window. I can see my objective. Twenty paces away. Fifteen if I take wide strides. Showtime.

I take short, loud breaths, quickly flicking my wrists. I unclip my seatbelt, letting it slide across my chest as it returns to its holster. My knees are bouncing, jostling my torso. I catch a glimpse of myself in the rear-view mirror. I grit my teeth and glare. I'm ready.

"Stay here. I'll be back soon. Keep an eye out for...well, for anybody, really." I don't look at Ken as I talk to him. I'm in the zone.

"You sure? You might need back up." Ken goes for the door handle. I wave him down.

"Stay. I'll be fine." I exit the car before he can object.

The bell rings as I open the door. The smell of eggs, sausages, and grease greet my nose. I blink to adjust to the fluorescents. I nearly slip on a puddle of orange juice. A woman with a yellow apron apologizes as she bends down with a filthy rag. I step past her and enter the main diner.

It's a usual crowd for a weekday lunch. Two bankers who'll never rise above their level are tearing into a plate of nachos, probably wondering whose funeral the other one will have to attend. A group of flannel-clad truckers sit at the counter, sipping an endless stream of coffee as they talk about sports. A couple (tourists, judging by their clothes) are putting on their jackets, leaving a meager tip as they scurry to the door. The waiters stroll between chairs and stools, in no hurry to clean up the messes or get anyone's order. Everyone here moves like they're in slow motion. A pocket of the world that marches out of step with everything else. A collection of pathetic losers.

Focus. I'm not here for them. I'm not going to make a grand speech about their failings. I'm here for one thing. I'm here for one man. And he's sitting in the booth at the far end.

A large chocolate cake lies in front of him. Not a slice; a whole cake. A half-full milkshake sits next to it. He's hunched over his plate, his long hair obscuring his face. He's tearing into the cake with a fork, shoveling the food into his mouth, spilling crumbs and icing over his face. He doesn't stop to chew or clean; he just eats.

Two men are sitting next to him, both wearing yellow clothes, both devouring a bowl of chicken wings. I can hear their slobbering from here. He's wearing his purple and gold ensemble. Even in public he has no shame. He puts his fork down and clears his throat. He grabs a napkin to wipe his mouth. I get a good look at him.

Smit.

He's exactly where Greg said he would be. It's one of the few solid pieces of intel we have. Ken was running errands one day and spotted Smit here. He went out a few more times to verify it. Every Wednesday at noon, Smit saddles into this diner for lunch. Rain or shine, no matter what, he's here.

He's gotten fatter. He has an extra chin and his fingers resemble thick rolls of quarters. His face is slick with sweat and his robe is covered in stains. His cheeks are bloated, already flushed red from the exertion of eating. His thighs are flabby tree trunks, spread wide so they don't rub against each other. All his weight is pushed to his limbs. His stomach is relatively lean, only slightly bulging over his waist. He looks like an inflated sex doll with a deflated center. How is that shape even possible?

He's talking to his men. He's wagging his fork at them as he talks. He points at the chicken wings, saying they're a vanilla option. He says everyone back home would've picked them. His members need to be creative. They need to be bold. They need to follow their guts. His two sheep nod and grab the menu. They call a waiter over and ask for three plates of burgers, hot dogs, and onion rings, all deep fried. Their server looks appalled, but the men insist. Smit nods as the waiter takes their order to the counter.

His eyes are still sharp, even under his heavy brow. They dart back and forth over his members, studying their reactions. He's always on, even in a two-cent diner. Everything's a game to him. He loves manipulating these idiots. He loves convincing them to shovel mounds of garbage down their throats. He gets off on it.

"Table for one?"

The woman with the yellow apron is standing in front of me. She's holding a pen over a notepad. She tapping her foot, brushing a loose strand of curly hair out of her eyes. I shake my head.

"No, no, I'm meeting a friend." I point at the toad in the booth.

The woman shrugs and walks behind the counter. I stare at Smit. He's no intellectual pushover. And he beat me last time. I walked in blind and I blew it. But now I've got my plan. He won't be ready. I'm going to win. I step forward.

I manoeuvre past a waiter carrying a tray of empty glasses. I walk past the truckers, offering a grunt as a greeting when one of them notices me. Smit's too busy ripping a chunk from the cake to notice me. A few more steps. I clear phlegm from my throat. His cronies are receiving their first plate, salivating. Someone else is here.

He's tucked away in the far corner. His mud-covered boots are propped up on his booth seat. Half-eaten scrambled eggs and bacon rest on his table, next to a cup of coffee. A newspaper obscures his face, but I can tell it's him. I can tell by the hat and the smoke.

Blume.

He folds his paper on his lap and takes a sip of coffee. He scans the diner, lingering on Smit. He spots me. He sits up straight. He looks me up and down. He runs his tongue over his lips, thinking. I tap my hand on my leg. I don't have time for this.

Blume looks between me and Smit, connecting the dots. His eyes widen. He raises his eyebrows and jerks his head at Smit. I sigh and nod. Blume smiles and brushes his thumb over his moustache. He tosses his paper aside and scooches to the edge of his booth. He spreads his arms, nodding at Smit. I have permission.

Blume and Smit in one place. A gun and two bullets would solve all my problems. I shake my head and approach the booth.

I tower over Smit. His goons notice me before he does. They drop their food and scramble to their feet. Their fists are drawn, ready to do...something. I smile. Ken could turn these boys inside out before they'd have a chance to think. I cough. Smit, fork still in mouth, looks up. A massive smile bursts across his face.

"Hey, Solomon, right?" Smit scratches his head.

"Yes. You're Smith, right?" I give a plastic smile.

"Smit. Simple mistake. Good to see you, man. Good to see you." Smit sucks in his gut as he stands up.

Blume's licking his lips, waiting for one of us to throw the first punch. Stay calm, stay calm. Smit leans in close and wraps me in a hug.

"Damn good to see you. Missed that stern jawline of yours. I kid, I kid." Smit's shouts in my ear.

I peel away from him, wiping his spit off my cheek.

"Take a seat, take a seat." Smit slides back to his spot.

I sit across from him. He waves his men away. They point at me. He chuckles and shakes his head. He points at the door. They nod and retreat outside.

"Always good to have some privacy, don't you think?" Smit cleaves the icing from the cake.

I let the faintest smile tug on my face. I scratch my finger on the table, digging a small groove into the wood. Smit sucks on his fork, slowly drawing it out as he licks the chocolate. He stares at his plate, barely acknowledging me. I've played this game before. Whoever speaks first loses. I can wait.

There's a massive smile on his face. It covers his entire face. He's proud his life has led him to a cheap, heavy cake in a roadside diner in the middle of nowhere. It's everything he could want. He's the dog who ate the cat who ate the canary.

Smit runs his straw over the bottom and sides of the glass as he slurps his milkshake. He's close enough to touch. My enemy, the man who's been ripping us apart. Here in this booth, with just the two of us, only one thought is running through my brain: God, he's ugly.

He's a man, that's all. An unimpressive one. He's hunched over a slab of food, dwarfed by the red booth cushions that loom behind him. He's let his body decay into gelatin. I fold my arms and flex my biceps, feeling them bulge in my hands. I glance at his arms as he finishes off the last drop of milkshake. There's no comparison. His skin droops from his elbows. It wobbles as he moves. He has two sacks of pudding taped to his shoulders. He's pure flab.

A fleck of chocolate flies onto Smit's cheek. He doesn't notice. He enjoys another bite of cake as the speck clings to his face, refusing to fall to the floor. I can't believe I was intimidated by this walking joke. In the harsh light of the diner, he's just a pig. I was overwhelmed when I first met him. All of the pomp and circumstance, his entire getup and performance; they flustered me. I thought he was bigger than he really is. He's a small man you wouldn't notice if he bumped into you. Removed from his compound and his followers, he's disappointingly average. A misled man in over his head.

I lean back in my booth, letting the cushions deflate against my weight. I look at Blume. He's still on the edge of his seat, but the excitement had faded from his eyes. He knows the chances for a fight are dropping with every second. I wave at him, flashing a toothy grin. He scowls and returns to his paper. Smit pushes his glass away. He meets my stare. He's ready to break. I can see the winner's circle already.

"Hey, you want a piece?" He shoves the chocolate-covered cake under my nose.

I flinch. He holds the fork there, letting crumbs fall onto my lap. I tilt my head. He pushes the cake closer to me. I shake my head.

"Oh, c'mon, you've got to try one bite. Seriously, it's some of the best cake I've ever had. I'm not bullshitting you. I swear to...well, to me, it's superb. I don't know what they do back there, I don't where they get this chocolate, I don't know how they make this icing, but it is..." Smit brings his fingers to his puckered lips, then blows them away as he makes a "smack" noise. I continue to stare at him.

"Honestly, it's the only reason I come here. I'd marry this cake if I could. If it were a person, I'd fuck it right on this table. I wouldn't care if everybody was watching. I'm not lying to you. It's goddamn orgasmic. You've got to try it. C'mon, give it a bite." Smit waggles the fork in front of me, dancing it near my eyes.

"Uh...no... thanks." My lips barely separate as I speak.

"Not even one bite? One little morsel? You won't regret it." Smit leans forward, pressing his gut against the table.

"I'm good. Thanks, though." I guide the three prongs away from my face.

"Suit yourself." Smit shoves the piece into his mouth.

He polishes off the cake. It's something to behold. The fork just passes his lips when it's back at the plate, spearing another brown chunk. It's a conveyer belt of gluttony, a constant stream of food hurtling into his gullet. His fork clatters onto the porcelain. He burped as he wipes his face. He stretches his mouth into another disgusting smile.

"Sorry about that. Had to finish it off. Now, what can I do for you?" He clears his throat, letting out a phlegmy cough.

I look out the window. Smit's lackeys are smoking cigarettes and playing rock-paper-scissors in the parking lot. They keep drawing paper. These are the wits we can't seem to beat.

"Small entourage you've got there." I jerk my thumb at the Mensa applicants outside.

"Charles and Josh? Oh, they've been dying to leave the compound and I couldn't say no. Besides, I don't need a big security detail at a diner. Unless you're going to stab me." Smit laughs. I don't.

"I usually see you with a bunch of cronies. Makes you look big. Right now, it's like someone left you in the wash too long." Now it's my turn to laugh. Smit joins me.

"The wash. That's pretty good, that's pretty good." Smit slaps the table.

We stare at each other, wearing our plastic smiles, searching for an attack point. Smit knows what I want.

"You're right, a crowd always makes me seem large. Classic trick. To be honest, Charles and Josh were the only members I could take to the diner. I couldn't spare anyone else. They're too busy with our new recruits." Smit's smile widens. Now we've begun.

"You mean you're busy with the members you stole." I jab my finger at him.

"My members. My followers. My people." Smit pokes the table with each sentence.

"No, they're my people. I've been leading them for years. They're my—"

"You getting anything?" A waitress stands over us.

"I'll have a refill." Smit passes his milkshake glass to her.

"I'm fine, thanks." I wave her away.

"Paying customers only. You can't stay in the booth." She points at the exit sign.

"We just need to talk." I gesture at Smit, but the waitress shakes her head.

"Paying customers only." She looks at the line cook behind the counter. He flexes his arms, staring me down. Now there's a stud.

"Oh, for… Fine, fine, I'll get something. I'll have a… a coffee. Black. No sugar. Small." I fucking hate coffee.

"Sure thing." She disappears behind the counter.

I look at Smit, trying to piece together our interrupted conversation. He picks up a cake crumb, placing it on his tongue.

"Right, right, like I was saying, they're my members and I—"

"They don't see you. They don't listen to you. They don't follow you. They're my members. They live at my compound. They wear my robes. They hear my speeches. They follow me." Smit raises his chin, making his smile look even fatter.

"You stole them."

"Didn't we have this conversation already? I'm not rehashing it. It's boring. Don't bore me." Smit's smile curls into a sneer.

"Bore you? I'm not your dancing monkey, you entitled—" I slam my mouth shut to stop myself from going too far. Diplomacy first.

"Entitled what? C'mon, finish it. I'm an entitled what?" Smit cups his hand to his ear.

"I'm sorry. I didn't mean to snap there. I'm just a…a passionate man. I care about my people." I regulate my breathing. Stay on topic, stay in control.

"I care about them, too. That's why they're with me instead of you. They're in better hands." Smit leans back, resting his head on the booth cushion.

He's trying to bait me. I can see it in his face. I won't bite. Stick to the script.

"Smit, three members left my compound today." I lower my voice.

"And we're glad to have them." Smit tips an invisible hat.

"What are their names?" I cock an eyebrow.

"Pardon?" Smit raises his head from the cushion.

"The members who joined you today. The people you stole. What are their names?" I keep my eyebrow raised.

Smit taps his fingers on the table, scraping his nails. He clicks his teeth. He opens his mouth, then closes it, thinking. He's racking his brain for the names. It's an almost-convincing charade. Finally, he gives me a half-smile.

"Can't say I know. Didn't get a chance to meet them, not properly. They arrived at my compound as I was heading out for lunch, so..." He shrugs.

"Darryl. Joel, and Chris." I pulled those names out of my ass. I barely talked to those men. Today's exodus was the longest conversation I've had with any of them. But that's beside the point.

"Fascinating." Smit can't hide his annoyance behind his veil of apathy.

"I know more than their names. I know everything about them. I've steered them away from disaster and destruction. I've watched them grow into men, real men. I...care about them." My voice cracks at the right moment.

"Uh-huh." Smit shifts in his seat.

"I care about all my people. They're my children. I know that might sound weird to you, but it's true. I'm their father, keeping them on the straight and narrow. But you're not letting me do that." I rap the table with my knuckles.

"I'm not interrupting your speeches or getting in your way. If your people want to see how the other half live, I can't stop them. It's not my place. I'm not their nanny. I just open the door; they have to walk through it. I won't force anybody to do anything they don't want. I'm simply showing folks an alternative. Your members have heard my message and some are clearly curious. And if more of your people are leaving you for me…" Smit shrugs.

"Cut the crap." I slap the table. I see Blume peeking over his newspaper. A trucker is staring at me. Stay calm, stay calm, stay calm.

"You know very well th—"

"One black coffee." The waitress slides the cup in front of me.

"Oh, uh, thanks." I nod and push the cup to the side.

"Get it while it's hot." She's smacking on a big wad of gum.

"I will." I give a strained smile, signalling her to leave.

"No good in waiting. Heat's the only thing that makes it drinkable." She scratches her head, sending loose hair tumbling on my lap.

"Thanks for the tip." My words come out in one extended sigh.

"She's right, you know. Cold coffee's bad coffee." Smit smirks.

I look at them, struggling to keep my anger from showing on my face. I grab the cup and take a loud sip. It burns as it rushes down my throat. I put the cup down and give a thumbs-up.

"Good stuff." I turn to Smit, trying to pick up my last point.

"That all you having?" The waitress doesn't move, her gum smacking getting louder.

"Yeah, I think so, yes." I don't look at her. Focus on Smit, focus on the plan…

"Could you pay now, if that's all yer having?" She holds out her hand.

"What? Why?" I want to rip her head off.

"You look like the dine and dash type." She rubs her nose.

"I've been coming here for years. I've never done that." I'm offended. This food pimp is accusing me of theft. Smit can barely suppress his laughter.

"I've never seen ya." She shrugs, just like Smit. The apathy is overwhelming.

I bite my lip and look at her greasy palm. Smit's covering his snickering with his right hand. I fish out a ten-dollar bill from my pocket and slam it into her hand. She doesn't ask if I want change as she walks away.

"Strict coffee rules here, I guess." Smit is close to cackling.

I take another sip of my coffee, letting Smit get out his giggles. He shakes his head and chuckles. I clamp my teeth on the rim. I let the liquid garbage swish around in my mouth. I set the cup on the table and point my thumb at him. He quiets down, still wearing a big smile.

"As I was saying…" I search for the right word to bring us back.

"What were you saying? I lost track after that...coffee interrogation." Smit lets out another laugh.

"I was telling you to cut the crap." I lean in close, shooting my words right into his face.

The smile sags. He can see what's in my eyes.

"When you tell me you're not doing anything, when you tell me you're not luring members away from my compound, you know you're talking shit. A big heaping mound of shit. And I won't accept it." I make a slashing motion through the air.

"Solomon…" Smit raises his chin. He's about to launch into a speech. I know the posture. I cut him off.

"You can peddle your crap to your followers all day and night. You can tell them they're on the right path and they've made the right choice and they're all going to get blowjobs eight days a week. But don't try to sell it to me. You've been harassing my people. Your goons show up every week and yell at my members to drop their things and hop into their disgusting cars. You sneak propaganda into my compound. You do everything you can to poach my followers because you can't find your own. You've been running a campaign against my compound. Admit it." My spittle flies into his face.

"Fresh milkshake." The waitress puts a glass of the fatty drink in front of Smit. He doesn't acknowledge her. He's focused on me. He nods.

"We might be...aggressively targeting your compound. Nothing out of bounds, mind you. More of a side project, really." Smit gives another feeble shrug.

"You're leading my people down a dangerous path. I want you to stop." I fall silent.

He slurps his milkshake. He licks a layer of cream from his lips. He looks out the window, watching his followers punch each others' shoulders. He rubs his eyes.

"You want me to stop...what? Succeeding? Growing my compound? What?" He scratches his chest.

"I want you to back off. I want you to stick to your plan and let me stick to mine." Ease off the aggression, pump up the humanity.

"But finding new members is part of my plan. Sorry if it conflicts with yours. I can't control which one people find attractive. Buyers' market." He takes loud slurp of his milkshake.

He's biting on the straw. I'm getting to him. I smile, leaning in closer.

"Smit, I don't hate you." I cover that lie with so much honey it sounds like the truth.

"The feeling's mutual." He raises his glass to me.

"I'm being serious here. I want us to talk. No jokes, no tricks, no runarounds. I want to have a conversation, alright?" I point at my heart.

"Fair enough." Smit puts his glass down and, amazingly, doesn't roll his eyes.

"We're just two guys. That's all. Two guys trying to be leaders. We dress up and we make big speeches, but when the chips are down, we're just men." Some more than others...

"Speak for yourself." A smirk creeps back on his face.

"Smit…" I sound like a disappointed schoolteacher.

"Yes, yes, fine, serious conversation." His lips return to even level.

"As men, we're fallible. We make mistakes." I resist the urge to gesture at his guards.

"Every day." Smit nods.

"Exactly, exactly, it's a struggle to be right, to do right, all the time. We're making it up as we go." I tap my temple. Smit nods again.

"Smit, when I saw my compound for the first time, when I saw the buildings and followers and everything else, you know what I thought?" A dash of secrecy to reel him in…

"Jackpot?" Smit rubs his fingers together.

"I thought, 'Oh, shit, I have no idea what I'm doing.'" We both share a chuckle, mine put on, his…less so.

"It's true, it's true, I'm not kidding. I almost dry heaved. I had to wipe my hands down with three different towels before I shook any hands so I wouldn't soak their palms. I was a mess." I bug out my eyes.

"Oh, man, classic, classic, I've been there. I swear, it was worse. Listen…" Smit scoots out of the booth and stands over me.

"It was our first official day as a compound. I mean, we'd been letting people in, getting everyone settled, making sure all our pieces were lined up, you know, the standard shit. But this was our first real day. Everybody was crowded into this pop-up tent we'd built. It's 100 degrees, we're crammed shoulder to shoulder, you can smell the sweat in the air, it's awful. I'm standing in front of these people. I have to make this big welcoming speech. I've never done anything like it before, so I have read from this stack of flashcards. My hands are shaking and I keep clearing my throat. The crowd quiets down and they stare at me. And I look at them. And I look down at my cards. And back at them. And back at my cards. And back at

them. I open my mouth and...I run out of the tent to throw up."
Smit opens his mouth and pretends to heave.

He holds his hand next to his mouth and drops it,
wriggling his fingers. His hand flops on the table. He makes a
gagging noise. I laugh and nod.

"Oh, it was nasty, man, completely nasty. It streamed
out of me for a minute. Everybody listened to me hurl out my
breakfast. And probably my dinner. I wiped my mouth, stood up,
turned to the tent...and vomited again. Totally brutal. That patch
of grass is still brown. Awful stuff." Smit has been flinging his
arms everywhere, nearly clobbering the waitress as she passes by
with a tray full of glasses.

"Crazy. So what did you do?" I rest my chin on my
furled fist.

"I spat out the leftover chunks, marched back into the
tent, and delivered my speech. I don't remember much else, but I
got through it." Smit slides back into his booth.

"You got through it. I thought so. You got through it
because you were passionate, because you had something to say.
You didn't quit. We've got that in common, yes?" Time to bring
it home.

"Yeah, yeah, I think so." Smit takes a quick sip of his
milkshake.

"Different sides, same coin. Cut from the same cloth.
Two peas in a pod..." I rattle off a dozen clichés.

"Yeah, sure, we're a couple of peas." Smit darts his eyes
at the window. He doesn't know where I'm going.

"Sorry, I didn't mean to ramble there. I know
philosophically we...differ, there's no denying that, but that
doesn't have to define us. We don't have to be enemies." I give
my voice a slight tremble.

"I didn't think we were." The plastic smile crawls across
Smit's face.

"We've argued, we've debated, we've insulted each
other. You've stolen my members, I've stormed into your
compound, and so on and so on." I rotate my hand.

"But I want you to know I respect what you've built. I respect your commitment. I respect your talent. I respect you." The words come out of my mouth like bile.

"Mutual." Smit tips an invisible hat at me.

"Because of that respect, because we're just two men sitting in a diner, I want to tell you: Stop tampering with my members." I raise my hand before he can object.

"Please, let me explain. I know you have to expand your compound. It's natural. It's what I did when I started. I grabbed every Tom, Dick, and Harry I could find. I wanted to swell my numbers. But I'm not where you're at right now. I'm at a crucial juncture. My people are at a crucial juncture. They can't be torn between you and me. They have to focus on what matters." I point at the ceiling.

"We don't have to be friends. We don't have to like each other. We might disagree on nearly everything. But I hope you see eye to eye with me on this. I hope you can respect me enough to leave me with my remaining members. I hope you can honour the sanctity of my compound. I hope you can let my people find their peace. I know you'll do the right thing." I fold my hands.

The waitress walks over to us. I wave her away before she can open her mouth. She sighs and vanishes behind the counter. Smit's followers are sitting on the hood of a car, flicking pebbles at the highway. Ken is pacing in a small circle, kicking up a cloud of dust, pretending he isn't staring at our booth. The truckers have fallen silent as they clean their plates, having exhausted their reserves of road tales. Blume has lost interest in us. He's polishing off his coffee while he tosses his newspaper across his table. It's just me and Smit.

He's looking at his milkshake, swirling the straw in the mixture. My words weigh down on him. I watched his face as I spoke. I saw his smug facade dim as he absorbed what I was saying. I saw his eyes narrow. I watched him try to process my speech.

He keeps spinning the straw. He coughs and rubs his nose. The silence is oppressive. I do nothing to relieve it. I've pushed him as far as I can; all I can do now is let him fall off the edge.

More staring, more swirling. I've won. It's written all over his face. I struck a chord. I weaseled into his heart and took a strong stab. He's fallen for my sob story, for my desperate plea. Of course it wasn't true. I despise everything about Smit. I don't respect him anymore than I respect Blume. He's simply an obstacle. I played to his sympathy. Quick, easy, effective.

He can't stop staring at his straw. Well, maybe it wasn't a complete lie. Some of the tremble was genuine. I meant what I said, somewhat. I want to help my people. I don't want to be tangled up in this nonsense. And I sense that Smit doesn't either. Deep down, past all the hedonism and arrogance and narcissism, he's a leader. As a leader, he wants what's best for his people. He wants to promote and protect his flimsy beliefs. I can respect that, as a concept. So, we'll go our separate ways. We can manage that much.

Smit stops swirling. He nods. He leans forward. I meet him at the middle of the table. He swallows. Victory.

"You can drop the act. It's just the two of us. Let's do business." Smit holds out his hand.

"Smit, I want to than—" My brain brings my mouth to a screeching halt.

What did he say? I wasn't paying attention; I was getting ready for the next stage of the conversation. But I know he didn't say the right thing. It sounded...off. I play his words in my head. He doesn't apologize or agree with me or ask how we can go forward. He said we should do...business? That can't be right.

"I'm sorry, what?" I blink.

"Let's do business. I'm sure we could work something out." Smit keeps his hand extended.

I nod. Okay, we're back on track. His response threw me. He made it sound like we were... I'm not sure, actually. Actors? Con men? Something like that. It didn't sound right. But

I've caught up. Clear as day now. That's just the way he talks. We can definitely do business.

"Glad to hear it. I knew you'd come around." I give his hand a firm shake.

"I know an opportunity when I see it. You and me? Cha-ching." He rubs his fingers together.

I squint my eyes. He wants to profit off our...mutual separation? How would that work? Maybe he wants a payout for his cooperation. A nice stack of cash to encourage him to respect our borders. It wouldn't surprise me. He's always got one eye on the bottom line. I'll check the coffers when we get back to the compound. There must be some spare change lying around.

"Right. Absolutely. Cha. Ching." I flash a thumbs-up.

"Now, how were you thinking of doing it?" Smit pushes his glass away.

"Oh, uh, well, nothing complicated, really. We let your current batch of...appropriated members stay where they are. No need to pull them out now. You revoke your promotional material and make sure your men don't visit anymore. Send any stragglers back my way. We go our separate ways. No muss, no fuss. We can get on with our spiritual ascension and you can get on with...whatever it is that you do." I push my thumb up even higher.

Smit stares at me. His eyes are glazed over. Great, I lost him. It was too much to expect him to pay attention. He was probably dreaming of pudding pools or double-fisting a pair of calzones. Dumb motherfu— Calm, calm, stay patient. Don't snap at him, not when you're this close. I inhale.

"What the hell are you talking about?" Smit shakes his head.

"Which part are you having trouble with?" I keep my smile frozen in place.

"All of it. The whole thing... What were you talking about? Separate ways? Why are we talking about that?" Smit tilts his head.

"Because we're trying to figure out the best way to keep our compounds apart. I was just pitching a rough sketch, but if you've got a better plan..." I jerk my thumb at him.

"Apart? I thought we were discussing business." Smit yanks at his ear lobe.

"We are..." I feel as confused as Smit looks.

"What business are you talking about?" Smit straightens his back.

"Our ascension. I thought I made that clear. I want your compound to leave us alone so we can complete our journey. We need to find our inner peace before we—" Smit cuts my speech short with his snorting and chuckling.

"Jesus, you can't turn it off. The dial's always cranked at 10, huh? You breathe this shit." Smit wipes crumbs off his shirt.

"Smit, I'm not playing with you. I want you to leave my compound alone. If you keeping tampering with-" I can't finish talking before Smit waves his hand to dismiss me.

"Oh, drop it already. You don't have to impress anybody. I'm the only one here." Smit smacks his knuckles into his palm.

"I'm not acting, you clod." My smile curdles into a glare. I feel the blood rushing to my face. I offer this punk the olive branch and not only does his break it over his knee, he starts mocking me. Little fucker.

"Yeah, yeah, sure, you're living the story. I worked with a theatre troupe for a year, I know the drill. But be real with me. We could do something big. We're both successful, we're both driven, we're both rakishly handsome. Well, me more than you. Imagine what we could accomplish." Smit locks his fingers together.

"Together?" I spit out the word like it's arsenic.

"Absolutely. If we pooled our resources, we could run this town. Hell, we could run this whole county. We'd have Blume and every other glorified meter maid deep in our pocket. We'd be..." Smit whistles.

I see the ravenous hunger in his eyes. I can hear his heart beating from here. I can smell his arousal.

"You want to be...partners?" I flick my finger between him and me.

"One hundred percent. I've kept tabs on you. I had to check out the biggest dog in the yard. And, buddy, I am impressed. You're little more...extreme than I'd like, but that sells. You know how to pump the gas to get butts in seat. You've got hustle, just like me. If we worked on this whole compound thing, we'd go to the next level." Smit raises his hand above his head.

I blink. I just listened to the most deranged sales pitch of my life. It was like a pedophile trying to get me to join a hot stock on panel vans. Smit licks his lips like a dog. He's deranged. How could he think we could work together? It's like boiling a premium steak in spoiled milk. A hundred reasons for rejecting him hurtle through my brain. I settle for the diplomatic one; I still need to steer him back to the right conversation.

"Smit, I don't think our compounds would be a good match. Logistics alone would be a nightmare. How do you keep track of that many people? But more than that, fundamentally, I think our groups are just too...different." I stay even-keeled.

"How so?" Smit raises his eyebrows.

Another hundred answers run through my head like tickertape. I bite my tongue before the most...visceral response leaps out. I offer a friendly laugh.

"Well, Smit, simply put we've clearly got...different aims. Nothing wrong with that, really. My compound is concerned with issues that go beyond this world. We're all about elevation. Your compound, from what I've gathered, is more preoccupied with...earthly pleasures. You're focused on the flesh, the here and now, immediate sensations." That's the best way to describe a bunch of filthy, horny pigs.

"That we do, that we do." Smit stick his tongue out.

"Right. That's your domain. It's not a...wrong path. But it's not ours. We keep our eyes on tomorrow. We're concerned with the next step. I don't think our union would benefit either of us. We'd water down our messages. We'd never get anything done. We'd be shells of ourselves. I think we should keep our two worlds separate." I plant my fists on the table and push them to the edges.

"Yeah, I mean, when you put it like that, we probably should stay apart. Too many differences. Totally." Smit nods.

"Glad you agree. Now, if we could get back to my original point, we sho—"

"Of course, we can make the necessary changes." Smit pats one of my fists.

"Changes?" I don't like the way he's looking at me.

"Yeah, you know, whatever helps the rubes fit in. I can tweak my stuff, maybe make it a little more strict. You can tone down some of your parts, because believe me, they're pretty intense. I'm sure we can find a nice middle. Whatever works." Smit's smile reaches new, perverse heights.

Holy shit. He's a fraud.

I stare at his plastic grin. I had this whole thing wrong. My plan was built on a false premise. I thought I was dealing with a hedonist, a man only concerned with his own satisfaction. I thought I was going to talk with a man who had built a religion around his own shaky convictions. I thought his beliefs were flimsy and flexible and egotistic, but I at least thought they were real. I thought his compound was built on a foundation, however repugnant, that he wouldn't stray from. I thought I was dealing with a misguided believer.

But I'm dealing with vapour. He's a huckster. That hunger in his eyes isn't fueled by a misplaced ideology or a poorly-written creed; it's just naked greed. I'm seeing Smit, the real Smit, in widescreen. He's nothing more than a cheap grin and an open palm. He doesn't care about his compound or his people. He only cares about stuffing his pockets.

He doesn't see me as a spiritual rival or an equal leader. To him, I'm just a face with resources. He doesn't want to beat me to prove the superiority of his faith or expand his reach; he's

just looking for money. He sees me coming here, hat in hand,
ready to talk, and he smells an opportunity. He thinks he can
latch onto me and suck up some extra dollars. He doesn't care if
he has to jettison his entire philosophy; they were empty phrases.
They were the words he thought would get him rich, words he
can dispose of at any moment. He can discard his whole belief
structure because it was a smokescreen. He'll take any shortcut
to his finish line.

How could I have missed it? It's clear as day. All that
energy, all that bravado, all that smarm; they were nothing more
than con man calling cards. He sounds like a used-car salesman
because that's exactly what he is. His words were calibrated to
give people exactly what he thought they wanted. He found a
way to make quick cash from a lot of people and exploited it. He
grabbed a hammer and started smashing an open nerve.

Smit doesn't believe a word he says. He can't even rise
to the level of a base hedonist. He'll take any path that widens
his wallet. This is all a game to him.

I'm not dealing with an equal; I'm dealing with a
parasite.

"Well? We going to sit here all day or are we going to
hammer out a deal?" Again, Smit extends his hand to me. I slap
it away.

"I'm not working with you." My voice is cold.

"No need to be greedy. It's a big pie. We can both have a
slice." Smit mimes cutting with an invisible knife.

"I'm not working with a fraud." I fire the sentence out
like a bullet.

"Ouch. You know how to cut a guy." Smit rolls his eyes.

"I'm going to leave now. Have a good day." I start to
scooch out of the booth.

"Jesus, what's your problem? I'm offering you the keys
and you're heading for the door? Get off your high horse and
think about it. Hey, listen to me." Smit grabs my arm, pulling me
back to my seat.

"What? Do you not like me? Is that it? You don't think
we can be buddies? Look, I'm sorry I stole your members. It was
just business. And what I'm offering you now is business. This is
a great opportunity. We can help each other." Smit squeezes my
arm.

"My work isn't business." I pry his fingers off my bicep.

"For fuck's sake, could you drop the gimmick for five
minutes? I know I'm the first normal person you've seen in a
while, so it must be hard to turn off, but I need you to be real
with me." Smit rubs his eyes.

"It's not a gimmick, you toad." I feel my composure
slipping.

"Well, does it include being an idiot because..." Smit
closes his mouth and considers me.

We stare at each other. I bore my eyes into his, refusing
to blink. I burrow into him, pulsating my entire mind into his
eyes. I communicate everything that words can't say.

"Holy shit." Smit leans back in his seat.

"What?" I keep my eyes trained on him.

"You believe this crap. You've bought into your own
brand." Smit is half-smiling.

"Of course I believe it. That's why I'm the leader."
Anger edges into my voice.

"Wow. I never thought... It explains a lot. You really...
Wow." Smit slow claps.

"Wow, a fraud who thinks everyone else is a fraud.
That's fresh, that's really fresh. They broke the mold when they
made you." I curl my lips into my mouth, trying to suppress the
anger from exploding on my face.

"Heh, again, you really know how to cut a man down.
I'm wounded, truly. You're one of a kind. An honest, real-life
cult leader. I never thought I'd meet one. It's an honour." Smit
salutes me as he chuckles.

"I'm glad you're enjoying yourself. You think this
whole thing's a big joke." Fury is seeping through my pores. I'm
filled with cold-blooded rage. This little fucker is leading the

biggest con in the state and he has the balls to laugh at me? To my face?

"A good joke, too. A man builds an entire compound centered around a, quite frankly, insane belief. He attracts hundreds of people to his cause, all of them willing to obey his every command. He could do anything his heart desires. He could scratch any itch. And what does he do? He subjects himself and everyone else to mind-numbing drudgery. He sucks the flavour out of life because that's what his religion is about. And the best part? He actually believes it. He refuses to cash the best cheque in the world because he thinks he's doing something important. He thinks he's going somewhere. It's fucking hilarious." Smit lets out a high-pitched giggle.

I see myself grabbing Smit by the neck and pounding his smug face into the table. I see myself climbing on top of him while he screams. I see myself grabbing his milkshake glass and smashing it on the corner. I see myself stabbing the broken end into Smit mouth and grinding it. I see myself squeezing his throat with my blood-soaked hand. I see myself laughing...

I keep my hands below the table. I hold a lid on my simmering anger. I can't touch him. Too many witnesses. Well, one witness, really; the one with a gun and a badge. If he saw me touching Smit, he'd use the former before he'd use the latter.

"Hilarious? Let's talk about a man who preaches, day after day, night after night, that people need to join him. He surrounds himself with lobotomized followers. He leads a faith he'd betray in a second if it lined his pockets. He's living a lie, one he can't tell any of his followers about, because he doesn't know how they'll react. They might get violent. So, he keeps his mouth shut and peddles nonsense he doesn't believe. He's trapped in a lie he created. That's funny." I don't pause for a single breath during that speech.

"See those two idiots out there? I could walk out there right now and tell them I have to leave for five years and they won't hear from me. I'll vanish. You know what they'll do? They'll wish me a good trip. Then they'll go back to stuffing their faces and staring at the TV, just like everybody else at my compound. All of my followers have one directive: Satisfy yourself. They don't need me around to blow their noses or wipe their asses. Do you think this is my first rodeo? Do you not think that I've run dozens of businesses before? Where do you think I got the money to start this dog and pony show? I've always got an exit strategy. Before I start anything, I build a back door. I can walk away any time I like. Can you?" Smit's smirk almost seems sentient.

"I wouldn't walk away because I felt like it. I'm not a sociopath." My neck strains. I'm speaking too much from my throat.

"Different strokes." Smit dusts his hands.

I'm arguing with a child. Next we'll be hurling our feces across the diner. I raise my chin.

"Look, Smit, we both came here with different ideas. I'm dedicated to my people and my cause. You clearly take a more...cynical approach." Diplomacy is the only way I'm going to get anything out of this misbegotten trip. It doesn't help suppress my bile, though.

"A smarter one, too." Smit truly resembles a toad.

"Right, fine, whatever. We let our emotions run away from us a moment ago. But that doesn't mean we have to walk away from this table empty-handed." I'm appealing to his wallet.

"Lay it on me." Smit wipes a dribble of saliva from the corner of his mouth.

"Smit, why did you start your compound? Of all the things you could've done, why'd you found a religion? You could've stayed in Malibu or San Francisco or New York or whatever decadent cesspool you crawled out of, and continued drinking, whoring, and snorting your way into oblivion. You could've stayed in your medicated bubble. Why'd you come to the middle of nowhere and start preaching?" I'm genuinely curious.

"Because I was bored." Smit shrugs and he looks at me like I asked him why the Earth is round.

Holy fuck, it just keeps getting worse. The thorn in my side, the man who laughs right in my face...was bored. He became my competitor because he wanted a little excitement? Fuck me rigid.

"Bored?" I grind the word up with my teeth.

"Yeah. It happened about a year ago, I was living in Louisiana. I was making...deliveries for the, let's say, "extra-legal" element in town. Good money, nice hours. One day, I realized I was bored out of my skull. I didn't want to go into work that day, or any other day. I thought about to do with my life. I didn't get far there, so I flicked on the TV and you know what I saw? A preacher. He was right there on the screen, like he was waiting for me. He was standing in a big church and he was hollering about damnation and salvation and all that nonsense, and every person in that room was cheering and crying and shoving their money in a basket. He was making cash hand over fist. Light-bulb moment. I thought to myself, 'Now, that looks like something I could do.' So, I spent a few months practicing my speeches and writing down 'holy scripture' before I bought that patch a land for peanuts. People started rolling in and I started preaching. And I've got to say, I haven't been bored since." Smit looks proud at his little story. His eyes are even watery.

What a load of shit. This worm was too lazy to go to work one day and he got inspired by some huckster in a cheap suit? He's in my way because he watched television? I'm fighting an overly ambitious couch potato. Even Joseph couldn't have seen this guy coming.

"Great. Okay, so you decided to preach because you wanted excitement in your life. I can understand that. Who wouldn't want to spice things up a bit? It's fun for you. It's just a game." I try not retch.

"Yeah, I guess so." Smit nods.

"But, you see, it's not a game to me. I didn't start my compound because I felt like it. I didn't attract hundreds of followers to alleviate my boredom or feed my ego. I didn't build a new faith for cheap thrills. I had a higher calling. I've taken every step forward because I was meant to do it. My compound is my world. And you have tampered with my world. You have thrown it off-balance. I need you to back off so I can restore it. I know you don't respect what I've created. You think it's a joke. But I need you to leave us alone. I need you to stop stealing members and spreading out flyers. I'm asking as one person to another. I'll throw in some money if that's what it takes. Please, for my people's sake, leave us alone." I never thought I'd sound so desperate when I walked into the diner, but this conversation has drifted away entirely from my script. I'm grasping in the dark.

Smit bites his lower lip and looks at the ceiling. He circles his thumbs around each other. He tilts his head left and right, back and forth, over and over. He lets out a big gasp of air.

"No." Smit waves his hand.

"Smit, what's your price? I'm sure we can work something out. Tell me what you want and we'll go from there." If he wants me to grovel, he's in for a rude surprise.

"I don't care about money." Smit actually says that with a straight face.

"Stop jerking my chain." I give him a death glare.

"I don't. I mean, yeah, I do. Of course I care about money. I'm not an idiot. But I don't have to worry about money, not right now. I'm in a good spot. I'm more concerned with entertainment. And I think you'd be a great source. So I won't take your money." Smit licks his lips.

"What, you want me to fucking dance for your cooperation?" My body tenses up again.

"No, no, nothing that crude. I want to fight you for your compound." Smit rubs his hands.

"What?" I blink.

"Yeah, the more I think about it, the more I like it. I want to take your compound from you. I want you to give me the keys. Yeah, it could be really interesting." Smit is looking at the ceiling.

A hole has opened in my stomach, forming a pit that's pulling down. I can see what Smit sees. He's planted the idea in my head. It plays out in crystal-clear definition. He's striding into my compound, blowing past the gate, gold-robed entourage in tow. He's flanked by followers, my followers. I'm standing at the center square, clutching my tattered robe close to my chest. Ken and Greg are sitting beside me, exhausted. They're the only ones left. Smit walks up to me and holds out his hand, grinning. His group forms a circle around me. They're chanting. I squeeze my collection of compound keys in my palm before passing them to Smit. He holds them above his head, triumphant. I fall and—

Nonsense. Utter nonsense. I'm letting my mind race away from reality. One speech from Smit and I'm already envisioning the end of my compound. I'm frazzled. This whole conversation has thrown me. I'm letting him get to me.

"That's, uh, that's quite a scenario you've cooked up." I clear my throat.

"You think so? I like it, too." Smit's voice swells with pride.

"But it's not going to happen. It's fantasy. You think you'll take away everything I've built just like that? You think you'll be able to swoop in and pick us clean? We wouldn't let it happen. We're not going to roll over for you. We'll fight you for every inch. You'll only walk away with a broken nose and a bruised ego. You won't beat us." I gesture outside at Ken, who, standing next to Smit's two blithering idiots, looks even more imposing than usual.

"What was it, three members that switched sides today? I've lost track of all our new arrivals. You've probably got a better count than me." Smit forms a "W" sign with his fingers.

I open my mouth, ready to fire back with an arsenal of invective, but I stop myself. He's baiting me. He wants me to blow a gasket and yell at him until I'm blue in the face. He wants to keep me off track. I'm not losing his game because I'm not playing it.

"Smit, you're being childish. I'm giving you a chance to walk away from this powder keg you've set up. If we keep going at this pace, we'll both wind up bloody. We'll trade punches until we collapse and our followers move on. We don't have to go down that road. You can back off and focus on your compound. Build your brand or increase your fortune or do whatever it is you business majors do. Leave me to my work and I'll leave you to yours. I'll even throw in a monthly...incentive if that'll make you happy. We can both be winners here." I've laid my cards on the table, my best offer. I've prostituted my compound's finances to this egomaniac.

"Man, you make it sound more fun than I imagined." Smit claps and giggles.

Fuck.

"It's not supposed to be fun, you chucklehead. It's work. Real, honest work. And you're fucking it all up." Well, I've lost my cool. Can't say I didn't try.

"Christ, I can almost see your vein pop. We're going to have a blast." Smit bangs his fist on the table.

"You're talking about destroying people's faith, their purpose, and you think it's going to be fun? What's wrong with you?" I shake my head.

"Oh, they'll be fine, you sanctimonious windbag. I'll look after them. You've got my word. I swear on...whatever you believe in." Smit holds his hand over his heart.

My mouth is slack-jawed like a caveman who just saw fire. Smit is literally shaking with excitement. He looks like he's about to explode. I can feel the glee radiating off of him.

"Can't you bother someone else?" For fuck's sake, I sound like a fifth-grader asking the playground bully not to take his lunch money. Am I going to break into tears next?

"Eh, not really. This town's pretty quiet. You're the only game in town. Man, it's going to be awesome. I'm going one-on-one with an honest, true-blue believer. I get to tangle with someone who really believes what he's selling. I'm amped." Smit thumps his chest.

Another non-believer who wants to take the piss out of someone who sees the truth. A man who wants to drag everyone down to his level. Typical. Smit's just got more resources than most agnostic assholes.

I can't argue with him anymore. He's shoved his flag in the ground and he won't move it. I slide out of the booth and stand up. Smit gives another mock salute. I lean over the table, looming in front of him.

"Stay away from my compound or I'll use you for fertilizer." I mean every word.

"Why don't you fuck off? I'd like to have my seconds in peace." Smit slaps on his plastic smile.

I see my untouched cup of coffee. I tip it forward, spilling the black liquid over the table. Smit curses, moving out of the way as it stains his pants. I'm already halfway to the door. It's a small victory.

CHAPTER TWENTY-FIVE

I'm in a blur.

A vise is squeezing my chest and my head. It fastened itself to my body the moment I stepped out the door. The weight of everything smashed down on me. The full realization of what had just happened crashed into me. My knees buckled. It collided with me in waves, striking me over and over. I'd stepped out of a bubble into a minefield.

We drew the battle lines. That's what happened at the diner. That was nothing more than a declaration of war. Smit wants a fight. He wants to tear us apart and I let it happen. I followed his bait. I could have talked us into a real solution. I could have talked his ear off and made him agree with me. But I didn't. I just cursed and spilled coffee on his lap. I threw my script in the trash and danced to his tune.

In the back of my mind, in a place I don't want to admit exists, I liked it. I could feel my blood pumping and my heart galloping as Smit laid out his plan. It was anger and hatred, yes, but hidden in the reeds was an unmistakable feeling: Exhilaration. I wanted to slug it out with him, to bleed his compound dry, to rub his face in the mud. I didn't care about ascension or purpose or higher callings; in that moment, I only wanted win. I was just as lustful for violence as the man with no principles. I was the animal scratching at the walls.

Standing outside the diner, these feelings overwhelmed me, suffocated me. The rush of arguing with Smit faded fast like a heroin comedown, leaving me lightheaded. I was woozy and jelly-legged, as if I'd been in a fifteen-round boxing match.

Ken walked up to me. Smit's goons were behind him, boredom having reduced them to walloping each other in the shoulder. Ken said hello, but it was like he was standing behind a waterfall. He grabbed my arm, yanking me back into the present.

He asked me how I was doing. Autopilot took over as I nodded and said I was fine. He asked how the meeting went. I repeated myself. I climbed into the car before he asked a follow-up question. We peeled away from the diner. I saw Smit past the grimy window, hunched over a sloppy Joe, red meat and sauce smeared on his face. My great enemy.

The ride home was a collage of houses, fields, and trees. Ken asked more questions. I answered them as best I could. I think I did. I wasn't there. I was in my head, grappling with a tsunami of thoughts.

I got out of the car and walked through the compound. People in the fields or working on buildings. I told Ken I needed to meditate. I told him to find Greg and help him with...anything. Ken asked if I was sure, but I was already headed to the forest, disappearing among the trees.

Now I'm standing next to the river, looking down at the flowing water. The world seems...distant, as if it's been tuned to a lower definition. I feel removed from it. I'm barely here.

War. It has everything Smit wants and nothing I need. He stands to gain the most, while I stand to lose...all of it. Every scrap I've built. Of course he wants to battle me. He's a taker. He's a vulture. He hasn't built a thing in his life. His entire religion is a hodgepodge of stuff he saw on TV. Zaan is nothing more than a fool's idea of what faith should look like. Smit looks at me and he sees a real innovator. He sees someone who created something. He sees a ready-made compound he can enjoy at his leisure. He sees something he can take.

Zaan isn't based on anything concrete, so Smit can make it into whatever suits him. He can mold it to adapt to anything, to appeal to anyone. That's how he coaxed my weaker followers out of their shells; he played to their base instincts. Zaan is whatever you project onto it. It's clay in your hands. It's a child's idea of freedom.

How can I compete? I offer structure, order, discipline, salvation. I offer something intangible, something indescribable, something that can save your life. But I don't give it away for free. You don't get a participation medal. You have to earn your ascension. Your deliverance comes through hard work and sacrifice. My compound is for strong people to find inner peace.

Smit offers the coward's way out. He preaches sex, and drugs, and gluttony. He gives people exactly what they want, not what they need. If the average person has to choose between true salvation or living like a human pig, they'll pick the sty every time.

I expect too much from people. I think they'll always try to be better. I think, deep down, people want to ascend. But they don't. They want to stay mired in the muck. I have to drag them every step of the way or they'll tumble back down.

Maybe I'm using the stick and neglecting the carrot. The sacrifices, the confessions, the long hours; maybe it's all too much to ask. If I gave an inch here or there, if I loosened the slack, maybe people would stay. If made things a little easier, maybe they would—

Shut up. That's Smit talking. There's nothing wrong with what I'm doing. It's as good as it was the day we started. If we're losing weak members to temptation, good. Only the strong should remain. Besides, when I crush Smit, and I will, they'll all come back on their knees. I have to stay the course. I repeat this line over and over. I half-convince myself. It'll sound better in the morning, after sleep has cleared my head.

The blur recedes to the edges of my eyes. I'm in the present, mostly. I look at the cavern. The site of our future victory. In this light, it doesn't look inspiring, or hopeful, or promising; it just looks gloomy.

I look at the moon. It reflects off the river, giving the water a pale glow. It's a relaxing slice of white—

Shit. I'm supposed to meet with Sandra.

I burst out of the forest and stroll through the compound. Not a soul in sight. Lights beaming through windows illuminate my path. I rub my temples.

A twig snaps. I freeze, grinding pebbles beneath my feet. I dart my head around the compound. I peer into the long shadows behind buildings and trees. I hold my breath. I strain my ears. A faint breeze is the only thing that greets them. I'm sure I heard a snap. I quicken my pace, keeping my head on a swivel. I watch for any movements, any darting figures or running silhouettes. As if I don't have enough problems, now I'm paranoid the killer is waiting around the corner to give me a rope necktie. The killer: another knife pointed at my gut.

I reach the door of the sermon hall and I pause. Nobody's here. If the killer was going to strangle me, he would have done it in the woods. I'm bathed in lights from the surrounding buildings. They're like a security blanket. The killer wouldn't strike here, not in the open. I'm fine. I'm safe. I tilt my neck to the side and I hear it crack. My back feels stiff and frozen. I'm carrying all this tension in my body. Each problem is a brick stacked on my shoulders. I have to carry everything or it'll all collapse. It's killing me.

I rotate my shoulders and stand on the balls of my feet, bobbing up and down. I flick my arms and sigh, trying to get loose. If I think about everything at once, I'll crumble. If I think about Smit, and our dwindling numbers, and the killer stalking our compound, and Blume lurking around the corner, and, oh, fuck, fuck, fuck, I'm so goddamned screwed. It's too much, it's way too much. I'm going to—

I slap my forehead.

I'm letting my mind run around without a leash. I can't let it jerk me from one panic attack to the next. It's not my guide; it's a tool. Use it.

I have to remove the bricks. I'll slide each of them of my back until I can stand up straight. If I move them all at once, they'll just fall apart and crush me into a red paste on the ground. I have to be a surgeon, not a bulldozer.

I'll start at the top. I'll take the smallest brick and I'll toss it aside. I'll start with Sandra.

She's behind this door. She should be. I can't remember when we exactly agreed to meet. It was definitely night time. That's usually when I schedule meetings. So, she should be in here, waiting for me. Always best to make a late entrance. People are more impressed when you show up than when you're already there. When I burst through the door, I'll have the advantage. As long as she's in there. Which she should be. She's never late. I think. I don't really know. Fuck, I slept with this woman and I barely know anything about her. Is she punctual? She seems like the type. Ah, crap.

I pace in front of the door, chewing on my thumb. I wait five minutes, then another, then another. I stare into the patches of light, looking for any figures. Nothing. It's getting late. No one would be this tardy. She's definitely in here. Or she completely forgot about it and she's curled up in bed. No way she'd forget. Who could forget about me? She's in here. She's absolutely in here.

I pat the door. I let the film projector play out the scene in my mind. I throw the door open, letting in smash into the walls. She'll pivot around, stunned and—No, no, too forceful, too much like a sermon. I need a more personal touch. Restart.

I push open the door and immediately close it as I enter the hall. Sandra will be sitting on the stage, expectant, anxious. I'll stride over to her and—No, be humble. This isn't a grand speech. Let her down easy. Again.

I'll walk to her wearing a bittersweet smile. She'll rise to greet me and lean in for a kiss. I'll hold her at arm's length. She'll be confused. I'll explain everything. I'll explain that our...encounter was a test, one she failed so resolute—No, don't be the executioner. Once more.

I'll tell her last time was a mistake. I wasn't thinking straight. What we did was...inappropriate. I'll tell her I'm sorry for what I did. I'll tell her it'll never happen again. She'll be upset, naturally. She'll say it's nothing serious, that we don't have to be prudes. She'll try to coax it out of me. But I'll be strong, chaste, firm. She won't sway me.

She'll get angry. She'll feel betrayed, misled. Maybe she'll curse me or scream. There may even be tears. But in the end, we'll walk out of this hall as leader and follower, nothing more. Another success under my belt and a brick off my back.

I push open the door. Sandra's standing onstage, her back facing me. She's far upstage, peering behind the curtains. She's holding the red cloth between her knuckles, balling it up into a wrinkled mess. She's turned the stage lights on, cloaking her body in soft gold. I click the door shut. Sandra turns around and smiles, dropping the curtain. I nod. She steps forward, moving to the center of the glow. I make my way down the aisle, listening to my footsteps echo in the room.

"Quite the rendezvous. I've never seen this place so...dark." Her grin widens.

I nod again, presenting a tight-lipped smile. Stick to the script. I'm going to wipe that smile off her face. With every word, it'll droop lower and lower, until it vanishes. I reach the lip of the stage.

"How're you doing?" Sandra cocks her head.

I nod again, climbing onto the stage. I can't open my mouth. Words can't escape. Calm down. It won't be like Smit. You've laid it all out. You've done it before.

I'm standing in front of Sandra. She parts the hair from her face. She clears her throat. We lock eyes. She chuckles, looking away.

"So, uh, what did you want to talk about?" She's biting her lip.

My script is gone. I'm staring at a white page. I tear through my thoughts, but I can't find anything. I'm standing in front of this woman and I don't have a clue. I'm lost. Sandra smiles. I open my mouth. A wheeze comes out. I grab her shoulders. I plant my mouth on her. She runs her hands over my back. We stagger away from the spotlight. We get tangled in the curtain. We disappear from the stage. We tumble down, down, down.

CHAPTER TWENTY-SIX

Jason Neary stayed in Joseph's car.

Joseph dropped Jason off at a bus station. Jason had enough spare cash for one ticket. It could take him anywhere in the country. He saw his home town on the listings. He could have gotten off the road. He could have slept in a real bed. He could have gone back to his old life.

Jason felt the gnawing in the back of his head. His hand twitched when he reached for the ticket counter. He stepped out of line. He saw Joseph filling up his car at the gas station. Jason walked over to him. Jason asked for another lift. Joseph nodded. Jason hopped in the passenger seat.

They drive for days, weeks, months. Joseph is behind the wheel, then Jason, on and on and on. While one drives, the other sleeps. Or studies the map. Or rambles on about some story. Or stares out the window.

They find work where they can. Someone always needs a roof shingled, or a fence painted, or a toilet unclogged. They count their money at the end of the day. If they're clutching bills in both hands, they go out for beers and food before checking into their hotel. If they're holding enough for one hand, they crash at a motel. If they're rubbing pennies together, they sleep in the car. They share a frayed blanket as they recline in their seats. Joseph usually rolls over in the middle of the night, leaving Jason exposed. Jason never reaches for it. He doesn't want to be rude to his host.

The car's always too cold when they fall asleep and too hot when they wake up. Their small rotation of clothes reek. The air conditioner only puffs out a feeble stream at the driver. When they're driving down the desert at noon, they have to peel their skin off the leather. They always smell something roasting.

Jason doesn't complain. He's experienced much worse over the last few months. This car is a nice break. He lost track of time. He thinks they've been on the road for two months. It's really three. Joseph has no destination. He's just driving. He doesn't talk much about his plans. He doesn't talk much, period. Jason doesn't even know his last name. He has no idea why Joseph is letting him tag along. Joseph seemed excited when Jason hopped in the car, but since then... Jason doesn't think about it too much. He doesn't want to spoil his luck. He'll ride here as long as he can. Then he'll... Well, he doesn't think about that too much, either.

One day, Joseph pulls up in front of a grocery store. There are four other cars in the parking lot. It's a slow Wednesday afternoon. They're in a town that's not on their map. They've eaten their last can of pineapples. They haven't found any work in days. Joseph turns to Jason.

"What's your stance on stealing?" Joseph drums his fingers on the wheel.

Jason looks at the store. Rusted bars cover its windows. A senior couple hobble into it. The automatic doors screech open. The sign above them has been faded to oblivion, leaving only a white space. This place is on its last legs. Jason puts his hands on his stomach. He can hear it churning and growling. His mouth is dry and twitchy. His entire body is tired. He's on his last legs.

Jason looks at the store. He looks at his belly. He looks at Joseph. He shrugs.

"So, you wouldn't mind if I walked in there and... procured us some food for the road? Just enough for the two of us, mind, nothing extravagant." Joseph pulls the key out of the ignition.

Jason shrugs again.

"Good to know. I need you to make a scene." Joseph steps out of the car.

"Uh, what?" Jason stumbles out of his seat.

"Nothing big. I just need you to stand by the front door and get people's attention. Get a crowd going. If you could attract the security guard, that'd be perfect." Joseph points at the obese man half-asleep in a steel-folding chair past the door.

"How... how do I make a scene?" Jason leans over the roof.

"I dunno. Say what's on your mind. That usually gets people's attention. I'm right behind you. Once you get going, I'll slip in and out." Joseph pats Jason's hand.

Jason has a hundred questions. His heart is hammering. His palms are sweaty. His mind is screaming. But he doesn't want to be an ungrateful guest, so he walks to the store.

Jason steps to the doors. They slide open, beckoning him in. He steps back and lets them close. He bites his lip. He looks back. Joseph is tapping his wrist. Jason swears to himself.

A man and his daughter approach the store. He's limping on his right leg while he nurses a beer belly. She's covered in acne and a pair of braces protrudes from her mouth. They're bickering over what flavour of chips to buy. Jason's reminded of home.

Jason steps in front of them. They don't notice him until the father bumps in Jason. The father apologizes and tries to sidestep him. Jason puts his hand on his chest. The words start flowing.

"Pig. This is what you want? This dead husk? You're just a mouth. All you care about is filling your hole with more poison. You're killing yourself and you're too stupid to see it." Jason jabs the father.

The father is stunned. The daughter is upset. People in the parking lot are staring at them.

"You're all fools. You're sleepwalking through life. You just buy, consume, and repeat. You don't think. You don't feel. You're barely human." Jason's face is turning red.

The father starts to shout back. Jason shoves him. The father shrinks away. A circle of people has formed around them. Someone boos.

"Cretins. Fools, all of you." Jason points his finger at different people in the crowd.

Jason shouts and curses, flinging his arms everywhere. The security guard shambles into the circle. Jason slaps him. The guard goes to grab him, but Jason dodges away. He runs through the parking lot, yelling.

Jason spots Joseph slipping out of the store with two bags tucked under his shoulders. Jason dives under the guard and slides across the hood of a car. He jumps into the passenger seat as Joseph puts his foot on the pedal. They're on the highway.

"Man, that was incredible. I caught some of it from inside. The way you went off... Damn, it was great to see. Where'd you get it?" Joseph laughs as he tears into an apple.

"I...I don't know. I just started talking and...it happened." Jason stares at the road as he chews on a granola bar.

"Oh, yeah, you do. That stuff doesn't come out of nowhere. That was some buried shit. Felt good, didn't it?" Joseph thumps Jason's chest.

"Yeah. Yeah, it kinda did." Jason smiles.

They laugh and replay the scene all day as they dig into their food. Joseph keeps nodding and patting Jason's shoulder. That night, in the car, Joseph doesn't roll over. Something changes. Joseph can't keep his mouth shut. They spend hours talking. Joseph explains how he worked in real estate. He hated himself. He kept waiting for something better to come along, something more exciting. But nothing did. He was staring down the barrel of thirty and he had nothing to show for it. So, he sold his stuff and hit the road. He knew that one more day selling houses and he would've drunk himself into a coma.

Joseph wants to learn more about Jason. He lets him ramble on about his office job, about Donna, about riding the bus home every day. Jason talks about the gnawing feeling. He talks about the sheet of the glass between him and the world. He talks about the pit he can't escape, the pit that eats him alive. He talks about everything.

"Everyone has that feeling, that sense of loneliness. We have a pit we can't escape. We fill it with jobs, and hobbies, and food, and sex, and television. We clog it with poison and hope it stays quiet. But it never does." Joseph is sitting on the hood of the car.

"What should we fill it with?"

"We shouldn't fill it at all; we should accept it."

Jason nods and sips his beer. Joseph raises his bottle and they clink the tops together. They watch the sun set, content.

They don't work odd jobs anymore. They find convenience stores, grocery markets, all-you-can-eat buffets, anything with crowds and food. Jason screams while Joseph steals. Jason never has a script; he just yells whatever's in his head. By the time someone takes a swing at him or calls the cops, they pile into the car and vanish. Joseph always scouts the joint. He plans out his route, what he needs to get, how much time he needs, where Jason should stand, everything. He lays out the entire event.

Jason doesn't think about home much anymore. He's found someone he can talk to, really talk to. Joseph actually listens to him. Jason is only reminded of home when he's gearing up for a speech. He only thinks about it when he's angry.

They're peeling down the highway. Joseph's behind the wheel, dangling a half-eaten apple out of the open window. Jason is reclining in his seat, stretching his legs. He's holding the map over his face, tracing his finger through the roads and buildings that litter the country.

The engine sputters and shakes, jolting Jason upwards. Joseph drops his apple as the car bounces. He pulls over to the side and hops out. They pop up the hood and a wave of black smoke blasts their faces. They step back, coughing. Joseph covers his mouth with his shirt and waves his hand through the cloud. He peers at the engine. Jason joins him. They have no idea what they're looking at. They flick a few gears, hoping it'll knock something loose. Jason remembers something he saw as a kid. He hauls a water jug from the trunk and pours it over the engine. Steam shoots up, creating an awful hissing sound. The smoke fades away. Jason and Joseph shrug.

Joseph turns the key in the ignition. The engine shudders and wheezes, refusing to start. They wait for thirty minutes, staring at the open road. They turn the key again. The engine grinds and moans, but the car doesn't move.

Joseph puts the car in neutral while Jason stands behind it. He pushes, hoping to give it a running start. The ground is slightly sloped, giving him a little momentum. Joseph stands by the driver's door, keeping one hand on the wheel while he pushes. The car starts to roll. Jason slips and lands in the dirt. Joseph cranks the ignition, forcing the engine to life before it fades away. The car rolls to a stop. Joseph rests his head on the steering wheel. Their car is dead. They're surrounded by scorching heat, endless road, a cloudless sky, and miles of faded grass. They've been on this road for hours and they've only seen four other cars.

A rock formation looms in front of them, barely fifty meters away. It's slouched over on the side of the highway, reaching for the sky until it curves and plateaus. It's the only source of shade they can see. They roll the car under the formation. They decide to climb the structure. Jason bounds up it, digging into the dirt as he ascends the slope. Joseph takes his time.

Jason reaches the plateau and he scans the horizon. He follows the road, keeping track of it with his thumb. He spots a faint cluster of buildings in the distance, no more than five miles away. They could walk there. Jason sighs. They aren't going to die out here. Joseph gets to the plateau and nods as Jason points out the town. Joseph looks at the sun, which is speeding towards the west. He clicks his teeth.

"We might as well stay here tonight. Everything's probably closed down there anyway. We'll head out in the morning." Joseph goes down the slope before Jason says anything.

They huddle under the formation as they eat processed sandwiches and warm juice. They watch the shadows grow towards them as the sun disappears. They sleep in the car.

When Jason wakes up, Joseph is gone. Jason pops open his door and tumbles to the ground. He rubs his eyes as he stumbles forward. He blinks at the formation, only seeing a blurry blob. He's forgotten where he is. He yawns as Joseph comes barreling down the slope, munching on the last of their apples.

"Ready to go?" Jason jerks his thumb down the road.

"You know, I been think we should stay for a bit." Joseph tears a chunk out of the apple.

Jason blinks again.

"Yeah, look around. It's quiet. It's beautiful. There's nobody else around. We've down nothing but rip off dime-stores and drive down the road. We've got to escape the grind. This is the perfect place to relax. Just the two of us. It'll be great." Joseph spreads his arms wide. Jason looks around. Between the highway and towering formation, he feels small, insignificant. This place unnerves him. He wants to get back on the road. He wants to keep moving.

He looks at Joseph, who hasn't let him down yet. Joseph, the only genuine person he's met. Joseph, who knows what Jason's been through. Joseph seems to love this place. Jason thinks if he listens to Joseph, maybe he'll like it too. Maybe he'll like their vacation. And, of course, he doesn't want to be a bad guest. So, they stay. They sit on the plateau. They walk through the prairie. They climb over rocks. They talk. They lay on the ground in silence. They relax.

The next day, they decide to stay a bit longer. Joseph only has to persuade Jason a little. Jason resists less and less each day. They stay for days, for weeks, for months. Jason agrees with Joseph; it's the perfect place. They forage for food. They find a brook with fresh water. They find wild berries to eat. They lay traps for rabbits. One time, they even manage to catch a deer. They live off the land. Time slips away.

Jason spends most days walking through the prairies. He runs his hands over the grass. He has no distractions, no excuses. It's just him and his mind. He lets it wander. He thinks about his past life. He thinks about the hollowness that ate away at him. He doesn't shrink from this feeling. He lets it wash over him. He sees a wasted life, one that tried to find meaning in a city without any. Before, he couldn't articulate why he ran; he just did. Standing in the prairie, surrounded by silence, he sees himself. He sees a man too afraid to say anything. He sees a man who curled up into a ball. He sees a man he despises. He ran because he had no other option. He ran because he had to. He ran because that feeling in his gut, the feeling that knew it had to move, took over. Now, in the prairie, Jason listens to that feeling.

Jason works. He skins the rabbits for their meals. He starts the fires at night. He scours the highway for tools. He does immediate work, necessary work, fulfilling work. He does work that matters. Jason only sees Joseph in the morning and the evening. Joseph collects berries and water as the sun rises, serving them in the car as breakfast. They talk about their plans for the day. Joseph gives Jason a checklist. Sometimes, Joseph will walk along the highway with Jason, looking for that perfect trinket. Or he'll ensnare a rabbit, holding its carcass above his head. Or he'll wander the fields with Jason. But usually after breakfast, Joseph ascends the slope.

Joseph spends most of his days on the plateau. He unscrewed the hood from the car and uses it for shade. He stares over the road and the prairie. A wild beard grows over his face. He scribbles his fingers in the dirt. He talks to himself. Sometimes Jason can hear him shouting, but he can never make out any words. Joseph turns the plateau into his temple.

At night, they sit by the fire, roasting a rabbit over the spit. They tear into their meat, singing their lips. Jason describes his day, talking about every animal that crossed his path, every knick knack he found in a ditch, every stray thought that crossed his mind. Joseph listens, nodding and occasionally asking a question. By the time they've polished off their food, he's exhausted. He retreats to the car while Jason stares at the dwindling fire.

On and on and on it goes. They ignore cars they speed by. They ignore people who slow down and stare at them. They ignore the blistering heat and their chaffed skin. They ignore everything but what's necessary: Food, water, and work. Joseph on his plateau and Jason in his fields; they've boiled themselves down to the essentials.

One night, Jason starts the fire without Joseph. He heard screaming earlier in the day, the loudest yet, but he hadn't thought much of it. Jason spears the rabbit and spins it over the flames. He looks over his shoulder, seeing nothing. He removes the rabbit from the fire and starts to cut into it when Joseph appears.

He nearly crashes into the fire. He grabs the rabbit and bites off a big chunk. He's twirling his fingers and stamping his feet. He can't stop chuckling. Jason doesn't know why, but he joins him. It's infectious. He jumps to his feet and grabs the rabbit, biting into it. They stomp around the fire. They pass the rabbit back and forth until it's nothing but shredded fragments on a stick.

Jason falls to the ground, out of breath. Joseph stays on his feet, waving his arms up and down. He tugs on his beard. He flicks his fingers.

"This is the life, isn't it? This is the real life." Joseph slaps his fist into his palm. Jason can only nod.

"This is what life should be. We aren't meant to scramble around in cities or fight over raises or find a bigger house to store all our crap. We're meant to work, actually work. We're meant to find something useful and do it. We have to cut out all the extra bullshit and the pointless distractions. We have to narrow it down to working and thinking. That's all we need. That's what we're supposed to do. That's what living is." Joseph kicks up dirt as he paces in front of the fire.

That night, Jason doesn't get a word in edgewise. Joseph talks for hours, long after the fire's reduced to embers. He talks about a world where you know what you're doing at all times. You have a purpose you're working towards. He talks about people who understand what they have to do. He talks about removing themselves from the rest of the world, saying it's too toxic to be saved. He talks about finding a place for people like them. He talks about making a new world.

Jason sinks to the ground as Joseph talks, resting his head on a rock. His eyelids fall down. He hears Joseph speak as he drifts away. He sees the world Joseph's talking about. He sees the pillars rising from the fields. Every night, Joseph talks about work, about rebuilding, about a new world. Every night, Jason nods in agreement and falls asleep to Joseph's voice. Every night he sees the pillars.

After another night of speeches, Joseph grabs Jason's shoulders and shakes him. Jason yells and punches the air, clipping Joseph's chin. Jason can't think to apologize before Joseph drags him to his feet. The sun is barely peeking over the horizon. Jason rubs his eyes and wets his mouth. Joseph pushes him towards the slope. Jason groans and starts walking.

Joseph runs ahead of him, disappearing over the plateau. Jason uses his hands for support as he climbs up the slope. He slips, covering his face with dust. He huffs as he pulls himself to the peak. Joseph is overlooking the highway, staring at the city. Jason walks to him, squinting past the sun. He rubs is arms to warm up.

"We're looking the wrong way." Joseph pivots.

He guides Jason to the other side of the plateau. They look at the endless stretch of prairie. Nothing but a sea of green.

"This is what we need. All the land we can see. We need something where we can build. We need room for people. We need space." Joseph spreads his arm.

Jason raises his eyebrows. Joseph chuckles and points at a patch of grass.

"That's where we'd have a sermon hall. Somewhere we could preach the truth to our people. And over there we'd have a garden. And over there we'd have a center square. And over there..." Joseph points to every square inch of the prairie.

Jason sees the pillars rising from the fields, and so much more. He sees buildings packed together. He sees crops ready for harvest. He sees people working, thinking, striving. And he sees a man on a hill, cloaked in white, talking about the path to salvation.

Jason and Joseph spend all day on the plateau, laying out paradise.

CHAPTER TWENTY-SEVEN

I'm in Hell.

I'm lying on my side, naked. My hair droops over my face, knotted and sweaty. I feel...sticky.

The curtains are drawn in front of me. I see a hint of the stage past their skirt. Sunlight streams past the fabric, bathing me in a red glow. I see a faint outline of my hand painted crimson in the darkness. I can only see a layer of red surrounded by an air of black. If I've died, I've landed far south.

I raise my head, propping it on my arm. I run my tongue over my teeth and lips, wetting them. I crack my jaw. I adjust my eyes to the darkness. I can see faint shadows of the sermon hall. I breathe and feel my body wake up. I'm not dead.

I sit up, peeling my skin off the floor. I scratch my neck and look down. The source of all my trouble. I couldn't keep it in my pants. Idiot. I don't look back. I know what's there. I can hear it snoring. I don't want to see my shame. Not yet.

My clothes are piled together next to the Weight. No, actually, they're on top of the Weight. They're discarded on it like it's a laundry basket. I used the symbol of repentance, my trump card, the final test, as a clothes hanger. I might as well have rubbed my crotch on it.

I roll to my knees and stand up, feeling my back groan. I grab my clothes and turn them outside-in, slipping them on. I trip as I pull my legs into my pants, nearly smashing my face into the Weight. How appropriate.

I stand in front of the curtain, holding its slim opening. I flex my knuckles, trying to prepare myself. Once I step out of this darkness, I'll have to confront...what I did. I'll have to...I don't know. I can't wait forever. I tear the curtains open, letting the sun blast me in the face. I stagger onstage, slamming the curtains shut behind me. Stale daylight trickles into the sermon hall. It must be noon, maybe later. A sea of empty chairs looks at me, judging. I can barely hear the sounds of the compound past the door. I'm sealed in an oyster, deaf to the world.

I wander to the podium and lean over it. I rub my eyes. I open the drawer at my waist level. It's full of pencils, photos of members, a list of names, everything I might need for a sermon. A sheet of paper is buried beneath all that, crumpled and faded. I fish it out and read.

It's an old sermon speech. Something from a few years ago. I'm congratulating our newest influx of members for making the leap with us. I'm asking them to prepare themselves for bigger jumps from higher cliffs. I'm talking about sacrificing our lies, our half-truths, our conveniences, for something greater, something real. I'm asking people to forget what they learned out there. I'm telling them self-denial is the only way to get through life.

My speech is covered in pen scratched and crossed-out words. Some sentences are underlined or circled. Arrows dart across the page. I must have rearranged it at the last minute, maybe as I was onstage. Heh. I've been writing the same few speeches over and over. I just shuffle the words around a bit. The core message doesn't change. It doesn't have to. I fold the paper and shove it back in the drawer.

I look at the pillars. They're a beautiful sight. Bold without being distracting, elegant without being opulent. They're everything my compound should be, everything my people should be, everything I should be. They're exactly what I pictured when I saw them rising out of the ground. These pillars are...are...they're...

Fucking hell, I'm a fraud.

I stare at the podium. I grasp the sides of my head and yank on my hair. I grind my teeth. I can't block what's coming. There's no wall of drunkenness this time. There's no hangover defense or blackout shield. There are no holes in my memory. I remember everything in pristine quality. My sobriety gives me no way out.

We fell past the curtains and tumbled to the ground. I kissed her everywhere. She tore my clothes off. I grunted. She moaned. We rolled on the floor. I held her close. She whispered in my ear. I closed my eyes with her in my arms. I slept with Sandra. Again.

I'm a worm. I surrendered to my base urges with barely a shrug. I grabbed her. I wanted to do it. No alcohol was nudging me along, no intoxication was fueling me. It was just me and my desires. I didn't fight; I gave in. I slept with Sandra because I wanted to. Because it felt good. Because I could.

I've taken my transgression and I've multiplied it. I slept with a member of my compound, a subordinate. I was in complete control of my faculties. I instigated it. And I did it in the sermon hall, of all places. I desecrated our temple.   I want to crawl into myself and never come out. I look back at the pillars. I'm unworthy of them. I'm a liar. I don't deserve to preach. How can I teach what I don't even follow? What's wrong with me? This isn't how it's supposed to go. I'm meant to be better than this. I'm meant to—

Maybe I'm wrong. Maybe I've always been wrong. Maybe I was just a guy who could make a good speech, shake a few hands, and flash a nice smile. Maybe, when rubber hits the road, when it really matters, I collapse. Maybe I deluded myself into thinking I was a leader. Maybe I never had to test myself. Maybe I was just a smokescreen.

I'm no better than Smit. I lie to get what I want. I don't believe in what I preach any more than he does. I built my faith on sand so I can change it whenever I want. We're the same. I'm nauseous. The sermon hall is spinning. I grip the podium, trying to steady myself. The pillars seem to grow, surging towards me. I shrink away. Something's screaming in my head, condemning me. I can't quiet it. I'm suffocating. I'm trapped here, trapped in this moment.

I see Smit's face. His smile is frozen. I can't look away. I grind my knuckles into my temples, but the screaming doesn't stop. My head is pounding. I see myself standing at this podium.

It's from another time. It's another person. I'm giving a speech. I'm talking about hard work. I'm talking about ethics. I'm getting choked up. My eyes are watery. Lies. All lies. I don't believe any of it. If I did, I wouldn't have... I wouldn't have done... I wouldn't have betrayed—

Arms wrap around my stomach.

"Morning"

Everything stops. The voices, the spinning, Smit, all of it. Nothing but me and silence.

I look at the door. It's beckoning me. It's only forty paces away, thirty if I really tried. I could bound down the aisle and burst outside. I could run to the river. I could...What? What could I do? Wash myself? Go for a swim? Sink to the bottom? I could drown myself... No, no, I can't avoid my responsibility. I have to face what I did. I have to own up to it. I have to turn around.

The arms are squeezing me tight. Hot breath blows on my neck. A warm body presses against my back. I can smell the excitement, the anticipation. I can't run from this. I let my body go loose, fighting against the tension. I grab the fingers and peel them apart, letting them fall to the side. I step forward as the arms fall back. I turn around.

Sandra. She's wearing her clothes, thank fuck. Her hair is a jumbled mess, flattened on one side and tangled on the other. A contented smile fills her face.

"How're you?" She arches her back.

"Fine." I keep one eye on the door.

"Get a good sleep?" She massages her jaw as she yawns.

"Hmm, well, you know." I briefly raise a tense smile.

"Oh, I do." She winks at me.

I scratch my neck. She sways her arms back and forth. Seconds crawls along. She opens her mouth. Fuck, fuck, fuck, I can't do this.

"Well, uh, I'd better get to work. Lots to do. People to see. Burning daylight. I'll see you later." I back away from her, ready to jump off the stage. I need to regroup. It's too real right now. I need space. I need—

"You're leaving?" Sandra tilts her head.

"Uh, yeah, it's pretty late, um, pretty late in the day and, eh, I've got a bunch of stuff to, uh, to deal with. So, I'd better...deal with it." My face spasms with half-smiles and apologies. I'm close to the edge. One quick hop down and then a beeline for the door.

"You have to leave right now?" Sandra steps towards me.

"Um, yes, yeah, uh huh, got to go. Seize the day and... all that." I'm an inch from the edge. Get out of here and I can deal with this later. Almost there.

"You don't time for a little...?" Sandra nods at the curtain.

I stop. She's biting her lower lip. Time apart isn't going to fix this situation. She'll keep hounding me. And she might let it slip to someone and... I'll be fucked. She's a ticking time bomb I have to defuse.

"Time?" I step away from the edge.

"Yeah, not too long, I think. Three minutes at most, judging on last time." Her smile grows as she places her hand on my chest.

Looking at her in the harsh light of day, I see everything that made me give in. I see her striking eyes and her olive skin and her smooth lips. I see every feature and blemish. I see a person I can talk to, someone with fire, with dedication. I see a follower with devotion. I see someone worthy to stand in this compound. I see someone I have to crush.

"Sandra, this is wrong." I take her hand off my chest.

"Yeah, I thought it was a little...sacrilegious. Your room then?" She starts to walk off the stage. I grab her wrist.

"No, what we did was wrong. What we did last night...it was inappropriate." I force myself to look her in the eye.

Sandra blinks. She slides her arms out of my grip. Her smile fades. She pushes the hair out of her face.

"How so?" She folds her arms.

"You know why." I clear my throat.

"I need something better than that." Sandra rolls her eyes.

"We...we're supposed to resist pleasures of the flesh. It's one of the tenets. We're supposed to rise above something tawdry like...sex." I feel my face getting red.

"And you think people here actually do that? Because you're in for a surprise." Sandra looks at me like I've knocked a screw loose.

I scowl. Of course I know what goes on in the living quarters. Does she think I don't pay any attention? I see people darting off into the woods, holding hands, and unbuckling belts. I see the looks couples give each other from across the sermon hall. When I walk the grounds at night, I hear the noises. It's the most natural thing humans know how to do.

"I know what goes on in my compound. I know what people do here." I'm sweating.

"So what's the big deal?" Sandra throws her hands in the air.

"Because it's wrong. It's weak. Just because everyone does it doesn't make it right." I run my hands through my hair. Why can't she get it?

"It's just sex. What's the big deal?" Sandra is right in my face.

"No, no, you're not...you're not listening. It's...it's wrong. We have to be better. We have to be..." I pinch the bridge of my nose. The pounding is getting louder.

"We all work hard. What's wrong with a little fun now and then?" She slides her hands around my waist.

I'm muttering. I can't find the words. I twist back and forth, locked in her embrace. The pounding grows.

"Give me one reason why we can't go behind the curtains again. One."

I grind my teeth. This room is shrinking. The pounding is thunderous. She doesn't understand.

"Just one. Tell me. Please."

I look at her. She likes me. She wants to help. But she doesn't get it. She won't listen. I can only hear the pounding

"I want to know. Tell me. C'mon, tell me. Tell me, tell me, tell me."

Her voice works in unison with the pounding. They hammer on my head. A relentless barrage. I can't think. I can't move. I'm stuck. Alright, alright, alright. I'll say it, okay? I'll fucking say it. Just stop this goddamn pounding. I'll say it.

"Because I have to be better than everyone." I tear away from her.

We look at each other. My eyes feel like they're about to bug out. Sandra looks like she's been slapped. My words hang in the air, smothering us. I know I should take it back. I know I should be humble and contrite. But my mind is drifting to the backseat. Instinct is taking over.

"Better?" Sandra chews on the word.

"I mean, well, I have to be the leader here, of course. It's my job, my duty. So I can't stumble with any tenet. I can't be a slouch, right? I can't screw up. I can't take my eye off the prize. It'd be inappropriate, improper, indecent. I'd be a fraud, you see. I can't have that. No, no, no. Not right at all." My mouth keeps spewing out nonsense phrases. I can't stop.

"O...kay. But you said 'better.' What do you mean?" She won't let go.

"It's like I said: I'm a leader. A leader's obviously someone you need to look up to, someone you respect. You can't listen to someone's rules when you know they're breaking them. I've got to the example. I've got to be the standard." I have a dim sense that if I keep talking, this problem will go away.

"Right. The standard. The standard we're all going for. You've always said we can reach it together. You've said we'll be even. But now you said you'll be better. I...I don't get it." Sandra frowns and rubs her left temple.

"Slip of the tongue, really. Didn't mean anything. Completely pointless. Obviously I want to be better than what I am now. I want all of us to be better. I want us to build each other up. I don't want to be better than everybody else. I want to be on equal footing with all of you." I'm trying to sell vapour.

"You meant what you said. I saw your eyes. It was real. It was the same look you had last night when... You meant it." Sandra glances at the curtains.

I'm stuck in the backseat, trying to grab hold of the steering wheel. I can't control myself. This pounding has overwhelmed me, pushed me out. I'm on autopilot now. I can only nudge myself in the right direction but I can't guide the ship. I have to ride the wave. Sandra found a flaw and she's holding a magnifying glass over it. She's sunk her fingers in deep. She burst open a fire hydrant and now everything's starting to flow. I can sense another surge rising to the top. I can't suppress it. She couldn't let it go and now...

"Well, I meant it a bit. Only in the abstract. A leader has to be better. That's what makes him a leader. He stands above the herd. I don't want to lord it over anyone, of course, but people have to know who's in charge. People have to know who to follow. I have to raise us up from the mire. I have to be the beacon." I cringe, but the words don't stop.

"The beacon?" Sandra's frown morphs into confusion.

"Exactly right. I have to keep myself pure. I wasn't meant to be part of the flock, following orders and listening to sermons. I'm supposed to be on this podium speaking the truth. I'm meant to be on top of the heap. I'm better because it's part of my path. It's my destiny. I can't stoop down to everyone else's level. I'm supposed to be the one who rises to the highest heights. I can't break my own rules. I need to be better." I wish I wasn't saying everything this way, but...

"Jesus." Sandra's jaw is slack.

"That's why I can't be mucking around with you. I can't let you keep me from my path. I'm supposed to be pure. I can't afford to make the mistakes everyone else does. I can't fuck up, not now. Last night was a...was an error on my part. I won't do it again. You can't interfere with my ascension." I finally shut my mouth.

Sandra rubs her chin. Her face is blank. She scrunches her nose and spits on the floor. She looks me up and down. She clicks her teeth and sighs.

"Egomaniac." Her voice doesn't tremble or quake; she's monotone.

The word slams into me. I crawl back to the driver's seat, scrambling for a response. I try to think of a retort, of an apology, of anything. Nothing comes to mind. Sandra doesn't wait for me. She looks me in the eyes, shaking her head. She walks past me and hops off the stage. She doesn't look back as she heads for the door.

I watch her leave. I want to tell her I'm sorry. I want to tell her that I need her. I want to tell her she's exiled. I want to, at least, tell her not to talk about our conversation with anyone. I don't say anything. I watch as she opens the door. I watch as she steps outside. I watch as the door slams shut.

I'm alone in the sermon hall. All I can hear is the pounding.

CHAPTER TWENTY-EIGHT

My office is a tomb and my robe is a headstone.

I prop my legs on the desk. My chair creaks, splitting the silence of the room. I stare at the ceiling.

Today crawled by. I stumbled around the compound, trying to keep up appearances. I cheered on builders and I chatted with planters, but it all sounded hollow. The pounding in my head wouldn't let me think straight. I hope no one noticed. I spoke with Ken and Greg for updates. Same shit, different day. We've got no leads on the killer. We're still losing members. We're still unprepared for the ceremony. Rewind the tape and play it again tomorrow. I could barely muster the energy to tell them to keep trying. I felt so goddamn tired.

I spent all day with my head on a swivel, darting my eyes over the compound looking for Sandra. I kept expecting her to march up to me, nail me in the gut, and tell everyone what I did, what I said. My toes curled every time I rounded a corner. My heart was in my throat.

But I never saw her. She wasn't in the fields or in her garden. I checked the living quarters, but I only found her rumpled cot. She must have gone into the forest to clear her head. That's what I should have done. Maybe she jumped ship to Smit's side. No, that wouldn't suit her, no matter how bad I fucked things up. Maybe she decided to cut her loses and hit the road. Maybe she figured she'd be better off anywhere else. That'd probably be for the best, for both of us.

I spent the afternoon at the center square, watching for Sandra, for Smit, for errant followers, for everything. I had to distract myself from the pounding. I watched the sun set as people filed into the cafeteria. Ken and Greg gave me a quick salute as they disappeared behind a building. I sat there, staring down the path that leads to the open road. It stretched out wide, ready to consume anything. It was pitch-black when I shuffled into my office.

My robe hangs in front of me. The moon reflects off it, giving its white fabric an eerie glow, the only source of light in the darkness. The only sign of life. My headstone. I drag my feet off the desk and walk to the robe. I haven't really looked at it for a while. Between the serial killer and Smit and my midnight trysts, it's faded into the background. I slip it on, deliver a sermon, and hang it up again. I haven't had any reverence, any respect for it. It's simply been a scrap of cloth. I rotate one of the sleeves. I slide my arm in and out of the hole. I run my fingers over the chest. I close my eyes. I can feel the electricity, the energy. I can see it for what it really is.

It's my armour. It's my uniform, the only uniform I've ever needed. When I wear it, I become a leader. All the bullshit slides away. I can be myself, completely. Everything I want to be, everything I want this compound to be, is bundled up in this robe. It's the symbol of purity and strength we all should follow. We should be radiant and glowing, perfect images of white brilliance. We should be something to be admired. We should...we should...ah, fuck.

My eyes are watery. I blink, but it just makes things worse. My vision is blobby and distorted. I wipe my eyes with my palm. I look back at the robe. I'm unworthy. I don't deserve to parade it around the compound. I don't deserve to wear it when I'm onstage giving a hollow speech. I don't deserve to wear it anywhere. I'm a fraud.

I've done nothing but failed for months. I've failed my people by letting a killer rampage through our compound. I've failed my faith by letting Smit suck it dry. I've failed myself by indulging in my basest desires. I've let all my teachings fall to the wayside. I'm unworthy of this robe. I'm unworthy to lead. I'm unwor—

Something knocks on the door.

Every muscle tenses up. I peek out the window, but I can't see anything on the porch. I flex my fingers. Minutes roll by. I don't hear another knock. Could it be Greg? He could have a lead on the case. But why wouldn't he ask me to open the door? Maybe it's Sandra. She wants to talk, but she's too angry to actually speak, so she just knocked and now she's waiting for me to answer it. Maybe it's the killer... Oh, fuck, maybe it *is* the killer. Maybe he knocked on the door to lure me outside so he could wrap a noose around my neck. Oh, shit, shit, shit.

Hold on. If he wanted to kill me, he would have done it by now. I'm the main attraction. He could sneak in here while I'm asleep and strangle me. That's a comforting thought. But he hasn't done it. He must be...afraid of me, yeah, that's it. He doesn't think he can take me. He's not behind this door. I'm going to open it and he won't be there. Fuck, I hope so...

I throw the door open.

No one's here. I look around the corners before ducking back inside. Nothing. Did I imagine it? Maybe a bird smacked into the door. I grab the handle when I spot something on the porch.

It's an orange arrow. It's made of construction paper and it's coated in fresh paint. It's taped to the floor. It's pointing at the forest.

I should go to bed. I should close this door, lock it, and go to sleep. I've dealt with enough today. I don't need any weird arrows laid out by...who the fuck knows. I should slam this door shut. I stare at the arrow. I feel an itch in my legs. My brain is tugging me forward. I shouldn't go out there, but... I want to.

I look back at my robe. If this is some prank by a member, it'd be best if they could recognize me straight away. I'd stand out with the robe. It'd be a perfect signifier. No one would fuck with me.

I enter the forest with the robe draped over my shoulders. I hold a lantern in one hand and a letter opener in the other. Just in case.

Arrows litter the ground. They're plastered to trees. They lead me to the river.

This place feels...wrong at night. I shouldn't be here. The river seems dangerous, murky. I see more arrows to my left. They form a loose trail along the river bank. I can see where they lead: The cavern.

I grip my robe close and follow them.

CHAPTER TWENTY-NINE

Jason Neary is standing the middle of a cavern.

Joseph is next to him. Jason can see his faint outline. They're surrounded by candles that shimmer in their alcoves. They provide little warmth from the cold that envelops them. No one knows they're here. They're lost to the world. They entered the cavern this morning. They've been lighting candles, chanting, and exploring the chamber, preparing for rebirth.

They found this cavern weeks ago during a hike. It was obscured by trees and bushes. They'd stumbled across something special. They knew it the moment they saw it. The cavern was the crown jewel of their property. Not even the landowner knew it existed. Months ago, when he led them on a tour, he didn't come anywhere near the cavern. He showed them the river and the forest and the open fields. He walked them through the disintegrated barn and the crumbled homestead and the hole in the ground that served as the bathroom. He showed them every dead patch of grass, every rodent infestation, every overflowing hornets' nest, but he never showed them the cavern. He didn't know about it. He didn't realize what he had.

Joseph and Jason knew. They knew as they hurtled down the highway and saw a "For Sale" sign teetering into a ditch, its arrow curving down a dirt road. They knew as they drove through the path, drifting further from the noise, from the clutter. They knew as they passed a rusted gate. They knew as they gazed over a wide expanse of green. They knew they'd found home.

They'd been on the road for weeks after their time on the plateau. They needed a place where they could build paradise. They needed land, and lots of it, to attract similar people. They needed something secluded, something removed from the city screams. They needed the plateau writ large. The field where they'd expanded their minds wouldn't do. It suited two people, not two hundred. It was too close to the city, too close to temptation. Joseph told Jason they needed an oyster, not an ocean. Jason agreed. He always agreed with Joseph.

They drove from city to city, county to county, state to state, searching for the land they saw in their minds. They looked through abandoned parks, dirt-poor farms, and empty prairies. They all lacked something, something neither men could describe. They were too small, or too barren, or too snug next to a town. There was always a flaw that spoiled the land.

"We're not looking for good enough." That was Joseph's constant refrain.

But when they rattled down that dirt road, they'd found something better than good enough; they'd found perfection. It was like someone had unspooled their thoughts and painted them into the Earth. It had everything they needed. It would be their paradise.

The landowner hadn't cared that they'd found their home. He just wanted to unload an unprofitable property. He was desperate, but not stupid. He saw Joseph and Jason's faces when he walked them through the fields and forests. He smelled their hunger. And he knew when to strike a good deal. He sat in his office trailer hitched to his pickup truck and he said a number to the men. Jason blinked. Joseph said other numbers, but the landowner repeated the same number over and over. They were at a standstill.

The men returned to their car and drove into town. Joseph went to a bank while Jason went to another. They emptied the accounts from their past lives. Joseph took out a loan. They pulled money from every pocket they could find. They piled it all in the landowner's hand. He tipped his cap, handed over a stack of papers, and drove off. It was theirs.

They aren't thinking about building anything now. Joseph is wearing a black cloak that brushes the ground. Jason is standing hip-deep in a pool. He feels the sharp rocks beneath his feet. He rubs his arms as his teeth chatter. He's naked. Joseph wades into the pool and stands behind Jason. He places his hand on Jason's neck, rubbing it. Jason shivers.

"Are you ready?" Joseph drums his fingers on Jason's neck.

Jason stares ahead at a lone candle. It flickers but it does not fade. He nods. Joseph shoves Jason's head underwater.

Jason sees only darkness. Water rushes to his eyes, blinding him. His mouth fills with liquid, some of it trickling down his throat. His knees scrape the ground. He keeps his eyes open, but he can't see anything. Joseph yanks Jason's head back to the surface. Jason coughs out a sliver of water.

"Do you give it all up?" Joseph slaps Jason's face.

"I do, I do, I do." Jason nods.

"What did you see?" Joseph points at the water.

Jason doesn't say anything. Joseph shoves his head back into the pool. Jason stares into the darkness, looking for something, anything. He gazes at the mass of black. His lungs ache.

His face breaks the surface. Joseph slaps him. He shakes his head, trying to focus.

"What did you see?" Joseph grips Jason's shoulders.

Jason sputters and mumbles, looking for an answer. His head returns to the water. He burrows in hands into the dirt, fighting through the darkness. It doesn't change.

Resurface. Slap. Blink.

"What did you see?"

Nothing. Underwater. Struggle. Darkness. Nothing. Jason is getting dizzy.

"What did you see?"

Nothing. Water blasts his face. The darkness mocks him. His lungs are exhausted.

"What did you see?"

Nothing. Jason is going limp. His eyelids are fluttering. The darkness just sits there, unmoving, unknowable. Jason returns to the surface. He feels a slap as he coughs out a torrent of water. Joseph leans in close.

"What did you see?"

Jason shakes his head, crying. Joseph puts his palm on Jason's forehead. He breathes deep.

"Last chance." Joseph pushes Jason back down. Jason squirms in the water. His lungs beg for air. He thrashes his arms and legs. Joseph holds him down.

Jason stares ahead. He's going lightheaded. His chest is on fire. He feels himself fading away. He looks into the darkness one last time. He sees something. It's faint, but it's there. Something buried beneath the darkness. It shimmers. He swims towards it. Joseph releases his grip. Jason paddles through the water, his lungs exploding, but he barely feels it.

He sees a glow. It's nearly crushed in the blackness, but he can see it. Only he can see it. Only he can touch it. Buried treasure in the gloom. Jason feels warm. This glow is what he needs. It's order. It's the way forward. He grabs it and holds it close. It disappears. He rotates his body and looks above. He sees the candles shimmering through the water. Stars. He bursts through the surface, devouring air. He stumbles to his feet before collapsing near the pool's edge. He grabs a candle and holds it in his palm. He stares at the flame. A flickering beauty.

He looks at Joseph, who's standing in the middle of the pool. His soaked cloak clings to his body. Jason nods and raises the candle. Joseph smiles and bows.

In the cavern, they've been reborn.

CHAPTER THIRTY

They're all dead.

Three pale faces stare up at nothingness. Their eyes are blank slates. They don't move. Their bodies bob in the shallow pool. They could be meditating. Their throats are all slashed. Ribbons of blood leak from their necks and down to the water. Their clothes have dyed into a dark shade of red. Dry plasma is caked on their faces. The spilled liquid shadows them in crimson. They're drowning in a puddle of gore.

They're lying in a pool in the cavern. It's barely deep enough to cover my shin. It rests deep within the cave, far from the moonlight. My lantern provides the only illumination. A lonely place to die.

Their limp bodies form a triangle. A head touches another person's feet. That person's head brushes against another pair of feet. The third body completes the set, returning to the first corpse's feet. Rope connects the bodies at their ankles and necks. They float, but they never separate. A perfect shape of order.

Ken and Greg are standing next to me. Ken is hunched over his knees, heaving. Greg is holding his hand over his mouth, muffling his sobs. I ignore them. I don't know how long they've been here. I don't know how long I've been here. I turn my head, holding my lantern forward. I see dark blobs in the cavern. I see towering teeth and hidden alcoves. I see another pool, a wider one, a deeper one. You could swim in it. I have. There used to be candles here.

I return to the bodies. I watch them spin in their triangle, trapped in the pool. All their work, all their sacrifice, all their struggles, all their endurance, all their pain, every step of their lives; it all lead to this. This is where they've wound up: Floating in their own blood.

I followed the arrows along the riverbank and up the hill. They led into the cavern, like I knew they would. I stood at the mouth for minutes, staring at the final arrow. I knew what I was going to find. Deep down, I knew. I knew I should go back to the compound, find back up, prepare myself. I knew I shouldn't step into the cavern. I had to find out. I had to satisfy my curiosity. So I put my foot in the darkness.

Now I'm here. I didn't notice Greg and Ken enter the cavern. They must've been working late and they saw an arrow. They followed the path and they saw what I saw. They satisfied their curiosities. So we stand here, staring, locked in place, not daring to utter a word.

I let my arm droop, allowing the lantern to swoop down, creating a brief dance of shadows. My whole body feels heavy. My head wants to sag into the ground and never come up. I want to collapse in a pool and drift away. I want to make it stop.

I can't fall apart. That's what he wants. That's what they all want.

"We need to get rid of those arrows." I push the words out of my mouth.

Ken straightens up, still sucking back air. Greg swallows and wipes his eyes. They look at each other. I see everything in the corner of my eye. I can't look at them yet. I can't tear away from the triangle.

"It'll be morning soon. If people see any arrows, they'll follow them right here. They'll see...they'll see what we see. We'll have mass panic. We need to get rid of those arrows." My mouth tastes like chalk as I speak.

"You're worried about hysteria after we just found three murde—?" Greg steps forward, but Ken grabs his arm.

"I'm aware of what're we've found. I know you're upset. I'm...upset, too. But we can't let this spiral out of control. We need to get rid of those arrows." I watch the triangle spin, and spin, and spin...

Greg pulls at his hair. Ken takes him aside. They whisper. I can't make out any words. Ken's voice is a steady

monotone. Greg's voice lashes out. They fill the cavern with a
hissing sound. I watch the head of a corpse bump the side of the
pool, scraping its skin. Ken and Greg return. I force myself to
look at them. Ken's face is stone trying to hide any cracks. Greg
is beet-red and teary-eyed. They nod. I bow my head.

"Thank you. I know this is...appalling. But you are my
champions, my titans. We'll fix this, I promise." I pat their
shoulders. Those words were more for me than for them.

I tell them to come back once they've removed the
arrows. I tell them not to speak with anyone. I tell them I'll
watch over the bodies. They leave me in the darkness, alone with
the triangle. They'll find the strength to keep going. They lean
on each other. They'll make it to the other side. They have to.
We all have to.

I look over the cavern. Any nook, any cranny, any dark
spot would be the perfect place for...him to watch. Watch and
wait for a moment to step out and—

No. If the killer was here, he'd have attacked me by
now. He didn't lure me here to kill me; he brought me here to
mock. It's all a show to him, a game. He's laughing at us. I shake
my head. I can't think about him right now. I look at the triang—
No, they're bodies, people, not a shape. And they don't deserve
to stay this way.

I take off my robe and fold it into a corner. I wade into
the water, staining my clothes. I plug my nose so I don't gag
from the smell of blood. I push the bodies to the side, untying the
ropes one by one. I destroy the triangle, letting the bodies drift
apart.

I grab the nearest corpse and haul it onto the cavern
floor. My hands are slick with watery gore. I reach under the
body's armpits and drag it away from the pool. I reach the thin
stream that stretches out to the river. I can see hints of the
outside through the small opening in the wall. I lay the body
down and cross its arms. I look at the face. It's a woman. I
recognize her.

She was a builder. She worked all over the compound. She helped build a greenhouse for the planters. She stayed there after the sun went down and everyone had gone to dinner, hammering on boards. She mostly kept to herself. But she worked hard. She always thanked me after a sermon. She always shook my hand. She had a strong grip. She was dedicated.

And now she's here.

I wipe the blood from her cheeks and brush her hair out of her face. I return to the pool and grab another corpse. It's heavier than the woman. I place it next to her and study the face.

He was a builder as well. I remember his voice. He was always the loudest person during a sermon. He stomped his feet the hardest and screamed at the top of his lungs. One time, he grabbed me in a bear hug and nearly bruised my ribs. He had passion.

And now he's here.

I straighten his shirt and I return to the pool for the last body. It's lighter than the other two. As I set him down, I look at his face.   He was a planter. Not a great worker, but a dutiful one. The quietest man in the compound. You had to lean into his mouth to hear what he was saying. He gave me a bouquet once. He said I was making a difference, at least to him. He had faith.

And now he's here.

Three people. Three followers. Three believers. They struggled to make this compound better, to make themselves better. They worked to improve their lives. They gave up everything for their paradise. And now they're here. Dead in the middle of a cavern. Covered in blood and water. This was all they got.

I collapse to my knees and look over them. I barely feel the tears as they fall down.

CHAPTER THIRTY-ONE

My hands are cracked rocks attached to twigs.

My fingernails are chipped and lopsided, overly long or short and jagged. My knuckles are white, ready to burst through the skin. My palms are covered in cuts. I haven't washed or slept in days. I close my eyes, but I don't drift away. My ears prick up at the slightest sound. My heart never lets off its jackhammer rhythm. I can only see the pool and the bodies and the blood when I got to bed. My mind won't let me rest.

During the day, numbness washes over me. I wander from building to building, watching followers. If they notice me, I'll say something vague and move on. I'm stuck on autopilot. I'm trapped in a dead body. My brain knows I should be rallying, should be fighting back, should be finding the killer. It knows what I have to do, but I can't connect it to my body. There's this thick wall of exhaustion between them. My body's beaten down. I'm stuck in a haze and I can't get out.

I raise my hands and let them fall down on the podium. The microphone picks up their landing, sending a "thumping" sound throughout the sermon hall. I tap my middle finger, watching it flex. I let the other fingers join in, drumming them on the wood. I can feel a slight sensation in them, something familiar. I'm rebooting myself, one piece at a time.

I look up. All my followers are coated in blood. Their bodies are covered from head to toe in gore. They're all staring forward, all blank. Their throats are slashed. A collection of corpses displayed like mannequins. The floor runs red as the blood flows towards me. The walls start to seep with the stuff. Everything turns crimson. I smell the plasma in the air. I feel a cut growing on my neck. I feel blood pouring over my chest. All my followers sink into the gore, lost. I start to fall. I disappear beneath the waves. All I see is red.

I blink.

I'm in the sermon hall. My members are here, all clean, all with intact necks. There's not a drop of blood on me. I'm fine. We're all fine. And they're all staring at me. I'm still drumming my fingers. Someone coughs. Did I even start the sermon yet? Was I talking before I spaced out? How long have they been waiting? How long was I gone? Why can't I remember? Stay calm, stay calm. They won't notice anything if you don't show it. It was all part of the act, all part of the show.

I stop the drumming. I wave my hands in a jazz hands salute and give a chuckle. A few people join me.

"A little musical interlude for you morning sermon." I grab the microphone.

I run my hand through my hair, straightening it. I smooth out the wrinkles in my robe. I look over the crowd, nodding at certain members. The last two rows are completely empty. I feel a twinge of anger beneath my haze. I scowl and pace onstage, bumping the microphone on my chest. I didn't think about this sermon at all yesterday. This morning, I stumbled out of bed, threw on my robe, and went to the stage. I think. I don't know how I got here.

Come on, think, think, think. I don't need much; a little kindling, that's all. I can spitball the entire speech, I only need a starting point. Come on, people are looking at the door. They're talking to each other. They're shaking their heads. Come on, one topic, that's all I need. One, that's it. Damn it, think. Think, think, think.

"Justice." My arm shoots out.

"People think justice is an individual concept. It's something that's meted out on a case-by-case basis. An individual commits a crime, an individual pays the price. Justice seeks out the guilty individuals and punishes them. The punishment for a sole criminal means justice is done. Society is just because it excised its lone perpetrators. But we know this is a lie, don't we?" I lock eyes with a feeble-looking planter in the front row. He nods.

"Of course we do. Justice isn't a personal judgment; it's a communal activity. We all have to participate in justice to make it work. It's an ongoing event. We have to make our world just every day. We can't let justice be reserved for special occasions. As a group, as a collective, we make this compound just." I feel my words chipping away at the haze. My body feels looser.

"But this sword cuts both ways. If we are all just, than our compound is just. If one of us is unjust, if even one of us is guilty, then we are all guilty. An individual is a reflection of his surroundings. An unjust person can only exist in a world without justice. We create the culture we inhabit. We make this a place of virtue or a place of vice. There is no in-between." I shake my head.   "When we find ourselves lacking, when we see weakness in us, when we know we're being unjust, we can't ignore it. We have to face our failings head on. We have to repair any harm done to justice. There is only one balm that can cleanse us: Confession." People applaud. They're happy we're in familiar territory.

"I've sensed something lacking in our compound lately. There's been an... absence, yes, that's the word, absence. We've drifted away from justice. We haven't stayed the course. We need to confess, all of us, together, right here, right now." I point my finger down.

"We need to confess and cleanse ourselves. Let go of your sins and step into the light. Don't shy away from the truth. I won't be excluded from this, oh, no. Listen: I used to have a weakness for sex. It nearly ruined me. I, Solomon Neary, was a sex addict." I glance around the room for Sandra. Nothing.

"See? See how easy it is to let go off all that weight? Come on, here we go." I step off the stage and wade into the crowd with the microphone. Everyone jumps to their feet.

I shove the microphone into the feeble planter's face. His wheezy sigh seeps through the speakers. He looks at the ground and shrugs. I tap the microphone.

"Come on, you've done it before. We all have. Get it out. Let's start sharing. You want to get started?" I yell over him. The crowd claps.

"Well, uh, um, I, uh, oh, I know, I know. Okay, I'm, uh, I'm a deep sleeper." The planter smiles. The crowd goes quiet.

I resist the urge to bury my head in my arm and scream. All my rhetoric and the best this amoeba can muster is heavy eyelids? Is he mocking me? Is he taking the piss? I can feel the haze creeping back into my mind.

"Uh, it's a real problem. I've slept through entire sermons. Uh, not that I want to. It just happens. I mean, I let it happen. I slept all day once. Didn't get up once. I'm trying to beat it. So...yeah." The planter offers a weaker smile and looks at his seatmates for reassurance. There's a smattering of applause.

I yank the microphone away from him. He shrinks, trying to disappear behind a bulky builder. He nearly derailed the sermon. I could feel the energy leaving people as he spoke. He battered their enthusiasm. He drained the room. Just move on. Don't dwell on it.

"Alright, yeah, sure, good start. Anybody else? Come on up and confess your sin. Let everybody know. Let's move forward. No burdens, no weights, no regrets. Let's loosen those shackles. Come on now." I walk down the aisle.

A bald builder grabs my elbow and steers me to my side. He's sweaty and trembling. He leans down to the microphone.

"I work too hard." He snickers.

"Oh, he works too hard? That's quite a sin. I think we all wish we could have that one, don't we?" The crowd chuckles as I shoot daggers at the builder. He gets the message and straightens up.

"Well, uh, I mean, I do too much. I don't leave, uh, anything for my co-workers to do. I hog all the work. It's not right. I'm sorry." The builder bows his head. I rub it and move on.

A planter is jumping up and down, flailing his arm in the air. I cut past the people in front of him. I can smell the eagerness on him.

"What have you got for us?" I pass him the microphone.

"Oh, thank you so much. Man, where to begin? Like, I've got so many things to confess. Okay, first off, I'm crazy lazy. I'll slink off to the river all the time and just sleep. My friends will all tell you. I'm allergic to work sometimes. Maybe I could get baldy to cover my shifts. Oh, I'm joking, I'm joking. What else, what else? Oh, I'm obsessed with gossip. It's my favourite. I've tried to kick it, but I just can't. I'll talk shit about anybody to everybody. I need to stop. Man, it's a problem. Oh, and I struggle to be humb—" The man trails off as I swipe the microphone out of his hand.

"Alright, wow, you said a mouthful. Several mouthfuls. Let's give him a round of applause for being so honest." The audience claps as I massage my temples. How is an egomaniac that oblivious in our compound? He should've been weeded out on day one. Is he a spy for Smit? If he is, he's a terrible one. If he's one of my followers, he's also terrible. Dumbass.

I walk through the crowd, listening to a barrage of banal, minor, self-serving sins. People backpedal and sidestep with excuses and rationalizations. No one says anything real. No one really opens up. The haze fully descends over my eyes.

"I steal food from the cafeteria. Only sometimes, though. Like, once every six months. And only if I'm really hungry."

"I lie to my friends. Small lies, but still..."

"I used to sleep through some of your sermons. I mean, I'd be here, but I'd be asleep. I'd hide behind a pillar and close my eyes. I don't do it much no more. No, sir, definitely put that stuff behind me."

"I can't focus. Sometimes, I'll be in the field and I'll just drift away..."

"I don't really understand a lot of what we..."

"I could do more to help our..."

"I would take..."

"I wish..."

"I..."

A man is sitting down near the door. Everyone around him is standing up, waiting for their turn with the microphone. Why isn't he joining them? He's leaning back in his chair, looking at the ceiling. His hands are in his pockets. His eyes are half-closed. His head lolls to the side. He's...he's bored.

The haze snaps. I'm awake. My body is shaking. My hands are curled into fists. I stare at the man. Everything else is pushed to the margins. I have tunnel vision; I only see him. I only see this lazy, insubordinate little shit sitting on his ass. I only see another traitor.

I march past my followers, holding the microphone close to my chest. I brush eager hands aside and barrel towards the door. I stand over the man and thump my hand on the microphone. He jerks his head and notices me. He slowly sits up straight.

"Why don't you confess for us?" I nearly smash the microphone into his teeth.

The man gazes at the microphone. He blows his lips into it. He scratches the back of his neck. He looks at me and shrugs. This fucker shrugs at me during a sermon. My left eye twitches. He must be working for Smit. He's here to make me look bad. Or, worse, he's just a non-believer, someone here for the cheap thrills. It's a joke to him. He's fucking with us.

"I think you've got something to say." I drop the microphone before I finish talking.

I grab the man by the bicep and haul him to his feet. Barely any muscle on him. So he's lazy, too. I drag him down the aisle, cutting through the crowd. People clap and jeer. The man barely resists. He sighs, as if the whole thing is an inconvenience. Little bastard.

I push him onstage and jump up. The crowd stomp their feet, waiting for the Honour.   I send my open palm careening across the man's face before he can get to his knees. He falls back, clutching his cheek. Someone in the crowd gasps, followed by loud applause. I unleash a series of slaps, throwing his head back and forth. The crowd continues to stomp, but lighter, gentler. What, it's too much for them? Now they lose their nerve? Forget them. It's about me and him.

The man scoots away from me, shaking his head. He holds up his hands and asks for a break. I raise my arm as I tower over him.

"Confess." I don't need a microphone to be heard; the whole room is silent.

"I...I, uh, I guess I could, uh, work harder sometimes." The man's face spasms as he stammers out his confession.

It's not real. I can see it in his eyes. He doesn't mean a word he said. He's just giving me what he thinks I want. He thinks he knows me. He's mocking me. Another insult.

My slaps rain down on him. He scurries to center stage, but he can't escape me. Some people chant with each slap, but a lot of people are quiet, murmuring. My fingers crack on his nose, bloodying it. The plasma streaks down his face and onto his clothes.

"Confess." I catch my breath. My hands are stinging.

"Sir, can I...can I please go? I'm not...I'm not feeling it today. Maybe get someone else. This...this is weird. Get someone else, please." The man inches to the edge of the stage.

He wants a break? He doesn't want to confess? He's telling me what to do? My fist collides with his jaw. The man sinks to the floor. Only a few people are cheering. I can hardly see them. Everything's clouded by this...fog. I want to pulverize this man. He's mocking all of us. He's refusing to participate, refusing to confess. He thinks the rules don't apply to him. He's desecrating our faith.

I leave the man in a heap and walk behind the curtain. I see the spot where Sandra and I...knew each other. I don't let it stop me. I see what I came for and I seize it. I pull the Weight through the curtain. More gasps. The man, touching his bloodied face, groans. He crawls to the edge, but I run and grab his legs. I drag him to center stage, flip him over, and connect with a quick slap. I move the Weight and plant it on his chest.

"Confess." I rest my hand on the Weight.

"Everything. I did everything. I, I cheated, and I lied, and I swore, and I, uh, slept around. I don't do enough work and I sleep in and I don't pay attention. I'm weak. I'm so, so weak. Please, I..." The man's face is a smear of blood, drool, and snot.

He's a trapped weasel. He's trying every trick he knows to escape. He's not looking deep enough. He's lying. I climb on top of the Weight. I feel it sink into the man. He wheezes. No one is cheering now.

"Confess." I jab my finger in his face.

"What...what do you...want?" The man's face is turning beet red.

I feel a valve loosen. A torrent rushes from my mind to my mouth. Everything pours out in a full-throated scream.

"I want you to confess. I want you to tell everyone your sins, your real sins. I want you to tell the truth. I want you to admit you're faithless. I want you to admit you have no idea what you're doing. I want you to tell everyone you've failed them. I want you to admit you're a fraud. I want you—" I stop.

The man can't breathe. I'm squeezing the life out of him. My entire body is tense. I'm choking on anger. I look at the crowd. They're frozen in silence. My head is pounding. I roll off the Weight and shove it off the man. He takes a deep breath and rolls to his side. He's whimpering. His face is a scarlet mess. I could've killed him...

"That's...that's why we...we need to confess...always. We need to...to be honest with each other. We need to...tell the truth. Someone look after him. End of sermon. I'm sorry..." I retreat to the backstage area.

I grab the curtain and sink my head into it. Where did I go? I wasn't teaching a lesson; I was hurting someone. I enjoyed it. My heart was racing. I could taste the excitement. I wanted to destroy something. Fuck, I'm losing my mind.

Something taps my shoulder. I spin around, fist curled. It's Ken.

"It's Smit. He's here."

CHAPTER THIRTY-TWO

I'm watching Smit preach.

He's standing at the front of the gate. His goons loom in the background, parked near the road, sitting on their black car. A ball of smoke surrounds them. People are gathered around Smit, listening to him. My people. He's here, in my compound, in front of my people, preaching his poison.

He's gotten fatter since I last saw him. I don't know how that's possible. His fleshly cheeks vibrate every time he moves his mouth. His gold robe can barely conceal the rolls of fat in his stomach. His hands are thick cuts of meat with sausages attached. He's a balloon about to burst.

I can't hear him, but I know he's preaching. His eyes dart over the crowd, pointing at certain members. He smiles and laughs. A few people join him. He points at the sky and shakes his head. He looks right past me and gestures at the sermon hall. He laughs again. He flicks his fingers in the air. He makes a slashing motion with his arm. He holds his hand over his chest and nods. Again, some people join him.

I'm standing at the centre square. Ken is with me. I'm staring at Smit, lost. My brain can't process what's happening. It's like a bizarre dream, but it's real. I'm not hallucinating. Smit is in my compound. He strolled past the gate and started talking to my followers. He's brazen enough to preach his filth at my home.

He's desecrating the air with every word that crawls out of his mouth. His presence here is an affront to taste and dignity. He's infecting my followers' ears with garbage. He's lowering our collective IQ. He's a virus begging for a vaccine. Does he have no decency, no shame? I would never preach at his compound. I would never cross that line. I'd let him live in peace.

This is the exact kind of man Smit is. It's all a game to him; he's just taking the next logical step. He wants to win and this is the natural move: Preach on the enemy's home turf. It's a show of strength. He's playing for keeps.

My feet are rooted to the ground. I can't move. I can taste blood in my mouth; I must be chomping on my inner cheek. Shock, anger, whatever it is, it's paralyzing me. I can only watch this fucker pretend to be a leader in my compound.

I need to stop him. I need to cut through the crowd and shut him down. I wouldn't say a anything. I wouldn't debate him or reason with him. I'd just walk up to him and strike him down before one more word can slip through his smug mouth. He's fall to the ground, covering his nice clothes in dirt. His followers would rush to stop me, but they'd be too late. I'd land on his chest and dig my finger into his eye. I'd slowly peel it out, slapping away his hands as he screamed. Once he was a Cyclops, I'd ask Ken for a knife. He'd oblige. And as I spilled Smit's lunch on our compound grounds, I'd tell everyone to watch. I'd tell them to listen. I'd tell them to learn. As the light faded from Smit's eye, I'd make everybody—

Ken taps my shoulder. I shake my head and look at him.

"We need to stop this. Now." He wipes the sweat from his forehead as he points at Smit.

I nod at Ken. My right hand feels sore. I look down. It's clenched into a fist, its fingernails embedded in its palm. I unfurl it, wincing. I'm holding a fragment of the sermon hall curtain. I don't remember tearing it off. I don't remember how I got to the center square...

I run my hand over my face and compose myself. I let the fragment fall to the ground. I inhale and start walking. I reach the edge of the crowd. I can see Smit through the mass of people. I poke a member in the back. He doesn't notice me. I poke him again. Nothing. I shove him. He spins around, a retort on his lips. I raise my chin. He looks to the ground and bows his head, shrinking away from the crowd. I've still got something.

I make my way through the gathering, shoving members to the side. Most disperse when they see me. Some stick around. I'll give them a show. I can hear Smit preaching his nonsense.

"My friends, and I hope I can call you my friends, you've been fed a steady diet of lies. You've been sold a false bill of goods, as they say. I know a scam when I see one and trust me, you are being scammed. You've been told the only way to paradise is through denial and misery. That's pure madness. You torture yourselves half to death for nothing. Life is hard enough already; why make it worse? Who even knows if there's a paradise at the end of this crazy journey? In your final moments, you don't want to be filled with regrets; you want to be satisfied. You want to know you lived to the fullest. That's what Zaan is all about. We enjoy ourselves as much as we can for as long as we can. Sounds pretty good, right?" Some members nod as I burst into the front.

Smit grins. He gives me a mock bow. Everything I hate distilled into one man. I glare at the crowd. They back off. I march to Smit. He winks at me.

"Leave. Now." I point to the gate.

"I'm here on a humanitarian mission. I'm trying to save these lost souls. You don't want to stop my good work, do you?" He's a parody of a leader. I want to vomit on him.

"Get off our property." Every impulse screams at me to pulverize him. I need to be in control with everyone watching.

"Friends, there is a better way forward. You don't have to stumble in the dark. Zaan is the light. Follow it and you'll never be lost." Smit waves at my followers.

"Stop lying and leave. Now." Don't let him bait you. Stay calm.

"Lying? That's what you call it? Friends, do I look like a liar to you?" Smit brushes past me and addresses the crowd. People look down at their feet.

"My people can smell bullshit. And you reek." I use my sermon voice, making sure everyone hears.

"You wound me, sir, you wound me." Smit holds his hands over his stomach as if he's been stabbed.

"I'll do worse than that if you don't leave now." This time, only Smit can hear me.

"Can't wait." Smit gives me another wink and moves closer to the crowd.

Ken is standing on the edges. He looks at me, waiting for the signal. I gesture at Smit's gaggle of lemmings up the road. Ken nods and moves to the gate, watching them.

"Friends, Solomon calls me a liar. Now, I like to exaggerate, I like to use colourful language, I like to get people excited, but I never lie. I'm sure you can see that. I'm not trying to deceive you or lead you astray. Nothing could be further from my mind. I'm simply presenting options." Smit holds his hands near his chest like they're scales.

"Options?" I snort.

"Yes, options, exactly right. You fine folks have been stuck in column 'A' for months, maybe years. You've had the same meals, the same chores, the same everything, day in and day out. Now, over here, you have column 'B.' That would be Zaan. It's something different. It's not just offering you a change of scenery. It gives you something fresh every day. It's a new adventure when you wake up. You die in the evening and you are reborn in the morning. Zaan is constant renewal. These are your options." Smit bounces his hands.

What a garbage sales pitch. He wouldn't get past the front door of any respectable house in America. Nothing but vagaries and empty promises. He's selling vapour. But people are nodding. They like his offer. They want to hear more. I step in front of him.

"Those aren't choices. You're comparing salvation to damnation. There's nothing better about your option. It's hollow, just like you." I look my followers in the eye, staring them down.

"Look at the way you're glaring at your people. You're threatening them. You're telling them how to think." Smit waves his finger in my face. I swat it away.

"I'd never do that." Damn, I sound too defensive.

"Is that so? Well, let's take a quick survey. You, there, Mr. Slackjaw, mind answering a question?" Smit saddles up to a particularly dim-looking member.

"Uh, sure." The man scratches his nose.

"You ever feel like your erstwhile leader is directing you down a certain path, regardless of your personal input or inclination?" Smit slings his arm around the man's shoulder.

"Uh, what?" The man frowns.

"You ever feel like someone's thinking for you? You ever feel like you're not really in control?" Smit squeezes the man's arm.

"I mean, sometimes, maybe. Like, I'll listen to suggestions, for sure. I like to hear other opinions. I mean, no, no, I, uh, I make my own choices. We all do. Yeah, um, yeah." The man darts his eyes between Smit's smug face and my withering glare.

"Seems like you can't make up your mind about who makes up your mind." Smit shakes his head and peels his arm away from the man.

"This man there is not free. He's following the carrot and avoiding the stick. He hasn't made a real choice in years. I'll bet he's not alone." Smit gazes over the crowd.

"Who here was taken against their will? Who's here under duress?" I look at everyone. No one raises their hands.

"Who came here voluntarily? Who made the choice to cross the threshold? Who here makes the decision to wake up every day and get to work?" Everyone raises their hands, some a little slower than others. I make a mental note of the late ones.

"We make free choices every second. We're not shackled by our urges. We're not slaves to our impulses. We make the conscious choice to be better. We choose to be more." I spread my arms. A smattering of applause.

"You've tricked these fine people. They thought they were going to find the road to salvation, to paradise. But you offered them one false choice after another. 'Work every day or be damned. Listen to me or be damned. Obey me or be damned. Never ask questions or be damned.' Blah, blah, blah. You browbeat people into choosing one option. You make everything else seem like poison so your snake oil looks like medicine. But it's not. It's killing these people." Smit's voice thunders throughout the compound. He's been practicing (and ripping me off).

"Just because my way is the right one doesn't mean people have to choose it. They can quit and drift back into despair. It takes real strength to choose the right path, strength you can't understand. It's easy to make your choices. It's simple. Your way is weak." I wipe the spittle from my lips. Composure. I have to look like a leader, not him.

"At least I'm giving real choices, not a lie. I'm offering you folks something you can touch and feel. I'm offering reality." Smit places his hand over his heart. His voices quakes. Sickening.

"Reality, damnation, all the same thing to you, right?" Fuck, that was way too catty. I sound like a teenager.

"Listen to that absolutism, people. This is a man who can only see in black and white. This is a man who looks at the world and sees only binaries. This is a man who judges things as wrong or his way. It must be disheartening, no?" Smit extends his hand to a woman in the crowd. She looks like she's about to nod when I step in.

"We see the world how it really is. We don't sugar coat it or try to find excuses. We're not trying to escape. We're looking for the only way forward, the right way." I meet the woman's eyes. She sinks back into the crowd.

"You keep saying that. 'The right way.' How do you know, without a doubt, that there is a right way at all times for all people? How did you become judge of all things? Were you assigned the position in an election? Did the heavens part as your role was revealed to you? Or did you just appoint yourself?" Smit is yelling in my face.

Where do I start to respond? That speech is a minefield. He's layered it with every accusation imaginable. I open my mouth, but Smit's already playing to the audience.

"My friends, standing here with all of you, as your oppressor looks on, it's clear to me what's really going on in this compound. You don't follow a religion; you follow the whims of one man." Smit points his finger at me like a spear.

I have to shut this down. I nod at Ken, but he's staring at Smit's lackeys. I curl my fists as my blood boils.

"Whatever Solomon wants is law. That's the only rule that applies here. He doesn't care what you think or how you feel, just as long as you choose him. He doesn't follow the creed because he doesn't believe in it. He thinks he's above all of you. He thinks he's your master." Smit is storming back and forth. It's a stream of verbal vomit.

"Look at him. He doesn't wear the clothes of a builder or a planter; he wears nice robes, just like me. But he's supposed to be one of you, right? He's not supposed to be a 'hedonistic degenerate' like myself. Hypocrisy, that's what he preaches. He lives apart from you in his nice home. He doesn't do any real work, not the work you folks do. He lords over everyone. He doesn't want to liberate you; he wants to keep you in the chains of his twisted faith. Your 'religion' is as corrupt as him." Smit's face is beet red. I'm grinding my teeth.

"You don't have to stay in bondage. Zaan will show you the path, the true path. Zaan will liberate you. Come with me and finally be free." Smit tilts his head to the sky and spreads his arms wide. He's met with small pockets of applause.

Smit smiles at me. My tongue is lead. He's miles ahead of me. I came here to send him away; he came here for a knockout. I have to speak. I have to say...something.

"You're nothing but...but a charlatan, spreading lies and, and... misinformation. My people know better. You need to leave, you...fraud." I jerk my hand to the gate. My mouth is mush.

Smit laughs right at my face. A full-throated belly laugh. He can barely contain himself. He keeps going and going. His laughter fills the air. He wipes his eyes and looks at me.

"You're the fraud. I'm promising freedom for these people. Freedom from you, a tyrant." Smit chuckles and shakes his head.

Enough. He needs to leave. I have to stop the laughter.

I lunge forward, grabbing Smit's collar. I wind my fist back to my cheek. I feel a stab in my gut. I release my grip. I crumple forward.

Smit's knee is in my stomach. I'm bent over it. I'm gasping for air.

Smit grabs my shoulders and pulls me up. He sends me down to the dirt with a punch to the face. I barely feel it when he kicks me in the back and slaps my head for good measure.

I'm huddled up on the ground, wheezing. My body stings. I can't move. My brain is trying to catch up.

Ken rushes to my side. I can't hear him. I'm looking up at Smit, blood and drool dripping out of my mouth. Smit adjusts his robe and smooths down his hair. Ken rises to his feet, fists raised, but Smit's goons are already here. They form a wall behind Smit. Ken hesitates. I have enough strength to shake my head.

Smit bends down and wipes the dust from his knees. He flicks dirt flecks off my face.

"That was fun. Let's do it again sometime." Smit pats my shoulder and stands up.

"Your leader is as weak as his faith. You don't have to follow him anymore. Come with us and start a better life. Enter Zaan. We'll be waiting for you." Smit bows and walks to the gate.

I hear his footsteps recede. I watch the feet of several members follow him, their voices filled with supplications. I hear them disappear down the road. I watch my followers drift back into the compound. I hear absolute silence fall.

I stay there on the ground, humiliated.

CHAPTER THIRTY-THREE

Jason Neary is afraid of heights.

His knees wobble as he climbs the ladder. He's scaled up and down it for months, but it hasn't gotten easier. He reaches the top and flops on his stomach. He gets to his feet and dusts himself off. Joseph is already here. They're standing on a roof.

Jason peeks over the edge. The flower bed below him looks like it could cushion his fall. The wheelbarrow next to the bed looks like it could cripple him. Jason shuffles away from the edge.

Joseph whistles. Jason turns to him, shielding his eyes from the sun. Joseph holds up a bundle of cloth. Jason nods and crouches on his knees. The cloth leads from Joseph's hand across the roof, crumpled and wrinkled. It ends in a heap at Jason's feet. He grabs it and unfurls it as he stands up. He twists it outwards and grips it by the corner. Jason and Joseph walk to the edge, bending down at the roof's corners. A thick nail rests on the shingles, nearly teetering over the side. A hammer sits beside it.

Jason hears a banging sound. Joseph's getting to work. Jason lays the cloth down and pins it to the roof with his elbow. He pushes most of the cloth over the edge, letting it dangle in the air. He keeps a tight grip on the edge. He grabs the hammer and the nail with his free hand. He positions the nail over cloth, finding the right angle. He keeps his fingers spread wide over the cloth as he brings the hammer down. With five strokes he's done.

Jason lets go of the cloth. It starts to slide away, but the nail holds it close. Jason looks at Joseph's end. His cloth section is clinging to the roof while the bottom part flutters in the wind. Joseph and Jason nod at each other. Joseph shouts to someone below him, pointing at the forest. Jason wraps his fingers around

the corner and brings his head over the edge. The cloth is
scrunched up near the top and loose threads dance on its sides,
but it looks good. He can read it, even upside down: "All
welcome."

Joseph said he saw something like this at a college once.
He'd been there to meet a girl or score some drugs or something
like that. Joseph said they had a banner hanging over their meal
hall. It was there all year. It was a reminder. Joseph said it'd be
perfect for their first building. The cherry on top. A little extra
thing for their office.

Jason pulls away from the edge and lies on his back. He
watches the clouds slowly drift in front of the sun. Fat white
tumours inching their way across the sky. Jason smiles. He turns
to his side and sits up, resting his legs over the edge. He looks
over the compound. Some new faces intermingle with the old
ones. Greg (Jason thinks that's his name) darts across the fields,
guiding farmers to their new plots. A group of builders stand
over an empty square. There's a buzz in the air.

It's been one year. One year since they stumbled across
this place. One year since Jason died and was reborn. One year
since he and Joseph decided to spread out. All this happened in
one year.

Everything blur together into one continuous weave. All
the long nights spent in the cavern meditating and thinking and
screaming. All the quiet evenings wasted swimming in the river,
looking deep into it. All the blistering hot afternoons spent
hunched over reams of paper as they tried to hammer out every
last detail of their creed. All the cold mornings dedicated to
learning how to command a crowd. All the minutes, and hours,
and days, and weeks, and months devoted to building shelter and
practicing their words and preparing for the first arrivals.

One day, Joseph told Jason he was leaving. Jason's heart
clenched, but Joseph assured him he'd return. Joseph said they
needed more recruits. He said they needed to spread their
message as far as they could. Joseph left Jason in charge. He

smiled as he hopped in the car and drove down the road. Two weeks later he was back with a truckload of eager followers.

That's how things went. Joseph would help around the compound, he'd preach with Jason, he'd write down more scripture, but before long, he'd get the itch. He'd tell Jason they needed more followers. He'd speed out of the driveway, always returning with more people. He'd always be back a little later than the last time. The first time Jason was on his own, he nearly had a panic attack. But he stumbled his way through until his friend came back. Every time he was left alone, the panic lessened.

Jason studies the faces milling through the compound. He tries to memorize them, tries to engrave them in his mind. He's met them all at least once. Everyone who comes through the gates talks to him. More and more lost souls come every week, but he makes time for all of them. He's been where they are. He's been them.

A mountain of a man walks beneath Jason's dangling feet. He's hauling a bag of seed. He flops it on the ground and wipes his brow. The man spots Jason and flashes him a thumbs-up. Jason returns the favour as the man picks up his bag.

"How are you?" Jason feels a hand clamp on his shoulder.

Jason stands up and gives Joseph a hearty grin. Joseph slings his arm over Jason's neck. He leads him to the middle of the roof. The best view of the compound. Everything's laid out like it should be. It all looks perfect.

"Ready for your first solo sermon?" Joseph pats Jason's chest.

"Made for it." Jason raises his chin.

Joseph chuckles and looks over the compound. Jason enjoys the warmth of the sun as he gazes over his home. They've made a good life.

CHAPTER THIRTY-FOUR

I'm jelly.

I'm slouched in my chair. My chin is tucked into my chest. My blinds are drawn, only letting in sliver of moonlight. I'm in a cocoon of darkness.   I'm holding a glass of water to my cheek. It still stings. It was beet-red when I looked at it in the mirror an hour ago. Smit put all his weight behind that punch.

I'm stuck in a loop. I see everything play out in my head over and over. I'm at the gate. My people are behind me. Smit's jowls glisten and shake as he speaks. I tell him to leave. He keeps talking. I lunge for him. I plummet to the ground. Everything goes sideways. Smit recedes down the road. My followers look down at me. They turn away. I'm alone in the dirt.

I'm at the gate. My people are behind me. Smit is there. I fall down. Smit disappears. People look away. I'm alone. Gate. Smit. Speech. Punch. Fall. Disgust. Alone. Over and over and over. My mental projector won't stop playing it.

The images I can't budge from my brain, no matter how I deep I sink into this chair, are my followers' faces. They looked like they'd just seen a dog with mange get a shotgun barrel kiss. They weren't shocked or outraged; they were quiet. They shook their heads. They pitied me.

I shoot a gasp of air at the ceiling. I'm fucked. I'm royally fucked. All those other times when I said I was fucked? I was an idiot. Those were just warm-up rounds to this prime fucking.

Smit exposed me. He humiliated me in my own compound in front of my followers. He talked circles around me. I could barely get a word in. My brain failed me. I stumbled while Smit charged ahead with a plan. I played catch-up the whole time. I was never in control, never leading the debate, and everyone could see it. I looked like an amateur. Smit left me naked and confused while everybody watched.

I could've had Ken escort him out before he ramped up his speech. I could have told my followers to get back to work. I could've stayed in the background and let Smit spin his wheels. He was looking for a fight; maybe he would've faltered if he didn't have one. But I didn't do any of that. I cut to the front of the crowd and started yelling. I had to prove I was the better man. I had to shut him down with everyone watching. I had to win. I gave Smit exactly what he wanted. I strolled into his trap with a smile on my face.

I got angry. The one thing I absolutely, positively needed to not do, I did. I let my temper overwhelm me. I got flustered. People didn't see a leader or a preacher; they saw a petulant child bawling his eyes out and stamping his feet. They saw something that disgusted them. And Smit smacked me to the ground. The cherry on top of this shit sundae. He didn't even attack me. I lunged at him. I snapped first. I lost my cool and got physical.

I didn't even fucking win. I had the element of surprise. I could've pummeled him before he could blink. I could've at least saved some face by coating the ground with his blood. But, no, I was too slow. I've gotten soft. Smit introduced his knee to my stomach and I crumbled. I couldn't beat an obese hedonist with a surprise attack. Fuck me.

I want to disappear into this chair. I want it to swallow me whole and dissolve me into its leather skin. I want it to leave no trace. But I can't. No matter how far I sink down, I can't leave. I'm still here. I'm still me.

How can I face anyone tomorrow? I've been emasculated, humiliated, and defeated. Smit completely bested me. He played his plan to perfection. After that display, who would follow me now? Who in that crowd would listen to a man who was so thoroughly dominated by that walking grease stain? Who will take me seriously after today? Certainly not the ones who left with Smit. Their minds are made up. Smit's victory was

all the proof they needed. They walked over my limp body
without a second glance.

The ones who stayed did so out of...what? A lingering
sense of faith? A notion of duty? Pity? They stayed because they
felt they had to, but they won't stick around for long. They'll
come to the same conclusion as the other deserters. They won't
be able to follow a man they can't respect, a man who can't
defend his own faith. They'll slink away.

But while they're here, they'll make everything worse.
People will ask them what happened at the gate. The ones with a
sense of propriety will hold out, but eventually they'll all spill
their guts. They'll regurgitate Smit's words, maybe make them
more palatable. They'll talk about my defeat. They'll whisper
how they have doubts now.

The rumours will spread. From one ear to another the
story will grow and distort. Smit will become a glowing Adonis
while I'll morph into a crushed worm. The story won't resemble
a sliver of reality, but it won't matter. People will believe it.
Even the people who ignore the story will have a gnawing sense
of suspicion in the back of their minds. Before long, I'll be
preaching a sermon to a room full of doubters.

Our leak will turn into a stream. Our followers will
trickle out the gate and follow the path to Smit's arms. We'll try
to stop them, try to convince them, but it won't matter. There'll
be nothing we can do, nothing I can do. They won't listen to the
man with the glass jaw.

In the end, it'll be Greg, Ken, and I standing in the
cavern. Some sacrifice. A great end to our story.

Fuck, fuck, fuck. It can't go this way. We're meant to be
an impenetrable shell. Nothing's supposed to break through. But
we're cracked. We've let in Smit, and the killer, and doubt, and
fear, and weakness, and everything else. We're exposed.

This is the deepest pit. This is the bottom of the barrel.
I'm down to the dirt.

This is the test Joseph told me about. I've stared down
countless tests over the years, but this one is different. This is the

test I've been waiting for. Joseph said it would come when we were vulnerable, when we were drained. This is a test that strikes when we don't want to fight.

I have to meet it. I can't let Smit, or the killer, or anyone else beat me. I have to rally the troops. I have to seize the reins. I have to climb back to the plateau. No, I have to go beyond the plateau. I have to scale the mountain to the peak. This test presses me to the dirt so I can rise even higher. This is my chance to succeed. This is a prime opportunity. I have to stand up.

I don't move. I recite the words over and over in my head, but I don't budge from my chair. My body is one with the leather. I'm wedged deep in my cocoon.

I understand the words running through my mind, but nothing happens. I know how important this test is, how crucial our work is, how vital it is for me to get up. But I can't. I know the words, but I can't connect to them. I hear them and I don't feel the fire. I'm behind a veil. I'm numb. I want to wallow in my misery. I know it's childish and useless, but I'm struggling to care. I can't help myself. I just want to sink.

My mind screams the words at me, hammering them into my skull. I sigh. The best I can do is lean over the desk. I touch the rock. I found it here when I got back from my...embarrassment. It was stationed dead-center on my desk. It's placed over a letter. I know who it's from. The rock hasn't budged. I roll my fingers over it. It's surprisingly smooth. I grip its base and start to lift it, but I stop. I know I should read this letter. I should tear it open and get it over with. I know I'm making things worse by waiting. I let the rock fall.

The door opens. I tense up. I see the bulky silhouette due to the lantern in his hand: Ken.

"Just finished the final sweep, sir. Greg and I checked all the usual spots. Nothing new." The words crawl out of his mouth. He's dead on his feet.

"I thought so. Thank you anyway." I nod.

"Do you need anything else, sir?" Ken catches a yawn before it spreads over his face.

I rub my finger on the rock. I chip at it with my fingernail and move it side to side. I look at the lantern. A flickering island surrounded by this sea of pitch black. Ken and I are consumed by it. We're stuck in the darkness and we can't see a way out.

We shouldn't be here. This is not our place. Ken wasn't made for this life. He wasn't built to skulk around the compound in the dead of night, looking for a serial killer. He wasn't built to fend off attacks from a rival compound. He wasn't built for all these complications. He was built to protect me and follow my orders. He was built to keep me safe, to keep us all safe. He's not cut out for this work in the shadows. He's a simple man who solves simple problems. He likes things black-and-white. He's been living in grey for months and it's killing him.

This work is killing all of us. Greg's unkempt hair and heavy-lidded eyes spiral further out of control every day. He can barely hold himself together for his daily status reports. He's running on fumes and when those fade away, I don't know what he'll do.

Ken's no better. He puts on a brave face, but it's covered in cracks. His shoulders droop and his head sags the moment he's out of the public eye. His body always tilts to the ground, as if he's going to take a permanent nap. He wants this whole thing to end. He wants a break.

And me? Well, I know how I'm doing.

We don't deserve this. We're meant to be standing tall, not hunched over in defeat. Someone else should be in our place. Someone else should be wasting away in the darkness. Smit should be in our hell.

I can see him chained to this chair. I see him smothered under the weight of his failures and inadequacies. I see him crumpled and deteriorated as the darkness engulfed him. I see him beaten beyond hope. I see him suffer.

I'm in the room with him. I see myself as I should be, as I was always meant to be. I'm wearing my robe. It glows in the darkness. I'm about to lead our final sermon. I'm about to finish my years of hard work. I'm looking at this shriveled prune of a man, my supposed rival, the person who thought he could rub me out. I gaze down at this shattered fool and I laugh.

Smit reaches his hand out to me. He's trembling. He moans as he peels himself off the chair. His eyes are watery. He wants me to lift him up. I'm his only lifeline in the dark. I'm the only one who can save him.

I walk out the door.

Smit needs to pay for what he's done. It's not about revenge; it's about self-preservation. He wants to tear down everything we've built. Whenever we've faced a threat to our compound, we've gotten rid of it. We've preserved our home. Smit is no different; he's just another threat. He needs to go. He needs to...

I look at Ken. My right hand, my sword, my will. The man who will do anything to protect this compound. The man who knows what's at stake here.

"Ken, would you kill Smit?" I stop moving the rock.

Ken is stone. The lantern casts a long shadow over his face. Brief flashes of yellow lines dart across his eyes. I lean forward.

"Ken, you've protected this compound for years. You've made our lives safer. Whenever there's been a problem, you've fixed it. We're in your debt. We're facing a crisis. Smit is bleeding us dry. Do you understand?" I peer through the darkness, trying to see his face.

More silence. Ken is a statue. I can't even hear him breathe. I swallow.

"He's a threat. And you're quite good at removing threats. I'm asking you a question: Would you remove a threat to our way of life, no matter what the cost?" I fold my hands and rest my chin on them.

The lantern continues to dance through the silence. I stare at the granite before me. Ken bends over the desk, stepping into the light. His face is blank.

"I'd do whatever's necessary for the compound." Every word out of his mouth is flat.

Ken is steel, but there's a crack. His eyes betray him. He doesn't want to match my gaze. He doesn't want to look at me. He's scared.

What am I doing? I'm looking at my most loyal follower, my one true believer. He'd do anything for me, even something that sickens him to the core. He'd listen to my every command because of his unshakable faith. He's pure.

I wanted to throw that all away. I wanted to taint him. I wanted to spoil his soul. I wanted him to do something he could never take back, something that would haunt him. I can't destroy my only real follower. I can't damn him. I stand up and grab the lantern. I walk around the desk and put the lantern in Ken's hands. I pat his shoulders and nod.

"You're a good man. Forget what I said. Get some sleep." I squeeze him.

Ken can't hide the relief in his eyes. He nods, bows, and shuts the door as he leaves. I'm alone. And I'm standing up. I look at the chair. I found enough energy to escape it and talk with Ken. I had a purpose, for a moment, and it got me on my feet.

I look at the letter. It begs to be opened. I drum my fingers on the desk. While I've got the energy, I might as well rip this bandage off. I grab a spare lantern from the other side of the room, light it, tear open the letter, and start reading.

Solomon,

I'm not great with words, so I'll cut to the chase: I'm leaving the compound. You probably saw that coming. Hell, you might be relieved. Sorry, I didn't mean to... Anyway, I'm sorry I couldn't say goodbye in person. I'm not great with farewells, not in person, anyway.

I wanted to tell you I'm sorry I made you uncomfortable. To me, it was just sex. There's nothing special about it. Two animals humping, that's all. But I could tell it was more than that for you. It was a violation. For that, I'm sorry.

But, I'm not leaving because of that. I'm leaving because I can't follow you. When you looked at me after that night, when you told me how dirty you felt, how wrong we were, I saw you. The real you. I saw a man driven by ego. I saw a lost boy.

I still believe in our faith. But I can't follow you anymore. How can I, when I know you don't believe what you're preaching? You built this place for you.

I hope you find your faith, your real faith. Maybe you'll make a good leader some day. Take care.
Sandra.

I sink back in the chair as I read the letter over and over. I clench the rock. With the light from the lantern, I see a marking on its bottom. I bring it close to my face. It's an engraving of my name. A grave marker.

I drop the rock to the floor as I lean into the chair and stare at the ceiling, letting the darkness wash over me.

CHAPTER THIRTY-FIVE

I'm standing in the middle of a field.

Barley brushes my chest. The wind pushes me back. The sun is glaring in my eyes. I tuck my chin and squint. Rows and rows of crops stretch out in every direction. The horizon is a perfect line. Everything is flat.

My jaw clicks. It spasms and contorts, trying to detach from my face. I grip it tight, forcing it to stay still. I feel my skin rumble and wriggle as I touch my cheeks. My body is rubber.

I spin around, looking for a landmark. There's nothing. The wind wallops me, but it doesn't make a noise. My head is a bowling ball trying to drag my body to the ground. I hold it up by the hair. I step forward. My foot squishes into the moist ground. I feel worms squirming beneath me, digging at my toes. I move my other foot. It pushes deeper into the dirt. I take another step. My foot tumbles through the ground. I take another step. My foot cuts through the soil like a flamethrower through ice. I take another ste—

I can't move. I pull on my back leg, but something holds it down. I strain to lift it, but nothing happens. My back leg is submerged in the ground. Everything from my knee down is covered in grime. The black ooze swirls around it, gurgling and frothing. I shoot my front foot forward, but it doesn't budge. I'm trapped. I reach for the barley, but they slip through my fingers. They disappear behind the horizon. Just me and the ooze.

I tear at my legs, trying to yank them free. I push away the ooze, but it never stops coming. I'm in the middle of a river. I get the gunk stuck to my fingers. My hands turn black. I scream, but I can't hear myself. The ooze stops flowing. The gurgling stops. It's firm as a floor. I'm wedged in tight. I see one remaining piece of barley. It's close enough for me to reach it. I stretch forward, nearly flopping face-first into the goo. I grab the barley and it doesn't break. It might be strong enough to pull me out. I grip it tight as I start to tug. I feel my feet moving. I can feel the ooze breaking apart. I keep pulling. The chunks of solidified muck fall away. I'm almost there. I'm—

Sinking. The barley is gone. I'm waist-deep in the ooze. It's rising to my chest. My legs are pinned down. I can't turn around. I'm locked in. I'm falling.

On the horizon, I see something. A collection of blobs. They dance and jiggle. They become more defined. They're outlines of people. Faded shadows. The sun rotates out of my face and shines on them. I see who they are. They're all here. Blume, Ken, Greg, Joseph, Smit, Sandra. They're all standing on the horizon, out of reach. They're smiling. I can hear their laughter. They're moving in a circle, hands interlocked.

I yell. I splash my arms in the ooze. I cup my hands around my mouth and bellow. I thrash and wave and plead and moan. They can't hear me. No one sees me. No one knows I'm here. The ooze rises to my nipples. Splashes of the black tar hit my face as it laps against my body. I'm nearly gone. But I can still see everything on the horizon.

Blume steps away from the circle and gives a quick salute to Smit. Smit returns the favour. Blume jumps backwards and disappears behind the horizon.

I can't feel my legs. I don't even know if they're still attached. I'm just a torso now.

Ken pulls Greg out of the circle and holds him in a tight embrace. Sandra, Smit, and Joseph applaud. Greg points down and tugs on Ken's shirt. Ken shakes his head and looks around. I holler at the top of my lungs. Ken shrugs. He and Greg vanish past the horizon.

The ooze inches past my shoulders. Every part of me is cold.

The trio is spinning fast now. They're a blur. Joseph darts outside of it and lights up a cigarette. He wipes his brow and peeks beyond the horizon. He gazes forward, shielding the sun from his eyes. He sees me. I know he does. I look into his eyes. He chuckles and gives me a thumbs-up. I scream. Joseph nods and leaps forward, plunging into the ooze. I see his raised thumb as it sinks beneath the waves. He doesn't re-emerge.

The ooze is spilling into my mouth. I'm drowning. But I still have a front row seat.

Smit and Sandra stop moving. He grabs her waist and she drapes her arms around his neck. They sway back and forth. There's music somewhere.

The horizon disappears behind four walls. Pillars shoot up next to me. A ceiling blots out the sun. I'm in the sermon hall. Sandra and Smit are on the stage. They're dancing. I'm on the floor. The ooze is still with me, still inching up my face, but I can move. My feet touch the floor. I fight against the tide as I surge up the aisle.

Sandra and Smit twirl and spin. There's applause. I fight the layer of ooze as I march past the empty seats. My hands break through the surface. The muck is clogging my nose. I keep going. Smit dips Sandra as they finish their dance. The music stops. More applause. Sandra and Smit look at each other. They both laugh. They lean in close.

I'm screaming, filling my mouth with ooze. I'm almost at the stage. Just a few more steps. The goo is clouding my eyes. Smit looks at me and grins. He puts his lips on Sandra's mouth. They're frozen.

I reach the stage. I climb up and crawl on my knees. Something's pulling me down. My fingers tremble as I reach for Sandra. I touch her hand. She turns her head and—

Darkness. I'm completely submerged in the muck. I'm smothered by it. I can't breathe. It's wrapping around my throat. I can't...breathe. I...can't...

I open my eyes. I'm bent over my desk. Something is wrapped around my throat. I reach my fingers to my neck. I feel a cord.

I jerk forward, but something slams me back to the desk. I tear at the cord, but a hand bats my fingers away. I shoot my legs out and plant them on the floor. They give way as someone kicks my feet loose. I feel hot breath in my ear.

"It's time." Oh, God, it's him.

I surge forward, gripping on the desk's edges for support, but he slams his fist on my hands. I scream, but only a hiss crawls out of my mouth. I can't get any air. I dig my fingernails into my neck. Blood pours down as I wriggle my fingers between my throat and the cord. I pull forward, creating an inch of space. I suck in a deep breath and cough it back out. I go for another gulp when the cord constricts even tighter, trapping my fingers.

I flail my arms behind me, hoping to land a hit, but I only tap his stomach. He pushes me harder into the desk, rubbing my face in the wood. I snap my head back and feel it connect with his nose. The pressure lets off for a second. I breathe as fast as I can before he squeezes tighter. I thrash and roll on the desk. I grab for pencils, sheets, anything I can get my hands on. They tumble over the edge. I heave forward. The cord stays fixed to my throat as we tumble to the floor.

I'm facing the ceiling. He's sitting on my stomach. He's pulling the cord ends in two different directions. I can only see his mouth. I can only see his smile.

My legs go limp. My fingers are gnarled. My hands pat the ground, looking for a lifeline. I'm gurgling. Everything is going black. This can't be it. No, please, don't do it. I don't want to die. Please, don't kill me. I had so much more...

My hand falls on something hard. I grab it and swing it up. It smashes into his jaw. The cord loosens. Blood splatters on my cheeks. I gasp. He touches his face and looks at me. He reaches for the cord. I smash into him again. He reels back. I sit up. I'm nearly at eye level with him. He yells, a high-pitched shriek, and grabs the cord. I bash him in the mouth. He teeters and crashes to the floor. He blinks. I strike face again and again and again. I'm screaming. His eyes slam shut. He's breathing, but he doesn't move.

My body is shaking. I stumble to my feet before collapsing back to my knees. I'm face to face with his unconscious body. I kick at it and scramble to the wall. I rub my hand around my neck. I can still feel the cord. I focus on breathing.

My body is crashing. The adrenaline is dying off. I slap my cheek. I need to be here. I'm still clutching my weapon in a death-grip. I unfurl my fingers. I'm looking at my name. It's the rock.

I let out a chuckle. It sounds like a punctured tire. No one hears it. Just a private thing between me and the killer.

CHAPTER THIRTY-SIX

I'm nursing my neck.

My throat is on fire. Every inhalation feels like gargling gravel. The skin is burned. I've been drinking nothing but water for hours.

Three lanterns surround me. They're perched on wooden stakes planted in the ground. They slant to the side, dangling the lanterns over the flowing river. They're the only illumination in the darkness. Them, and the moonlight.

The forest is dead still. We didn't hear a thing as we walked through it. Everything was frozen, as if we'd wandered onto a deserted movie set. The only sound comes from the gurgling river. Ken is sitting on a rock, chin resting on clenched fists. Every one of his muscles is tensed. I can see it from here, even with the flickering lights. He stares down at our guest.

There's not another living soul around. It's just the three of us: Me, Ken, and the killer. What a trio.

Ken didn't believe me when I dragged him out of bed. He nearly walloped my chin when I poked his side to wake him up. I managed to duck out of the way before he could clip me. I let Ken figure out who I was before I leaned back in.

Ken opened his mouth, but I covered it with my hand. Greg rolled onto his back on his side of the bed. He held my finger to my lips and nodded at the door. Ken went to wake Greg, but I grabbed his wrist. I needed to keep this as quiet as possible for now.

We grabbed a lantern, moved outside, and silently shut the door. I waited for a moment to see if Greg was stirring. Once I was sure he wasn't, I guided Ken to the middle of the compound. He noticed the red mark on my neck before I could say anything. He hit me with a barrage of questions. I tried to slow him down, but he kept going and going. I knew we only had a few hours before the compound was crawling with followers. Our window was about to slam shut. I slapped him, and he stopped talking.

I massaged my throat and collected my thoughts. I told Ken everything. I told how I'd nearly died. I told him who was in my office. But all that came out of my mouth was a thin rasp. I managed to squeeze out one word: "Killer." Ken's eyes widened. He swiveled his head, bringing his fists to his chest. I pointed at my office. Ken frowned.

I grabbed Ken's wrist and walked him to the office. I barged through the door and pointed at the unconscious lump loosely tied to my desk. I gestured at my neck, the bloodied cord, and the man. I wrapped my hands around my neck and "throttled" myself, then I pointed at the body.

The colour drained from Ken's face. He nodded and picked up the killer. I led him to the river, keeping an eye open for any late-night wanderers. Before word of this got out, we needed to act. We needed to get answers. And we needed somewhere...private to ask our questions as loudly and firmly as possible.

It's still dark now, but I can feel the sun inching its way to the horizon. We've got two hours, tops, before the early-risers tumble out of bed. And who knows how long it'll be for Greg to figure out where we are. Or for a random member to stumble across us during a morning walk. We have to move.

"Give it another go." I flick my hands at Ken.

Ken bends down and cups his hands in the river. He splashes the water in the killer's face. His messy hair moves to the side, and a layer of dirt on his cheeks morphs into mud, but he doesn't wake up. Ken spits and clenches his jaw.

I shake my head. I look up the river. I can't see the cavern through the gloom. Not even an outline of it. But I can feel it looming over us. Watching. Waiting. Judging.

I clear my throat and rub my neck. It's tender, but I can speak in short bursts. That's something. I'm going to need to talk when he finally wakes up. I dip my toes in the river. Relaxing. I stand up, sinking my shins in the water. It's familiar and calming. It's my center.

I close my eyes and let my body sway with the current. I try to let go of the panic that's gripped me for the last few hours. I slacken my shoulders. I can't be a terrified rabbit. I need to be on point. He needs to answer for what he's done and I'll pull a confession out of him. This is no different than any other confession. He's a sinner and I'm going to expose him. I've already beaten him. He took his shot and he lost. He's been humbled, defeated. He'll be open to a confession.

But what do I say? How to go forward with this? What kind of questions do I ask? Where do—?

No. I have to leave those worries in the river. If he senses any hesitation, he'll clam up. A person like this only responds to strength. I'm the hammer and he's the nail. However long it takes, he's going to bend.

Water splashes my legs. I open my eyes. Ken is standing in the river with me. Violent ripples surge away from him.

"He's up." Ken nods.

I clap Ken's shoulder as I climb onto the riverbank. I straighten my robe and grab a lantern from a stake. I make my way to the rock. There he is, bound and gagged next to the stone. His arms are pinned behind his back. His ankles are tied together. We stuffed a rag in his mouth. He thrashes and squirms, bumping his head against the rock. Every part of him is shaking.

His eyes are focused on the river. He's staring at the opposite bank. Even as he jostles and struggles, his eyes never move from the bank. His face is turning red as he strains against his bonds. I move in front of him. He looks up at me. His eyes narrow. He stops moving. He's still.

He's a mangy dog. His arms and legs are wiry and covered in dark hair. His clothes are tattered and filthy. Brown smears cover his chest and pants. He's wearing a tank top with a faded logo of a surfer. His pants are shredded pajama bottoms held up with a loop of rope around his waists. Holes and tears dot his clothes, exposing leathered flesh. There's a tattoo of several birds flocked together on his right knee. His fingernails are pitch-black.

An unkempt beard covers his face, obscuring his chin, mouth, and cheeks as it connects with his disheveled head of hair. Cuts and scars adorn his exposed skin. One runs from beneath his left eye to his nose before it vanishes in the beard. His lips are cracked. This is the source of our troubles: A fucking vagrant.

His eyes are bright blue. They never blink. He stares at me. He doesn't look away for a moment. His eyes follow me as I study him. They're empty and cold. He's looking at me like I'm an insect or a stray animal that just pissed in his yard. He's disgusted.

I match his gaze, refusing to blink. He's unnerving. He's not like anyone I've met. But, there's something familiar about him. Something I've seen before. It's like I've lived this moment already. Not the time to contemplate. You're letting him psych you out. Get to work. I take the rag out of his mouth and toss it away. Drool pools from his lips, but he doesn't say a word.

"Quite a number you did on me." I pull down my collar so he can see the red line.

He doesn't look at the mark. He doesn't laugh or smile or nod. He doesn't acknowledge it. He continues to stare at my eyes.

"Close shave for me. Lucky thing you're so shit." I smirk.

He continues to stare.

"Who are you?" I shove my finger into his chest.

He continues to share.

"Who are you?" I bump my knuckles on his ribcage.

He continues to stare.

"Where are you from?" I press down on his knee.

He continues to stare.

"I want some answers. Where are you from?" I slap him.

He moves his head back in place and he continues to stare.

"Look, you're going to talk. I'm going to get some answers. So I'll ask again: Where are you from?" I flick his ear.

He continues to stare.

"Why did you do this?" I bop his nose.

He continues to stare.

"No one knows you're here. We can do whatever we want to you. You might as well talk. Why did you do this?" I lean in close.

He continues to stare.

"Why did you try to kill me?" My forehead bumps into his.

He continues to stare.

"Last chance. Why did you try to kill me?" I grab his collar and shake him.

He continues to stare.

"Fine. Let's try something else." I shove his head down as I stand up.

I nod at Ken. He lifts the killer to his feet and drags him into the river. I stay on the bank.

Ken backhands the killer's mouth, sending blood and saliva flying. He drives his knee into the killer's gut, who doubles-over. Ken punches his jaw. He lets the killer falls into the water. He lands near the bank, directly below me. Ken kneels on top of the killer and rains his fists down.

Ken is silent. The only sound is flesh pounding flesh. He'll pummel the killer into paste if I let him. Maybe I should. But we need answers. We need something to take back to the people.

The killer grunts and winces with each blow, but he doesn't talk. He doesn't plead for mercy or beg off. He takes the beating. I crane my neck to look at him. There's something about him. He reminds me of...I don't know what.

Ken hauls the killer back to his feet. The killer spits out a stream of blood. Ken towers over him.

"You could drown here and no one will know." Ken's words sound like ice.

The killer tilts his head. He looks past Ken, to the other riverbank. He nods.

"Fine. I'll speak to the liar." The killer jerks his head at me.

Little fucker. When this is over, I'll—

No, no, you're letting him bait you. You're in control here, not him. I crack my jaw and nod at Ken. He lets the killer go, who collapses into the water. I enter the river as Ken steps to the side. The killer struggles to his feet as I stand in front of him.

"Speak." I fold my arms.

The killer stares at me. His pupils are dancing as they look me up and down. He leans to the side to see my profile. His body is vibrating. A smile breaks out over his face.

"How's Sandra?" His voice is lit gasoline.

I blink. He didn't say that. I imagined it. I've still got her on my mind. There's no way he said her name.

"What?" I keep my voice steady.

"Sandra. Your little backstage fuck. How is she?" The killer bites his thumb, grinning.

How? How does he...? Has he been watching me? No, no, stop, you're letting him into your head. He's just fucking with you. He doesn't know anything. Stay cool, stay cool, stay cool.

"What are you talking about?" My voice cracks. Dammit.

"How's Jessica? She was in the cafeteria, right? Melanie? She was a feisty one. Susan? She would go anywhere, wouldn't she? Lauren? Quite the catch." The killer ticks off numbers with his fingers.

How does he know these women? They haven't been here for years. No one knows them. I barely knew them... No, wait, I never knew them. He's talking gibberish. I don't know these women.

"What are you going on about?" I keep an eye on Ken. I don't want him to hear the wrong thing from this lunatic.

"All your friends. They were very close to you, weren't they? Very intimate. Very hush-hush. Don't want it to get out. Oh, no, no, no. Just between us." The killer makes a shushing sound.

I slap him. He bends over and touches his cheek. He straightens up and looks at me. His smile is gone.

"Serious business. I understand. Very serious. You're a leader. But do you tell people what you do when you're alone? Do you tell them what you do with your robe? Do you tell them what you do in the garden? Do you tell them you don't know what you're doing? Do you tell them you're a fraud?" He opens his mouth to continue, but I punch his nose.

I look at Ken. He has no idea what's going on. I'm losing control here. I grab the killer by the collar and pull him in close.

"Who the fuck are you?" I spray spittle over his face.

The smile returns. He flashes rows of crooked, yellow teeth. I grimace when his rotten breath reaches my nostrils. He leans into my ear.

"I'm just someone who found his way."

CHAPTER THIRTY-SEVEN

There was a man.

He worked in a post office. He lived in the same city he grew up in. Most of his friends had moved away. He planned to move to Hawaii once he had enough money.   But his mother got sick. She never got better. She spent all day in bed. The man had to support her. He had to take care of her. So, he put his life on hold.

He drove around the city delivering parcels. He ate his lunches in the backroom, watching the flood of letters trickle in and trickle out. He listened to customer complaints and wrote them down. He unclogged the toilets when they backed up. He went to the bar after work. He got home every day at 6. He made his mother a salad. He crushed a handful of pills and tossed them in the greens. He climbed the stairs, feeling his shoulders and knees ache. He knocked on the door. He heard the reply. He turned the knob.

His mother would always be staring out the window. She'd smile when the man walked into the room. He'd put his hand over her forehead as she held the thermometer in her mouth. She'd straighten up in the bed as he snapped open her table. He'd lay the salad in front of her as she said grace. They'd eat dinner together watching TV. She'd fall asleep to the buzzing glow. The man would slink out of the room and pour himself a drink in the kitchen. He'd stand out on the porch and watch the cars drive by. He'd crawl to bed. He'd wake up and start over. Every day.

He'd go to work, drive around the city, grab a drink, make a salad, watch TV, stare at cars, and go to sleep. It was a single blur. It was predictable, ordered, safe. It was a simple life. The man thought it was alright, all things considered.

Then his mother died. Her eyes were vacant, hollow. The man knew. He sat next to her and watched the ball game before calling the hospital. He felt cold.

Her family came for the funeral. They didn't know him well, but they apologized and shook his hand and patted his shoulder. Brothers, and sisters, and husbands, and wives gave their condolences.

Friends from high school came back to say goodbye to her. They'd always liked his mother. The man heard them talk about their new jobs, their new families, their new lives. They asked the man what he was doing. He'd start to talk, but he'd see their eyes glaze over. He'd see them look at their watches. He'd fall silent as they said hello to someone else. The man sat at a table and watched the people he used to know talk to each other. He sat there and entertained the onslaught of well-wishers.

The man spoke at the funeral. He thanked everyone for coming. He watched as the casket was lowered into the ground. He tossed down a clump of dirt. He mourned her. She was buried in a cemetery near the post office. He walked past it every day. After work, before he got a drink, he'd stop at her grave. He'd say something and shuffle along.

All he could picture were her eyes. That was the only memory of her he had left: Those empty eyes. It was senseless. The man couldn't shake the eyes from his mind.

He sold her house and moved into an apartment in the city. He was sandwiched above an arguing couple and below a dance instructor. A neon sign from the strip club across the street bathed his room in cold light. He filled the room with furniture and appliances and toys, but it always felt empty. He hated it. But he couldn't live in that house.

He stayed at the post office. He couldn't say why, but he stayed there nonetheless. He had every reason to leave. There was nothing holding him back, nothing tethering him to this city. He had more than enough money to move to Hawaii. But he didn't do it.

He thought about leaving. He looked up homes and jobs in Hawaii. He even booked a plane ticket. But he couldn't board the plane. He couldn't take that step forward. He was afraid. So he stayed at the job he hated in the city he despised.

Years later, he was delivering a package to house outside the city. The recipient wasn't there. The man had some time to kill, so he kept driving. He drove past schoolhouses and community centers and fast-food chains. He drove past the county line. He checked his watch. He needed to get back to work. He needed to turn around. He pressed down on the gas pedal.

He couldn't explain what he was doing. He didn't know what had snapped in his brain. He just knew he couldn't go back. He couldn't face that city again. He couldn't check in for another day of work. He couldn't sleep in the apartment for one more night. He had to escape.

He drove for hours, days. He didn't stop to eat or sleep. He kept his hands glued to the steering wheel. He drove until the truck ran out of gas in the middle of a back road. He grabbed a bag and dumped its letters out. He slung it over his shoulder and started walking. He walked through highways, villages, towns, cities. He did odd jobs for money and food. He slept wherever he could be warm and dry. He didn't follow a map. He didn't have a destination. He just walked. He knew he had to find...something. He knew he'd find it out here.

One day, he walked into a farming town. It was noon. Most stores were closed for lunch. The man sat down at the town square benches to rest. He closed his eyes. He heard a voice. A preacher was speaking under the gazebo. He was yelling at people crossing the street. He was laughing and cracking jokes. He told everyone to listen. He said he had something important to share. The man walked to the gazebo. The preacher smiled at him. He asked for the man's name. The man told him. The preacher told the man his name: Joseph.

Joseph told the man there was more out there. Joseph said they were destined for something great. Joseph said he was on a journey and he was looking for company. Joseph asked the man if he'd like to join him for a drive. The man shrugged and said yes.

They hit the road in Joseph's car. Joseph asked the man about his life. The man told him. Joseph nodded and listened. The man could see a smile tugging on his lips.

Joseph said the man was right to run from the city. He said everyone needs to look for their purpose. He said most people give up and settle down somewhere comfortable. Joseph squeezed the man's wrist and grinned. He said the man was an exception. He said the man was walking down the right path.

They drove for days. They talked about everything. The man nodded as Joseph spoke about a place, a special place where people find real meaning. The man thought Joseph made a lot of sense. The man thought he'd finally found the something he'd been looking for.

Joseph took the man to a desert. They parked under a rock. It towered over them, its plateau shielding them from the sun. They camped out there, spending days gathering food and wandering through the fields. Joseph said this was how life is supposed to be. Joseph said life can be boiled down to work and sacrifice. Joseph said the world only makes sense when you struggle; it's only reasonable when you force it to be. The man had to agree.

Joseph took the man to the top of the plateau. He showed the man everything. The man saw pillars shooting to the sky. He saw fields of fresh crops. He saw people sacrificing their time, their efforts, their sins, all on the altar of this compound. He saw a place dedicated to meaning, real meaning. He saw people working towards a common goal. He saw a world that made sense. Joseph showed the man paradise.

The man followed Joseph his home. They parked near the woods and they walked through the compound. Joseph explained every building, every feature, every mound of dirt. He pointed at workers in the fields and builders on top of a roof. The man waved at everyone he met. They smiled back at him.

Joseph and the man reached the center square. Another preacher was standing on top of a box. He was wearing a white robe. He was flanked by a giant covered in muscles who never stopped scanning the compound. A man with a clipboard was off to the side, making notes. A group stood in front of the preacher. They were dead quiet.

The preacher's voice echoed through the compound. He threw his hand to the sky and slammed it down on his open palm. He pointed at individuals and grabbed their foreheads, massaging their temples before throwing them back into the crowd. His head was on a swivel, bobbing and weaving. His entire body bristled with energy. His robe rippled and flowed with his every movement. It was a part of him.

The man walked into the crowd while Joseph stayed behind. The man bumped his way to the front. He stared at the preacher. He listened to the preacher's words. The last puzzle piece slid into place.

The man saw the entire picture. He heard the preacher's promises and his guarantees. He heard him lay out a plan for salvation. He heard him talk about sacrifice, real sacrifice, and what it could do for the soul. He heard the preacher say everything the man was feeling. It was like the preacher had reached into the man's head and flicked on the light bulb.

The man could only see the preacher. The world melted away. The man had found a leader, a true leader. He'd found someone he could follow. When the man heard the preacher talk, he knew he meant every word. He could feel the sincerity. The preacher believed in a better world. He believed in his people. He believed in the man.

The preacher bowed and hopped off the box to roaring applause. He wandered into the crowd, shaking hands and thanking everyone. His bodyguard stayed on the fringes. The man pushed past five people and seized the preacher's hand. The preacher blinked. The bodyguard stepped forward, but the preacher waved him off. The man shook the preacher's hand up and down, nearly tearing his arm off. The preacher smiled and patted the man's shoulder.

Joseph introduced the man to the preacher. He told the preacher why the man was here. The preacher's smile grew. He congratulated the man and squeezed him in a tight hug. He told the man he'd made the right choice. He told the man he was among friends. The preacher told the man his name was Solomon.

The man watched Solomon wade through the crowd touching hands and patting heads. He nodded at Joseph, who grinned and receded into the compound. The clipboard guy ushered the man into an office. The man answered hours of questions and filed reams of paperwork. He was escorted to his new home. He was told he was now a planter. He stepped into his new life.

The man sat in his cot and made a vow. He promised not to waste this opportunity. He wouldn't squander his time anymore. He would be the model follower. He would be just like Solomon.

Every day, the man woke up with the sun. He rushed to the cafeteria and wolfed down his meal. He scurried to the field and started working. He kept his head down. He didn't speak to anyone. He toiled away until the whistle blew. That was his favourite sound. He stormed past everyone and burst into the sermon hall.

The man always grabbed a front row seat. Sometimes he was asked to sit in the back, but he didn't mind. Solomon had a reason. The man jostled in his seat, waiting. When Solomon walked onstage, the man would be the first one on his feet. He'd clap, chant, and scream the loudest. He'd hang onto every word. He'd beg for the Honour. He was there.

After the sermon, the man devoured his lunch before rushing back to the field. He stayed there until the sun was a thin whisper on the horizon. Once he finished dinner, he went to his cot, meditated, and went to sleep. He'd wake up and start over again. Every day.

The man suppressed himself. He didn't indulge or make excuses. He sacrificed his time. He didn't let his past life creep into his mind. He didn't think about his old job or the city or his friends. He didn't think about the shackles he'd throw off. He devoted himself to the compound. He gave everything to the compound. The man never complained, he never questioned, he never stopped. He'd purged every pleasure he knew. But it was a good life. He finally had a purpose. He believed.

One night, he was walking to his cot from the field after staying there for longer than usual. He saw Solomon's office door open. For reasons he couldn't explain, he stayed in the shadow of a building. He watched.

He saw a woman emerge from the office. Her hair was a mess. Her clothes were disheveled. She looked around the compound before darting into the night. The man blinked. Solomon stepped through the door. He wasn't wearing a shirt. He scratched his crotch. He went back into the office.

The man shook his head. He was seeing things. There had to be an explanation. He was jumping to conclusions. He should go to his cot and forget what he saw. But he stayed in the shadow. Solomon came outside with a lantern. He was wearing his robe. He disappeared into the forest. The man followed him, his mind screaming.

The man found Solomon kneeling in the river. He was weeping. The man crouched behind a bush and listened. He heard Solomon berating himself. He heard Solomon confess to what he'd done with the woman. He heard Solomon forgive himself. He heard Solomon crawl out of the river and leave the forest. The man sat there, stunned. Solomon had succumbed to the pleasures of the flesh. He'd given into his desire. He'd done what he'd condemned in countless sermons. The man sat there until the sun came up.

The man spent the next few days looking for the woman. He scanned the compound and the sermon hall for her. He never found her. He heard rumours that someone had left the compound. Her name was Jessica. No note, no explanation, nothing. The man felt the weight on his chest lighten. Solomon must have rejected her. He must have seen his error. He made her leave for both their sakes. Solomon was still the leader the man knew he could be. There was hope for him. He knew he should let it go.

But he didn't. He spent night after night camped in the shadows, watching the office door. Weeks rolled into months. Nothing. He relaxed. Solomon had reformed. He had made one mistake. We're all entitled to a slip-up. The man was satisfied. He was ready to leave it alone when he saw the door move.

This woman stood on the porch and stretched. Solomon joined her and slapped her ass. She kissed him before disappearing into the night. He watched her, smiling, with his robe draped over his shoulders. The man couldn't look away. He stayed in the shadow until it retreated from the sun. He stumbled to the field, grabbed a hoe, and went to work.

He felt a pit in his stomach. He finally accepted the truth. He couldn't ignore the facts anymore. Solomon was breaking the creed. He was succumbing to his desires and he didn't care. The man smashed the hoe into the ground over and over, tearing the soil. His fingers stayed wrapped around the handle all day, going from beet red to pure white. He thought about nothing but Solomon. He kept picturing the leader staring at the woman. He kept seeing Solomon's smile. He kept envisioning the robe draped over Solomon's shoulders like a common towel. The man seethed.

The man returned to the shadow that night. He kept his eyes glued to the door. This time, the woman stumbled out of the door. She was clutching her cheek. Tears were running down her face. She collapsed in the dirt, sobbing. Solomon stood in the doorway, covered in darkness. He pointed at the gate. The woman crawled to him, but he slammed the door shut. She sat there for minutes, crying. She stood up, wiped her face, and walked to the living quarters. She emerged with a bag over her shoulder. She cast one look at the office, spit on the ground, and walked through the gate, swallowed by the night.

The man wanted to run to her. He wanted to tell her it wasn't her fault, that she was manipulated by a liar. He wanted to tell her not to stray from the path, that the creed was true even if the leader was not. But the man did nothing. He just stood in the shadow. He found out later her name was Melanie.

The days melted away. He woke up late, gobbled down breakfast, and slumped to the fields. He bumped into people, staggered in others' work areas, and pounded the same lump of dirt for hours. His co-workers asked him what was wrong. He said nothing. They said he was dragging them down. He told them fuck off. They complained about him to the managers. The man was taken aside and chewed out. He was told he wasn't pulling his weight. He was told he could be expelled.

He nodded and apologized, but he barely heard them. His mind was focused on Solomon. He was obsessed. Everything else was secondary. He didn't care about work or food or people. He was a ghost during the day; he only lived for the night. He only lived for the shadow.

Weeks trickled by. The man stood in his perch and watched the door. Nothing happened... He knew Solomon hadn't reformed, hadn't rejected his ways. He knew an addict couldn't stay sober forever. But he hoped he was wrong. He hoped Solomon had the strength. He hoped his leader hadn't abandoned him.

The third woman dashed those hopes. She sauntered out of the door one night. She held her head like she owned the compound. Solomon, completely naked, leaned on the doorframe as she left. She blew him a kiss as she returned to the living quarters. Solomon caught it. The man retched.

This fling went on for months. It was the same routine every night, but the man never missed it. He had to bear witness. He didn't know what else to do. He wanted to scream the truth from the rooftops. But who would believe him? Who would the people trust: A follower who's neglected his work for weeks or the faultless leader? All the man could do was watch.

One night, the woman emerged from the office and sat down on the porch. She was shaking. Solomon sat next to her. He was wearing his robe. He grabbed her hands and patted them. He talked. The man couldn't make out the words. The woman tried to speak, but Solomon shook his head. The woman looked confused. She stood up, but Solomon pulled her down by her wrist. He stuck his finger in her face. She nodded. Solomon left her on the porch. She stayed there until the sun started peeking over the horizon.

Later in the day, she was standing in front of the gate. A small crowd was there. The man stood to the side. The woman was holding back tears. She said she had to leave. She said she didn't belong here anymore. She said she had to find her own place and sort herself out. Everyone shook their heads. Friends hugged her as her eyes turned to waterfalls. She waved as she walked down the road. Her name was Susan. Solomon watched the whole scene from his porch.

The man's anger curdled into rage. He felt impotent. He was stuck watching a feeble man destroy lives through his weakness. He stood in the shadow, letting his fury fester.

One night, a woman walked up the porch and knocked on the door. Solomon answered it and welcomed her inside. The man stepped out of the shadow. He had to see more.

The man approached the porch. He peeked his head over the window. He peered inside. It was dark, but a lantern near the bed provided enough light to see what was happening.

Solomon was on top of the woman. They were both grunting. They were smiling. Solomon kissed her everywhere. He groaned and rolled off of her. They cuddled and slept. The man slunk against the wall and sat down. He shook his head. Solomon was a snake.

The man never saw the woman go to Solomon's office again. She left the compound with no note, no fanfare. Most people barely noticed she was gone. The man eventually found out her name was Lauren.

All those women. Who knows how many the man didn't see? This charlatan had ruined all of them. Solomon hadn't sent them away to save them; he did it to assuage his guilt.

The man returned to the window every night. The shadow wasn't enough anymore. He watched Solomon drink bottle after bottle of whiskey. He watched him drunkenly stumble through the office reciting old sermons. He watched Solomon stare at his robe and cry. He watched Solomon peer through the darkness looking for...something. He saw the lost boy pretending to be a man. He saw the fraud.

After every tryst, after every bender, after every long, lonesome night of staring into the void, Solomon would go to the river. He'd stand in the water and berate himself. He'd talk about stepping down or running away. He'd call himself a liar. But he'd always forgive himself. He'd always give himself another chance. He's always emerge from the river with new resolve. He'd always vow to be better. He'd always break that vow.

The man's fury degraded to disgust. Solomon sickened him. The man couldn't stand the sight of him. Solomon was an impostor. The man hated him.

Every sermon became torture to sit through. The man slumped in the chair near the door. He endured endless lectures from the insecure wreck onstage. Every speech made the man cringe. The words rang hollow coming from the drunk in the white robe. He didn't mean a word he said. The man wanted to run onstage and pummel Solomon.

The man punished himself in the fields, trying to find that spark again. He believed in the creed. He wanted to ascend. He wouldn't let Solomon derail him. But the pit in his stomach gnawed away at him. He couldn't stop thinking about Solomon. That fraud had tainted this place for the man. It was desecrated land now. The man would never find peace, not with the fake at the helm.

The man was surrounded by blind idiots. They thought Solomon could do no wrong. They thought he was perfect. They'd follow this fool off a cliff. The man was choking on disgust. He could barely breathe. All his hatred was poisoning him. He would drown in it. He had to escape.

One day, he was working by himself in the field. He felt the same sensation come over him that had pushed him past the county border. The same sensation that had pulled him into Joseph's car. He dropped the hoe and walked into the forest. No one saw him leave.

He stumbled through the woods. He climbed a hill, never looking back. He found a cave, crawled inside and slept. He woke up in the darkness. His whole body ached. His neck cracked as he sat up. Pebbles fell from his back. He was cold. He shuffled outside and greeted the sun. He closed his eyes and soaked it in. He felt good.

Past the trees, he could see glimpses of the compound. He heard voices wafting through the air. He looked around the cavern. He saw a trail leading down the hill and further into the forest. He knew he should follow it. He knew he should get as far away from Solomon as possible. But his feet didn't move. Something held him in place.

He stayed near the cave. He camped on its backside, away from the compound. He snapped branches off trees for shelter. He created a fire pit. He nestled into the earth. He collected fruit that grew around him. He stalked rabbits and deer. He shoved anything edible into his mouth. He was always looking for his next meal. There was no down time, no rest. He was constantly surviving.

The man returned to the compound from time to time. Always under the cover of darkness. Always when no one was around. Always for supplies. He raided the cafeteria for plates and knives. He swiped blankets and sheets from empty cots. He pinched hoes from sheds. He needed these things more than they did. No one noticed anything was missing.

The man built his own world in the forest. He was sealed off from everything. Not a soul knew where he was. He wandered endlessly through the forest. He talked to himself. He contemplated the creed. He ignored Solomon and considered the words. He still found them powerful. He still believed in sacrifice and denial and struggle. He still thought they were the best path to salvation.

Months bled into years. The man had no idea what he looked like. He shed all forms of decency or manners. He became pure will. He only focused on staying alive. He slept, hunted, ate, and thought. He distilled himself to his essential elements.

One day, as the man was roasting a rabbit over his fire, he realized something: This was the way life was supposed to be. This was what everyone should strive for. There were no buildings, no sermons, no liars; just the man and the woods. He was living the creed how it was meant to be lived, how Joseph had described it. He was the truth.

The man didn't feel a pit in his stomach anymore. That emptiness that had gnawed on him for years faded away. He didn't worry; he just lived. But one thing always spoiled his mood. When he sat in front of the cavern and looked down at the compound, he felt the wave of disgust surge over him. Those people were still being misled. Nothing had changed, he was sure of it. Solomon was still weak and he was still dragging everyone down with him. If only they could live like him. If only they could see the truth.

Despite himself, the man felt drawn back to the compound. He didn't go for supplies; he'd stopped needing them long ago. He went to the outskirts of the compound to observe. He wanted to see if things were as bad as he'd remembered. He hid in the bushes and watched.

The people worked themselves to death. They slaved away in the fields and assembled buildings and screamed themselves hoarse at every sermon. Even Ken and Greg, the arms of the fraud, worked hard. This compound was a testament to self-sacrifice. But it all meant nothing if the head was tainted. And Solomon was still poisoned. The man followed him as he wandered through the compound, spouting empty platitudes and rhetoric. Solomon presented himself as a thoughtful leader, but the cracks always showed. He'd degraded even further than when the man last saw him.

The man sat on the other side of the river every night, waiting for Solomon. His patience was always rewarded. Solomon would throw himself into the stream, begging for forgiveness and absolution. He would confess to every sin he condemned in his sermons. He would lambast himself. But, like clockwork, he would let himself off the hook.

The man couldn't stay away. He couldn't stop following Solomon. The leader's transgressions piled up into a hideous collection of failure. The man stalked him from the forest, never letting him out of his sight. He followed him in his office, around the compound; he even found Solomon's garden. It was a car crash he couldn't turn away from. The man had to do something. He had to fix things. He just needed inspiration. Solomon gave it to him.

One afternoon, the man heard Solomon talking with Greg in his private garden. The man heard them discuss the ceremony. The man heard them talk about everyone's last voyage. The man heard them plan mass suicide.

All the pieces fell into place. This had been the plan from the start. This had been what Joseph had wanted. This was supposed to be the ultimate reward. The man loved it. It made perfect sense. It's what he'd been striving to do. That's what they'd all been working towards. Death was the best solution.

The man sat in the forest and realized what he was meant to do. He had to free the people. He couldn't let Solomon do it; he'd fuck it up. He didn't deserve to lead the final step. The man wouldn't let him ruin it. He had to save these people. He had to send them off right.

The man chose his targets. He watched people. He found the members with the most faith, the true believers. He found people who deserved the perfect send-off. He grabbed his knife. He stood in front of the cavern. He watched the sun set. He knew his target's movements. He knew what he had to do. He took the

knife and ran it across his arm. He watched the blood flow. He
felt that sensation take him over again. It sent him down the hill.

The man found his target. He pulled him into the woods.
He said a quick prayer. He let them know it was going to be
alright. He ran his knife over their throat. He watched them
thrash and gurgle. He smiled. He disappeared into the night.

The man kept his eye on Solomon. He watched the
leader unravel. He saw Solomon lash out. Solomon put on a
brave face in public, but he couldn't hide from the man.
Solomon cracked in his office and the man saw it through the
window.

The man kept going. He liberated people and planted
them in Solomon's garden. He left a trail for Solomon to follow
into the cavern. The man saw Solomon crumble. He saw the liar
face the inescapable truth. The man saw Solomon finally receive
his punishment.

The man waited as Solomon reached his lowest point.
He waited until Solomon was lost. He waited until Solomon was
on the brink.

The man entered the office. He wrapped a cord around
Solomon's neck. He started pulling. The man would give
Solomon something he didn't deserve: A proper send-off.

The people were ready for a new leader.

CHAPTER THIRTY-EIGHT

The killer stops talking.

The smile is plastered on his face. He held it as he told his little story. A granite grin.

I look at Ken. He inched closer and closer as the killer spoke. His mouth is agape.

I'm cold. I shouldn't have let him talk about the women, or the drinking, or the river. I should have stopped him. But I couldn't move. He paralyzed me. Jessica. Melanie. Susan. Lauren. I can see their faces. They were a lifetime ago. I paid my debt for those mistakes. I scrubbed myself clean. I picked myself back up. Who is he to judge?

The killer keeps looking at me, unblinking. He makes my skin crawl. These eyes have been following me for years. He's been watching my every move, my every word, my every private moment. This creep has stalked me around my own home. I feel violated.

I shake my head. I'm letting him psych me out. He told his pack of lies and now I'm doubting myself. No, it's worse than that; Ken is doubting me. I see it in his eyes. He heard the slander that poured out of this filth's mouth. Ken believes those awful things about me. He doesn't trust me.

No. I'm not losing my last real believer because of some nutjob's half-cooked bullshit. I'm not what he said I am. I raise my head and look down at the killer. I move to the side, grabbing Ken by the arm. We step farther into the river. I face the bank to keep my eyes on the killer. He doesn't budge.

"Ken, you know he just told a big whooper, right?" I wrap my fingers around the back of his neck.

"...yes, of course, sir..." Ken's eyes dart to the water. Fuck.

"Ken, he made that stuff up. You don't believe it, do you?" I raise his chin. I'm shaking.

Ken meets my gaze. He bites his lip. He shakes his head.

"I need you on my side, Ken. One hundred percent. We have to work together. Do you understand?" My voice cracks. Panic is winning me over.

"I...I do. It's just... what he said. The way he said it. It all sounded...real." Ken glances at the killer.

I slap Ken across the face. My palm stings. My heart is hammering on my chest.

"Real? He sounded real? The homeless vagrant who just confessed to murdering our friends sounded believable to you? He makes you doubt? After all your time here, after all your work, you're going to let this psychopath throw you off? That's what you're telling me?" I keep my voice to a low growl.

"No...I just...oh, fuck, I don't know. The way he looked at you and the way you looked at him...He sounded like he was telling the truth. I just....I just don't know." Ken rubs his face.

Sweat trickles down my back. He thinks I'm a fraud. The last person on my side and this lunatic took him away. Ken thinks I've deceived him this whole time. Oh, fuck, fuck, fuck. This can't be happening. No, no, stop panicking. It doesn't help. You're in control here. Not them. You. Always you.

"Ken, you know me. Better than anyone. You know me, right?" I touch his elbow.

"Yeah...I mean, I think...yes..." Ken pulls at his hair.

"I'm not speaking as your leader; I'm speaking as your friend. It's Solomon. It's me. You've known me for years. Am I those things he said?" My fingers dig into his neck.

"...No...no, I don't think so...no, you're not." Ken locks his eyes with mine.

"Ken, if you doubt me, if you question my integrity, if you're not comfortable with what we're doing here, I want you to leave. I want you to get out of this river, walk through the woods, and cuddle up with Greg. No judgment, no punishment, no lecture, nothing. You can walk away and let me handle this...scum. I'll do what I have to do alone." I step back and spread my arm to the forest.

Ken scratches his head and winces. He looks between me and the forest. He shuffles his feet, sending water ripples crashing into my legs. The killer doesn't move. Ken looks at him and frowns. He inhales and arches his neck. He nods.

I try to hide the relief from my face. I've got nothing to celebrate. I've only dampened the fuse; it could relight at any moment. The killer planted the seed of doubt in Ken's mind; it'll fester and grow. I'll have to spend days, weeks, fucking months, to get him completely back on my side. And even then, there'll always be that niggling hesitation in his brain when he listens to me. He won't be pure anymore. The killer took that from me. One more thing to add to his list.

"If you're staying, you're here to the end. Whatever happens, whatever's said, I need you on my side. I need you to trust me. Can you do that?" I'm asking Ken, my most loyal member, if he can follow me. Madness.

"Y-yeah, I can. I will. Sir." Ken taps his finger against his chest.

I turn around. The killer is staring at the riverbank. I want to close my eyes and have the river swallow him whole. But nothing's that simple. I slog through the water and stand in front of him.

He tilts his head as he looks at me. He licks his lips, keeping his smile wet. His neck twitches.

He's deranged. He took our scripture and twisted it into this dark perversion. He took my teachings and warped them to suit his worldview. He hated us all for no reason, so he used my words to justify it. He's a madman who's convinced himself he's a zealot. He's piss pretending he's gold.

That's how I'll beat him. He's constructed a small box for a worldview. It's too tight to let anything in. But if I can batter it enough, it'll break. I need to prove how he's failed our faith. He'll fall to his knees and beg forgiveness. Then we can...well, we'll figure that out later.

What did he say at the end? He attacked me because he wanted to take my place? There we go. I breathe through my nose and open my mouth.

"So, you want to replace me?" I straighten my back as I peer down at him.

"That's one way to see it, I suppose. One way through a small keyhole. So, so small. I wouldn't replace you. I wouldn't become you. I'd be better. Much better." The killer bobs his head up and down.

"Better?" I raise my eyebrows.

"Without a doubt. I know what this place really needs. I know what faith is. I can lead these people down the right path. Ken, Greg, all of them. They'd be better off with me. I know it and you know it. You can feel it. Yes, yes, yes, I'd be a much better leader than you." The killer's smile grows.

"So, you'd build your leadership on a pile of corpses, with mine at the top." I tap my chest.

"Ugly image. But true, I guess. It's not so bad. It's part of the plan. It's all been part of the plan. You have to burn so we can rise from the ashes. You're just a necessary sacrifice." The killer shrugs.

My skin crawls at the idea of this lunatic stuffing me under the floorboards and replacing me. I want to slap the taste out of his mouth. But I turn to Ken and force myself to laugh. My voice cuts through the air. I throw my head back and make my stomach heave. Ken half-smiles, confused.

"Well, there we go: He's just as greedy as Smit." I jerk my thumb at the killer while I roll my eyes at Ken. He slowly nods.

"Smit...Smit...Sm-it." The killer rolls the name in his mouth. His eyes light up.

"Oh, the fat one from the gate. The one who beat you. I like him." The killer winks.

"You would. You're both trying to destroy my compound. You're both power-obsessed. You're both frauds. I'm sure you'd be pen pals." I give my eyes another roll.

"Hmm. Maybe. Maybe I'd be his friend. Maybe I'd have to destroy him. Who knows? You'll have to introduce us." The killer holds up his bound hands and pulls on the rope.

"You haven't even met Smit and you're thinking about killing him? Depraved." I shake my head.

"No, not depraved. Right. I'm right. I know what I'm doing. I'm—" My hand connects with his lips before he goes on.

"Everything you've done is wrong. You didn't save those people; you slaughtered them like animals. You slit their throats before they could defend themselves. You didn't even have the courage to fight fair. You hid like a coward." I jab my finger in his face.

"Coward? Pot, meet kettle." He snaps his teeth at my fingers.

"You could have marched on the stage during a sermon and challenged me. You could have debated me. If I'm as weak as you claim, it would have been easy. You could've mopped the floor with me, right? If I'm such a fraud, you could have sent me running. You could've seized the brass ring. But you didn't. You never stepped onstage. You stayed in the woods. You know why?" I flex my fingers.

"Cleaner air." The killer licks his top lip.

"Because you were afraid. You knew you had nothing to stand on. You talk about faith, but you don't have the strength to rise with it. You lived in the dark because you knew you'd wither in the light. You don't have conviction. You want to run away and shirk your responsibilities and pretend you're a true believer. People relied on you and you disappeared. You're a fake. And you knew everyone would see you for what you really are if you stepped into the compound, if you challenged me face to face. So you stayed in your shadows and took out your frustrations on whoever was unlucky enough to be in your way." I kick my leg forward, sending water flying.

The killer's smile falters. His brow furrows. The anger smoldering in his eyes erupts to the forefront. He clicks his teeth together. Keep hammering.

"You projected all your failings on me. I'm not perfect. Of course I'm not. I've slipped up from time to time. Who hasn't? And that's all the excuse you needed. You made me into your personal monster, one you could blame for everything that's gone wrong here. I became the symbol of everything you hate about yourself. You convinced yourself I was a fraud and you were a real believer. And that led to one conclusion." I make a slicing motion across my neck.

"Execution." The killer's voice is laced with excitement. Goddamn, he's so fucking creepy. I blank for a moment.

"...Right. You wanted to kill me and take my place. You wanted to lead these people. But not because you're a believer. You want to be the leader because you want the power. You want control. You want to tell people how to live. You want to yank their chains. You're not guided by faith; you're guided by lust." My spittle flies into the killer's face.

"Hmm." The killer scratches his nose, leaving my spit untouched.

"There's nothing special about you. You didn't kill those people for a grand cause. You didn't stalk our compound to pass judgment. You didn't try to murder me because you thought the people needed a better leader. You did all of that because you wanted to. You didn't follow our creed down this path; you made it yourself. You're a lunatic." I wave my hand in his face.

I step back. I exhale, letting my shoulders relax. Not a bad speech, not bad at all. Could a fraud do that, motherfucker? Could a fraud expose you for what you really are? Could a fraud tear you to shreds like I just did? No, he couldn't. I'm the real deal, bitch.

The killer clears his throat. He tilts his head from side to side. He's mumbling.

"What's that?" I cup my hand around my ear.

"Not a fraud, not a fraud, I'm not a fraud. You're the fake. Not me. I'm real. You're a liar. I know what I'm doing." The man chews his fingernails.

"Clearly. You've definitely got all of your screws sealed on tight." It's my turn to smile.

The killer bites of a chunk of his thumbnail and spits it into the river. He's shaking. His eyes lock with mine. They twitch and tremble. The killer closes them and breathes. He opens them and stares right through me. His pupils are motionless. His smile inches up his face. He snorts.

"Fancy, fancy talk. You were always a good talker. Tried to trick me there. Tried to make me doubt. But you can't do it. I have faith. Not like you. Nothing like you." The killer wags his fingers.

"You're right. You're not like me; you're beneath me. You're beneath all of us. You're not worthy to judge this compound. You're just a murderer." I don't break eye contact.

"It's not about power. It was never about power. I don't care about your titles. I want to save those people. I want to rescue them from damnation. I want to save them from you." The killer jerks his head at me.

"Bullshit. If you wanted to save people, you'd stepped out of the forest and spoke to me like—" The killer's hands leap to my face. I jump back.

"Wrong. You're always wrong. I couldn't win them your way. I couldn't win with words. You twist them, make people confused. You make them depend on you. I couldn't beat you if I spoke at your sermon. I'd be fighting empty words with empty words. Gasoline to the fire. Nobody would listen to me. More white noise. More distractions. I'd lose. Can't have that." The killer shifts his weight from foot to foot.

"So you took a shortcut. Whoa, just like a real believer." My voice drips with sarcasm.

"I had to give them something real. I had to show them. I couldn't say it. I spoke with blood. I had to remind people what living feels like. I had to remind them about pain, about fear. I had to wake them up. I had to speak my way." The killer furls and unfurls his fists.

His voice has become a deathly rasp. I can barely hear it over the river, but it wriggles into my ears. My skin shivers.

"You've never show them anything real. You've let people live in lies. You'll let this compound wither and die. You'll allow these people to waste their lives. You won't even know you're doing it. You'll tumble off the cliff while everyone holds your hand." The killer tugs on his beard.

"You fucker. How dare..." I can't think of the words. I'm lost in his gaze.

"I know who you are. We're the only two who do. You don't know what you're doing. You're stumbling in the dark. You're a lost boy with too much power. You will fail." The killer is right in my face.

I feel queasy. My eyes are watery. It's like he reached in my chest and... pressed a button. My heart is pounding.

He knows. He sees me. No, stop don't let him— Fuck, it's true. I couldn't admit it but—Goddammit, stop. It's what he wants. He wants to—Jesus, I'm lost. I'm a fake. He's- Fuck, fuck, fuck, calm down. This isn't helping. What do I do? Oh, fuck, what do I do?

Stop. My brain shuts down. I breathe and look at the killer. He's still smiling. I nod. Stay focused. Stay here. This is confessional like any other. Stick to the script. After a member confesses, what do I do? Exactly right.

"You have done horrible things. Unforgivable things. You have strayed from the path." I ignore my shaking knees.

"If I have, I know my way back. Do you?" The killer flashes his teeth.

"After everything you've done, after the horrors you've committed, do you want salvation?" I place my palm on his forehead.

The killer steps to the side. He looks at me. I refuse to look away. He cranes his neck forward. His lip curls into a frown. He sighs. His eyes are...sad? He opens his mouth. I lean in.

His spit lands on my right cheek.

Everything goes black. When I come to, I'm holding the killer under the water. My hands are squeezing his shoulders. His face is clouded by bubbles. We're deep into the river, almost up to our waists. I have to plant my feet to stop myself from being swept away.

I gave him the olive branch. After everything he's done, he doesn't deserve a single courtesy. But I gave him dozens. I let him speak. I listened to him. I gave him a chance for salvation. I allowed him to save himself. And he spat on my fucking face?

The killer grabs my arms, digging his fingernails into my skin. I push deeper, soaking my robe. I'm nearly squatting in the river. Ken is standing next to me. He's saying something. I can't hear him. My head is pounding.

This fucker attacked my leadership, my faith, my people, my character. He's questioned my integrity. This guy, the little troll who lives in the woods and shits where he eats, feels justified in questioning me. He's ruined my life and he's still mocking me. I'm the better man. He's a coward who couldn't face me. He had to attack me while my back was turned. I'm better than him. I'm better than all of them. I'll prove it.

I pull the killer's head out of the river. He coughs up a stream of water. I hold him by the collar, standing over him as he sits on the riverbed. His messy hair droops over his face, obscuring it. Ken is tapping my shoulder. I turn to him.

"Sir...is, uh, is everything alright?" Ken's eyes are shaking.

"All part of the confessional." The words managed to sneak out of my clenched jaw. Ken slowly nods and steps back. I peer down at the killer. He's stopped coughing. He pushes the hair from his face. He looks at me and grins.

"Surprised. Almost thought you'd do it. Knew you wouldn't." The killer spits into the river.

"Do what?" I pull him up.

"What I tried to do to you." The killer rolls his eyes into the back of his head and makes a gagging sound.

I held his life in my hand...No, I still hold his life in my hand, and he's making fun of me. He thinks I'm weak. He thinks I couldn't end him. One little push would prove him wrong. One underwater dip and he'd... No, it takes strength not to be like him, not to smother your problems.

"We're not playing your game; we're playing mine. You remember confessionals, don't you? A chance for someone to unload all their sins and receive their just punishment. Even if you spent years out year eating pine cones and sleeping in your shit, even if you've forgotten how to clean yourself, you remember confessionals. Right?" I shake the killer.

"Ye-es. Favourite thing to watch. Best part of the sermon." The killer nods.

"Well, welcome to our private sermon hall." I spread my hand over the river.

"Hmm." The killer shrugs.

"This is your last chance. I'm giving you a shot at retribution. You've already confessed your sins. You've let that weight off your chest, but it's still shackled to you. It could drag you under, down to a place you can't crawl out of. Your past could kill you." I let the killer sink into the river.

"There's no crowd. Who are you playing to?" The killer strains his neck to keep his head above the water.

"I'm 'playing' for you. I'm giving you salvation. Just take my hand. Beg me for forgiveness. Submit to me. Admit you were wrong. You have to want salvation. And when you do, when you accept it into your heart, we'll take care of you. We'll make sure you get help. We'll bring you back into the fold. What do you say?" I extend my free hand to him.

"Fold's no good if it's run by you. I believe my own way." The killer tries to spit on me again, but it falls back and lands on his forehead.

I plunge him back into the water. He'll break. I'll wear him down and get him to say the words. He'll kiss my feet. Then, well, I can't take him back to the compound. Even a broken animal can still bite. Even if he begs forgiveness, we can't accept him. Some things can't be pardoned. We'll have to... It doesn't matter. We'll sort it out later. But I will break him here. I will prove myself. I will beat him. I raise him up. He shoots out a volley of water. I slap him.

"You're being purified by the water. It is washing away your sins. But you have to accept it. You have to accept my salvation. Will you do it?" My knuckles are turning white from the grip on his shirt.

"Don't...need it." The killer shakes his head.

Back into the water. He's a goddamn murderer. He's slaughtered our people. He threw the compound into chaos. He turned Ken and Greg against me. He tried to kill me. Me! He's a rabid dog that needs to be put down. But he still denies me. He still pretends he's better. He still mocks me. I'm grinding my teeth.

He comes up. His face is red. He's gasping for air. I don't let him rest.

"Salvation. It's yours. Just take it. Now." I throttle him.

"W-worthless." The killer smiles. He fucking smiles.

I shove him into the river. I'm a joke to him. I'm funny to him. He's amused. After everything he's done, he doesn't deserve to smile. He doesn't deserve to fucking live.

He rises. Ken leans in close. He looks worried. I ignore him.

"Salvation. Do it." My voice is guttural.

"No... thanks. Waiting for...something better." The killer chuckles.

Water engulfs him. Aren't I allowed to fail? Aren't I allowed to make mistakes? I'm human like everyone else. Sure, yeah, maybe I...knew those women. Maybe we gave each other company. But I sent them away, didn't I? I punished myself. I promised to be better. I was better. I'm entitled to slip up now and then. It's part of the plan, part of my tests of faith. And I passed them. I never gave up. I'm still the leader. I'm still in control. I am...

The killer bursts to the surface. He can barely open his eyes. Ken says something. I don't hear him.

"Take my salvation. Please." I try to smooth over my voice.

"Wish I...could. Really." The killer drops his smile.

We look at each other. He shakes his head. His eyes fill with disappointment. He's ashamed of me. I bash him into the river. He's not fit to judge me. No one is. No one has to right to question me. I know where we're going. I know the path. Joseph laid it...No, I laid it out. Only me. No one can judge me. No one. The killer is dead weight in my hands. Ken is yelling at me, but I can't make him out. It's just me and the killer.

"Salvation. Salvation. Salvation." I shake him with each word.

"Weakling..." The killer winks at me.

Dirty. Little. Fucker. I'm the strongest one here. Who else could've gotten this far? Who could've held this whole thing together? Me. Only me. I'm the only one with true faith. I've led my people to greatness. I've conquered myself. I've done it all. This bastard is worthless. He can't follow our creed in the woods. You can't obey our faith without me. This compound is nothing without me. These people are nothing without me. I'm nothing...

The bubbles stop. The water settles. I can see the killer's face. He's smiling at me. It's frozen and distorted. I let go off his shirt. He floats away.

I stare at my hands. My fingers are gnarled, trapped in the moment I killed him.

I walk out of the river. I'm aware of Ken shouting something. He's wading through the water, trying to catch up to the body. I'm walking. I can feel my body move. Everything's faded and blurry. My legs have taken over. My mind is fog. But I know where I'm going.

I'm stumbling to the cavern.

CHAPTER THIRTY-NINE

Jason Neary strides through his compound.

He looks at his hands. They're trembling. His head feels light. He's riding the high from his sermon. It ended three hours ago. He's been surrounded by progress. Workers swarm over new buildings, hoisting up wooden beams with rope. Planters haul bags of soil to the fields. People dart across the compound, shouting instructions. Everyone keeps moving.

Jason sees new faces everywhere. People who've flocked to the compound over the last few months. People he's only talked to once. People whose faces he can't remember. People who tripped over each other to get here. He's surrounded by followers. Jason stops at the centre square and admires the compound. It's been one year since they opened the gate. One year since the first people signed up. One year since he started preaching. They hit the ground running and they never stopped. In one year, they've built a community.

Jason sits on a crate. "Supplies" is sloppily written on its side. Jason closes his eyes and runs through his mental checklist. He just finished the sermon (a particularly good one, if he's being honest). He needs to drop into the office and take care of a bit of paperwork. Then he should check on his garden. After that, a few quick rounds in the compound to see where everyone's at, a meditation session by the river, some brainstorming for tomorrow's sermon, dinner, then bed. A perfect system. No surprises, no distractions; just work. He opens his eyes.

Greg is standing over him. Jason blinks, nearly teetering off the crate. He stands up.

"List of new recruits for you, sir." Greg hands his clipboard to Jason.

Jason takes the board and flips through it. A swath of eager faces greet him. He nods, tilts his head, and makes a few grunting noises, pretending to read. Jason paid attention to Greg's first reports, but he's slowly tuned them out. Day after day after day; it's too much information. Jason doesn't want to clutter his mind. But he doesn't want to hurt Greg's feelings. So he stares at the clipboard for a minute every day.

"Looks good. Can't wait to meet 'em." Jason tosses the clipboard back to Greg.

"Yes, they're very excited to meet you, sir. They traveled a long way to get here. Like, really, really far." Greg marks the clipboard with his pen.

"Yeah? Where from?" Jason cracks his neck.

"Uh, I can't pronounce it. Small town. Not on the map." Greg flips through the clipboard.

"Well, let's make sure it's worth their trip." Jason claps Greg's shoulder and start walking to his office.

"Absolutely, sir, absolutely. They can't wait to see your sermon. They said Joseph told them all about it. He must travel far..." Greg keeps pace with Jason.

"He's always spreading the word. Always out... Speaking of, have you seen him? I need a word." Jason nods at two passing planters. They giggle. Nice faces.

"Joseph? I saw him go into your office right before the sermon. Haven't seen him since. No, wait, I... No, actually that was Michael. You know, the builder? They've got similar faces. I always get them mixed up. And they're always in the same place. One time I called Michael Joseph when they were working on the living quarters and it was a whole thing..." Greg chuckles. Jason doesn't notice.

"My office? Perfect. Thanks for the report, Greg. You're a lifesaver. Catch you around." Jason ruffles Greg's hair as he walks to his office. Greg turns around and almost gets decapitated by two builders carrying a wooden beam.

Ken is standing in front of Jason's office. His arms are folded as he constantly scans the compound. His eyes light up when he sees Jason. He waves. Jason returns the favour.

"Great sermon today, sir, really great. Top-notch. One of your best. I've been thinking about that...stuff for days and you just said it all. You reached in my head and put my thoughts out there. I mean, they were your thoughts, but...you know..." Ken's face turns red.

"I like to think they're our thoughts. I just say 'em." Jason climbs the steps.

"Damn, I couldn't have... You nailed it. That was...damn, you're right." Ken's smile seems to stretch past his face.

"So, how's life for the world's deadliest bodyguard? Break up any fights?" Jason throws some light jabs at Ken's stomach.

"Naw, everyone keeps to themselves. They know what happens when they scrap. But I'm staying sharp, sir. That Kevin guy... Ever since he hugged you after a sermon. Don't like the look of him. What do you think?" Ken leans in close, as if someone is listening.

"I think hugs are pretty harmless. But trust your gut." Jason pats Ken's belly.

"Thank you, sir. I will." Ken gives a quick salute.

"Greg said Joseph might be in here. You seen him?" Jason points at the door.

"Joseph? No, not for a while. I haven't been here long, though. Want me to check?" Ken grabs the door handle.

"I got it. You hold down the fort here. You never know when a riot might break out." Jason smiles as he opens the door. All the curtains are closed. Jason throws them open and invites the sunlight inside. His office is immaculate. Nothing out of place. Just the essentials. Paradise.

Jason doesn't see Joseph. He checks the bed. Nothing. Jason double-checks the office, but he doesn't find him.

He runs through his speech as he searches. "Joseph, thank you for your recruitment efforts. It's been tremendous. But we need you here. We need your guidance. I need your guidance. You can't be running around all the time. You need to lay down your roots. Damn, is that too pushy? Maybe if I..."

Jason sees a letter on his desk. It's bright red. He tears it open and sits down. It's Joseph's handwriting.

Jason,

I'm a better speaker than a writer, so I'll be blunt: I'm leaving the compound. For good this time. You probably didn't expect this. Or maybe you did. I don't know. Maybe you're happy to be rid of me. Sorry I couldn't say goodbye in person, but I really had to be going. And I didn't want you to try to talk me out of it.

I wanted to tell you I'm proud of you. When I found you, you were lost. You were nothing. I rebuilt you. Together we made something special. We made a place of principles. We made something strong. We made this compound. I can't thank you enough for your help.

But I've realized something: This place is for you, not me. You want to create a legacy, something permanent. But I have to move. It's my hardwiring. I need to be on the road. I love the idea of this place more than the actual thing. I'm not ready to tie myself down. I need to be out there. I need to follow my path. I hope you understand.

Of course, I still believe in our faith. I haven't lost my mind. I'll practice it wherever I wind up. I'll spread the word to everyone I meet. I'll send as many as I can your way. But I can't stay here. This place is your destiny, not mine.

Stay faithful, my friend. It's up to you now. Lead these people. Stay strong. I know we'll meet again. You're going to make a great leader. Take care.

Joseph.

Jason reads the letter for hours. The sun retreats and shadows creep over him. He stares at the door, waiting for

Joseph to come bursting in with a smile on his face. He never does.

Jason leans back in his chair. He feels the weight settle on his shoulders. He understands what he has to do. He's alone on the mountaintop.

His hands are still shaking.

CHAPTER FORTY

I'm standing at the mouth of the cavern.

My hands are still shaking. They twist and tremble next to my legs. I barely notice them. I overturn a rock behind a bush. I dig past the surface and see a yellow bar. I pull it from the ground and dust it off. Our emergency flashlight. In case something ever went wrong in the cavern. In case the worst happened. Joseph thought of everything. He laid it all out. Then he left.

I enter the cavern. My footsteps echo around me. Darkness threatens to swallow me whole. This place doesn't feel sacred; it's cold and hollow. I'm walking into a tomb. I tense my fingers to stop the shaking. I furl my digits, wrapping them around an invisible...neck. I see the killer. I see his body under my hand. I see him drowning in the river. I feel the air bubbles float past me. I feel his body stop. I hear his laughter.

He was a true believer. He followed our faith to the letter. He was one of few who really believed. And he was completely psychotic. Fuck, what does that tell you? What does that say about us? About me?

I could have saved him. I could have shown him the way. No one's beyond help. I could have pulled him up from his pit. I could have saved him.

Instead I killed him.

Could I have saved him? Did I have that power? If he had taken my hand, if we had climbed out of the river together, what would've happened? Would I have brought him before everyone? Yeah, that's what I'd do. I'd make a big show. I'd have a cloak draped over his face. I'd build up the suspense, explain what's happened to our missing members, let the shock settle him, reveal how we captured the culprit, bring the crowd to a fever pitch, then tear the cloth away. I would have forced him to his knees. I would have slapped and punched and kicked and beaten him down. I would have torn a confession out of him. I would have dragged him through the crowd, letting them spit and smack him, exacting their revenge. I would have humiliated him as penance. I would have soaked in the cheers. And the killer? We'd probably keep him locked under the cafeteria until the final sermon. I'd call it additional karma. I'd try to forget about him. I'd convince myself I'd done the right thing. I'd ignore the pit in my stomach.

Maybe I wouldn't have done that. Maybe I wouldn't have let the crowd near him. I would have probably realized they'd tear him to shreds. And they'd never be able to trust me after keeping the bodies from them. I'd have thought about the compound's psyche. No, I'd have thought about my ego. I'd have to preserve it. I would have told the killer I forgave him, but he couldn't stay here. I would have told him he has to pay his dues somewhere else. I would have gotten Ken to drive him into another state. Ken would have made sure it'd be somewhere remote, somewhere secluded, somewhere from which he couldn't find his way back here. We would have packed him in the car and I'd have watched them speed down the road. I would have wiped my hands of the killer. Every day I would tell myself I'd saved the compound by excising a virus. I'd convince myself I'd done the best thing for the killer, that the one thing he needed was isolation to reflect on his sins. I'd prepare for the ceremony and let the killer fade from my mind. I'd ignore the pit in my stomach.

But maybe I wouldn't have even gone that far. Maybe I would have just killed him. Even after he'd taken my hand, after he'd begged for forgiveness, after he'd asked for help, maybe I would have refused him. Maybe I would have told him he's beyond redemption. I would have said a parasite needs to die so the herd can live. I would have told him he can't be allowed to corrupt our air. I would have told him assaulting me is a capital offense. I would have wrapped my hands around his neck and squeezed. Ken would have tried to stop me, but I would have told him it's for the good of the compound, the good of our souls. I would have told him it's necessary. Ken would have backed off. I would have felt the killer's heartbeat in my hands. I would have felt it stop. I would have watched the light melt from his eyes. I would have been horrified. But my brain would have justified it. I would have told myself I had passed another test. I had removed the tumour from the compound. I would have rationalized my way out of murder. I would have told Ken to dispose of the body quietly. I would have returned to bed and tried to sleep. I would go through the rest of my life convinced I had done the right thing. I would feel good about myself. Whenever my hands trembled, I would block out the thoughts. I would ignore the pit in my stomach.

Those are the things I would have done if we'd stepped out of the river together. A lot of thoughts would be running through my mind, but saving him wouldn't be one of them. It's not in me. I can't save people. I can put on a show and say the right words and act like I know where I'm going, but saving someone? Really, honestly saving someone? I don't know what to do.

So I didn't save that wretch. I saw a desecrated soul screaming for help, and I killed it. I drowned it beneath the river. I had a real problem and I smothered it. I'm no better than the lunatic I left floating in the water. I preach forgiveness and when I have a chance to do it, I flush it away. Just one more hypocrisy to throw on the pile.

I shine the flashlight on the ceiling. Jagged rocks jut down at me, threatening to fall and impale my torso. They're covered in a green slime. They look like cancerous teeth. Fuck, it's a gloomy place when you really look at it.   My feet splash on something. I look down. I'm standing on a small stream no wider than my foot. It's flowing away from something. I trace it with the flashlight. It curves around a boulder. I follow it.

I enter a small chamber. It's circular and constrictive, barely big enough to hold five people. I've never been here before. The stream stretches across the floor. It's flowing from a collection of rocks against the wall. The chamber is right next to the main room, the place where I was reborn. How have I never found this place before?

Because I don't pay attention. I only saw this place as a room to simulate drowning. I didn't explore because I wasn't curious. Whenever I come here it's just to recreate my initiation. I told myself I wanted a reminder. I always orgasmed. Christ, was I just trying to justify a fetish? I used this place as my weird playground. What's wrong with me? I wasn't sacrificing anything or raising my consciousness; I was masturbating. I created an excuse to get off. Fucking idiot, fucking idiot, fucking goddamn idiot.

I lean on the wall next to the rocks and sink to the floor. I rub my temples. Smit called me a true believer; he saw it in my eyes. That's how he knew he could beat me. The killer called me a fraud; he saw it in my eyes. That's how he knew he could beat me. Which one am I?

I bang my head against the wall. Pebbles fall at my feet. My arms dangle between my legs. I feel a breeze. I look at the rocks. I see a hole. I move to my knees and put the flashlight in my mouth. I grab a rock and roll it to the side. The hole widens. I grab another rock, and another, and another. They cover my hands in slime. The light bobs up and down. I keep going. The rocks are piled to the side. The stream flows from the hole. I tuck my chin into my chest and crawl through.

I'm in a smaller chamber. It can barely fit me. I have to hunch over. A pool lies before me. I found the starting point. I walk to the edge and stare into the dark water. I can't see the bottom. I point my flashlight down, but it only illuminates the sides, it's a pit.

I take my shirt off and fold it on the ground. My pants and underwear join it. I'm exposed. The air is harsh. I sit at the edge of the pool, letting my legs swirl in the water.

I've betrayed all of my beliefs. Did I even have them? Did I just convince myself I had faith? Did I just trick myself into believing? I believed the lie. I told myself I had faith. I told

myself I was a leader. I told myself I'd honour my beliefs. And I
pissed all over them. I didn't have the strength to live up to my
ideals. I wanted to believe. I tried. I really did. I heard Joseph's
words and I accepted them. I vowed to be better. I promised
myself I wouldn't fall back on my own ways. I told myself I
would let the past go. And I couldn't do it. I couldn't escape
myself. Whenever things got hard, whenever I had a crisis,
whenever I couldn't stand the pressure, I snapped. I submitted to
the person I wanted to get away from. I took the easy way out. I
gave up.

The women. The drinking. The outbursts. The self-
centred moping. They weren't rare. I fell into them over and over
and over. Then I'd promise myself I'd stop. I'd make the women
leave, I'd pour the liquor down the drain, I'd whip my back until
it bled. I'd swear to change. I'd say I'd passed another test. And
things would be fine. I'd be the leader I wanted to be. I'd know
what to say and what to do and where to be. I'd be perfect.

Then they'd find me. It always started with women.
They'd come for advice or counselling or confession. They'd
want one-on-one sessions so they could take the weight off their
chests. I'd listen and say the right things. Then they'd make their
moves. They'd put their hands on me. They'd kiss me. Before I
knew it, we'd be tumbling down together. They'd always take
me off the path. They'd drag me back into Hell and I had to claw
my way out. I can't shoulder all the blame. If they'd just left me
alone, I'd be fine. If Sandra could've just...

No. I can't use them as an excuse. I knew what I was
doing, every time. Whenever I took them to the sermon hall for a
personal confession, I knew where we'd wind up. I had a
hundred chances to stop it, but I never did. I wanted to do it.
They trusted me and I exploited them. I used them to forget
myself. I sought those women out. I needed a release. I'm to
blame.

Everything else would spiral out from there. I'd try to
silence my guilt with drinks. I'd promise to stop. I'd tumble
further and further down with them. I'd scream during my

sermons, ranting about myself. I'd pummel some poor follower and pretend it was a confessional. I took out my hatred for myself on everyone. Then I'd wake up. I'd go to the river and float in the water. I'd think about sinking to the bottom. I'd think about following the current away from the compound. I'd think about swimming to the other bank and starting to walk. But I didn't do any of those things. I didn't free my followers from me. I couldn't let myself give up. I'd remind myself why I was here, why people needed me, why I couldn't fail. I'd forgive myself, every time.

After that, I'd start cleaning up. Banishment for the women, rehab and punishment for me, and in a few days we'd be back to normal. I'd force myself to forget what I'd done. I'd shove those thoughts into an abyss where they couldn't crawl up. I'd go about my life until another woman found me. I was trapped in a circle I couldn't see.

I'm the problem. Not the women, or the booze, or Smit, or the killer; me. I'm everything that's wrong with this place. I've been pretending to be a leader when I can't even control myself. I'm a lie. I shiver. The water is freezing. I don't move. The pool is beckoning me, asking me to fall inside. I could get lost in there. I could sink to the bottom. I can't look away.

I'm afraid. I've been afraid every since I left my job. I was sitting at my desk and that feeling just grabbed me. The vise around my chest. It told me I had to move. I had to get out of that office. It told me to run or I was going to die. It didn't make any sense. But it kept insisting and insisting. It ordered me to run. So, I listened. I ran past the cubicles, past the water cooler, past the elevator, past everything. I burst out the door and I didn't stop. I ran through the city all day. I reached the highway as the sun kissed the horizon. I slept in the forest. I felt warm. I was smiling.

When I woke up covered in pine needles, the feeling was gone. I was sober. Fear stood in its place. Cold, rational fear. I walked to the road. I knew I couldn't go back to work. I couldn't say why; I just knew. But I didn't know where I was going. I had

no idea what I was doing. I just walked. I let my fear gnaw away
at me.

I met Joseph. It all came so easy to him. He had a plan.
He knew what to do. He explained everything to me. He took me
under his wing. He showed me the way. When we lived under
that plateau, when it was just the two of us, I was happy.
Everything was simple and pure. I knew my purpose. It all made
sense. I felt the embers of the feeling that had forced me onto the
road. I felt good.

We built the compound together. We gathered people
together. We created a religion together. It was comforting.
When everything was easy, I could believe. But that's not real
faith; that's convenience. Then Joseph left. I was alone. There
was no one with me in the office. I started to feel the weight.
And the fear came back. I realized something: I have no idea
what I'm doing.

So I reached for the bottle. Just to take the edge off, I
said. I took the edge off every night. Then she came to my office.
The first one. I don't remember her name. She wanted to talk. So
we went to my room and I fell into the circle.

I grab the flashlight and dive into the pool. I swim down,
struggling to keep my eyes open. I can only see a dark blur. I
reach the bottom and start tearing at the dirt. I pull and throw
rocks to the side, clawing downwards. There has to be a way out.
There has to be an escape route. I need to get out. I need to get
away.

I stop digging. I let my body float in the water. The
flashlight falls to the ground. My lungs groan, but I don't swim
to the surface. I can't run anymore. I can't escape. I have to stay
here. I have to face what I am.

I'm not a leader. I don't think I ever was. I just dressed
like one. I propped myself up on things I didn't believe and
ideals I never reached. I'm lost. Ever since that day in the office.
Ever since I stepped out the door. I've looked and looked and
looked. I never found it. I never figured it out.

The killer said I was a fraud. Smit called me a true believer. They were both right. I believed in the wrong things. I deluded myself into thinking I was a good man. I fooled myself. I repeated Joseph's words over and over until I believed them. I convinced myself I had faith. I built a cocoon of lies and made myself think they were true. I lived in my own deception and called it reality. I was a believer. But my beliefs were shallow, fragile things. They shattered with the slightest touch. I was fanatic over papier-mâché, not Holy Scripture. I worshiped a smokescreen.

The killer saw a phoney while Smit saw a devoted lunatic. They saw the same man. Smit looked at the surface man, the mask I presented to the world. The killer found the broken shell that lurked behind the facade. They both saw the same onion; the killer simply peeled back the layers.

I'm faithless. I don't believe Joseph's teachings. I've done nothing but spout empty words and make excuses. I've hurt people. I've led them down the wrong path for years. I've steered them away from salvation.

They deserve a better leader. They deserve someone who can pick up the pieces and move forward. Someone who can guide the compound back to the path. A light in the dark. Someone better than me. Greg could do it. He has the passion, the real belief. He'd struggle, I know, but Ken would be by his side. They could go forward together. They could rebuild after my destruction. They could make something real.

Bubbles float past my face, jiggling as they spiral away. I look up. I can see the faintest hint of the surface. It's a dim splash of light in the dark. My lungs are begging for air. My lips are aching from having to stay shut. My heart is working overtime. I need to get out of this water. I need to breathe. I have to go. Now.

I could swim to the surface. It would take five strokes to rise out of this muck. I could burst out of the water and take one long gulp of air. I could climb over the edge and put my clothes on. I could stumble out of the cavern and greet the night. I could make my way to the compound and explain everything to Greg and Ken. We could work something out. We could find a way forward. I wouldn't have to leave. I could make things right. I could fix everything. I just need to get out of this pool. I just need to breathe.

I don't move. My hands limply sway in the water. My feet scrape the floor, bumping against rocks. I stare at the opening. My body demands air. It screams at me to swim. My chest is churning. I feel faint. I need to breathe. But I continue to float.

I never believed. I talked about sacrifice, but I never made one. I demanded discipline and I always exempted myself. I put my interests first and ignored everything else. I've weaseled out of real consequences my whole life. I ran from my office when I couldn't take the pressure. I ran from the city when I couldn't stand the noise. I ran from my responsibilities when I didn't want to own up to them. I've held onto my petty ego and vanity. I've clung to my old life, the old me. I've prostituted my faith for a fleeting glance of pleasure. I've wasted my life.

And now I'm lying in the bottom of a cavern pool. No one knows I'm here. Ken might guess that I'm in the cave, but he'll never find this spot, not in time. I'm alone. Just me and my impulses. I have a choice, an actual choice. I can swim to the top and find another excuse to pardon myself. Or I can stay here and float.

It's time to let go. I've kept a desperate clutch on my life and it's ruined everything. I held onto my insecurities and they tore my compound apart. I let a killer into our home and a huckster to our front door. I avoided our teachings because I thought I knew better. I didn't know a fucking thing.

It's time for faith. Honest, true faith. I have to stay in the water. I have to stay in this sunken place. I need to submit. This is all part of the plan Joseph told me about years ago. Everything that happens to us is part of the final purpose. Every moment, every setback, every success; they all lead to the endgame. I was meant to be in this pool. I was meant to float in the bottom. I was meant to drown.

I'm making a real sacrifice. I'm throwing away my earthly distractions. I'm letting go of my poisons. This is part of the plan. I believe. I believe. I believe. My lungs are screaming. I ignore them. This is where I belong. This is where I'm meant to be. I believe. I believe. I believe...

My brain feels heavy. Everything's distorted. I'm losing my... I don't know where... I'm in a cloud. It's murky. I don't... I can't leave. I need to stay. I need to...

I see a flash. I spin around. I feel a current brush across my face. I swim forward. I bump against the wall. I trace my hands over the rock. I feel an opening. It's a hole, just big enough to fit through. Or are there two? Or three? I can't think. I don't know what...

It's a sign. It's part of the plan. It's telling me what to do. It's pushing me forward. I climb through the hole and enter a tunnel. It's cramped. I grab the walls to push myself forward. Everything's black. I twist through corners and turns. My lungs are weeping. Everything's blurry. I feel woozy...

I see Joseph. He's standing in front of me. He's in the tunnel, but he's not cramped like me. He's standing. He's waving at me. He sinks into the water. I keep going forward. I see Smit. He's laughing. I keep going. I see Greg. He's looking down at me. I keep going. I see Blume. He's smiling and shaking his head. I keep going. Ken extends his hand to me. I keep going. The killer wipes blood from his chin and nods. I keep going. Sandra just stares at me. I keep going. I wind through the tunnel. I'm moving up. They keep looking at me. My lungs beg for mercy. My brain is mush. Everything's dim. I feel weak. I see light. I push forward. I burst through the surface.

My mouth slams open as I suck in the air. Water trickles down my throat, making me cough. I thrash my arms everywhere. My eyes are closed. My hands land on a cragged rock, breaking the skin. Blood slides down my wrist. I lean over the rock. I breathe. My head feels like it could float away. My brain is scrambled. I can hear my heart pounding in every bone in my body. I don't see Joseph, or Sandra, or any of them now. My mind is full of melting colours and bright lights. I'm nauseous. I don't care. I breathe.

My legs feebly paddle in the water. My arms are clinging to their sockets, crying in agony. My stomach is double-tied in knots, too compressed to let a drop of water in. My neck feels like it's about to explode. My eyes want to retreat into my skull and down my throat. Every part of me is in pain. I ignore it. I breathe.   I let all of this pain and nonsense slip away. I focus on breathing. I relish the air on my lips. I feel it fill my chest. I savour every second.

I'm alive. Unless this is the afterlife. Would I know if I was dead? Would I be able to tell? There'd probably be a sign. There'd be some way to know where you are. They wouldn't leave you in the dark. It wouldn't be like this. I wouldn't be floating in the water in darkness. This isn't the afterlife. Unless we were all wrong about what comes next. Maybe my corpse is floating at the bottom of that pool while I'm here. No follow-up, no next step, no nothing; just a void. Maybe this is all I get. Maybe—

I slap myself. Stray water shoots out of my mouth.

I'm doubting the plan again. I'm questioning Joseph's wisdom. I'm not that person anymore. I killed him. I trusted the plan and it led my through the tunnel. It brought me to the other side. I'm alive. This isn't the afterlife. This isn't what Joseph described we'd see when we crossed over. This isn't the end. I'm here for a reason. I open my eye.

I'm in another chamber. Moonbeams stream through cracks in the rocky ceiling. Stony daggers dangle over my head. I'm floating in a pool, larger than the last one. It's a nearly-perfect circle. It must be shaped like a funnel, with the tunnel widening as it goes to the top. I'm perched on the edge. I move my feet close to my body. I can touch the side. I stand up. This pool's big enough to fit the whole compound. Hell, it could probably accommodate Smit's followers, too.

I lean back and sit on the edge. I dangle my feet in the water. What a perfect spot. Ken and Greg could host their sermons in here. It'd be something different, something just for them. There must be a better way in than my tunnel. I'll find the entrance and tell them all about it. It'll be my parting gift to them, my apology present. That's why I was taken here. I'm a messenger for Ken and Greg. I'm going to show them their new home. I smile. I swing my legs out of the water and shake them dry. I feel cold, but it's hardly noticeable. I turn around. I stop breathing.

A mountain is standing in front of me. It spirals up to the roof of the chamber. It's perfectly smooth. Ridges dot its sides; natural stairways. A platform juts out at its center. A stage in the cave. A sermon mount. My head is screaming. I massage my temples, but it doesn't stop the throbbing. My mind is diving and flipping. I don't understand. This mountain, this platform, they seem... I can't make sense of it. My brain is splitting apart. I feel sick. I don't understand. I don't—

The flash. When I was down in the pool, right before I found the tunnel, I saw a flash. I didn't know what it meant. But I understand it now. The flash showed me what to do. It showed me this chamber. My followers were standing in the pool, draped in robes. Torches surrounded them. They were holding goblets. I was standing on the platform. Ken and Greg were by my side. I was giving my final sermon. I told everyone to drink. I led them to salvation. I fulfilled my purpose. That's what I saw in the flash. I saw the truth. I saw everything laid out as it should be. I saw my destiny.

I pull myself to my knees. My head is still throbbing. My brain doesn't matter. I have clarity. I have vision. I have purpose. This is why I'm alive. I can't be killed or exiled. I was brought here for a reason. I'm a leader for a reason. All my failings, all my missteps, all my stumbling in the dark; they were part of the plan. They were the steps that led me here. How could I not see it before?

I'm going to do it. I'm going to save everyone.

CHAPTER FORTY-ONE

I'm pacing at the edge of the compound.

The sun is creeping over the horizon. Everyone's heading off for work. I'm hidden behind the trees. I have so much to do. Oh, so much to do. I can't stop shaking. I have followers to save. Here, and elsewhere. I have to save the people who've been kidnapped by that smiling nihilist. I have to pull this compound back into order.

I have to restore the faith. No more half-assed speeches or empty rhetoric. I have to create a beacon in the darkness, a guide for the lost. I have to rebuild. I have to reclaim my power. No, not reclaim; it was never mine. I had empty power, weak power, power of theatrics. I commanded hollow words and useless actions. But I'm ready for true power now. I'm ready to assume my role. I'm ready to lead this compound. I'm ready.

I can see the cavern from here. It looms over the trees. The place of my rebirth. A symbol of everything this compound should be. Maybe I should go back there to clear my thoughts and prepare everything. I don't want to blow this. Yeah, maybe, I need to refocus up there. Shouldn't take long. I'll come back tomorrow. No big deal. I can—

I slap myself. I'm overthinking again. That was the old me, the dead me. I drowned that man in the cavern. I don't need to think or scheme anymore. I know the plan; I just have to follow it. I have to trust it. I have to ignore the ringing in my brain. I'm not letting my thoughts distract me.

I straighten my back and flatten my hair to one side. I stretch my jaw, hearing it crack. I bounce on the balls of my feet and flick my wrists. I take one step into the compound. My brain tries to rein me in. It tries to paralyze me, tries to make me doubt, tries to stop me. I narrow on one thought, one overriding sensation. I let it wash over me. I've let everyone down. I've steered this compound into near-destruction. I've danced over oblivion. But I have a chance to fix everything. Time to make amends. I walk into the compound.

I stroll past the centre square. How many women did I send away in the middle of the night from there? How many impromptu, uninformed sermons did I deliver from that bench? No, I didn't do that; a dead man did. He's not going to poison this place anymore.

I see the planters working in the fields. They're almost silhouettes against the rising sun. I wave to them. They don't see me. They keep their heads down. This place is falling apart because of me and they're still focused on their jobs. They understand what's important. Heroes.

My feet and head feel lighter with every step. I see why I was brought back. Workers staying on task. People helping one another. A living, breathing compound worth saving. An organism on life-support, but still kicking. I'm meant to be here.

Two builders are carrying a plank horizontally. I squint my eyes. They're the men who nearly decapitated me with a board a few months back. Feels like a lifetime ago. It was, I suppose. I duck under the board. I smile at the men, clapping. They tilt their heads, eyebrows raised. I lean my face forward. They grunt and walk towards a building.

Planters and builders walk past me, some lost in conversation, some busy with work, some aimlessly wandering. They all meet my gaze. A few nod at me. One gives me a toothy grin. But most look elsewhere. They're more interested in the ground than me. They give me a wide berth. I part them like the sea.

They're right to distrust me, to be disgusted by me. What have I done to earn their admiration? I've screamed nonsense from the podium, I've shirked my responsibilities, I've failed spectacularly in front of Smit. Fuck, I nearly beat a man to death and called it an "honour." I've embarrassed myself time after time. But that's over. I'm going to save them. I'm going to take them to the promised land.

I walk to my office. I see a woman working in a garden. She's kneeling in the dirt, ripping away at weeds. Her back is to me. Her black hair is tied into a loose ponytail. I can hear her grunting. She reminds me of Sandra. I couldn't leave everything behind in my corpse. I had to hold onto some things, things to remind me of my failings, things to keep me straight. I'm going to live with what I did to Sandra. I spoiled her faith. I threw her off the path. If she were here I'd crawl on my stomach and beg for forgiveness. I'd do anything to make it up to her. But she's not here. And I have to live with that. Wherever she is, I hope she's...fine.

I reach my office porch. The home of my failures. Long nights of self-serving misery. I shove the door open. Ken and Greg are standing over my desk, leaning into each other. They're arguing. I can't make them out; it's a mess of words. They don't notice me. They're too busy slamming the desk and shouting. I lean against the doorway. They've done everything for me. They've sacrificed all they have for our cause. And I've failed them both so completely.

Greg turns his head and stops talking. He rushes over to me and grabs my arm. He looks at my eyes. He's blabbering about my condition or something like that. The ringing in my head makes everything fuzzy. I grab him in tight hug, sweeping him off his legs. Greg tenses up. Can't blame him. Last time I touched him, I was accusing him of being the killer. I bring my mouth to his ear.

"I love you." I kiss his cheek.

I let Greg go, who stumbles to the side. I smile and wag my finger at Ken.

"Your turn." I sprint across the office and leap onto Ken with a hug.

I float above the ground as I embrace him. He keeps his arms to the side, letting me slide to the floor. I reach up to his head.

"I love you, too." I smack my lips on his chin.

Ken wipes my saliva off his face. Greg spins me around and grabs my jaw. He squeezes my cheeks and turns my head from side to side.

"Sir, are you alright? When's the last time you drank? Did you eat anything in the forest? Can you hear me? Sir?" Greg snaps his fingers next to my ears.

"Greg, please, I'm fine. I'm completely sober." I slide his fingers off my face.

"You're not sick? Nauseous? Bloated? Seeing double? Triple? You can see, right?" Greg waves his fingers in front of me.

"I see everything. Healthy as a horse." I flex my biceps.

"Nothing wrong with you? Everything's above board?" Greg looks me up and down.

"Never better." I flash a toothy smile. Fuck, I don't deserve to feel this good.

"Oh. Okay, then." Greg shoves me.

I tumble into Ken's chest. He pushes me forward, then leaps between Greg and I. Ken hold his arms up to separate us. Greg bounces on his feet, glaring at me. I don't move.

"What the fuck? You disappear in the middle of the night after murdering a man, you make Ken fish the body out of the river, you let us worry about it for 12 fucking hours, then decide to come back and kiss us? What's wrong with you, you absolute..." Greg loses his energy and starts pacing.

Ken's hand is on my shoulder, his fingers squeezing me. He shakes his head, pleading. Greg looks at me, nervous. His surge of bravado has dissipated, leaving frayed nerves. He chews his thumbnail, his whole body tense, preparing for an assault. The room is silent. My high disappears. This is how my most loyal followers view me: A violent abuser. They think any form of dissent or argument will be met with brutality. They're right, of course. That's exactly how I treated them. Yesterday, I would've dragged Greg into the garden for shoving me. But I'm not living in yesterday.

I peel Ken's hand off my shoulder. I smile at him and put my hand on my chest. I take a deep breath. Ken steps to the side. Greg's fists are curled. I walk forward.

"You're right." I bow my head.

Greg doesn't say anything. Ken doesn't move. The silence continues.

"You're absolutely right. I shouldn't have fled. I shouldn't have left you two behind to clean up my mess. I shouldn't have done a lot of things." My voice cracks.

Greg can't stop blinking. His fists have flattened out. Ken is a statue.

"Greg, for more than I can say, I'm sorry." I extend my hand.

Greg stares at it. His arms are glued to his sides. I don't move. Greg glances at Ken. He slides his palm across mine and lightly curls his fingers. I shake his hand and pull him close.

"I mean it. And I'm going to make it up to you." I pat his shoulder and let him go.

Greg rubs his hand and shuffles towards Ken. I pull the curtains, bathing the room in darkness. I grab two chairs and plant them in front of the desk. I spread my arms wide over them as I look at Ken and Greg.

"Please, take a seat. We have a lot to discuss." I tap the chair cushions.

Greg and Ken look at each other. Greg inches to the door. Ken shakes his head. He sits down, tense. Greg joins him, his legs bouncing. I clap their shoulders and position myself behind the desk.

"Do you know what I did after my very first sermon?" I plant my hands on the desk. Greg and Ken shrug.

"This would've been a bit before your time. Greg, I think you might've come a week after it happened. No, wait, it was three weeks after. I remember because I was filling out your form and I kept asking you for the date. I couldn't get it through my head. You just kept repeating it. You had a little suitcase full of... Not important, not important." I wave my hand.

"Anyway, you two weren't here yet. We were a new group. We were raw. Joseph had delivered the first few sermons. They were immaculate. I can't even describe them. I just sat in the front row and took notes. You guys have seen him in action, you know what I'm talking about." Greg nods and rolls his eyes. I get the hint.

"Sorry, sorry, I'll get to the point. So, one day, Joseph asks me to go onstage. He tells me to say what's on my mind. Just let the scripture flow out of me. He didn't give me any time to prepare. He asked me to speak while I was in the front row, with everyone staring at me. I couldn't say no. I'd look like an asshole. So I jumped onstage." I feel a trickle of sweat running down my neck as I remember.

"It was a dream. I said all the right things. I talked about sacrifice and self-denial and every other cliché in the book. I said exactly what Joseph wanted me to say. I asked members to confess and I soaked up their applause. It was everything I thought it'd be. Hell, it was more." I chuckle.

"When it was over, I went to the river. I wanted to savour the moment by myself. So I sat on the bank and I thought about my speech. I threw up." I rap my knuckles on the desk.

"It was a stream of vomit. It went everywhere. It flowed out of me in one continuous blast. I don't mean to be gross, but it was a torrent. I threw up my breakfast, my dinner, and stuff I'd forgotten I'd eaten. My throat was burning, but it wouldn't stop. By the end I was coughing up saliva. My body heaved but I didn't have anything left in my stomach. I collapsed on the bank and watched my island of hurl float away." I grimace. That was far too graphic. I could've stopped at the second sentence. Judging by Greg and Ken's faces, they're wishing I'd stopped at the first.

"So, I lay there in the grass, huddled into myself, watching the river roll by. I massaged my neck and spat out loose chunks. I listened to my stomach, ready to lean over the water if another load was coming. I breathed. Nothing happened.

No more vomit. And as I lay there, I tried to figure out what had happened." I pat my belly.

"At first, I blamed it on bad food. Our cafeteria wasn't exactly fine dining. Not that we wanted it to be. But it wasn't a paragon of sanitation. Maybe there had been some cross-contamination with the meat and veggies. Maybe I'd eaten too much. Maybe my body was doing one big purge as it got used to my diet. A final cleanse of my old toxins." I point at my gut.

"But I dismissed that idea. I'd been eating our food for months. I'd thoroughly purged my body of the old poisons. Our cooks were well-trained. They wouldn't cross-contaminate. I'd never seen anyone else throw up their meals. It couldn't have been the food. It was something deeper." I wag my finger. Ken narrows his eyes and leans forward.

"It must have been nerves. That's what I told myself. I'd just completed my first solo sermon. And it was a complete surprise, as well. I'd been thrown into the deep end without a life preserver. And I'd knocked it out of the park. But once I stepped away, once I went to the river on my own, once I reflected, my nerves caught up with my body. All that overstimulation I'd suppressed crashed into me and I overreacted. My body became super-charged and it had to evacuate its contents. I just had a little...post-show vomit. No big deal. It won't happen again. I just popped my performance cherry. It'll be all good from here. Smooth sailing ahead. I kept telling myself that over and over." I rotate my hand.

"But I didn't believe it. My brain wouldn't accept it. I'd performed before. I'd spoken in front of crowds. I never got nervous before; why now? No, it was something else. And as the moon started to peak its head through the clouds, as I stared at the river, as I really looked at myself, I realized what it was: Fear." I swallow. Greg is leaning forward next to Ken now.

"I had no fucking clue what I was saying on that stage. I just parroted all of Joseph's talking points. I didn't make any original insights. I didn't strike upon some new observation. I didn't make that presentation my own. I just said what I thought

I was supposed to say. I stuck to the script because...because I didn't believe." I push down on the lump in my throat. Greg and Ken are stone.

"I didn't want to accept it. I didn't want it to be true. But it was staring me dead in the face. I couldn't escape it. After all the miles I'd traveled, after all the sweat and blood I'd poured into the wood and stone, after walking away from my life, I still didn't believe. I marched on that stage, preached in front of my people, and I felt nothing. I was the same person I always was. I was still me." I blink, clearing my watery eyes. Greg and Ken don't say a word.

"On that river, I saw the truth for the first time. My body forced me to see it. I was a lie." I rub my forehead.

"That was the first honest thought I'd had in months. I saw myself in full definition. I could have done a lot of things at that moment. I could've tried harder, or reflected, or walked away. But I didn't. I did the worse thing I could do: I stayed." Greg and Ken are emotionless.

"I stayed me. I ran back into my lies. I convinced myself I was a true believer; I was simply having a mini-crisis of faith. It happens to everyone. No one leaves their convictions unquestioned. This episode was merely an obstacle I would overcome. I'd be stronger for it. I was going to bask in my faith. I repeated those lines until I thought they were real. I tricked myself into thinking I was a pious man. I left the river, carrying my poison with me." I spit on the floor.

"Everyone's suffered since I infected this place with...me. My insecurities, my weaknesses, my doubt...I can't even say how much damage they've done. I've hurt the people closest to me. I've hurt you boys most of all." I sink to the chair, looking at Greg and Ken at eye-level.

"You two have worked yourselves half-to-death for this compound. You've pushed yourselves past exhaustion every day. You're real believers. And I repaid you with abuse, deceit, and misery. I exploited you. I'm an asshole, and worse. You deserve a better leader. You deserve a better friend. You deserve the truth. So I'm going to give it to you." I fold my hands on the desk.

"I was born Jason Neary. Both my parents are dead. I went to college. I worked in a cubicle in an office building in a crowded city. I hated my life and everyone around me. I had a pit in my stomach I could never fill. It crushed me. I was sinking and I couldn't see a way up.

"One day, out of the blue, I ran away from my job and hit the road. I walked for weeks, months, I lost count. I met Joseph. He told me about our wonderful faith. I wanted to believe it, so I followed him across the country until we landed here. Our Plymouth Rock. We planted the seed where a mighty tree would grow. That's where you boys come in.

"You lads lit this place on fire. You pushed us up higher and higher. People streamed into the compound. We had more followers than we knew what to do with. We were on a roll. And I was doing fine. Joseph wasn't around that much, but I found my groove with the sermons. I said exactly what I thought I should say. I did everything I thought a real believer would do. I was going to fake it until I made it.

"Then Joseph left, for good. You remember that note he left. I must've read it twenty times. I kept running the words through my head over and over again. I knew I had to step up. I knew all the weight had been placed on my shoulders. And, for the first time in a while, I felt that pit in my stomach.

"I held it together for a bit. I put on a strong face and made sure everything didn't fall apart. But that pit kept gnawing away at me. I couldn't silence it. Nothing I did made it go away. I pretended to be pious, but that wasn't cutting it anymore. I was all surface, no depth.

"So I crumbled. I'd drink. I'd sleep with every woman who winked at me. I'd make excuse after excuse after excuse. I'd crash down at rock bottom and keep digging.

"Then I'd run to the river, the one place where I'd been honest with myself. I'd see what I'd become, see all the rules I'd shattered, see what a mockery I was. I'd scream and curse at myself, shout my throat hoarse, everything I could think up as penance. I'd always stop at the edge. I'd peer over and I'd see what I'd have to do to make amends. I'd see the long road to redemption and I'd slink away. I'd dismiss my failings as mere hiccups on my true path. I'd promise to rise above them. I'd swear to be stronger when I emerged from the water. I'd take a dozen oaths of piety, chastity, and restraint. I'd crawl back to the compound, ready to start anew. Then I'd be back at the river in four months with the same problems.

"I was the criminal and the judge. I always found a reason to pardon my actions. I let my pit suck me into hell. I couldn't even see how miserable I was. I couldn't see the damage I was doing to our home. I had fooled myself into thinking I was the only real believer here. I thought I was complete, whole, a leader. I was empty.

"That's why our compound has fallen apart. That's why a huckster in a cheap robe can waltz in here and pluck out members in front of us. That's why people sneak away in the middle of the night. That's why a serial killer could flourish at our doorstep. They've all stemmed from my failures. Smit could sense my weakness. The people can see my obliviousness. The killer understood my lack of faith. They saw something in me I didn't want to accept. They saw the truth.

"Smit and the killer exploited that fact for all it was worth. Smit's been hammering us for months and I'm sure he's getting ready for the final blow. The killer thought he could replace me. And I've been too scatterbrained to do anything about them. I've let these cancers fester until they're nearly terminal. I've led this compound down to the hell I've created. I left the gate open and the barbarians are rounding the hill.

"You two are the only things holding this place together. You've made sure everything stays in one piece. You stuck by me, stuck with the compound. You showed real dedication. And I repaid you with abuse. For fuck's sake, Greg, I attacked you. And still you boys stayed. You kept us afloat.

"You guys are....are everything I should have been. You're true believers. You put your faith in this place because you know what it promises. You have sacrificed your time, energy, and sanity for this compound because your beliefs are unshakable. You are the examples everyone should follow. And if you'll have me, I'm ready to join you.

"Ken, when I left you by the river, I was lost. Somehow, I found my way to the cavern. I sank into a pool. I didn't think I was coming back up. I thought I might be more useful at the bottom. But I saw something. It was a flash, no longer than a second, but it showed me everything. A glorious vision. A glimpse of paradise, a paradise we can all share. I know what I have to do, what we all have to do. I know where we're going and I know how to take us there. But I can't do it alone. I need your help, one more time. I know I don't deserve it. I know you have every right to walk out that door. But I'm asking you to stay. I'm asking you to take us to the promised land. Will you help me?"

My hands go limp on the desk. I release all the tension from my neck. I inhale. There's nothing more to say. I'm vulnerable.

Ken and Greg have not moved for minutes. They're squeezing each others' hands, turning their fingers red. Their breathing is short. They don't look away from me. I keep my mouth wired shut. I can't rush this.

Greg brushes his shoulder against Ken's elbow. Ken mechanically turns to look at him. Greg blinks, darting his eyes between me and the door. Ken clenches his jaw and grunts. Greg nods, pats Ken's hand, and stands up. He walks to the desk. I rise to meet him.

"Ken and I are tendering our resignations." The words barely escape Greg's sealed mouth.

"Greg..." I don't know what to say

"Please, not another word or I will smash your face into this desk until you stop moving." Greg bares his teeth.

Impressive.

"You've been...fucking with us for years and you think you can say a few words, apologize, and we'll leap to your side? You've perverted... You've made a mockery of this place. I can't...I can't even begin to understand... You're a sick man, sir, a sick man. I'm going..." Greg looks away.

I could touch him. He's close enough for me to grasp his shoulder. I could tell him any number of things. I could get on my knees and beg. I could promise him the world. But to him, they'd just be words. I don't have the right to ask him for anything. I stay quiet.

Greg straightens his hair and shirt. He walks to the door and flings it open, blasting us with sunlight. He pivots.

"Ken, let's go. We need to arrange...well, everything, I suppose. There's so much..." Greg rubs the bridge of his nose.

Ken is staring at me. He hasn't budged from his chair. He's a statue. I return his gaze.

Greg says Ken's name again. Ken's head twitches. He looks at the door. Greg motions to the outside, tapping his foot. Ken stands up and starts walking. I've lost them. I should—No, no, I can't do anything. It's not my place. It's their decision.

Ken stops. He rotates. He walks towards me. He leans over the desk. I meet him halfway. Embers of anger burn in his eyes. He could crush my skull without breaking a sweat. He could make this place in his own image, his perfect ideal of faith. But he wouldn't last. Only I can lead us. He knows this.

Ken bites his lips. His gaze wavers. He's looking at me for...something. I slowly nod.

Relief flickers in Ken's eyes. He grunt and extends his hand. I seize it.

"You're not the same man." Ken's voice is a low rumble.

"No, no, I'm better. I swear to you." I put my free hand over my heart.

"You know what to do." Ken keeps a grip on my wrist.

"I do. I have a plan. It's going to work." My head won't stop nodding.

"You swear?" Ken's voice cracks.

"Yes. We're going to paradise. But I need your help." I squeeze his shoulder.

"...I'm with you." Ken jerks his head up and down.

I want to scream. I round the desk and wrapped my arms around Ken. He pats my back. This is fantastic. The sheep has rejoined the flock. He'll be-

"What are you doing?"

Greg is still standing in the doorway. His arms are dangling at his sides. He's staring at Ken.

"Ken, we can't stay here. He lied to us. We can't trust him." Greg tries to keep his voice level.

"He's not that guy anymore. I can tell. He's got a plan. We're getting our reward." Ken steps towards Greg. I move to the side.

"How can you believe him? It's just another....another lie. It must be. Why are you listening to him?" Greg tugs at his hair.

"I know he's let us down, but this is right. I can feel it. This is why we're here. We're finally getting what we deserve. He has a plan."

"Stop saying that. How many times are you going to crawl back to him? He's using you. We have to leave." Greg grips the door.

"I'm staying. I've...I've made it too far. I can't quit." Ken shakes his head.

"I can't stay here with him. I'm not living this lie." Greg steps through the doorway.

"Goodbye." Ken's voice is barely audible.

Greg stops. He looks at Ken. His eyes are trembling. Ken stares at the floor.

"You won't come with me?" Greg's voice breaks.

"I belong here." Ken scratches the back of his neck.

"But what about me? What about us...? Don't I...?" Greg chokes.

"I want you here, but I won't leave with you. The compound comes first." Ken looks Greg in the eyes.

Greg is about to break down. Ken is steel. I don't belong here. I tell them I'll be ready when they are. I slink out the back door.

My garden. God, I missed it. I stroll through the plants and flowers. They've begun to decay, but they're still marvelous. I sit in the middle of the green and cross my legs. I stare at the door.

I hear shuffling feet, raised voices, stomping, shouting, crashing. I don't move a muscle. This is their decision. I can't interfere. I wait among my flowers, submerged in the green. The door opens. Ken walks through. I stand up. Ken steps to the side. Greg, head bowed, is behind him. I approach.

Greg's breathing is halted. He looks at me. His eyes are bloodshot.

"I have to know it served a purpose. I have to know it meant something. Please, sir, tell me there was a reason. Tell me you won't let us down." Greg grips my shirt.

"I'm going to take us to paradise. This is one oath I won't break. Greg, you're going to be rewarded." I caress his hand.

Greg bites back more tears and gives me a crooked smile. He looks at Ken and nods. Ken wraps us in a hug. I regained my right hand and it retrieved my left one for me. I'm unstoppable. I break free from Ken's grip.

"We'll have time to celebrate later. We've got work to do. Greg, get the ceremony preparations done. I want everything running on schedule." I slap my fist into my palm.

"I don't know...yes, sir." Greg disappears into the office.

"Ken, get the car ready. I'll explain as we go." I salute him as he rushes through the door.

I look over at the garden. I'll be able to savour it soon. First, I need to deal with Smit.

CHAPTER FORTY-TWO

The road is quiet.

The moon is the only light in the sky. The stars are swallowed in the sea of black. The yellow lines rush under the car, illuminated by our dim headlights. The wheels rumble over the pavement. There's nothing around us. I can't see the billboards, or the suburbs, or the fast-food chains, or the houses. I think we passed the diner a while ago, but I'm not sure. We're a bullet speeding through the darkness.

Ken flexes his knuckles on the steering wheel. He's hunched forward, he's forehead nearly pressing against the window. His mouth is sealed shut. He hasn't said a word since I brought him to the cavern, since I showed him my plan. He just nodded and loaded up the car. My heart is trying to crawl up my throat. I wipe my face, peeling off a thick layer of sweat. My knee is bouncing in time with my heartbeat. I'm nibbling on my lower lip. I want to scream, but I hold it together. This is what I'm meant to do. I'm ready.

I turned the radio off miles ago. We need to focus. Tunnel vision. I haven't tried speaking with Ken. No point. He knows what he has to do. And so do our friends in the back. Ken pulls to the side of the road and takes the keys out of the ignition. We sit in the darkness, watching the highway for cars. Nothing. I grunt and open my door.

Ken pops open the trunk. Ken grabs two black bags, slinging one over his shoulder while carrying the other on the ground. I grab the third one and start to drag it. Ken flicks on a flashlight and pops it in his mouth, guiding us into the woods. I stay behind him, struggling with my load. The bag gets caught on rocks and twigs, nearly ripping it. I try not to think about what's inside. I bump into Ken. He points with his flashlight. I squint. There it is: The gates of Zaan.

Even in the middle of the night, it looks ridiculous. A disgusting monument to hedonism. They've added to it since I was last here. An iron-wrought eagle is perched at the top, surveying the land with its wings spread wide. A pair of snakes run away from it, stretching down the ground. The silver seems to glisten in the darkness.

Ken traces the flashlight up the gate, landing on the plaque. "Zaan: Indulgence is Salvation." The words seem painted with a fresh coat of gold. The light bulbs surrounding the sign have been turned off. I suppose even Smit worries about power bills.

This gate is why we are here. It is everything wrong with the world. We're going to bring their golden tribute to themselves burning down around them. I clap Ken on the back. He nods and stuffs the flashlight in his pocket. He hauls the bags to the gate and props them up vertically. One by one, he seizes them at the base and slides them up the bars, sending them to the other side. They land with a loud crunch. I wince.

I look around. I don't see any lights or hear any voices. Ken shimmies over the gate, landing next to the bags. I wipe my hands on my pants and step back. I break into a sprint and leap forward, clanging against the gate. My feet slip on the bars as I steady myself. I pull and pull and pull. I clamp down on my tongue. I grip the top of the gate, propping up my body with my elbows. I lean forward. The momentum carries me to the other side.

I land on the bags. Something sharp jabs into my lower back Ken covers my mouth before I can curse. I bite my lip. I nod at him and he removes his hand. I scamper off the bags. They look crooked, but they haven't torn yet. Ken takes his two as I take mine. We walk through the Zaan compound. Every step takes five seconds. We breathe through our noses. We stay in the shadows. I can barely hear us.

Only a few lights stream out from the windows. We hear idle chatter. It's too late for the revelers and too early for the eager beavers. It's the absolute dead of night. Most of them are asleep, unprepared. They've been sleeping their whole lives. Time to wake up.

Ken walks under a window and waits at the corner of a building, watching for any patrols. The main hall is right in front of us. Just a few more steps. I follow him, keeping my head ducked from the window. I hear laughter. Actually, just one, short laugh. I recognize it. I let my bag slide to the ground and I press myself against the window. I can't resist. Ken hisses at me, but I ignore him. I peek my eyes over the window ledge. There he is.

Smit is lying in a swarm of pillows. He's bathed in a red light. He's alone. He's naked. He's holding a turkey leg in one hand, tearing away at its loose meat with his teeth. He snorts and slurps as he chomps on the food. He's holding a comic book in one hand. I can make out a few lewd drawings. He turns a page and chortles, nearly choking on the turkey. He slams his chest to clear his throat. He rips off a piece of the bird, but it falls from his mouth, landing between the deep crevices of his crotch. He puts the comic book down and sticks his hand near his groin. He roots around down there for a minute, panting. He pulls out the chunk of turkey and eats it, wiping his lips.

I have to cover my mouth to stifle my laughter. This is my great rival. My arch enemy. This is the man who's nearly brought our compound to its knees. This is the leader who humiliated me in front of my people. He's a joke. I'm overwhelmed with embarrassment. I've been publicly dressed-down by this fat slob. He's pushed me to the limits. I was so caught up in my own bullshit, my own weaknesses, that I couldn't see Smit for what he really is: A pig in a suit.

Smit's no grand manipulator. He doesn't have the vision to rise that high. He just wants his little plot of land to eat and fuck and binge to his swollen heart's content. If he'd stayed in his world, he would've been fine. But he couldn't ignore that tiny in voice in his gut that kept saying "more." He couldn't resist taking what was mine. He couldn't stop himself from kicking me into the dirt. Now he has to reap what he's sown. And it's going to be a bountiful harvest.

Smit tosses the comic to the floor, along with the turkey bone. He stares at the ceiling, aimlessly scratching his belly. He sighs and closes his eyes. He's not a boulder for me to overcome; he's a roadblock. Looking at him splayed out on the pillows, exposed and decadent, I feel something close to pity. He's a small man who fooled himself into thinking he was a big player. He's forced himself into a battle he can't win. He can't see the dagger dangling over his head. I shake my head and slide away from the window. I grab my bag and I crouch-walk over to Ken. He grunts and scans the area. He nods and moves forward.

We approach the main hall doors and push on them open. Thank God they're too stupid to lock this place down. We enter the building, closing the doors behind us. Ken leads me down the aisle with the flashlight. The empty pews seem to be silently accusing us. We hop on the stage. We lay the three bags next to each other. Ken steps back, keeping an eye on the door. I sigh and rub my hands. I open the bags.

Here they are: Our three murdered members.

The idea came to me this morning as I was walking down the hill to the compound. My plan was coming together like a puzzle. I saw Greg and Ken taking their places at my side. I saw my followers flocking back to me. Everything fit, except one lousy protrusion: Smit.

I knew he had to go, but I couldn't see how to make him disappear. Murder was out of the question. There's enough heat on us; one wrong move and Blume will shut us down. Besides, his blood isn't worth the stain. And we don't have the time for an aggressive campaign to win back our lost members. I needed a quick solution that kept our noses clean while winning back everything we'd lost. Basically, a miracle.

I tossed it around in my head as I descended the hill, rejecting every terrible idea. It gnawed at me. I couldn't see an answer. Then I looked at the cave. And I remembered my three friends. I led Ken to the small pool where I'd laid them to rest.

They were still in place, undisturbed. Their skin was clammy and bloated, but they hadn't started to rot yet. They were in decent shape. Aside from being dead.

I explained to Ken where we were taking them. I explained to him what we were going to do with them. He nodded and grunted, staring at the bodies. When I was finished, he grabbed three bags and hauled our friends out the water. I couldn't ask for a better right hand.

We took them outside the cavern. Ken opened the bags while I stood over the bodies. I burned their faces into my mind. Two men and a woman. Victims of my incompetence. I failed these people. I let a murderer take their lives before their time. I allowed them to be torn from paradise. I will carry that load for the rest of my days.

I kneeled beside the bodies. I looked at the planter. His thin beard was stained with his blood, dark and crimson. I reached out to clean it, but stopped myself. They had to look untouched. They had to be perfect.   I placed my hand on their foreheads and said a small prayer. I told them they would be avenged. I told them I would find meaning for their deaths. I told them they had purpose. I kissed their cheeks and stood up. Ken sealed them in the bags and we descended the hill.

Now they're here, lying on Smit's stage. Even the dead are coming to Zaan. I allow myself a bitter chuckle. It distracts from this distasteful act. My stomach is churning. What we are doing is appalling. Ken knows it. Greg would know it if we'd told him. Every fiber of my being knows it. We are crossing a line I want to reseal the bodies and scramble back to our compound. I want to think of a better plan, any plan, instead of this...desecration. I want to pummel myself for even thinking about it.

But I look at our friends on the floor. I see their lifeless eyes, their butchered corpses, their ruined potential. I see the life that was robbed from them and I feel an anger boiling in my gut. I will give them meaning. What we are doing is necessary. We have no other options. We have to do this if we're going to have a future. We have to be bastards.

I grab the planter by the wrists. Ken bends down to help, but I shake my head. He's soiled himself enough. I drag the planter across the stage and drop him near the curtain. I flip him onto his stomach and pull his arms in different directions. I contort his legs in odd angles.

I grip the male builder's backside. I roll him down the stage, leaving blood smears on the floor. I bring him to the edge and give him one final push. He falls and crumples in a heap. His body is mangled as he stares blankly at the ceiling. Very natural-looking.

I haul the female builder over my shoulders. Ken looks away. I walk to center stage. My brain is screaming at me to stop, but I drown it out. I let the woman slip from my grasp. She crashes at my feet, landing on her side. She's staring down the aisle.

I step back and look at the scene. If I didn't know better, I'd say it was real. Nothing about it looks staged. Our friends are very convincing. Anyone could see what happened here. Anyone could draw the right conclusions. I tap Ken's shoulder. He turns to me, holding back tears. I pull him into a tight hug. He lets out one sob.

I pull away from him and I point at the door. He grunts and steps off the stage. I hop down and slide through the aisle. Ken holds the door open. I turn around, holding the flashlight forward. Our friends have done more for this compound than we can every repay. I bow to them and slink through the door.

We crawl across the compound, sticking to the buildings like glue. We reach the right one. I peer through the window. No one's here. I slide the pane open and wriggle my way inside. Ken stands guard while I fumble in the dark, bumping into chairs. I shine the flashlight around me. I'm in the right spot: Smit's office.

Just like the gate, it's more opulent than the last time I was here. Hundreds of posters of Smit litter the walls. His beaming, idiotic face stares at me from every angle. The chairs are decked out with platinum legs. The trophy case glitters from the overabundance of medals and statues. For some reason, a samurai sword is holstered on his desk. How the fuck does he get enough money for all this crap? He must be bleeding his members dry. I don't have time to think about that. Do my job and get out. I move to the desk and slide open the drawers. I reach into my back pocket and pull out the plastic bag. I hold it up to the flashlight to double-check.

The light reflects off the knives, freshly stained with my dead friends' blood. The rope, equally bloody binds them together. The tools of a killer. What else could they be? I pour the bag contents onto the desk. I place the knives into the drawers and close them until they're barely open. They definitely wouldn't be noticeable if someone wasn't looking. But if someone was...

I bunch the rope up and stuff it behind the trophy case, letting a small portion of the tail jut out, ~~noticeable~~ for the right person.

I'm done. I crawl through the open window and close the pane. I nod at Ken and we crouch our way out of the compound. I leap over the gate and land on my feet this time. We pile into the car and peel off into the highway. Ken knows where to take us.

We pull over on the road about three miles from Zaan. Ken's headlights illuminate a phone booth. Ken stays in the car as I get out. I enter the booth and pick up the receiver. I start breathing fast. I well up my face, summoning tears to my eyes. I quiver my lips. I insert the coin and dial the number.

"H-hello? Please, oh, God...I don't...Oh, God...Yes, yes, I'm sorry, I...Please help me. I'm at the, at the Zaan compound. There's blood everywhere. In the main hall there's...oh, God, they're all dead. He killed them. He...Please, send help. Hurry. He killed them all. Hurry, for God's sa—" I slam the receiver down.

I stay in the booth, wiping my face. I stare at the road. Minutes roll by. I don't look away. I hear sirens. I press against the booth wall, hiding my body. A car speeds past me, its lights flashing. I catch a glimpse of the driver. Blume. I could see his smile from here. He's followed by three other flashing cars. I know where they're going.

I return to the car. Ken is silent. A smile washes over my face. I turn to him.

"We're going to be alright."

CHAPTER FORTY-THREE

I'm staring at my naked body.

I set up the full-length mirror in my bedroom. I found it years ago in a yard sale and brought it back to the compound. I used it in a few sermons. Made the members look at it and confess to themselves why they were so weak and frail. I said they couldn't escape themselves or something like that. Pure gimmickry.

I put the mirror in storage after a couple of performances. I should have thrown it away, honestly. It was meant for the landfill. It was a symbol of vanity and self-obsession. It was worthless. I should have biffed it to the curb, but my hoarder instincts took over. I didn't want to lose it and find out I needed it a week, a month, a year down the road. I'd be livid. Couldn't have that. So I stuffed it in a spare closet and forgot it existed. That was...fuck, I don't know how long ago. Joseph was still here, I think.

I woke up this morning before the sun was up. It's been my habit for the last few weeks. I don't want to greet the day; I want to beat it to the punch. I find it easier to get out of bed than I used to. The earlier I rise, the more shit I can get done.

I sprang out of bed and started flexing my legs. I wiggled my fingers and woke up every part of my body. I yawned and massaged my jaw. I came back to life. The constant buzzing in my head was fainter than usual.

Flopping my arms back and forth, I walked to the window. A grey paleness hung over the compound as the last remnants of night retreated from the sun. I could see the dew on the grass. A bird settled on the ground, plucking away at the loose worms. They writhed in the dirt, burrowing back to their holes, but my feathered friend was too fast. He scooped them up and choked them down. He licked the plate clean. I scratched my stomach. It was a good final morning.

Greg wanted to run through every last detail one more time. Ken needed help with the lanterns. Members were waiting for a quick pep-talk sermon before they made their afternoon preparations. My mind should have been racing. But it was only focused on one thing: the mirror. It just popped into my head. I hadn't thought about it in years, but now it was all I could focus on. It wouldn't leave my mind. I had to see it. I couldn't explain why; my gut just told me to get it. It was completely irrational, but I didn't question it. My gut knows best. Much better than my buzzing head.

I stepped outside weaved through the compound. I came to a small shack next to one of the sleeping quarters. I fished the skeleton keys from my pocket and inserted them one by one into the lock. After thirteen keys, I felt the fourteenth one click as the lock went slack. I pulled the door open.

A thick level of dust greeted my eyes. I coughed and swatted it away. Stepping inside, I saw piles full of cleaning supplies, shovels, axes, cloths, and empty bags. Things we'd forgotten about, things we didn't need anymore. I walked through the wreckage, pushing aside rags and poles. There, at the back wall, I found it.

The mirror was coated in grime. I grabbed a loose rag and wiped it semi-clean. I saw myself. Its frame was pure black, chipped and cracked in some spots. I grabbed it sides and lifted it off the ground. It didn't crumble. I pull it out of the shack and closed the door. I dragged the mirror across the compound as the sun greeted me. I set it up in my bedroom. I wiped away the leftover grime. I stared at myself for a moment before someone called my name. I dashed out the door.

The rest of the morning was a blur. Greg talked a mile a minute as he explained every single piece of our plan while we walked through the compound. I did my best to listen and signed off on his report. I thanked him. He seemed grateful. Ken and I hauled crates from the car to the center square. We'd gone on a shopping spree a few days ago and it was almost time to show off the goods. I told everyone not to open their presents until tonight.

I gave a speech inside the main hall. Once more for old time's sake. Everyone was on their feet. They were vibrating. I told them to make their arrangements and to prepare themselves. I told them to enjoy the afternoon. I told them to be happy. I shook all their hands as they dispersed into the compound.

I returned to my office, drained. I was sweating. I peeled off my clothes and went to my room. I almost flopped on my bed when I noticed the mirror. I stopped. I saw myself. I've been staring at this mirror for hours. The body I'm looking at is unimpressive. It's pudgy and flabby. Two sizable breasts droop down, pointing at a round potbelly. The arms dangle limply at the sides, thin and frail. There isn't a hint of muscle anywhere. It's a weak shell. Unremarkable. Pathetic. Perfect.

I smile at myself. I have the most generic body imaginable. If you saw it on a beach, it'd meld together with the hundreds of other torsos. Anywhere else, I'm a nobody. But we're here. We're in my compound. We're in the place I've built. Me, a feeble, chubby nothing. I've risen above my physical limitations. I've attained so much. My body is a testament to the power of transcendence.

I look away from myself. My robe is draped over a chair. It's sitting under the window, soaking in the last few rays of sunlight. I drenched it in the river this morning, running it under the stream, almost letting it slip away. I wrung it out and spread it on the chair to dry.

I hold the robe close. I run my fingers through it, rubbing the fabric. I press it against my cheek. It smells rank. It's been run ragged. Stains and small holes litter its frame. It's on its last legs. You wouldn't sell it at a flea market. It's sublime. I hold the robe above my head and let it fall. My arms and head slide through the holes. The cloth unfurls down my body, just skirting the edge of the floor. I grab the rope I left on the bed, tying it around my waist. The robe goes tight. I can move, mostly. I look back at the mirror. The feeble creature I was saw is gone. I'm looking at a new man. The robe makes my chest seem wide and strong. My stance is powerful. I'm a leader.

I've donned my second skin, my armour. I've become everything I've aspired to be. I'm the image I want everyone to see. The interior has become the exterior.

I don't do it for vanity. I've finally let that go. I know who I am. I know what I've done. I've failed more times than I can count. But at this moment, in this room, I'm the leader they need me to be. I'm the person they want to take them through the forest, up the hill, and into the cavern. They need the picture of faith. They need the man I see in the mirror.

I look out the window. Everyone's huddled around the center square. Some are sitting on the ground, pressed together in silent prayer. Others are leaning against the buildings, cracking jokes. Some are holding each other close. They're all wearing white robes.

There's a divide in the crowd. The majority of the mob is positioned near the center square. But a small faction is lurking on the edges. They're a tight-knit group, eyes on the ground. I frown. I told everyone to welcome them with open arms. I know it's been short notice, but...

Ken is dragging one final box across the compound. He staggers past the outsider group and someone bends down to help. They carry it to the center square and slam it down. Ken slaps the man's back and shakes his hand. Some people applaud. The man's friends have followed him to the square. The majority thank the man for his help. The groups start to mingle. Ken sees me in the window and waves. I chuckle. He's smarter than he looks.

I keep my eye on the new group. They've been struggling to settle in. When they arrived at our doorstep a month ago, Greg wanted to turn them away. We were running fine enough with the numbers we had; any more people might through us off course. But how could I say no to them? Where else were they going to go? Without Zaan, they needed us.

The groups came in waves after Zaan fell apart. First were the true believers, the ones who said they'd been duped into joining Zaan. We let them in. Next came the converters, the people who'd bought into the bullshit and left our compound without a second glance. They pleaded for another chance. They said they'd seen the light. We let them in. Finally, we had the newcomers, the people who'd never stepped a foot in our compound. These were the true blue Zaan followers, the ones who'd been deepest in it. They said they needed a home, they needed guidance. We let them in. We let everyone in.

It was madness when Zaan fell apart. We only heard bits here and there from local town gossip. It took us a while to piece everything together. Sheriff Blume led the charge past the gates. The police found the bodies in the Zaan compound. They discovered Smit in a...compromising position with a chicken leg. They dragged him to the main hall and asked him to explain himself. He had no words. The cops badgered him with questions and he had no answers. Blume slapped Smit, but nothing happened. They stayed all night. The sun rose and they were no closer to the truth.

Then, some enterprising young rookie peeked into Smit's office. Something caught his eye. He opened a drawer. He pulled out a plastic bag covered in red. He ran outside.

The compound exploded. Everybody was screaming. The cops whipped out their handcuffs and stuffed people into cars. People fought back and the police bludgeoned them with batons. Blume called in reinforcements. The entire police department descended on the compound. Buildings were roped off. Evidence was seized. The followers were forced off the property. They walked down the highway as the police combed the compound. Some people said Blume couldn't stop laughing. In all the confusion, the police lost track of Smit. He slipped through the cracks and ran out of the compound. No one's seen him since.

And that was it. That's all it took to bring down the imposter. Three bodies and some well-placed "evidence." I gave

Blume an inch and he turned it into a mile. I lit the fuse and watched the explosion from the comfort of my home.

The investigation wound down. The cops put out an arrest warrant for Smit, but he'd be stupid to hang around here. He's probably in another state, trying to piece together his life. The cops released most of his followers; not enough evidence to detain them. And so, with nowhere else to go, they all came here. They trickled into our home and joined the family.

The police left the compound alone. The property's still sealed off, but they're long gone. They got all the evidence they need from it. The place is a ghost town. I returned to it one last time three weeks ago, by myself. I strolled through the front gate in the middle of the day. I wandered the compound for hours, savouring the silence. Rooms were stripped bare. Rabbits and mice scurried in the halls. It was as if no one had lived here for years. In a month, everything Smit had built had been erased. The party had gone quiet.

I made my way into Smit's office. His trophy case had been smashed and looted. His posters dangled limply from the walls, shredded and torn. Broken glass littered the floor. The desk was cracked and splintered. No more glamour, no more extravagance, no more anything. I didn't go there to gloat over a ghost; I had a mission. I'd spoken with a former Zaan member. He told me about a souvenir I had to see. He told me where to look.

I gripped the desk and pushed it to the wall. In its spot, I saw a small square on the floor. I kicked the dust away and found a latch. I gripped it and pulled the square up. I looked into a dark hole. I reached in and pulled out my prize. It was wrapped in a red cloak. I unfurled it and held it to the light. It was a golden staff twice as long as my arm. A horse head rested on the top, relaxed and poised.

I smiled as I walked out of the compound. Our ceremony could use a bit of pomp and circumstance. What better way to usher in a new era than with the remnants of our defeated enemy? Something good might as well come from Zaan. The staff is on my bed now. I grab it and look in the mirror, tapping my finger on the horse head. My outfit is complete. I'm ready.

I stretch my head and shake my body. I need to be loose. I raise my chin. That's when I see it in the mirror. A red line runs across my neck. It's faded now, but still visible. I touch it and feel the bump. The spot where the cord wrapped around me. The night I nearly died. My wakeup call. One last souvenir from the killer. One more reminder of what I'm here to do. One last memento.

I peek out the window again. The crowd in the center square has grown. People stream out of buildings. Private conversations trail off and die. Members hug each other. Everyone's finished their personal rituals. Ken is unpacking the boxes and handing out the lanterns. People are striking matches. Greg is approaching my office. No more delays. It's finally, actually time.

I cast one more look around my office before I fling the door open.

CHAPTER FORTY-FOUR

We are a snake of light weaving through the forest.

I lead the group into the woods. Our lanterns bob and flicker in the darkness. The glow of the compound recedes. The warmth of its fire fades away. We hear wood cracking and buildings tumbling down, but no one turns back. We don't live there anymore. No one will. Everyone keeps their heads down, their mouths sealed. They trudge forward, crunching the leaves beneath their feet. They have nothing left to say; they simply need to ascend.

I sink Smit's staff....No, I sink my staff into the ground with every step. It feels satisfying as it pierces the earth. I follow the path Ken and Greg cleared for us. They needn't have; I could walk this route in my sleep. But I appreciate their efforts. I appreciate them.

They're walking beside me, my left and right hands. Greg keeps turning around to do a head count of our members, worried some might slip away. He needn't concern himself, but I let him have it. He's entitled to his neuroses. Ken is staring forward. They're both carrying their lanterns in one hand and their clay chalices in the other. The rest are in the cavern. I gave the goblets to them before the other members. I shouldn't play favourites, but... Well, I'm allowed one last failing.

Everyone marches in a straight line, their faces etched in stone. They know what's coming. I didn't mince words when I told them. I could've spun it somehow, but they deserved better than that. They deserved the truth. I laid everything on the line. No metaphors, no big spectacles, no tricks. I just sat on the stage with microphone and talked to them. I told them what was going to happen. I told them what we were going to do. I told them what they would be leaving behind. But I also told them what they'd gain, what they'd see, what they'd feel. I told them about their reward.

There were walkouts, of course. A few members stormed out of the hall when I finished talking. They yelled at me, cursed me, called me crazy. Some tried to convince their friends to join them. I let them leave. There were about twenty quitters in total. They were all from Zaan. They joined us thinking they'd get more of the same. They never fit in. I wasn't surprised to see them go. They hadn't signed up for this. They were still in denial. They were still children. This place wasn't their destiny. But most people stayed. Where else were they going to go? They'd devoted years to this compound or to Zaan. They'd walked away from jobs, friends, families, their entire lives, to be here. They couldn't go crawling back; they'd come too far. They weren't going to walk away from their reward when they can practically taste it. They're ready.

We reach the river. The place where old Zeke choked on his own blood after a villager drilled a pitchfork into his back. The place where the killer filled his lungs with water until they burst. They place where I beat, tortured, and brutalized myself. So much violence for such a small place. But you can't see any of it. Nothing looks out of place. It's forgotten its past. After all, it's just a river.

We turn left. We climb the hill. The cavern is silhouetted by the setting sun. A few more steps and we'll be there.

I can't get the killer from my mind. I should be focusing on the ceremony, on our ascension, but I keep returning to him. I see him strangling me, laughing at me, drowning beneath me, judging me. I can't let him go. I don't even know his name. After everything he's done, I don't know what to call him. Greg checked the records, but he couldn't figure who he might be. We checked his clothes for any identification, looked around the woods for his campsite, but we found nothing. After tonight, no one will remember him. Once Ken, Greg, and I have ascended, there will be no witnesses to what he did. No one will find the grave I dug for him deep in the cavern. No one will think about him. It will be as if he never existed.

None of this would have been possible without him. He pushed me into the abyss and left me no choice but to climb up. He hammered our compound and made it stronger. He was the virus we needed to purge our system. He found purpose his own way. He stepped outside of my corruption and followed the faith. He made his own meaning. It doesn't matter that no one will know after tonight; he knew. I can respect that, in a way.

Our lanterns fill the cavern, chasing the darkness into the corners. I lead them past my baptism pool and through the twisting paths. I hold my breath as I squeeze into a tight passage. I inch my way forward. Looking up, with all our combined light, I can see the endless rows of stalactites dangling over us like daggers. It's a gloomy place. It's perfect.

I break through the other side. I wait for the others to join me. Their lanterns slowly light up the room like the rising sun. Members gasp as they take in the chamber. Clay chalices line the lip of the pool. I gesture to them. Members pick up the goblets as they gape at the size of the chamber. Some stand in the shallow end of the pool while others stay on the edges. Their lanterns illuminate the reddish water.

Ken and Greg are standing next to me. A million words run through my head. I don't say any of them. I pull my friends into a hug. I whisper in their ears. Greg sniffles. Ken squeezes tight. I let them go and nod. They smile at me and clap my shoulders. They enter the pool with their chalices.

Everyone is silent. They're staring at me. I hold my staff up high and march across the chamber. I reach the mountain and climb its jagged footholds. I balance my lantern and staff in one hand. I move slowly, trying not to grunt. Best not to spoil the mood. A ridge in the mountain gives out beneath my feet, sending rocks tumbling to the ground. I leap forward, planting my foot in another ridge. Not yet.

I pull myself up, dragging my stomach across the rough surface. Using the staff for support, I stand. I walk forward. I'm on top of my rocky stage. The final sermon from the mount.

I survey the crowd below me. Their eyes bore holes into me. They're united by faith. They've come together under one common cause. It's what I always envisioned: Beautiful people joined in harmony, ready to ascend. I can't even properly describe it. My words are cheap. I feel a ball in my throat. I rub my eyes. I hold the staff up straight and start my speech.

"Thank you for being here. Thank you for experiencing this moment. Thank you for taking this leap with me. I know it wasn't easy to get here. I know you've had to sacrifice so much. I know you've considered quitting. I certainly have. It's been a difficult path. Life beats you down every time it can. It's brutal and unforgiving. But you persevered. You never gave in. Because you knew how much worse it is out there. You knew how empty the world is. Life is scary, vast, and unknowable. We stumble in the dark, grasping for a light switch that isn't there. We have no idea where we're from or where we're going. We fill our lives with trinkets and medications to distract ourselves from the gaping holes in our stomachs. We're all lost.

"But you all made a decision to not be lost anymore. You made your way to my compound. You surrendered your past lives. You committed yourself to the faith. You stepped out of the darkness and into the light.

"Our faith is not a kind one. It does not give you a shoulder to cry on. It's been painful and ugly and unbearable at times. But it's our life. It's something we have that no one can take away. We've created meaning in this random world. We've built a beautiful home.

"And now, finally, we're at the end of the road. There are no more trials, no more sermons, no more sacrifices. We have made it to the finish line. We have climbed the mountain and we can see the valley. It is time for our reward. It is time for us to step through to the other side. It is time to transcend this petty world. It is time for a second life.

"Please, my friends, drink with me. Fill your cups and join me in paradise." I spread my arms wide, letting the staff fall away.

One by one, people dip their chalices into the pool. Water drips echo in the room as they raise their goblets to me. I smile and nod. They drink. I see Ken and Greg. They're holding hands. They look up at me and nod. I raise my hand goodbye as they drink. They were the best men I ever met, better than any of us deserved. I hope they knew that.

I close my eyes. I hear a thud. It's followed by another. There is a splash. Another. And another. More thuds. More splashes. They cascade and fall on top of each other. It's a wave of noise. It builds and builds. One more thud. Silence. I open my eyes.

They're all lying in front of me. Some float in the middle of the water, others are crumpled on the floor. Their lanterns are extinguished in the pool or smashed on the ground, their light slowly dying. A few members are holding onto each other. I see Ken and Greg huddled together at the edge of the pool.

They didn't feel a thing. Greg made sure of that. They simply drank and leaped into the void. They've worked enough; they deserve peace.

I leave the staff on the stage as I descend the mountain. No one left to impress. I walk past the bodies, closing their eyelids and parting their hair. They seem calm. I wade into the pool, gently pushing people out of the way. I reach the dividing point between the shallow and deep ends of the pool.

Everyone's gone. This place is dark again. Only a few active lanterns remain. I'm alone. I should do it. Now's the time. It's what I'm—

Someone's here. Someone alive.

There's light in the corner of my eye. It's moving towards me. I peer into the darkness. I see a face approach the pool. I almost laugh. It's Smit.

Of course he'd be here. One last test.

He's filthy. His face is covered in mud. His tattered clothes cling to his body. Cuts and scars litter his arms and legs. His knuckles are tightly wrapped around the handle of a lantern. His eyes are sunken and tired. He's lost weight since I last saw him. He's a broken-down animal.

"You sick fuck." Smit's voice cracks, as if he's using it for the first time in a while.

"It's good to see you one last time. It's a nice surprise." I flash him a toothy smile.

Smit stumbles into the pool, falling to one knee. He drops his lantern, extinguishing the light. He scrambles to his feet, thrashing in the pool. He screams. He kicks the water and strikes one of my members. He recoils, backpedalling to the edge of the pool. He wipes his hair from his face and looks around the chamber.

His face turns to stone. He scans the room, lingering on every...post-life person. He's trembling. He gags. He doesn't understand. Pity.

"What...you...why'd you...fucking Christ....you fucking....you killed...good Lord..." Smit covers his mouth.

"I did what I told you I would do all those months ago. I did what I'm here to do: I set them free." I rest my hand on a nearby member and close her eyes.

Smit's eyes are saucers. He's shaking his head. He runs his fingers through his hair. He grips the edge of the pool, flinching as corpses float past him. He refuses to accept the truth.

"This is what I've been building towards. This is the glory you tried to derail. This is our culmination. I did what you could never do, Smit; I gave them purpose." I push the woman to the center of the pool, rejoining her with her friends.

Smit zeroes in on me. His fists clench. He stands up. His lips curl into a snarl. Good. I wouldn't want a boring final conversation.

"You freed these people? You fucking killed them. You're a goddamn lunatic." Smit marches across the pool.

"Different perspectives, I suppose." I offer a shrug.

"Fuck you. Fuck you, psycho. You killed these people. Goddamn Blume and those other pigs have been hunting me when they should have been dragging you through the streets." Smit pushes a member aside.

"They have a good reason to be hunting you, Smit. You're a wanted killer, after all. Three bodies on your property looks pretty bad." I widen my smile.

Smit stops moving. His mouth droops open. It dawns on him.

"You did it." The words hiss out of Smit's mouth.

"Yes, yes I did." I nod. Even he deserves some honesty.

"You fucking bastard. You set me up. You planted those, those, those people in my hall. You hid that shit in my office. You, you fucking... Oh, Christ, I..." Smit's staggers around the water, clutching the sides of his head.

"I did what I had to do." I watch a lantern sink to the bottom of the pool.

"You killed your own people?" Smit wipes the drool from his mouth.

"They were taken from me. But I found a solution. I gave them purpose when I planted them—"

"Shut the fuck up. What are you talking about? You did all this for your retarded club? You ruined my life. I've had to live in the fucking woods like an animal. You took everything from me. You, you, motherfucking..."

I let Smit ramble on. He's earned one last outburst. I might as well give him this petty pleasure. He calls me a bastard and a murderer and a psychopath and every insult his feeble mind can dig up. He goes on and on and on. He screams and splashes the water and pushes bodies away. His face turns red. He pauses to catch his breath. I open my mouth.

"Smit, you lost because you were meant to lose. You didn't believe in anything. You only sought your own pleasures, your own vices. That gave you the advantage for a while. You stole from me when I was sleeping. But I woke up. And I realized what I had to do. I understood what boundaries I'd have to cross, boundaries you'd never consider breaking. I stepped over them. I caught you while you were sleeping. That's why I won. You were limited by your small ambition; I had no limits. There's nothing I wouldn't do to get this." I spread my arms wide.

Smit swallows and stomps over to me. He gets close to my face. He's panting. I prepare myself.

"I had you, you fucking shit. I had you in my fucking fist. I should have drove you out on a fucking rail." Smit's teeth are bared. All his niceties and manners; all forgotten. He's a trapped rat now.

"But you didn't. So we're here." I gesture to the chamber.

Smit grimaces. Doubt is creeping into him. He needs one more push.

"Smit, I have to know: How does it feel? How does it feel that your entire life, everything you experienced, everything you achieved, everything you dreamed about, all of it, only amounted to being my speed bump?" I grin at him.

I see the knife before I feel it. It comes rushing from Smit's hand. I let it sink into my stomach. I grunt, feeling the blade dig into my flesh. I bend over, holding the dagger in place. Smit doesn't move. We're statues.

I twist away, jerking the knife from Smit's grasp. I grab his neck and wallop his ear. I slam into his nose and throat. He stumbles backwards, flinging his arms everywhere. I fall forward, driving my knee into his gut. He wheezes and collapses. I land on top of him. My blood is dripping all over Smit. I keep going. I wrap my hands around his throat and push down, sinking him beneath the surface. Smit digs his fingers into my arms. I don't let go.

Smit looks at me as water crashes over him. His eyes are wild as he thrashes beneath me. I won't be denied. He kicks the ground, but he can't get away. My blood mixes with his air bubbles. I'm staring into Hell. It all led to this. All the talk, all the lies, all the deception, all the theft, every last bit of it led to this moment: Smit under me. This is my final task; eliminating the deceiver. It is our last revenge. We leave this world with everything while he leaves with nothing. Zaan dies as Smit drowns.

The bubbles stop. The scratching stops. The thrashing stops. Everything stops. I let go. Smit floats away, just another body in the pool.

I tumble to the water, sitting on the ground. I touch the knife and wince. It's lodged in deep. I leave it alone. I spit out a mouthful of blood and sigh. It's quiet. I'm the only one left. Smit was the last person on my to-do list. I didn't think he'd find my invitation, but here we are. Now it's just me.

I look at the edge of the pool. It's not that far. I could crawl to it and pull myself out. I could remove the knife and stitch myself up. Ken taught me how. I could go back to the compound. We've got a chest of money stored in my office. Our emergency funds. I could hit the road and start over somewhere new. I could spread the word to more people. Or I could just be alone. I don't have to die here. I've done my work. I can walk away. There's always more life to live.

That's what Jason would've done. If he stumbled into the compound, he would've taken the money and ran. He would've walked across America finding new excuses. He would've kept going. But Jason's dead. I'm not him anymore.

This is where I'm meant to be. To leave now, on the cusp of victory, would defeat the purpose, would defeat my purpose.

I could start over again. It'd be easy. But that'd only bring Jason back. And he has to stay in his grave.

No, this is my home. I can end it how I want. I can go out strong. I can step into paradise. This is where I belong. I've found it.

I sink into the water and open my mouth.

END